W9-BXD-240

THE REST IS SILENCE

ALSO BY THE AUTHOR

Billy Boyle
The First Wave
Blood Alone
Evil for Evil
Rag and Bone
A Mortal Terror
Death's Door
A Blind Goddess

THE REST IS SILENCE

A Billy Boyle World War II Mystery

James R. Benn

**Cuyahoga Falls
Library**
Cuyahoga Falls, Ohio

Copyright © 2014 by James R. Benn

All rights reserved.

Published by Soho Press, Inc.
853 Broadway
New York, NY 10003

Library of Congress Cataloging-in-Publication Data

Benn, James R.
The rest is silence : a Billy Boyle World War II mystery / James R. Benn.
p. cm

ISBN 978-1-61695-266-2
eISBN 978-1-61695-267-9

1. Boyle, Billy (Fictitious character)—Fiction. 2. World War,
1939-1945—England—Fiction. 3. Murder—Investigation—Fiction. I. Title.
PS3602.E6644R48 2014
813'.6—dc23 2014013450

Printed in the United States of America

10 9 8 7 6 5 4 3 2 1

For Debbie

If music be the food of love, play on . . .
Twelfth Night, Act I, Scene 1

The rest is silence. O, o, o, o.
—HAMLET, 1603 (SECOND) QUARTO

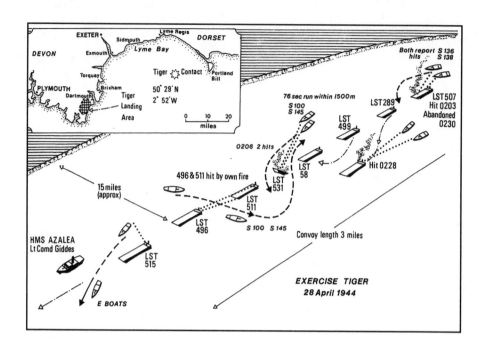

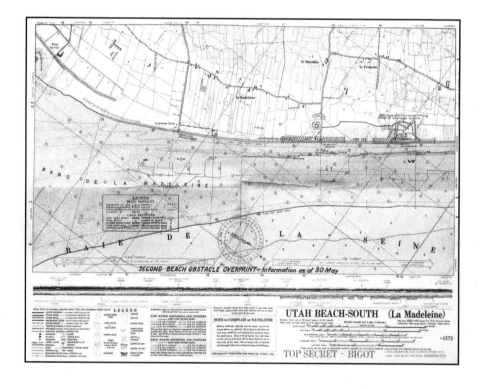

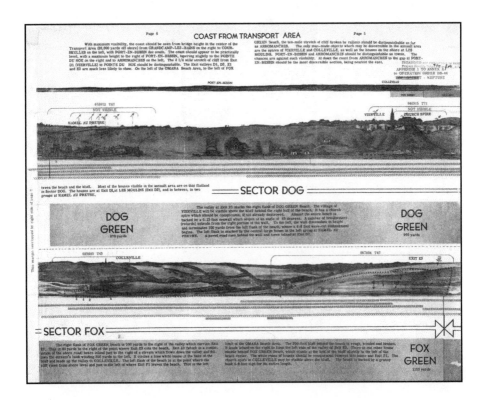

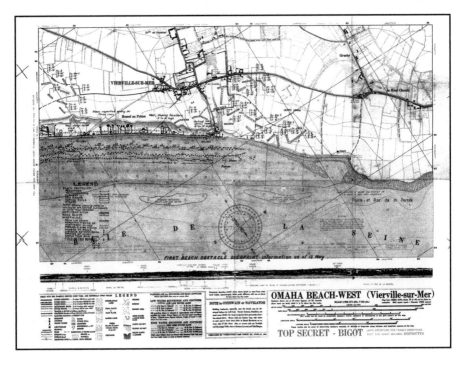

CHAPTER ONE

KINGSBRIDGE, ENGLAND
April 23, 1944

I KNEW I was in trouble when the coroner wheeled in the body, encased in a rubber sack, on a wobbly gurney with one wheel that wanted to go in any direction but straight.

Police surgeon, I should say, instead of coroner, since this is England, not the States. I'm happy to tell you more, if only to put off thinking about that smell. It's still coating the back of my throat and clinging to my skin, so here you go.

I'd been sent to Kingsbridge, a nice little town by the southwest coast of England. Picturesque, actually, despite the thousands of GIs everywhere, camped in fields, housed in barracks and barns, marching in every direction, whistling at girls, and tossing chewing gum to kids who trailed in their wake. The roar of trucks and tanks tore through the peace and quiet of this seaside town, as it did in plenty of others like it.

Allied forces were here waiting for word to invade occupied Europe. Everyone knew the invasion was around the corner. Not the exact time or place, but with all these soldiers, sailors, and airmen here, the anticipation was building up to a fever pitch. They *had* to go somewhere, and soon, or else the pressure and the stress of waiting would break even the strongest. Me, I was here because some poor slob got himself washed up on the shore near Slapton, a small seaside town not far from Kingsbridge. It would have passed unnoticed if the beach, Slapton Sands, wasn't being used to practice amphibious landings: the kind of landings that would soon be happening across the Channel, in France.

I work for a guy who's paid to get nervous about stuff like that, who sees conspiracies and danger in every unexplained event. Why did the corpse end up on this particular beach? Was he a German spy, a drunken fisherman, or a downed pilot? How come no one had reported him missing, no civil or military authority? Colonel Samuel Harding is an intelligence officer with Supreme Headquarters, Allied Expeditionary Force, and unanswered questions bother him, so here I am in Kingsbridge to fill in the blanks. I work at SHAEF as well. I have the flaming sword patch on my shoulder to prove it, not to mention orders signed by General Eisenhower himself giving me the authority to go anywhere and question anyone as part of this investigation. Helpful, if some senior officer wants to push a mere captain around.

That's what led me to Dr. Verniquet and his mortuary. The questions and the corpse. The smell was already overpowering, even though the bag was zipped up tight. The antiseptic smell of the tiled basement room, painted bright white, faded under the onslaught of decay. Think of a slab of beef left out in the sun for a couple of days, then add a dash of metallic odor and a tinge of vomit.

"Are you ready, Captain Boyle?" Dr. Verniquet said. He was short, with a shock of white hair sticking out behind his ears, marking the last stand of a receded hairline. He wore a stained white coat, and a lit cigarette dangled from his lips, probably to help mask the odor of decomposition, although in this case it might take an entire pack.

"Sure," I said, aiming for a nonchalant tone. I'd seen plenty of corpses, even fished a few ripe ones out of Boston Harbor back when I was a cop, before the war, and before my personal count of dead bodies skyrocketed. I'd witnessed a few autopsies as well, and even though I'd retched bile in the hall midway through my first, no one had seen me slip out. I'd managed to keep it together after that. Cops are supposed to always be in control, and that extended to the morgue. It was part of the job, a duty to the dead, and everyone expected you to get it done without putting your last meal on display. Especially my dad. He was a homicide detective, and he'd told me when I was a rookie not to disgrace myself when I got around to my first autopsy. That was easy. I simply hadn't eaten a thing that day.

"He's been in cold storage waiting for you to arrive," the elderly doctor said. "No one has claimed the body." He gripped the zipper and glanced at me. I nodded.

As he pulled the zipper open, waves of putrid stench washed over me, each worse than the last. I tried to breathe, but my body revolted at drawing in more of the rancid air. I blinked, trying to make sense of what I was seeing. Dark, bloated flesh, marked by pockets of greyish-white growth on the cheeks and belly. No eyes, no lips. Teeth bared in a hideous grimace.

"Show me the bullet wounds," I said, unable to focus my watering eyes, trying for quick, shallow breaths.

"Here," Dr. Verniquet said, pointing to a bicep, seemingly immune to the smell. "The bullet went through his arm. A minor wound." He tapped a pencil against a puckered hole on blackened skin, then drew on his cigarette and blew the smoke out his nostrils. I had never taken up the habit, but it looked like a good move. "He was killed by this shot to the head. Note the angle." He tapped his pencil again, first on an entry wound high on the forehead, right side, then on the exit wound above the left ear. Or where the ear would have been.

"He was shot in the arm while standing up," I said, trying to block out the barrage of odors attacking my senses. I forced myself to study the body, wishing I could simply bolt for the clean air outdoors. The arm wound was on a straight line. "Judging from the position of the head shot, the killer was above him when he fired the second shot."

"Yes. The victim may have turned away at the last second," Dr. Verniquet said as ash dropped from his cigarette. He turned his own head upward and to the left, this time using the pencil to demonstrate the trajectory of the bullet. "He was almost certainly killed in the water, or thrown in immediately after death."

"Because of the grave wax?" I asked. I instinctively held my hand over my nose, not that it helped much.

"Adipocere," Dr. Verniquet said, nodding. "The fatty deposits turn into a white, waxy substance when the body is immersed in water, as has occurred in this unfortunate fellow. But it never happens in the presence of insect life, so we can assume that he went into the water immediately."

The corpse's gut and cheeks were covered in the stuff, which looked like homemade soap mixed with candle drippings. It wasn't pretty, but all it told me was that he wasn't skinny when he was killed. The bottom of the rubber sack was awash in fluids I didn't want to think about. I pulled back the edges and studied the rest of the body. One foot was missing, the other without toes. His fingers were stubs.

"Fish food?" I asked.

"Yes," the doctor said. "Probably happened close to the shore, before he went out with the tide. Or came in with it. As you can see, there's nothing much left of the soft tissue on his fingers, so there's no hope of fingerprints. I'd put his age at about thirty. Five foot eleven inches in height."

That looked about right. What was left of him seemed to be in good shape, too. His chest was broad, and he had a full head of brown hair, darker in some spots. I ran two fingers through the hair and sniffed, trying to block out the overwhelming stench of decomposition and concentrate on what was in his hair.

"Oil?" I asked.

"Yes, he was covered in petroleum. He may have floated through an oil slick from a sunken ship. Could have happened at any point. Anything else?"

"No," I said, desperate for the sound of the zipper going in reverse. Dr. Verniquet obliged as I gripped the edge of a table to keep from fainting. "I didn't see any clothing," I managed.

"There wasn't much. It was all in shreds. Nothing as substantial as a belt or lifejacket. As you saw, the fish had been at him, and between being banged about on the rocks and exposure to salt water and sunlight, his clothing did not hold up well. What we took off was as decayed as he is." The doctor took a flat box from the bottom of the gurney and set it on a table as he trundled off, the broken wheel clacking in protest.

There were shreds of cloth, the colors of which had been bleached and stained to a dull reddish-brown hue. A uniform? Perhaps. Or workingman's garments. They had a rough feel, probably wool. Not a dressy kind of guy. No labels or telltale stitching where insignia might have been. Useless.

"I have been informed that I must list the cause of death as 'killed in action,'" Dr. Verniquet said a few minutes later as we sat in his office. There was a fresh cigarette in his mouth and an open window, which helped, even though the fragrance of decay still hung on my uniform and cloyed my nostrils. "By the highest authority, or so they said."

"If they were English, it must be MI5," I said. Killed in action meant an end to questions, at least officially.

"They were. You're the first Yank who's shown up to take a look. At least now I can put the poor chap in the ground."

"In an unmarked grave," I said.

"Certainly," Dr. Verniquet said. "I have no idea if he's German, French, or one of ours."

"How long was he in the water?" I asked.

"It's hard to say precisely," Dr. Verniquet said, grinding out his cigarette. "Minimum of a month, perhaps as long as three or four."

"Have other bodies washed ashore since the start of the war?"

"We've had our share," he said. "Especially in summer 1940, when Jerry attacked the Channel shipping. We had sailors and airmen alike. But then they focused on the London area, and we saw less of the war in the air this far west."

"Did any of them look like our guy?"

"Not a one," Dr. Verniquet said firmly. "None were badly decomposed, and all had their uniforms relatively intact. Some were still in life belts. And their wounds were horrible. When a few twenty-millimeter rounds or a machine-gun burst strikes the human body, the flesh rips apart. This man was shot at close range with a pistol of some sort, mark my words."

CHAPTER TWO

I WALKED OUTSIDE and breathed in the fresh air, happy for each cleansing lungful. The mortuary was on a side street near the police station, where Kaz waited for me in the jeep. His head was tilted back, his eyes closed as he made the most of the warm April weather and the low, slanting sun.

"I hope you haven't worn yourself out talking to the constable," I said, dropping myself into the driver's seat. Kaz smiled, then wrinkled his nose as he opened one eye.

"Billy, you smell horrible!"

"You would too if you'd spent time poking a decayed corpse." I filled Kaz in on what I'd learned—or had not learned from the police surgeon and asked what he'd come up with.

"Nothing, really," Kaz said. "I had tea with Constable Miller, who had no idea where the corpse might have come from."

"Tea? You had tea while I looked at a guy sloshing around in a rubber sack?"

"It wasn't very good, Billy. Day-old teabags, I daresay." For Kaz, that was roughing it. He was used to the finer and more expensive things in life. "Constable Miller is beyond retirement age and is staying on for the duration. He is a good man, and diligent in his own way, but he is not at the forefront of criminal investigation."

"Great," I said, noticing that Kaz was hanging half out of the jeep. "Is it that bad?"

"Perhaps we should drive. The wind may help," Kaz said. "In any case, the body was found on Slapton Sands, which is not in the good constable's jurisdiction. It is part of the army's Assault Training Center, and the soldiers who found him brought the body here to the mortuary."

"Constable Miller had no leads?"

"He said he took one whiff and decided it was an army matter. The military police declined, declaring that it was obviously not an American soldier, and that he'd been in the water long before they arrived in this area. The constable did refer me to Inspector Grange at the Dartmouth headquarters of the Devon Constabulary, who is in charge of the investigation, such as it is."

"No one wants a smelly corpse," I said, and started the jeep. I headed down Fore Street, the main thoroughfare in Kingsbridge. It was a narrow lane, hemmed in on each side by low, grey granite buildings, each one lower than the last as the road meandered down to the waterfront from the wooded heights above. We waited at an intersection as a long column of GIs marched by at a quick pace, heavy packs and rifles slung over their shoulders. Some were kids, maybe nineteen or twenty tops. I wondered how many of them would end up floating facedown in the Channel before too long. Youthful life could so easily be swallowed by the charnel house of war. I wanted to wash the stench of death away, but I knew it would return. It was all around us, waiting around each corner. Waiting for the invasion, across that cold English Channel.

The column passed, the tramp of boots on cobblestones echoing in the distance.

I drove on. Kingsbridge was at the head of a broad estuary that brought tidal waters up from the Channel a couple of miles to the south, providing a natural safe harbor for small boats. I'd noticed the fishing vessels when we drove in, all of them moored and resting on the muddy flats along the quayside. The smell of low tide and rotting fish guts wafted on the breeze.

"Ah, camouflage," Kaz said, working to keep a straight face. Kaz enjoyed a good laugh at my expense. And I didn't mind. Kaz was a good pal, the best. He'd been through hard times and lived through tremendous losses. The kind of losses that would have sent many tough guys to their knees. So anything that brought a smile to his face was okay by me.

Kaz, or rather Lieutenant—and sometimes Baron—Piotr Augustus Kazimierz, was Polish and had joined the Polish Army in exile when I was still in blue back in Boston. But he was a small, skinny guy, with a heart defect to boot, and the only work he could get was as a translator at the US Army headquarters in London. He spoke half a dozen European languages fluently, and was generally the smartest guy in the room, having won all sorts of honors at Oxford. But Kaz had always wanted to do more, and when I came along, he and I became a team. But that's a long story. Suffice it to say he's a Pole in a British uniform and I'm Boston Irish in Uncle Sam's brown. Kaz's uniform is tailor-made and mine needs to be ironed to look half as good.

Did I mention the scar?

I've gotten to where I don't even think about it. But when someone first meets Kaz, their eyes either linger on the scar or look away quickly, as if they'd glimpsed the price of war and found it too painful to bear. It goes from his right eye down the side of his face, courtesy of a killer who tried to take him out of the picture. He almost succeeded, too, but that's yet another long and complicated story. Kaz carries that jagged scar on his face, his wound visible to the world. A memory he will never shake loose.

Did I mention the Webley?

For a thin guy with glasses and a bum ticker, Kaz is a damn good shot. He wears a Webley break-top revolver and has used it to save my neck more than once. He's easy to underestimate at first glance, but that would be a fatal mistake. Has been, for some.

Did I mention Kaz came close to killing himself?

No, I didn't. Too much to get into right now.

"Let's talk to the fishermen," I said, pulling the jeep to the side of the road. Fishermen knew tides and currents, and we needed to know where this body had come from. I saw that Kaz understood. Like I said, Kaz is smart in six languages. He reached into the musette bag we kept in the jeep for emergencies. It was filled with chocolate bars, cigarettes, and other goodies from the PX. A little gentle bribery went a long way when all you wanted was information from guys suspicious of outsiders. We decided to deploy the Lucky Strikes.

"Good morning, gentlemen," I said, approaching a group of fishermen perching on a variety of tubs and crates near a row of a half-dozen fishing craft, keels in the mud of the estuary, lines tied snug to stanchions on the quay. On their laps was a confusion of nets being sewn or mended or whatever fishermen did with them. I got a couple of nods, but most didn't bother to look up. Yanks were tuppence a dozen along the southwest coast.

"Sorry to interrupt your labors," Kaz said, handing packs of Luckies around. That got their attention. "But we need your expertise."

"Those cigarettes would buy you a lot more than that, laddie," the oldest of the bunch said, with a wide grin that could have used a few more teeth.

"But not from us, eh, Alfie?" This from another grey-haired fisherman. It got a round of laughs.

"I wanted to ask about the tides and currents," I said. Before I could say more, Alfie beckoned me closer and raised his head, sniffing the air.

"Either you fell in a dung heap," Alfie said, "or you've been to see Doc Verniquet. Which means you're here about the body." He pocketed his smokes and grinned. "Ain't that right?"

"Dead on, Alfie," I said, which earned me a chuckle. Bringing a bloated, stinking corpse into town must have been hard to keep secret.

As the others lit up, Alfie studied me. "Think he was one of yours?"

"Too soon to tell," I said. "What I'd like to know is where he might have floated in from. You fellows must know the tides and currents better than anyone."

"Aye. But why should we help you?" one of the other fishermen said, blowing smoke from one of the twenty reasons. He was younger than Alfie, but not young enough for military service. In his forties maybe, or maybe his weathered skin and thick stubble had just aged him. "Your lot has shut down all the good fishing west of here, not to mention taken homes away from good people."

"Now hang on, George," Alfie said. "It was our lot who took over the South Hams, not the Yanks. And between E-boats and the Luftwaffe, the Germans have had as much to do with keeping us clear of those waters."

"Yeah, but we could still have stayed close to the shore," George said, "if it wasn't for the Yanks blowing up our homes."

"I'm sorry, fellows," I said. "But I don't know what you're talking about. We just got here from London to look into the body they brought in."

"The government evacuated the whole area. Our government, that is," Alfie said, with a hard look to George. "Right before Christmas, it was. Hard on everyone, especially the older folks. Some had never been more than one village away from home their whole lives."

"An old fellow from my village hung himself in his barn," George said. "He'd never been outside of Blackawton, said he'd die there rather than leave."

"I'm sorry," I said. "That must have been hard."

"It was," Alfie said with a nod. "But most of us feel we had to do our part. If it helps to get your lads ready for the invasion, it's the least we can do. The government gave us money, after all. It's not like we were bombed out sudden like. We had a month to pack up and leave, more time than many had after the Luftwaffe come over."

"More than three thousand people, I understand," Kaz said. "Nearly two hundred farms spread out over six parishes."

"Polish, eh?" Alfie said, pointing to Kaz's shoulder patch. "You know what it's like to lose everything to the war. Our complaints must seem petty."

"Loss is loss," Kaz said, with a sad smile. He looked away, studying the muddy riverbed. Kaz had lost more to this war than most people.

"Sorry," George said, after another glare from Alfie. "I know lots of folk have it worse. But I can't help missing it. We lived in Beesands all our lives, the wife and I. Fished out of there and made a good living, too. Plenty of crab and plaice out on the Skerries and beyond."

"The Skerries?" I said.

"Sand bank out in Start Bay," Alfie explained. "Off limits now, strictly for the navy."

"Aye," George said. "Ours and theirs. Jerry sticks his nose up this way now and then. The E-boats go out at night, looking for transports."

"They ever attack you?" I asked.

"No," Alfie said. "We skirt the coast and head west into the wider waters. Jerry likes to stay in the Channel, where he can run back to Cherbourg if things get too hot."

"You men know these waters," I said, getting back on track. "Any ideas about where the body could have come from? France maybe?"

"Naw," George said with a dismissive wave of his hand. "The currents don't carry north or south. East or west, depending on the tide."

"The Channel's like a sleeve," Alfie said. "Water goes in every day, like a man's arm into his shirt. At the narrow parts, it's a surge. Less so as the Channel widens, into the Atlantic or the North Sea. Here, it's strong, as you can see." He gestured toward their fishing boats stuck in the mud. "Two hours from now the tide'll come in, and in three we'll be heading out in deep water."

"In and out, four times a day," George said. "The inshore currents run about two or three knots an hour. More if the winds are favorable."

"Which means a body washed up at Slapton Sands could have gone into the water twenty or so miles in either direction and been stuck in the tidal currents until he washed ashore," I said. I figured the tides ran six hours apart, and at three or maybe four knots an hour, the currents could have carried him back and forth for quite a while.

"Could be," Alfie said, glancing at the other fishermen, who nodded their assent. "The winds have kicked up since last week, enough to bring him ashore."

"You haven't heard of any fishermen missing? Boats that didn't come back from the Channel?"

"No. If a man was missing, everyone within miles'd know if it. Of course, a body could have gone in right here, from the embankment,"

George said. "The estuary goes on for three miles before it reaches the Channel. He could have floated out with the tide and got caught up in the currents, washing up and down the coast until the wind took pity on him and returned him to dry land."

"Here, or anywhere up the River Dart to the east," Alfie said. "We're not much help, I'm afraid."

I thanked them for their assistance, such as it was. As we left, I took stock of their clothing. Corduroy or wool, plain browns mostly. A month or so in the drink and they'd look like the shreds Doc Verniquet had taken off the body.

CHAPTER THREE

I GUNNED THE jeep as we crossed the low stone bridge that arched the estuary, letting the wind whip the smell from my clothes. Mud flats and tidal pools spread out on either side as the salty aroma of the ocean grew stronger.

"I'd prefer the stink of death to actually dying," Kaz said, holding on to his cap with one hand and the seat with the other. I let up on the gas and drove sedately through a small village. Whitewashed stone cottages with thatched roofs sat close to the road, stark and bright beneath the slanting rays of the morning sun. A pub, a couple of shops, and then we were back in the midst of green fields. Aircraft roared overhead, descending as they passed us, heading for the coast.

"P-47s, I think," Kaz said, following their flight with shaded eyes. "Outfitted with the new rockets under each wing." The P-47 Thunderbolt was easy to spot. It was large for a fighter; long and wide, able to carry a heavy load of armament. We heard distant explosions, then saw the fighters climb gracefully in two groups, engines snarling as they vanished over the horizon.

"We must be getting close to the assault training area," I said.

"I assume we will wait until they are done with live-fire exercises," Kaz said. "Perhaps we can find a spot for a decent luncheon. We passed a pub in that last village. The dead can wait, after all."

"Let's find someone alive who can tell us what's going on first," I said.

"As long as they are not firing five-inch rockets at us," Kaz said. I had to agree. Kaz was up to date on the newly configured P-47s because General Eisenhower was coming down next week to watch an amphibious assault at Slapton Sands, which was going to feature a demonstration of the new rocket-carrying Thunderbolts. The general was interested in their capabilities against German tanks, which everyone knew we'd come up against all too soon. The Air Force probably had their pilots practicing every day so they'd look good when the brass was watching.

We came to a roadblock outside of Chillington, a village not rating more than a tiny dot on the roadmap Kaz held folded in his lap. A jeep was parked across the narrow lane, and a sign warning DANGER AHEAD was set up in front of it.

"Restricted area, Captain," said the military police sergeant, holding up his hand as he crushed a cigarette butt under one heel. His white helmet and white leather belt were spotless. He managed to sound pompous even when addressing two officers. "You'll have to turn around."

"Ike says I don't have to, Sergeant," I said as I passed him my orders. I couldn't help myself. Even though I come from a family of cops, I grew up hearing stories from my dad and Uncle Dan about the MPs they ran into during the last war. According to them, the snowdrops—so called because of their white helmets—spent way too much time and trouble keeping the fighting men from liquor and French ladies. Dad and Uncle Dan were both cops themselves. Detectives on the Boston Police Department, where I'd worked in the family business until this war came along.

"I've heard of SHAEF," the sergeant said, handing the papers back. "First time I've ever seen anyone from Supreme Headquarters. You're a long way from London, sir." He spoke evenly, but the sarcasm about officers from HQ was clear. I was thinking of a way to get even when Kaz spoke up.

"Sergeant," Kaz said. "Is the way ahead clear? Of bombs and explosions, I mean."

"You must have heard the P-47s, sir. They're done for the day. But they are running landing exercises down at the beach. May I ask your business here?" By now, his two companions had gathered around, probably glad of a break in the dull routine. One was an army private, the other an English constable with a rifle slung over his shoulder.

"You heard about a body washing up on Slapton Sands?" I asked, grateful for Kaz's interruption. This MP might have thought it'd be funny to send a couple of junior officers into a bombardment if I'd rattled his cage enough.

"Yes, I found it," the constable said. "Wish I hadn't. Horrible sight."

"They brought it through our checkpoint," the sergeant said. "That what you're here about?" He seemed friendlier now that we were talking about a gruesome corpse.

"It is. SHAEF wants to be sure it wasn't a Kraut," I said. "Mind if we borrow the constable? It would be helpful if he could show us exactly where the body was." The sergeant didn't mind. The constable's shift was up in an hour, and we could give him a lift back to Dartmouth. Besides, two guys could stand around and smoke as well as three.

"Tom Quick," the constable said from the rear of the jeep after we'd introduced ourselves. "Don't mind a drive to the shore, I'll tell you." Constable Quick was dark haired, with deep brown eyes and a confident way about him. He looked to be in his late thirties, maybe on the short side of forty. He wore his dark blue uniform well and handled his rifle like he was used to it. Bobbies had only been armed for the duration of the war, and some of them had never fired a shot in their lives.

"Boring duty?" Kaz asked as we drove off.

"It can be," Quick said. "But the worst of it is turning people back when all they want's to check on their homes. That's why I'm there, to provide a local face for the poor souls from the South Hams. Some try to sneak in, so we have to patrol the whole area. Sad business, really."

"Are you from the South Hams yourself?" I asked.

"No, I come from Newton Abbot. I'm assigned to the Dartmouth division; we work with the army quite often."

"What's the W.R. stand for?" I asked. Quick was wearing a British Tommie helmet with w.r. constable painted on the front.

"War Reserve Constable," Quick said. "I was a regular constable before the war, then I joined the RAF in '39. Served as a gunner on a Lancaster until I took some shrapnel in my leg. They invalided me out, even though it only gave me a slight limp. The police are undermanned enough to overlook a minor injury, especially if it gets them an experienced officer. Temporary duty only, though, until the end of the war."

"I was a cop myself, before the war," I said. "Back in Boston."

"Thought you might have been," Quick said.

"Why?" Kaz asked, turning to face Quick.

"Because he asks a lot of questions. A good copper never stops asking questions, does he, Captain Boyle?"

"No," I admitted. "Once you get the habit, it's hard to break. So I expect you asked some questions yourself after you found the body."

"Indeed," Quick said. "I didn't think he was a serviceman, and the Yank MPs were quick to agree. They had no reports of anyone missing, and the last thing they wanted was a case they couldn't solve. Besides, he'd been in the water a long time, probably since before the whole American army descended on the South Hams. I don't mean to sound ungrateful, but it's been a handful, let me tell you."

"Dr. Verniquet said he'd been in the water a month or more," I said, confirming his hunch. "And keeping the peace among thousands of GIs while guarding the border around the South Hams sounds like a huge job."

"It is, and the force is shortstaffed. A lot of the pensioners who came out of retirement at the start of the war have had to leave, and most of the younger lads have joined up. So it's up to the lame and elderly most of the time, but we manage, even with the black market to add to our woes. Which brings us back to our friend from the Channel."

"You think he was a criminal?" Kaz asked.

I slowed as we entered Stokenham, one of the villages emptied out by the government. It was a ghost town. Shops and homes along the main road stood with broken windows, open doors, and bits and pieces of furniture on the ground as if the buildings had spewed them out.

A curtain fluttered in the breeze, a frayed token of surrender. One house had burned, its roof caved in. At the center of town, dozens of GIs sat around a First World War monument, eating K-Rations. More came out of the Church House Inn by the side of the road, tossing their empty ration packs on the path. The village looked like it had been plundered.

"What's this?" I asked, shocked at the sight. I knew the residents were gone, but I had never imagined their homes and businesses would be treated like dump sites in their absence.

"Criminal, really," Quick said. "But the lads who come through here aren't the only ones to blame. At first we patrolled the area, but there weren't enough of us. Vandals and thieves had their chance before the army. So when the first troops came ashore, they found the homes wide open. The live-fire rounds they sometimes use for realistic training have only added to the destruction, as you can see. A house full of bullet holes is ripe for desecration. Most of these men probably think the entire area's slated for destruction."

"Or don't care," I said as I watched a large rat scurry into one cottage. We drove out of Stokenham in silence, until Quick got back to Kaz's question.

"I think it likely he was up to no good," he went on. "We had no missing persons who matched the general description, and I talked to some fishermen over in Paignton who said they hadn't heard of anyone lost in the Channel."

"We spoke to some in Kingsbridge who told us the same," Kaz said.

"Good," Quick said. "Plus there's the bullet wounds. Looked to me like a small caliber. What did Verniquet say?"

"Same thing," I said. "Probably a pistol, certainly nothing like a machine gun."

"Right. So I'm thinking a dispute between black marketers. This fellow's on the losing end of the argument and gets tossed overboard or off the end of a dock, and the tides keep him out in the Channel waters for weeks. Here, we're close now," Quick said. "Bear right."

We drove along a body of water to our left, a series of small, despoiled cottages to our right. At one time, it must have been a beautiful spot. On the other side of the water, low hills rolled across the horizon. The smell of salt air was sharp on the wind. As the road curved, we saw the long beach beyond the hills and a large beachfront hotel that had certainly seen better days. Gaping holes showed in the masonry, and smoking craters dotted the grounds.

"That's what the P-47s were aiming at," Quick said. "It was scheduled for demolition but kept in place for target practice. This stretch of beach is Slapton Sands; the water on the other side is called Slapton Ley. A few miles up the beach is the village of Slapton itself."

Several LCIs—Landing Craft Infantry—sat on the beach disgorging GIs. These weren't the small Higgins assault craft, but much larger vessels that could carry over two hundred men and deposit them on the far shore, with dry feet, via gangways on either side of the bow. They were designed as follow-up craft, so the good news was that if you were on one of these, you wouldn't be charging across the beach into machine-gun fire. Or at least, that was the plan.

GIs wandered about, clustered in small groups, smoking and chatting as if on holiday. A few officers yelled and hollered as they pushed the men off the beach and up the road we'd driven in on. If this was training for D-Day, no one was taking it seriously.

Quick directed us past the bombed-out hotel to the shingle beach, the pebbles making a continuous *click clack* sound as the waves washed over them, drawing them back into the deep. We left the jeep and walked a few yards as Quick got his bearings. The wind off the water was cold, and I buttoned up my trench coat as it flapped around me.

"Here, I'd wager, or close to it," he said. Slapton Sands was long and straight, hardly a curve or landmark in sight.

"He had petroleum in his hair," I said. "Have any ships sunk along this stretch of Channel?"

"Not for a while, no," Quick said. "Although there has been a lot of traffic. Landing craft, destroyers, escort and smoke-laying vessels, all sorts. Any of them could have leaked oil."

"Was anyone else around when you found him?" I asked.

"No, I was alone," Quick said. "It was one of the few days no landings were scheduled. I patrolled the village and walked down to the hotel, to make sure no one was about. That's when I found him. When the MPs came to fetch me, they called for a lorry to take him to Kingsbridge. They wanted nothing to do with it beyond getting him out of the area."

"So black market is your best guess?" I said, gazing out to the Channel. A destroyer moved offshore, one of the old four-stackers from the last war. It almost looked peaceful.

"It makes sense, doesn't it?" Quick said. "It explains why no one reported him missing. He probably wasn't local, maybe part of a gang moving in. We have so many Yanks quartered in Devon these days that it's black-market heaven."

"Did you question any of the local suspects?"

"Not me," Quick said. "You'd have to ask Inspector Grange. I believe he planned to, but I haven't heard from him about it yet."

"That's our next stop," I said. "We'll drop you off at your place, if that's where you're headed."

"Home is the division headquarters in Dartmouth," Quick said. "They have rooms for single men." I glanced at his left hand. I thought I'd seen him wearing a wedding ring. He noticed the look and stuffed his hands into his pockets. "Let's go, then," he said, and turned back to the jeep.

Nearby, an LCI revved its engine as it backed off the shingle, the last of the GIs having disembarked. About a dozen dogfaces took off their helmets and stretched out on the beach, lighting cigarettes and laughing.

"What the hell are you guys practicing for?" I said.

"The invasion, sir," a corporal said, standing, brushing off his pants, and tossing me a salute. "We just landed."

"You just landed on enemy territory, and the first thing you do is take off your helmets and bunch up for a smoke break? One mortar round could take out all of you idiots." I never enjoyed spouting off like a loudmouth officer, but I'd seen enough combat to know these guys didn't have a clue.

"Sure, Captain," the corporal said. "But this is only an exercise."

"Yeah. Be sure to tell that to the Krauts. Shape up, soldier, or you'll get your men killed." I gave him a hard glare, which wasn't my best face. I tried to think about Dad chewing me out when I was a rookie cop, and that helped. The corporal nodded and put on his helmet.

"Okay, men, spread out and move up to the road. Now!"

They did, but it was with the reluctance of children going back inside after recess. They dawdled and cast surly glances my way.

"They do not comprehend where they are going," Kaz said, whispering his words to the wind.

I knew he didn't mean a particular place. There were no map coordinates to mark the location. He meant that point in time and space where bullet meets bone, where grown men cry rivers of tears; the point you can never return from, even if you live to be ninety.

"How could they?" I said, and walked back to the jeep where Quick stood, hands still stuffed in his pockets.

CHAPTER FOUR

"WE'LL COME BACK tomorrow," I said, and washed down the last of my sole with a sharp, tasty ale. As Kaz mentioned, the dead can wait. They don't get tired or hungry, impatient or demanding. But they don't ever go away either, especially not the victims of murder. They're quiet but determined, unsettled by their violent end, present in every waking moment and some nightmares, reaching out for justice and remembrance. I can see the face of every victim I've ever known. After a case is solved, they retreat into the hazy recesses of memory, but they're impossible to forget. Maybe someday.

Maybe not.

We'd dropped Tom Quick off at the Dartmouth constabulary and gone to look for Inspector Grange. Quick had left us with hardly a word, a far cry from the friendly constable we started out with. The inspector was attending to a court case in Exeter and was not expected back today. That left us with only one move: lunch. The George and Dragon pub was a block from the station, with fresh fish and a view of the waterfront. Which meant a view of LCIs, LSTs, destroyers, and the odd fishing boat for as far as the eye could see. Dartmouth sat on the west bank of the River Dart, where it widened before flowing into the English Channel. It was well protected from the weather and the Luftwaffe, which made it a prime harbor for naval vessels training for the invasion.

"Good," Kaz said. "I'd like to get to Ashcroft as soon as possible."

"How long since you've seen your pal?" I asked.

"It was the summer of 1940," Kaz said. "David left Oxford to join the RAF, and had just earned his wings. He piloted a Hurricane during the Battle of Britain, then was sent to North Africa. We kept in touch, but I hadn't heard from him in months when I got his letter inviting me to visit."

"You're sure you don't mind me tagging along?"

"Not at all. David will be pleased to meet you," Kaz said, finishing his drink.

"Did he mention how serious his injury was?"

"He was rather silent on the subject, and of course I didn't press. The English are not the most demonstrative people, as you may have noticed. He may not wish to discuss it, even with an old friend."

Kaz and David Martindale had been friends at Oxford, where they both studied European languages. Flight Lieutenant Martindale was recuperating from injuries received in Italy. He'd been discharged from the hospital to rest at home, which was not far north of Dartmouth. He'd invited Kaz about a month ago, but a case we were on had kept him away. When we'd learned an investigation would take us to the Kingsbridge area, Kaz had written and set up the visit.

To be honest, we weren't exactly in demand at SHAEF. There was a shortage of murder—criminal murder, in any case—and other crimes that impeded the war effort. With the big invasion looming, it seemed as if everyone had been drawn in to the planning and training for D-Day, leaving little time or energy for our stock-in-trade.

Kaz and I, along with Staff Sergeant Mike Miecznikowski, or Big Mike as everyone from generals to privates called him, made up General Eisenhower's Office of Special Investigations. Our job was to deal with low crimes in high places that got in the way of the war effort. And to deal with them quietly, although quiet wasn't always in the cards. Every now and then the Brits borrowed us for some dirty work, which usually involved keeping me totally in the dark about everything until it was almost too late. We'd gotten in a bit of trouble because of our tendency to dig too deeply on our last job, and I half wondered if we had been sent here to get us out from underfoot.

Now all we had on our plate was the case of the rotting corpse. None of us needed to know anything about the invasion, for reasons of security. "Need to know" was the popular phrase of the day, often preceded in our case by "you don't." If you worked at SHAEF and weren't involved in D-Day, then you just sat back and watched everyone else scurry around being busy and important.

The fact that I understood why we were left out of planning for Operation Overlord—and I only know the code name since I'm nosy and can read upside down—didn't make it any easier to swallow. I hate being on the sidelines, no matter the logic. So when the opportunity came along to spend a few days at an English country home with a fancy name like Ashcroft, I thought, why the hell not? It's got to be a classy place, since Kaz only has classy friends.

Not counting me, of course.

We paid the tab and got into the jeep, Kaz unfolding the map to figure the best route to North Cornworthy, where his buddy's family estate was. Martindale's in-laws, to be precise. As Kaz studied the map, I noticed Tom Quick exit the police station. He caught my eye, then looked away. As he did, I realized something odd. He had said his injury left him with a limp. I hadn't paid much attention to his gait before, but as I watched him stroll away, I didn't see that he had any trouble walking. Kaz caught my look and saw it as well.

"It seems our Constable Quick has secrets," Kaz said.

"Or miraculous healing powers," I said. "He wouldn't be the first guy to exaggerate an injury to get out of combat. I can't imagine what it's like in a bomber at night, loaded with high explosives, as every gunner in Germany tries to blow you out of the sky." I pressed the starter and tried to put Quick out of my mind. He bothered me. The wedding ring, the sudden change in mood, the supposed limp—it all added up to something more than malingering. But what? And what did it matter anyway? Not my business.

Traffic was backed up with military vehicles in every direction. In a few minutes, we were idling on a residential street of neat red-brick semi-detached houses, flower boxes in spring bloom. A boy zipped by on his bicycle, his dark blue cap and leather pouch marking him as a telegraph messenger. Lace curtains fluttered in his wake, closing in relief as he passed each residence, until he braked and stopped farther up the lane, racing up the steps and knocking at the door of a house where moments before a wife or mother had been sitting in blissful ignorance that a husband or son had been killed in Burma or Italy, over Germany or under the sea, in any of the terrible far-flung battles of this war. That was what a telegraph meant these days. Bad news, each and every one. The traffic moved, and we watched as the boy stood at the door, clutching the telegram, waiting to confront the face of grief.

We drove out of town, past the red-brick Royal Naval College high up on the hills overlooking Dartmouth. The slopes were blindingly green in the sunlight, the River Dart flowed peacefully to the Channel on our right, and I was pretty sure I didn't smell like death anymore. I banished thoughts of corpses and Tom Quick from my mind. It was like playing hooky, something I'd been pretty good at back in Boston.

My mental vacation was interrupted by the blast of a jeep's horn behind us. "It's Colonel Harding," Kaz said from the passenger seat. "Pull over." We got out and approached the colonel's jeep. Several staff cars and other jeeps passed us, Harding giving a friendly wave to the occupants. I tossed off a lazy salute and Kaz did the British equivalent, palm out, with a lot more élan. As always.

"I'm glad I spotted you," he said. "Saves me a trip. I telephoned Ashcroft House, but a fellow named Williams said you hadn't arrived."

"What's up, Colonel?" I asked.

"We just finished a planning meeting at the Royal Naval College, preparing for upcoming maneuvers. I need you at Slapton Sands early tomorrow. The local police will be out in force, keeping people as far as possible from the exercise area, several miles out from the regular boundary."

"Why?" Kaz asked.

"There's going to be a live-fire exercise tomorrow morning, and we don't want any civilian sightseers anywhere near the place. Plus, with senior brass thick on the ground, we want to have as much security in place as possible. A lot of them will be out on ships observing from the Channel, but others will want to watch on land. To complicate matters, in a few days there's an even bigger exercise, codenamed Operation Tiger. All eyes are going to be on Slapton Sands, so I don't want any screw-ups."

"What's our job?" I asked.

"I need you to be my eyes and ears while I'm offshore with Ike. I spoke to Inspector Grange of the Dartmouth police, and he has agreed to provide a liaison officer for you."

"We were just looking for him," I said. "About the dead man who washed up at Slapton Sands."

"Grange was at the meeting," Harding said, hooking his thumb in the direction of the Royal Naval College up on the hill. "Any news on the body?"

"We met the constable who found the corpse. The general consensus is that it was likely a black-market deal gone bad. Colonel, if we're going to work with a local cop, Tom Quick would be the fellow."

"He is the constable who found the body," Kaz added. "He knows the area."

"Fine," Harding said. "I'm headed back to Dartmouth, so I'll see Grange and have Quick made available. Pick him up at police headquarters at zero five hundred." I groaned at the early hour.

"What are we looking for?" Kaz asked.

"Whatever shouldn't be there," Harding said. "Your theory of a black-market killing makes sense, but I'm not taking any chances. Watch for anyone who shouldn't be in the area. It's a long shot, but if there are any German agents around, they'd have a field day given half a chance."

"You want us there when they're using live ammo?" I asked. It didn't sound like a day at the beach.

"The cruiser *HMS Hawkins* will shell the beach from zero six thirty to zero seven hundred. Be at the checkpoint outside the restricted area before that starts. At zero seven hundred, the beachmaster will inspect the beach and give the order for the landing to proceed if it is safe. I want you two close by to make sure nothing goes wrong."

"What could go wrong?" I asked.

"Everything," Harding said. "Nothing. I don't know. That's why they call it the fog of war. I need you two close to the action. Now let's switch jeeps."

Harding had a field radio installed in the back seat, and he went over the frequencies we were to report on. "I'll be on one of the LCIs with General Eisenhower. If you see anything out of place, contact me immediately. Got it?"

"You don't think there's any threat to the general, do you?" I asked.

"The corpse on the beach probably was some sort of crook. Probably. Or some poor slob who stumbled into a black-market deal. Or a German agent coming ashore who got himself killed for what he saw. Very improbable, I grant you. But impossible? No. So don't get complacent. If Ike decides to come ashore after the exercise, I don't want to be looking behind every tree and shrub. I want you to do that before he gets there. Understood?"

"Absolutely, Colonel," I said. Sometimes Harding was an okay guy. Once in a while you could kid around with him. But most times, this was the essence of his personality: a hard-ass, take-nothing-for-granted kind of guy. He came out of the trenches of the last war in one piece, so I figured he had a right.

THE SKY WAS darkening as we turned off the main road and drove through the village of North Cornworthy. It had the usual monument at the center of town, a stone cross listing the names of the dead from the last war. It didn't seem like there were that many people left in all of North Cornworthy these days. The street was muddy, the one pub dark and uninviting, and the few shops closed. Whitewashed houses with greying thatched roofs stood amidst weeds and looming pines.

"Not much of a place," I said.

"Many of these small villages were devastated by the Great War," Kaz said. "Men from the same town served together, whole companies often wiped out in minutes. Then the Depression, another war, the young called up or working in factories, and soon only the old are left behind."

Outside the village, we found the turnoff for Ashcroft. We took a driveway lined by giant oaks and followed a gradual incline until the trees thinned out and we saw Ashcroft House, rising from the hill like a giant slab of stone. It was a low two-story structure built from the same grey granite as the stone walls in the area. The roof was slate, the only brightness provided by the stark white trim around the windows and doors. The main section had a wing off either side, and it looked like other parts of the house had been added over time. I wondered how old the place was. Centuries, at least, for the main house.

"This is some joint, Kaz," I said as I parked the jeep in front.

"Apparently David married well," he said as we grabbed our bags from the rear. "He and Helen met late in 1940 and married rather quickly. Wartime romance."

If anyone knew about love in a time of war, it was Kaz. He rang the bell. An elderly butler answered the door and told us we were expected, then shuffled off to fetch Martindale. The entryway was impressive. Gleaming marble floors and a wide staircase ascending to a broad upper landing, paneled doors lustrous with polish. The place smelled rich.

Double doors to our right swung open, and the butler stood aside as a figure emerged from the gloom of the unlit room. A good-looking man in a RAF uniform came toward us, a smile on his face. His blond hair was slicked back, and his step was quick and steady. It had to be Martindale, but at first I saw no sign of a wound or injury.

"Piotr!" he said, extending his hand as he drew nearer. "It's so good to see you."

As he came into the bright hallway and turned to greet us head on, I almost gasped.

It was his face.

"David," Kaz said, gripping his hand in both of his. I saw the slightest evidence of struggle cross his features as he worked to find another way to say it was good to see his friend. "It has been too long. I've missed you."

"And you must be Captain Boyle," Martindale said. "Kaz has told me so much about you."

"Don't believe half of it, Flight Lieutenant. Thanks for inviting me." We shook, and his grip was firm, but I detected a tremor in his hand. Still, he put on a good show. He'd been burned. Badly. But only the right side of his face. It looked as if the flesh had melted, then frozen into a hard, shiny skin. He'd had surgery, to be sure. His right eye was visible, but barely, peeking out from a slit that looked like it never closed. His nose was perfect on the left, a tight bump of scar tissue on the right.

"Glad to have you. And let's leave rank aside, shall we? From what Piotr tells me, I sense you'd rather not bother about it. I'll show you to your rooms, and you can wash up before dinner. Thank you, Williams," he said to the butler, who quietly departed. David waited until he was out of earshot.

"Look, Piotr, I'm sorry I never told you about this," David said, gesturing vaguely in the direction of his ruined face. "I should have prepared you. It must be a shock."

"It is a shock you are still alive, after all the battles you have seen," Kaz said. "And I have not come through the war unscathed either." He made the same small gesture toward his own scar.

"What, that little thing?" David said, and they both laughed, the kind of laughter that comes when two old friends reunite and pick up as if the intervening years had never occurred. Maybe this would be good for both of them. I kept a few steps behind, letting them chat as David led us upstairs.

"I don't know what to think," Kaz said later in my room. "I should be glad he's alive and has all his limbs, but what a price he's paid. I can't imagine what life will be like for David."

"It will be a life. Don't forget that," I said as I tied my field scarf, which the army insisted on calling a plain old necktie.

"Yes," Kaz said, with little enthusiasm. He stared out the window as I finished dressing. I'd brought my new tailor-made Ike jacket. It was a new short-waisted coat, based on the British army's battle jacket. General Eisenhower had pushed for the new design, and his name was linked to it, even though the quartermaster insisted on calling it the M-44 jacket. I wore it with my dark brown wool pants and chocolate-colored shirt. I looked pretty damn good—sort of a cross between an American gangster and a military intelligence officer. Bit of an exaggeration on both counts, but you get the idea.

Kaz looked elegant, but he always did. All his uniforms were custom-made, and for a guy with a small frame he wore them well. He removed his glasses and cleaned them carefully. I stood behind him and gazed out at the lawns and gardens below, the river in the distance, the sun lighting the horizon with reds and yellows. Below, a couple walked briskly toward the house.

The woman was tall and thin but big-boned, with a purposeful chin and a broad-brimmed burgundy hat that covered the rest of her face. She was gesturing with her gloved hands and seemed to be in earnest conversation with the guy next to her. Husband, probably. He held his hands behind his back, his head tilted slightly as if to catch her every word. He wore a tweed suit and a worried look.

"I wonder who they are," Kaz said idly. "And how they reacted to David's injury."

"Let's find out," I said.

CHAPTER FIVE

WILLIAMS DIRECTED US to the library for drinks before dinner. The hallway carpets were deep and plush, absorbing the sound of our footsteps. But not the voices coming from the library.

"You had better think of *something*, Edgar." A woman's voice, hushed but unable to contain itself. "We only have so much time."

"I will, I will." A man, probably Edgar. Kaz laid his hand on my arm and we backed up a few steps, not wanting to intrude. The voices followed us.

"Think of the children—although I don't know why you'd start now. You should have thought of them first, Edgar. We shall have to take them out of school. I've already warned them, and I told them it was all your fault."

"Why would you say such a thing, dear?"

"It's true, isn't it?" Her voice was lower, throaty and demanding. Edgar went silent as the clink of glassware echoed in the room. Kaz and I took that as our cue to enter. There were only two people in the room, the same couple we'd seen earlier.

"Hello," the man said, with no trace of the previous conversation in his greeting. "You must be David's guests. Edgar Shipton. This is my wife, Meredith. Sir Rupert is her father."

"Lieutenant Piotr Kazimierz, at your service. This is Captain Billy Boyle."

"But it's Baron, isn't it?" Meredith Shipton said as Kaz gave her hand a kiss. I settled for a limp shake. "At least, that's what David told us. I didn't know the Poles had barons, but why not?"

"Indeed," Kaz said. "Yes, I am a baron of the Augustus Clan and would be pleased to be addressed as such."

"And you, Captain Boyle?" Meredith said, turning her attention to me. She had penetrating hazel eyes, glints of green reflecting off the emerald dress she wore. Not a beautiful woman, but striking. She exuded health and strength, and I'd have bet she was used to getting what she wanted.

"From the Boyle clan of Boston. And I'd be pleased if you'd call me Billy."

"I think I shall," Meredith said, smiling over the cocktail raised to her lips. She seemed as delighted to meet an informal Yank as a Polish aristocrat. "Edgar, please see to drinks for our guests." Edgar did her bidding. He seemed used to it, and smiled as if indulging her, which I guessed he was also used to doing.

Kaz asked for whiskey and soda. I told Edgar I'd have whatever he was drinking, which turned out to be a large whiskey, no soda. It's a little trick Dad taught me. It establishes a bond and tells you something about the person you've just met. Everyone likes to be flattered, and showing you trust a person's taste in booze is gratifying to them. Every now and then, I end up with a Pink Lady, but it generally turns out well.

"You're both with SHAEF, I see," Edgar said as he handed me the whiskey in a cut-crystal glass that cost more than the whole bottle. "You chaps must be working day and night, what with the invasion coming up."

"We really can't say anything about that," I said. It was true, but not for the reason I led Edgar to believe.

"Ah, security, certainly. But all signs point to it, Captain Boyle. All of Devon's thick with American troops moving towards the coast. We see convoys every day, and tent cities springing up everywhere. The current witticism is that one can cross the River Dart at Dartmouth simply by stepping from one landing craft to another." Edgar chuckled, and I went along with the gag. It was almost true, from what we'd seen today.

"Do you live here, or are you visiting as well?" I asked Edgar. He looked to be in his late thirties, maybe too old for service, maybe not. I knew he had kids, and there was probably an exemption for an older married man with children. He had some grey flecked through his short brown hair and a bit of a paunch, but he held himself well.

"Here, temporarily," he said, and his eyes sought out Meredith. "We've recently returned from India. I was in the civil service there, and I'm looking for a position now. Meredith wished to visit her father, and Sir Rupert was so kind as to invite us to stay for a while."

"I'm sure the Foreign Office needs people with experience in that part of the world," I said.

"Edgar's already been to the Foreign Office, haven't you, dear?" Meredith said, gliding in between us. "Any joy?" I was pretty sure she knew the answer.

"Nothing yet, no." Edgar met her eyes dead on. A challenge?

"Did you enjoy India?" I asked Meredith, feeling uncomfortable with their exchange.

"I loved it," she said, clasping her hand on Edgar's arm as if there was no discord between them. "Father was with the civil service in the Raj as well, for eighteen years. I was practically raised there. I adore India, except for that creature Gandhi and the India National Congress."

"They're for independence from England," Edgar explained, catching the blank look on my face. I knew who Gandhi was; he was famous enough. But Indian politics was not my strong suit.

"And for the Japanese as well," Meredith said. "Some of them in the National Congress, anyway."

"The enemy of my enemy is my friend," Kaz said.

"What? Oh, of course," Meredith said. "Still, I don't see why they should look upon us as the enemy. So many Indian soldiers are fighting the Germans in Italy, aren't they?"

"How long were you there this time?" I asked Meredith, trying to turn the conversation away from British imperialism. As a good Irishman, I was bound to say something unpleasant before long, and I was a guest here.

"Only two years," Meredith said, with a hooded stare in Edgar's direction.

"Sorry I'm late," David said from the doorway, a well-timed distraction. "Helen will be down shortly."

"David, the baron and Billy are absolutely delightful. I'm so glad you invited them," Meredith said, smiling in David's direction. She didn't avoid looking at him, and Edgar served up a drink in no time. I was glad to see David readily accepted. The English are rightly famous for their stiff upper lips, but they also tend to hide the occasional inconvenient truth. David's face was a truth that some families, in their comfortable libraries on their country estates, might prefer to keep locked away. Or maybe my Irish was up, and I was being uncharitable to the whole race.

"Yes, I'm glad it worked out," David said. "It would be a shame to lose contact with old university friends, wouldn't it?"

"I agree," Edgar said. "I still correspond with several. You read modern languages at Oxford, if I recall. Which college?"

"Balliol," Kaz said. "A fascinating experience, with students from many nations.

"Yes," David said. "That was when there was still hope for a Europe without war. I thought understanding language would be a key to understanding people. Instead, we're learning to kill one another. But at least Piotr can put his knowledge to good use these days. Translation, isn't that what you do at SHAEF?"

"It was," Kaz said, and sipped his whiskey and soda.

"We work in the Office of Special Investigations," I said. Why not give Kaz a boost in the eyes of his pal?

"Investigating what?" Edgar asked.

"Whatever they tell us to," Kaz said. "We cannot say much more, unfortunately."

"Sorry, Piotr," David said. "I should have known you didn't earn that scar translating German."

"Are you spies?" Meredith asked, a hint of mischief in her voice. Or was she adroitly moving the conversation away from the subject of facial injuries?

"Glorified policemen would be closer to the mark," I said. "I was a detective in Boston before the war."

"Piotr!" David exclaimed. "A copper? Who would have thought?" Kaz smiled as his friend clapped him on the shoulder.

"David, please don't be so vulgar." A woman spoke from behind us.

"Helen, dear," David said, turning toward his wife. She was thin, with dark blonde hair that was outshone by her husband's vivid color. Pretty, in a timid sort of way. She wore pearls and a red silk dress that drew your eyes to every fold. David did the introductions. Helen smiled as Kaz bowed and kissed her hand. I could have kicked him. I blushed and shook her hand, which I could tell was not the highlight of her evening.

"Do I understand that you're with the military police?" Helen asked Kaz.

"What's this about the police?" Another voice, this one from an ancient lady wearing a dress that had last been stylish back when the kaiser was running things in Germany. She was small and thin like Helen, but she had Meredith's jaw and the kind of voice Sister Mary Margaret used to use when I'd done something wrong, which was every waking minute, according to her.

"Great Aunt Sylvia, come and meet our guests," Helen said, taking her by the arm.

"Don't shout, Helen! I am not yet deaf. Which one is the policeman, and why is he here? Has something been stolen?"

"Nothing has been stolen, Auntie," Meredith said, taking her hand and maneuvering her into a comfortable chair. "Helen misunderstood. This is Baron Piotr Kazimierz. He was with David at Oxford. Baron Kazimierz, this is Lady Pemberton."

"Charmed," Kaz said as he clasped her gloved hand and bowed. "Thank you for your hospitality."

"I'd say you were welcome, but the hospitality is not mine to give," she said, turning her raised eyebrows on me. "And this is?"

"Captain William Boyle, Lady Pemberton," I said, lowering my head a notch. I wasn't much for bowing to the English, even old ladies. I kept my hands clasped behind my back and left out my usual invite to call me Billy. I doubted she'd care to.

"Thank you, Edgar," she said, studying me as Edgar kept up his bartending duties with a glass of sherry. "It's nice to see some new faces, David. Sir Rupert invites people so seldom that one forgets the joy of fresh conversation. We seem to say the same things over and over."

"Sir Rupert Sutcliffe is Helen and Meredith's father," David said, filling in the rest of the family tree.

"Now what was this police business Helen hadn't grasped?" Lady Pemberton asked. She might have been old and wrinkled, but she wasn't forgetful.

"We are investigators, Lady Pemberton," I said. "For General Eisenhower. I used to be a detective, before the war."

"Goodness, Captain Boyle. The last time we had a police detective in the house was 1933—or was it 1932? When those jewels were stolen," Lady Pemberton said. "I did not care for the experience."

"I don't think Captain Boyle cares to hear about that," Meredith said. "He's our guest, after all."

"Well, there's a first time for everything," Lady Pemberton said in a disapproving tone. "You too, Baron Kazimierz? A policeman?"

"More like a spy, Lady Pemberton," Kaz stage-whispered. "A continental man of mystery." She liked that. I grinned in the direction of the others and noticed Helen. David was speaking to her, and she was casting her eyes everywhere but toward his. He was smiling, but she looked like she would burst into tears at any moment, her fist clenched white.

"I understand it was a case that brought you to Devon," Edgar said. "David said it was the only reason the baron could take the time to visit. Should we be worried about German agents lurking in the bushes?"

"Nothing so dramatic, Mr. Shipton," I said.

"Please, call me Edgar," he said. "We're really quite informal here."

"Okay, Edgar, if you call me Billy." Edgar was friendly enough, and chatting with him seemed less dangerous than jousting with the great aunt. "A body washed up on the beach in a restricted area. We're trying to identify who it was. Nothing much to it, probably."

"In the South Hams?" Edgar asked.

"Why do you say that?" I asked.

"Restricted area, you said. Fits the bill, close by. Never mind, don't bother to answer. Loose lips and all that. I hope you find whoever it was."

"Well, he doesn't match any missing persons, so it's doubtful anyone reported his absence to the police." I continued to watch Helen as we spoke. She moved around David, putting her right arm through his left, so she faced the unscarred side of his face. She relaxed and opened her clenched hand.

She couldn't look at his face.

Edgar went off to freshen his drink. He had the careful gait of someone who has drunk quite a bit and is working hard to hide it. Meredith motioned me to where she and Kaz were entertaining Great Aunt Sylvia, and I put on my best face for the old girl.

"The baron tells me you are related to General Eisenhower, young man," she said. "Is that true?"

"Yes, ma'am. I mean Lady Pemberton. We're related through my mother's family. I call him Uncle Ike—only when we're alone, of course—but I believe we are actually distant cousins."

"Hmm," she said. "One bristles at the idea of a foreigner, even one of our American cousins, telling the British army what to do. But he seems like a decent fellow. Is he?"

"The best," I said. "You can rest easy. He has the interests of all Allied soldiers at heart."

"Well, that may be, but does he have the worst interests of the Hun at heart as well?" Great Aunt Sylvia's eyes bored into mine, and I realized this wasn't just idle chitchat. She had a sharp mind, and it was a perceptive question.

"He's not a general to throw men's lives away for nothing," I said. "But he intends to win this war by destroying the enemy. Nothing short of unconditional surrender."

"Good!" Great Aunt Sylvia said. "That is what I wanted to hear. No talk of armistice like in the last war. What a mess they made of that. Having this happen all over again would be a disgrace to all those who died." Her face was vivid with rage, still fresh a quarter century later.

"You lost someone," I said. It was only a question of whom.

"My husband and my son," she said. "Lord Pemberton was a commodore on the battle cruiser *Queen Mary*. He was lost in the Battle of Jutland. Roger was a lieutenant with the Devonshire Regiment. He was killed at the Somme. His body was never found. Neither came home."

"I am sorry, Lady Pemberton," I said, my voice catching in my throat.

"As have I been all these years. I am the last of the Pembertons, living here by sufferance in the house and on the lands that should have gone to my son and his heirs. I have no wish for another generation to suffer such losses in the future. Tell your uncle to get on with it, Captain Boyle. Finish them off."

I said I would. I meant it.

Sir Rupert entered the library, and a deep silence. Everyone had been listening to Great Aunt Sylvia, and when she was done speaking, the only sound was Edgar pouring another drink.

"What's this?" Sir Rupert asked. "Has someone died?" He smiled at his jest and looked wonderingly around the room.

"Not recently," Great Aunt Sylvia said, and David stepped up to do the introductions. Meredith sat with her great aunt as the others hovered around Sir Rupert. He was middle-aged, dressed in a blue double-breasted suit that had been in style sometime during the previous decade. Not a surprise exactly. With wartime rationing, everyone in England made do with what they had. His face was long, topped by curly hair going grey. He had an easy air of authority about him, an acknowledgment that he was master of the house and a lot more besides. He stood with his back to Meredith and Great Aunt Sylvia, waiting for his drink as Edgar poured and David made the introductions.

"Sorry to keep you all waiting," Sir Rupert said. "I only got back from London an hour ago. More Foreign Office business."

"You are with the Foreign Office, Sir Rupert?" Kaz asked.

"They bring me in now and then," he said, accepting his whiskey and soda from Edgar with the kind of nod you might give a decent bartender. "After two decades in India, I do have some knowledge of the area, Burma and China included. I have retired from the Indian Civil Service, but it is rewarding to continue to be useful."

"Edgar was telling me he's back from India as well," I said.

"Yes, he is," Sir Rupert said, turning away and addressing the ladies. It was time for dinner—not to mention a new topic of conversation.

CHAPTER SIX

DISTRACTED SOMEWHAT BY the mussels in white-wine sauce, I watched my fellow diners. I had been expecting decent enough food by wartime standards, but it was clear rationing hadn't put a dent in the Ashcroft kitchens.

"Not bad, eh?" Sir Rupert said as he tucked into his own bowl. "We have a fellow on the staff who used to fish for a living. Gave it up to manage the grounds here when the war began. He still keeps a small boat. Brings in a good catch when it's safe to go out into the Channel."

"Safe from Germans?" I asked.

"No, safe from the weather and the American navy, Captain!" Sir Rupert said with a grin. "Crawford's boat's only little, no match for gale-force winds or those big wallowing landing craft. But if it's a calm day and he can avoid the larger vessels, he'll go out just beyond the mouth of the River Dart. Dartmouth, if you understand. We all benefit, so I don't begrudge him the time."

"We spoke to some fishermen in Kingsbridge today," I said. "It seems as if the war has taken its toll on them."

"Along the Channel coast, certainly," Sir Rupert said. "Crawford says the fish are plentiful, so perhaps it will be better than ever once the war is over."

As the first course was cleared, I leaned back and surveyed the table. Sir Rupert at the head, of course. I was on his left and Kaz across from me. Meredith and Edgar sat next to Kaz, while to my left were

Helen and then David. Great Aunt Sylvia faced Sir Rupert at the other
end of the table. The arrangement allowed David's ruined face to be
hidden from his wife, who spent most of her time talking across the
table to her sister.

Edgar offered to pour more wine for Great Aunt Sylvia, but his
was the only empty glass. David looked uncomfortable, and I wondered
whether Helen had made the seating arrangements. The conversation
was animated, but I noticed that Meredith and her father had not
exchanged a single word, or even looked at each other. I caught Kaz's
eye, and he gave the tiniest of shrugs, telling me he sensed the strange-
ness as well.

Lamb cutlets were served, and my surveillance was interrupted.

"Baron Kazimierz," Great Aunt Sylvia said, raising her voice to be
heard. "I hope you are not disappointed in the state of the household. We
live a simple life in Devon, much simpler than that in many smaller country homes. No footmen, no useless frills. I hope you do not disapprove."

"On the contrary, Lady Pemberton. I would not trade these fresh
peas for a dozen footmen," Kaz said. I hadn't thought about it, since
at the Boyle kitchen table it was strictly pass the potatoes and every
man for himself, but there was only one young girl bringing out the
plates. Williams, the butler, was nowhere to be seen.

"The early peas were picked from the greenhouse just today,"
Helen said. "Crawford again. Where would we be without him?"

"Are footmen hard to come by these days?" I asked.

"I would think so," Sir Rupert said. "But it's never been our style.
Even though the family has had its share of earls and lords, we've
always worked for a living. The upper classes tend to forget that they
got where they are today by dint of some distant ancestor who fought
and clawed his way to the top of the heap."

"My grandfather helped to build the mill on Bow Creek," Great
Aunt Sylvia said. "Not simply with funds; he helped to construct it.
The Pembertons were never afraid of hard work, believe me."

"The Sutcliffes agree," Sir Rupert said, nodding to Great Aunt
Sylvia. "Ashcroft will continue in that tradition." The table quieted as
a long-standing family dispute seemed to shimmer in the air between

them, seeking to take form. I could imagine the ghosts of Pembertons past at Great Aunt Sylvia's shoulders.

"You were knighted yourself, Sir Rupert?" Kaz inquired, moving the conversation to safer ground.

"Father is a Knight Commander of the Most Exalted Order of the Star of India," Helen said, with evident pride.

"It's what one gets for twenty years' service to the Crown," Sir Rupert said with a self-satisfied smile. At the other end of the table, Edgar set down his glass so loudly that Great Aunt Sylvia nearly jumped out of her chair.

Edgar's father-in-law had spent twenty years in India, had been knighted for his services, and was called to consult with the Foreign Office. Edgar had come home after only two years, and couldn't find a position anywhere. Was that the cause of the chill between Meredith and her father? Had he declined to help Edgar for some reason?

"Piotr, I hope you and Billy can remain with us for a few days," David said, the first words he'd spoken at the table.

"Yes, by all means," Sir Rupert said. "Have you concluded your business in Devon?"

"No, we haven't," I said, weighing the prospect of dinner the next few nights at Ashcroft against taking our chances at a pub or inn. "We're going to the South Hams tomorrow, the restricted area, quite early in fact. After that we'll wrap up our investigation in a day or so, I hope."

"Good hunting," Sir Rupert said, quite the jovial host. "You should both feel free to come and go as you please. Glad to have you."

"If you are sure it is no trouble?" Kaz said.

"You will find Sir Rupert is not given to idle platitudes when it comes to invitations to remain under his roof," Great Aunt Sylvia said. It was hard to tell whether that was a compliment or something else entirely. "Of course you must stay, so you and David can catch up properly. It's not every day we entertain the nephew of General Eisenhower, after all."

"Really?" Sir Rupert said, an eyebrow raised in my direction. I guess I didn't look like I could be related to the Supreme Commander.

"Yes," I said. I filled him in but kept it short. What I didn't tell any of them was that my folks had cooked up the idea of me working for Uncle Ike well before he became a big deal. You see, to my dad and Uncle Frank—he's a real uncle—the British Empire is pretty much the enemy, since we're all loyal Irishmen, and the Brits had kept their heel hard on Ireland for far too long. Both had served in the last war, and they lost their older brother in the trenches of France, so they didn't take kindly to the idea of another Boyle lost in a war to keep the English in control of half the world. I had no problem with that.

It was my mother who came up with the idea of getting in touch with Uncle Ike. He was from her side of the family, and at that time was working at the War Plans Department in DC. A perfect place to sit out the shooting war. Favors were called in, and soon I found myself a second lieutenant ready to join the staff of General Dwight David Eisenhower, duties unspecified. What we didn't count on was Uncle Ike rocketing to the top and taking me along for the ride.

What a ride it had been. From England in the early days to North Africa, Sicily, Northern Ireland, and Italy, then back to England. I was a captain now, and I saw things entirely differently than when I first arrived. I kind of missed the old me. He was much more certain—on the basis of knowing a whole lot less. I envied him.

"Good, it's settled then," David said. My thoughts had taken me out of the conversation, but I saw that Kaz was pleased to stay on. David looked relieved, and I wondered what he wanted besides renewing a youthful friendship. Occupational hazard for a cop. After chasing crooks and killers for a living, you begin to focus on the dark side of human nature and expect the worst of people. Maybe all David wanted was an old pal to keep him company at Ashcroft, where the residents weren't exactly warm and chummy.

Helen and David: the ideal couple, as long as she only saw him in profile, from the left.

Edgar and Meredith. A boozer without a job and his wife, who didn't speak to her father. Why were they here, unless it was to seek a favor from Sir Rupert?

Great Aunt Sylvia and her barbs directed at Sir Rupert. Or was that crack about invitations to live at Ashcroft directed at Meredith?

Sir Rupert himself was pleasant, but there was obviously something brewing between him and Meredith. And why the disapproval of Edgar? He was following in his father-in-law's footsteps, after all. That should be a plus for the old boy.

"Captain Boyle?" Sir Rupert said, with a look that said he'd had to repeat himself.

"Sorry, what was that?" I said.

"Can you tell us anything more about what brings you to Devon? If it's not too hush-hush, that is."

"It's really nothing much," I said. But all eyes were on me, and this wasn't exactly a top-secret operation. I decided to expand on what I'd told Edgar. "A body washed up on the beach at Slapton Sands. It's a restricted area, and that made my boss nervous. The corpse wasn't in uniform, and no one local has been reported missing, so we were sent here to determine his identity."

"A German spy, perhaps?" Sir Rupert said, obviously keen on the idea.

"Any reports of parachutists recently?" I asked, not answering his question. Best to let them imagine we were tracking down a dangerous nest of enemy agents. It was the least we could do in exchange for this fine food.

"The Home Guard did bring in a German bomber crew," Helen said. "They crash-landed in a field outside of Stoke Fleming, but that was two years ago."

"Do you suspect that this person was local?" Meredith asked.

"It's hard to say. We spoke to some fishermen who said the tides and currents could have carried him in from some distance."

"Talk to Crawford," Sir Rupert offered. "As I said, he fished the Channel waters. He might have an idea or two."

"Good idea," I said. And then the bread-and-butter pudding was served, and once again my attention was momentarily diverted. There was more talk of the indispensable Crawford, and how he kept the household in milk, butter, and eggs from the few cows and chickens on the estate. Given that the current weekly ration allowed two ounces of butter and one egg per person, Crawford was practically worth his weight in dairy products.

CHAPTER SEVEN

"I'M STILL NOT sure what to make of that bunch," I said to Kaz too damn early the next morning. We'd left before dawn for the Dartmouth police station. I'd thought about packing my bags and staying in town, but that would have put Kaz in a bad spot.

"David will fill me in, once we have a chance to talk," Kaz said, buttoning the top collar of his trench coat. It was a crisp morning, the sun a distant promise of warmth as it began to crest the horizon. "I am sure your own family might appear strange at first to an outsider."

"Doesn't everyone have an uncle in the IRA?" I said, taking his point. There was little traffic at this hour, and in no time we pulled up in front of the police headquarters, where Tom Quick was waiting.

"Didn't expect to see you fellows again quite so soon," he said.

"Sorry for the early hour," I said as he squeezed into the rear seat next to the radio equipment.

"No mind, I'm not much for sleep," he said. "What's this all about then?" We filled him in on Harding's orders and the little we knew about the upcoming maneuvers.

"Doesn't take much to make the high and mighty nervous," Quick said after we'd finished. It was hard to disagree. As we neared the coast, a thick fog rolled in, the breeze pushing the salt-scented air in from the Channel.

"Please don't drive us into a ditch," Kaz said from the passenger's seat. "I can barely see the road."

"Up ahead," Quick said. "Lights." I slowed and pulled over, glad to have found the roadblock without crashing into it. MPs stood at the closed gate. Ambulances, tow trucks, and other heavy vehicles were parked off the roadway, GIs nodding off in the cabs, waiting for the fun to begin. It looked like the army planned on something going wrong, which was sensible, since it always did.

"We have orders to check the beach after the bombardment," I said, showing my papers to the MP sergeant. "Still on for zero six hundred?"

"You got me, Captain," he said, handing the orders back. "They don't tell us much. It's supposed to end at zero six thirty, then the beachmaster goes forward to inspect. That's all I know."

"Is the beachmaster here?" I asked, buttoning up my M-43 field jacket. No field scarf or low-quarter shoes today. Combat boots and a wool shirt and sweater did the trick for this damp, chilly English spring morning.

"No, sir, he's inland with some troopers from the 101st. I can let you through at zero six thirty, but you might want to take it slow. You never know with the navy. Meanwhile, they got a field kitchen set up on the other side of those trucks. Help yourself."

We did. Coffee and bacon sandwiches made the early morning fog bearable. As we finished up, a sea breeze wafted through the fields, thinning out the greyness, but not by much.

"It's five past six," Quick said, checking his watch as we settled back in the jeep. "Or am I fast?"

"I have six after," I said. "We should be hearing the bombardment by now."

"Would the fog delay it?" Kaz asked.

"Not likely," I said. "Everything is strictly timed. The troops are coming ashore at zero seven thirty. Besides, the cruiser has radar; they could hit the beach in the dark of night." We waited another five minutes. The silence was broken only by the distant crashing of surf.

"We should radio Colonel Harding," Kaz said. I agreed, put on the headset and fiddled with the radio until I got the right frequency and gave our call sign. I got an ensign aboard the *Hawkins* who sent a message to Harding.

"Did he know anything?" Kaz asked when I'd signed off.

"Only that the rocket attack by the fighters has been called off due to fog," I said. "He said he'd track Harding down but that the brass was all in a tizzy. Ike decided to go back to Dartmouth when he heard the air attack was cancelled." It looked like the old hotel on Slapton Sands had had a reprieve. But if fog grounded aircraft for the real invasion, the reprieve would be for the Germans. Not an auspicious start.

There was nothing to do but have another cup of joe. As we drank, zero seven thirty rolled by. Still nothing.

"Can you radio the beachmaster?" I asked the MP sergeant.

"Don't have a radio, Captain. Don't even know what frequency he's on. Like I said—"

"Yeah, I know. They don't tell you anything. I know the feeling."

There was nothing to do but wait, which was typical of the army. Hurry up and get somewhere before dawn, then wait for hours for something to actually happen. When zero eight hundred came around, the MPs shrugged, opened the gate, and let us through. "Guess the bombardment was called off," the sergeant said. "The landing craft should be on their way to the beach by now, so it ought to be safe." He waved us forward.

"We're the only ones daft enough to drive in here," Quick said, hanging on to his seat in the rear as the jeep negotiated the ruts in the road.

"No reason for them to," I said. "Those are emergency vehicles."

"Then shouldn't they be closer to a possible emergency?" Kaz asked.

"It's the army, Kaz," I said. "No one moves unless they're ordered to. Don't worry." I hadn't been worried myself until Tom brought up everyone else staying behind. All of a sudden, it felt damn lonely to be driving through a deserted landscape in a restricted area, heading for the site of a canceled bombardment from a heavy cruiser.

We drove through Strete, past untended fields and cottages, and watched a herd of deer bolt for the woods as we disturbed their morning feed. The road curved along the coast, hugging a rise a few hundred feet high. I pulled over, the heights a ringside seat to watch the landings once the fog cleared. The Channel was dotted with LCVPs—Landing Craft, Vehicle, Personnel—or "Higgins boats" as the flat-bottomed tubs were commonly known. Each one carried thirty-six combat infantrymen, and there were dozens and dozens crashing through the surf, coming closer to the shingle at Slapton Sands.

"I can't see the cruiser," Kaz said, scanning the horizon with binoculars.

"It's too far out," Quick said. "Those big naval guns can lob shells for miles." Large LCTs and LCIs stood offshore, with smaller landing craft circling as they formed up for the run in.

As the Higgins boats drew closer, they were overtaken by half a dozen fast patrol boats—odd-looking craft, shorter than any PT boat I'd ever seen, about ten or twelve yards long at most. Three hundred yards from the beach, they stopped, and in seconds a terrific volley of rockets launched from each boat, bright flames coursing above the waves and slamming into the barbed-wire entanglements we'd seen put up yesterday. Most of the rounds hit, blowing gaps in the wire, leaving openings for the GIs about to land. The craft turned and made smoke as they headed back into the Channel.

"That's something new," Kaz said. "Very effective, but of course no one was shooting back at them."

"You can't have everything," I said, and started the jeep. "Let's head closer."

"Perhaps they canceled the naval bombardment in favor of those rocket boats," Kaz suggested.

"Impressive, but they're not quite the same thing," Quick said. "It'll take Jerry by surprise, but concrete isn't the same as strands of barbed wire."

Closer to the beach, we came upon the paratroopers we saw yesterday, sitting outside their entrenchment, smoking cigarettes. They waved, looking happy about the absence of 7.5-inch shells raining down near their position. We halted at the end of the shingle, watching the landing craft drop their ramps and men storm the stony shore.

"Kaz, would you contact Colonel Harding? We should let him know we're here."

"All right, Billy," Kaz said, getting out of the jeep. Quick and I joined him, stretching our legs and watching as hundreds of GIs poured out of the LCVPs and sloshed their way to the beach. Some made for the gaps in the barbed wire while other men with wire cutters worked their way through it. The rest bunched up behind them, milling about, waiting.

"That's not good," I said. "Their noncoms should be pushing them forward, getting them off the beach."

"Pity no one takes training exercises seriously," Quick said. "Whenever we practiced getting out of a Lancaster while it was on the ground, we'd end up laughing at how silly it all was. Especially Freddie." He smiled at the memory, and I had to admit he was right. Training was a game for most guys, even if what they were training for was anything but. I gave a sympathetic laugh and was about to ask who Freddie was when Kaz put on the headset and broadcast our call sign. I heard a faint screeching sound echoing out over the water and looked up, wondering if there were high-speed fighters overhead. But the sound wasn't right. It took a split second to register.

The cruiser *Hawkins* was shelling the beach.

The screeching grew in intensity, drawing everyone's attention, like a magician's distraction, masking a deadly trick. I could see the wire cutters stop their work as the GIs making their way off the beach turned and stared, everyone wondering what was going on, wasting precious seconds in bewilderment.

"Get down!" I hollered, hands cupped around my mouth. They were too far away to notice or understand. I could hear Kaz telling whoever was at the other end of the radio to stop the shelling, that the beach was crowded with men.

The first shells overshot the strand, hitting the Slapton Ley beyond it, sending plumes of water skyward. I could see a few men digging in, scraping at the stony beach with their helmets, but most scurried around, confused and unsure which way to go and whether this was part of the exercise.

The whistling threat came again, earsplitting and terrifying.

This time they had the range. Seven shell bursts struck the beach, sending bodies flying and men rushing in all directions, some swimming for the Higgins boats, which had already backed off the shore and were heading into the Channel.

"Stop the shelling!" Kaz roared into the microphone. "You are killing men on the beach!"

"Is that Harding?" I asked. He shook his head no. Tom Quick ran toward the beach, calling to the men to come to him and the safety of the road leading off the beach. Safe for now, anyway. A group sprinted in his direction, others running for the ruined hotel and seeking cover there. Another round of shells shrieked in, hitting right at the waterline, killing those who had sought refuge there.

"No, you idiot!" Kaz screamed into the radio. "There are men on the beach!"

"What's happening?" I hollered as Kaz handed off the microphone and earpiece.

"The ensign said the landings were delayed an hour. He insists the Higgins boats haven't gone in yet." Which made sense, given that we'd seen craft circling the larger ships on the horizon. The men now on the beach apparently hadn't gotten word of the delay.

"Find Colonel Harding," I said, trying to keep the panic out of my voice. "This is Captain Boyle."

"I sent a runner to find him," a tinny voice said. "But there can't be anyone there, the landing craft were ordered to wait an hour."

"Well *we're* here, goddamn it!" I yelled as another volley ripped the sky open. As the shells began their shrill incoming descent, I braced myself for them to hit. One struck the beach, another hit close to the hotel, and a third was screeching straight for us. I grabbed Kaz and threw him to the ground, covering his body, wishing I knew where Quick was.

I thought I would hear it, but I swear there was no sound at all, even when the jeep flew into the air, twisting and turning as metal and debris flew in every direction in silent slow motion. It finally came down on its side with a sudden, fearful loud crash of metal and earth, and then rolled, a black shadow of burning rubber and searing flame above me as I pressed my face into Kaz's shoulder. Then, nothing.

CHAPTER EIGHT

"BILLY," I HEARD Kaz say in a choked voice that drifted into my dazed mind. I tried to open my eyes, but it was useless; heat and darkness pressed out all other sensations. "Get off of me, I can't breathe."

"I can't move," I said, feeling my face pressed into the wool of Kaz's uniform jacket. There was pressure on my legs, and I became aware of a dull throb in my arm. I tried to rise, but a piece of metal was in the way, pinning my back to the ground.

It was the jeep. It had fallen on us, and judging by the working end of the gearshift a few inches from my eyeballs, it was upside down. That was the good news. The bad news was that it was on fire.

Burning rubber and blistering paint gave off an acrid spume of smoke that forced its way into my lungs and eyes. Kaz began to cough and hack, each spasm reverberating beneath me. I tried to call for help, but as I opened my mouth I drew in more of the smoke and felt the heat of the fire on the undercarriage, fanned by the wind and fed by the burst fuel line. It wouldn't be long before the tank went and we roasted in a fireball of Uncle Sam's Grade A gasoline.

"Heave!" A voice sounded from within a jumble of shouts and boots shuffling around the jeep. The side panel came off my back, and hands dragged me out as I kept a grip on Kaz and pulled him with me. "Clear!" Quick shouted as soon as Kaz was safe, and a dozen or so GIs let the jeep drop from their grip, scampering back from the flames licking out at them.

"Are you all right?" Quick asked, kneeling and looking into our eyes. For signs of shock, my mind dully registered.

"I think so," Kaz answered, dusting himself off. "Now that I don't have a jeep and Billy on top of me."

"I'm fine," I said, then noticed my torn pants and the red, oozing gashes on my legs. Plus my left arm was warm and sticky with blood. Maybe not quite so fine, I realized.

THE NEXT THING I knew, I was coming to in a field ambulance, my arm swathed in a bandage as a medic wrapped gauze around multiple wounds on my legs. Harding stood outside the open rear door, the medic telling him I'd be fine, nothing but superficial lacerations. I was about to say they didn't feel superficial, but then I remembered the dead on the beach, and the others who must have been grievously wounded, so I kept my trap shut.

"What happened?" I asked, struggling to sit up on the stretcher.

"Constable Quick tells me a shell narrowly missing taking your heads off," Harding said. "It flipped the jeep and tossed it on top of you. You were damned lucky it dropped the way it did. The seat well gave you space and protection."

"Colonel," I said, swinging my legs off the stretcher, "if I was really lucky I wouldn't have been stuck under a burning jeep while our own side bombarded the beach." Some people had the oddest way of looking at luck. "What I meant was, what went wrong with the shelling?"

"Misjudgment, error, incompetence," Harding said, glancing around to be sure no one heard. "Some of the transports were slow in forming up, so the naval commander delayed H-Hour by sixty minutes. The *Hawkins* got word, but some of the transports didn't. They launched on the original schedule."

"Which put men on the beach right under the *Hawkins*'s shells," I said.

"Yeah," Harding said, nearly spitting out the word. "You can't change plans once troops are underway. Someone always misses the message. Normally it'd just be confusion. But today it cost lives."

"I'm beginning to think this beach is jinxed," I said. "First the corpse, then this. Not to mention a flaming jeep."

"Keep it under your hat, Boyle," Harding said. "I've already talked to Lieutenant Kazimierz and the constable. They understand what happened here has to be kept on the QT."

"Why?" I asked. "I mean, it was an accident. Happens all the time in training."

"Not in these numbers," Harding said. "And there are other considerations you don't need to know about. So get back to your swank billet and rest up. Right now I have to get these bodies moved out of here. Your resourceful constable has come up with transportation for you, so get back and take it easy."

I didn't argue. It wasn't often that Harding told anyone to take a rest, and I began to worry that I was hurt worse than I thought. It sure felt that way as I eased myself out of the ambulance and looked around for Kaz and Tom Quick. They were in a jeep parked alongside of the ambulance, partially hidden. Tom helped me into the back seat as Kaz looked around like a furtive thief, which technically he was. He eased out onto the roadway, cutting in between two trucks. We followed as the deuce-and-a-half in front of us ground gears going uphill, the unsecured rear canvas cover flapping in the breeze. I caught a glimpse of limbs jutting out at odd angles from the darkness of the truck bed. A truck full of dead soldiers. As soon as we came to a side road, Kaz took it.

"You trade in ours for a newer model?" I said as Kaz floored it and headed inland, away from the concentration of men and vehicles, the quick and the dead.

"It was Tom who pinched it," Kaz said. "How are you feeling?"

"Still a little stunned," I said. "Since when do constables steal automobiles?"

"As it's an American military vehicle," Quick said, "I am participating in Lend-Lease, not stealing. Your Colonel Harding thought it was an ingenious rationale."

"It helped that the major we borrowed it from was a fool," Kaz said.

"How so?" I asked from my perch in the rear.

"He cursed the Royal Navy for the shelling. Called the captain of the *Hawkins* a British son of a bitch."

"General Eisenhower doesn't mind officers calling each other sons of bitches," I explained to Tom. "But he hates it when they say someone is an American or a British son of a bitch. Ike is all about Allied unity."

"Colonel Harding was too busy to discipline the major, but I knew he was furious with him. So he turned a blind eye to our enterprise," Kaz said.

"Well, it worked out well for us," Quick said. "Otherwise we'd still be waiting for a lift. It seems every other vehicle was pressed into service to deliver the wounded to hospital and the dead to wherever they'll be buried."

"How many?" I asked.

"We don't know," Kaz said. "Harding did the count of dead and wounded himself and wouldn't say. He threatened everyone within earshot with a court-martial if they spoke of the incident."

"It's not like Harding to worry about public relations," I said.

"I think it is more than that," Kaz said. "There's a secret he's not sharing with us."

"Need to know," I said, a shopworn phrase by now.

"And we do not need to know," Kaz said. There was nothing much left to say. We left the deserted South Hams and drove through villages and past fields alive with people, animals, and crops; everyday scenes that seemed to mock the devastation we'd left behind. Bodies and burnt houses, only a few miles from these peaceful hamlets where life continued much as before on this fine spring day. I wanted all these people to understand the sacrifice their neighbors had made, to know about the American GIs suffering in hospitals, and the dead tossed in trucks for a secret burial. Maybe they bore their own burdens of loss, or maybe they were oblivious to the world carrying on around them. It didn't matter. Deep down, I knew I simply didn't want to carry this secret locked up inside me. But orders were orders, as went the insistent logic of the army.

"Tom, how'd you miss getting hit by those shells?" I asked. "I seem to recall you were pretty exposed."

"I saw they were headed in our direction and ran," he said. "The force of the blast bowled me over, but the shrapnel missed me, thank God. After all the German ack-ack we flew through, I'd hate to go for a Burton courtesy of His Majesty's navy."

"A Burton?" Kaz asked.

"Buy the farm, go for a Burton, it's all the same. Die," Tom explained. "Burton is an ale. So gone for a Burton and never come back, see?"

"Why not?" I said, watching Tom for any signs of the black dog, as Churchill called his deep depressions. "You're all right, Tom? Just knocked down?"

"Look at this," Tom said with a grin, sticking a finger in a rip on the shoulder of his uniform jacket. "Shrapnel missed nicking me by half an inch." He was none the worse for wear. As bad as the shelling had been, it was new to him. It happened on the ground, not high in the night sky over Germany. That was my theory, anyway.

We dropped Tom off in North Cornworthy. He said his pal Constable Robert Carraher lived there and wouldn't mind the company. He'd hitch a ride into Dartmouth with Carraher in the morning.

WHEN WE ARRIVED back at Ashcroft, Kaz helped me limp inside. We'd concocted a story about an accident with the jeep, and I was sure that no one would pay us much mind. With all the military vehicles tearing around southern England, accidents were pretty much commonplace.

"What happened to you?" Edgar said as soon as we set foot in the hallway.

"Captain Boyle," Meredith said, following Edgar out of the library. "Are you badly hurt? Come, sit down."

"A minor accident," I said. "Our jeep came out worse than I did."

"What can we do for you?" Meredith asked, the concern on her face not what I expected. Haughty indifference, perhaps, or a cutting remark about Americans driving on the wrong side of the road. But this was a kinder Meredith.

"Nothing, thank you," I said. "I think I'll go lie down."

"Baron, you look hurt as well," Edgar said.

"I am fine," Kaz said. "A few minor bruises. Billy got the worst of it."

"Are you sure you wouldn't like to eat?" Meredith said. "We've just finished our luncheon, and there's plenty of food."

"I'm hardly dressed for it," I said, gesturing at my trousers where the medic had shredded them to get at my cuts and scrapes. But it dawned on me that I was hungry, and suddenly the appeal of hot food was undeniable.

"Perhaps a tray will be best for Billy," Kaz said, reading my mind. Meredith hustled off to organize food, giving orders like she ran the place.

Twenty minutes later I was in bed, munching on a cheese sandwich served with a bowl of fish soup and a glass of stout. My legs were stiffening up, and my arm ached, but at least I was on the right side of the grass for another day.

"You okay?" I said to Kaz, who was seated at a small table by the window, downing the soup without a single slurp.

"Yes," he said. "I am a little sore, but unhurt. Do you need anything, Billy?"

"Some shut-eye, that's all," I said.

"Thank you," Kaz said, standing at the foot of the bed. "You saved my life."

"It was my turn," I said. "I think we're even now."

Kaz laughed, the joy of cheating death yet again vivid on his face. He left, and as I lay there I thought about getting up, but my eyelids grew heavy, and I fell asleep as odd visions of Sir Rupert in a truck filled with dead men danced through my head.

CHAPTER NINE

THE NEXT MORNING I awoke to a knock on the door. It was Alice Withers, the kitchen maid, with my uniform from yesterday, or most of it. She had bright eyes, full lips, straw-blonde hair, and looked to be twenty or even younger. A cheery girl.

"Sorry to wake you, Captain," she said, "but the baron said you should be up, and I thought you'd want these things. I cleaned and stitched the shirt myself. The trousers were a lost cause, sorry to say." She placed the pile of clothes on the bed as I sat up.

"No problem," I said. The shirt looked like new, except for the tear, which had been expertly sewn up. "How'd you get the bloodstains out?"

"Cold water and spit," she said, giggling a bit. "Then you rub in salt and scrub with washsoap. It's how Mrs. Dudley taught me. I hope you don't mind."

"The old ways are often the best," I said, glancing at the clock. It was past time to get up. "Thanks, Alice." She giggled again as she shut the door.

I washed and dressed, wincing as pain shot through my protesting legs. I sat back down on the edge of the bed, overcome by the realization that I really had been lucky yesterday. A thirteen-hundred pound vehicle had been tossed in the air by a 7.5-inch shell and then fallen smack on top of Kaz and me in about the only position guaranteed not to crush the two of us into a red meat pie. Luck. How much did I have left? Those guys on the beach hadn't even met the enemy yet, and now some of them were six feet under before they'd fired a shot in anger.

I downplayed my injuries at breakfast, telling everyone I was fine even as I felt blood seeping through the thick bandage on my arm. I might need more of Alice's spit tomorrow.

"Are you sure you're well enough to travel, Captain?" Sir Rupert asked as he tucked in to his eggs.

"We're only going to Dartmouth, to talk with an Inspector Grange," I said. "Shouldn't be a problem."

"Edmund Grange, you mean? Of the Devon Constabulary? Decent man, he should be of help to you," Sir Rupert declared. "I sit on a committee for the Dartmouth Royal Regatta; I met him last summer while we were preparing for the festivities. Big headache for the police, I expect, but everyone enjoys the fun. It's all scaled back these days, thanks to the war, but it's a morale boost for the locals even so."

"Oh yes, the Mayor's Ball is the highlight of the week," Helen said, lighting up with enthusiasm for a brief moment. Then her face went blank, and she stared down at her plate. Maybe the notion of going to the ball with David this year didn't sit well.

"Give Grange my best," Sir Rupert said, a brief frown creasing his forehead as he watched Helen. "And I'm glad you're not badly hurt, or worse."

"Indeed," Great Aunt Sylvia said. "It would be a silly way to go, in any case. Tell me, Baron Kazimierz, have you family in Poland? It must be quite difficult for them, from what I hear."

"No, Lady Pemberton," Kaz said in a low voice. "I do not." The only sound that followed was Edgar tapping the shell of his soft-boiled egg. After a few minutes, the idle chitchat picked up again. Kaz and I excused ourselves and made for the jeep.

Family was a hard subject for Kaz. His was wiped out by the Nazis after the invasion of Poland. They had been wealthy—far wealthier than the residents of Ashcroft House—and his father had had the foresight to transfer the family fortune to a Swiss bank in case of war. He hadn't foreseen how quickly the war would be at his doorstep, however, and had missed his chance to leave the country. The Kazim-ierz family had been murdered as part of the Nazi plan to exterminate the intelligentsia. Businessmen, aristocrats, lawyers, and anyone who might resist were ruthlessly slaughtered. Kaz had had no relatives to squabble with and no one but me to confide in since he was maimed in the explosion that had killed Daphne Seaton.

It was our first case together. Kaz lost the love of his life and got that scar as a daily reminder. He took chances and sought death after that, but he was too damn lucky to find it. Since then, he's hung around to keep me out of trouble, I think. It's a good thing for him that trouble seems always to be right around the corner.

Maybe I should revise that bit about Kaz having no one else but me. There is a princess in Rome, but she's part of the underground, and he won't be seeing her anytime too soon. Again, it's a long story, but she deserves a mention. Sometimes broken hearts do heal.

"A hospitable bunch, but strange nonetheless," I said, if only to break the silence as we headed down the long driveway.

"I admit there are undercurrents of tension within the family," Kaz said. "That is clear. The question is, does it have anything to do with why David wanted me to visit?"

"It wasn't just for old times' sake?" We drove through the muddy streets of North Cornworthy, and I noticed the mill this time, down from the bridge that spanned Bow Creek. That was where Great Aunt Sylvia's grandfather supposedly put his own sweat into the construction.

"I do not know," Kaz said. "I think there must be something he wants to talk about. He seemed to relax when we said we'd stay, did you notice? Or it could have been the strain from his injuries. He is recuperating, after all, and still on sick leave. Perhaps it was a wave of pain that passed."

"Having a wife who can't look you in the face could cause a lot of pain," I said. "You didn't know Helen at all?"

"No," Kaz said. "I hadn't met her before. Whenever David men-tioned her in his letters, it was what you'd expect. She was wonderful, he couldn't believe how lucky he was, that sort of thing."

"Some people are fine when the going is easy," I said. "Wealthy girl gets a dashing, blond-haired RAF pilot who went to Oxford. Fairy-tale stuff. As long as the fairy tale plays out, she's the perfect wife. But then reality comes along when his fighter goes down, and the charming prince isn't quite so charming anymore. Life gets tough, and she doesn't know how to handle it, so she hides out on his left side."

"You could be correct," Kaz said. "And if so, I don't know what David might expect me to do about it. Perhaps he doesn't want her to look at his burns, did you think of that?"

"It didn't look that way to me," I said. "She was the one moving around to his good side, far as I could tell. Either way, he might want a shoulder to cry on. Ashcroft may not provide many sympathetic listeners, especially when it concerns one of their own."

"We shall see," Kaz said. We drew closer to the River Dart and heard the blast of a steam locomotive from the opposite bank. The green hills rose above the rail line as the engine pulled its long load toward the coast. "You know, our dead chap could have come from anywhere. He could have come from the north of England on that very train, got into a dispute, and been shot and dumped in the water that same day."

"Meaning we should widen the search?"

"Yes," Kaz said. "Contact Scotland Yard as well. If we assume he wasn't in the military, that narrows it down quite a bit. About thirty years of age, in decent condition, and engaged in a business that involves violence."

"You're right," I said, following his lead. "He might have had a criminal record that would have kept him out of the service. Good thinking, Kaz. Let's see what Inspector Grange has to say, and then we'll follow up, maybe call Inspector Scutt at the Yard."

I'd worked with Detective Inspector Horace Scutt of Scotland Yard a while ago. We hadn't seen eye to eye at first, but he was a good cop, and I trusted him. He was beyond retirement age, staying on for the duration. It had to be tough, dealing with a war and thousands of rowdy servicemen when you should have been tending roses or doing whatever coppers do when they turn in their badges.

We threaded our way through Dartmouth traffic, mostly military, and sought out Inspector Grange at the Devon Constabulary. This time we were lucky.

"Glad to help, for what it's worth," Inspector Grange said when we'd explained our assignment. He gestured toward two chairs in front of his desk and flopped down into his own. He was stout, with a thick grey moustache and even thicker eyebrows. He looked tired as he fired up his pipe. "I heard you chaps got caught up in that mess at Slapton Sands. God-awful."

"The only good thing is that it was a rehearsal, not the real thing," Kaz said. "Do you have any further information on our corpse from the beach?"

"I suspect you know as much as I do, if you've talked to Dr. Verniquet." He puffed to get the bowl hot and blew out a stream of smoke that filled the room with an aroma of ashtrays and wet socks.

"Guy about thirty, shot in the arm and then the head, in the water for three to four months," I said. "No missing person reports that match?"

"None from Devon, that much we know," Grange said. "Of course, that could be meaningless. It could be a local no one cared to report, or an outsider no one wanted to."

"Do you know many male civilians of that age who wouldn't be missed?" I said. "It's not like he was an old man off in the woods."

"I agree, Captain Boyle," Grange said. "If he had been local and unmarried, there would certainly have been a lady or two who noticed, what with most of the eligible men gone."

"And if he were married, his wife would have reported him," Kaz said.

"Yes," Grange said. "Although perhaps not, if she was the one who killed him."

"A wife would be more likely to shoot him in the heart," I said. "Not the head."

"I'll take your word for that, Captain," Grange said with a friendly smile. "But as it stands, I have nothing of value to report. I sent out word to the rest of the constabulary to ask around again about any man missing for a month or more. Pity there wasn't enough of the face left to use for a description."

"I know Detective Inspector Scutt at Scotland Yard," I said. "Would you mind if I contacted him to see if he has any information about anyone fitting the description?"

"Go ahead, if he'll act on it," Grange said, waving his pipe. "It's doubtful our chief constable would request assistance from the Yard for a minor case like this, but if you can get Scutt to assist informally, I'm all for it."

"Thanks, Inspector," I said. "I don't want to cause any problems."

"No problem if we get some help on this, Captain Boyle. We're short-staffed here, and we have it better than most."

"Why is that?" Kaz asked.

"Oh, the South Hams," Grange said. "When the government evacuated those villages, we absorbed the constables to help us cover the rest of Devon. Even so, we're short of younger men. Plenty of old-timers like me, not short on experience. But stamina, that's harder to come by. Many of our lads enlisted as soon as they could, and I can't blame them. But it leaves us in the lurch, especially with so many army and navy chaps coming in. Royal Navy, US Army, it doesn't matter, they all want to have a good time when they get a pass, and there's the devil to pay some nights. Plus we've had a rash of burglaries lately. A few well-to-do ladies have had their jewelry pinched."

"What about the War Reserve Constables?" I asked. "Tom Quick seems pretty sharp. He was a constable before the war, he said."

"Ah yes, Tom Quick is a good man," Grange said.

"Why is he not a regular constable?" Kaz asked. "His limp did not appear too bad."

"Limp?" Grange said. "Oh, his limp. I couldn't tell you. Dr. Verniquet decides who's fit enough for what. Now, anything else I can do for you?"

There wasn't. Not that he had done anything in the first place.

"That was odd, about the limp," Kaz said as we left the building.

"Yeah. He acted as if he'd never heard that was the reason Quick wasn't on the regular force," I said.

"And then he covered his tracks," Kaz said. "Not that it matters. But it bothers you?"

"Everything that doesn't make sense bothers me, Kaz. What's the story with Tom Quick? Where does all the tension at Ashcroft come from?"

"Not to mention our dead body," Kaz said as we got into the jeep.

"No," I said, my hand draped over the steering wheel as I looked out over all the ships anchored off Darmouth harbor. Destroyers clustered at the center of the river, and smaller landing craft huddled close by the docks. Fairmile Motor Torpedo Boats cruised out toward the Channel, the throaty rumble of their engines echoing against the hills across the wide river. "The body doesn't bother me. A guy was killed, floated around for a while, and then washed up at Slapton Sands. It makes sense. All we need to do is reconstruct what happened before he took a couple of slugs. Quick and the crew at Ashcroft, they're all unanswered questions and confusion. They all have secrets. The dead body is just an unknown. There's a big difference."

"I see your point," Kaz said. "But it is none of our business, really. Whether Quick has a limp or not, what David wants, why the overall tension at Ashcroft: these are all merely curiosities. Colonel Harding will want a report on our progress on the actual case, Billy."

"We've been going about this all wrong," I said, turning to look at Kaz. I think he'd been lecturing me, but I hadn't listened too much after the word *business*. "Most murders are about love or money. Assume money in this case. A criminal enterprise. So who should we talk to? A county detective is going to be as much help as a fisherman. We need to talk to a crook."

"Not that fellow in London," Kaz said. "The one who has the gang in Shoreditch?"

"No," I said. "I don't know what sort of reception I'd get. I'm thinking of Razor Fraser."

"The solicitor?" Kaz said.

"Yep. And he's closer than London, to boot," I said. Stanley Fraser was a lawyer whose clients were mainly known criminals. I'd questioned him on our last case, but it had turned out he had nothing to do with the crime in question. There's always a first time.

"Why would he help?" Kaz said.

"I'll try the carrot, and carry a big stick," I said. Fraser was based in Hungerford, more than halfway to London, but it was the only idea I had. He was connected to several major gangs, according to the police inspector who had come along for that last interview. Razor—so called because he got a client declared innocent after witnesses had seen him slit the throat of his victim—knew things. And one thing I'd picked up on was that he craved respectability. Maybe I could use that. If he knew anything—and it didn't mean selling out a rich client—he might go for it.

"We should get started," Kaz said. "It's a long drive."

"I'll go. You can spend some time with your buddy and snoop around Ashcroft," I said with a grin. I wanted Kaz to know I was joking, but I wouldn't mind if he dug up anything on the cast of characters in that family, just for laughs.

Kaz went to check the train schedules, and I returned to the police station. I told Grange I needed to use the telephone. He probably assumed I was calling Scotland Yard, because he let me use his office, telling the switchboard operator to put my call through. The operator made the connection, and after Fraser calmed down and I explained that this was strictly off the record, he agreed to see me that afternoon.

"You're in luck," Kaz said as we rendezvoused at the jeep. "A ferry leaves in ten minutes, and the train stops at Hungerford. If you don't spend too long there you can make it back this evening." The Dartmouth ferry shuttled people across the river directly to the station at Kingswear, which cut down on travel time. I figured two hours in Hungerford would be more than enough, so Kaz planned to pick me up later that night.

I paid my fare at the Dartmouth ticket booth and half an hour later settled in to a Great Western Railways car with the local newspaper. The big news was that the British government had banned travel and communications for all neutral diplomats. No more coded messages in diplomatic pouches, no flights to other countries where secrets could be passed on. The government had given no reason, but they didn't have to. D-Day. No one was taking any chances on a neutral diplomat friendly to the Germans getting out with any information about where or when.

It made me feel better about our case. If Great Britain was violating centuries of international law for security purposes, then maybe identifying this corpse was worth our time. It remained to be seen whether Razor Fraser agreed.

CHAPTER TEN

FRASER'S PLACE WAS a short walk from the train station on a quiet residential street. I still had a bit of a limp, and my arm was stiffening up, but a brisk walk felt good. Fraser worked in one side of a semi-detached and lived in the other. A gleaming brass plaque marked the office entrance, and as I opened the door I tried to recall the name of his receptionist. What I did remember was her manicure. She'd spent most of her time filing her nails, and I doubted she did much typing with them.

It didn't matter. Sitting at the receptionist's desk was Mrs. Fraser herself. Her nails weren't as perfect as her predecessor's, but she was actually working, typing away at a rapid pace.

"Right on time, Captain Boyle," she said. "So nice to see you again."

"Same to you, Mrs. Fraser. I didn't expect to see you at work. You're pretty fast with those keys."

"I worked in an office before we were married," she said. "And I got bored sitting around, doing nothing. Now Stanley and I are together all day, and we save on the expense, of course." She smiled, queen of her domain, having vanquished the competition.

"That sounds great," I said, wondering what Stanley thought about the staffing change. "Is he available?"

"Yes, go right in. But you've only got twenty minutes. We've got a new client coming in and you'll have to be done by then. A local, law-abiding client, I am pleased to say." She looked quite pleased indeed.

"They're the best kind," I said, and went in.

"What's this all about?" Fraser said as I sat across from him.

"What happened to the previous receptionist? Too receptive?" I figured if he was going to give me a hard time, I'd give it right back.

"She went off with a Yank," he said. "Dorothy and I decided to put her skills to use. It's worked out well for us."

"That must be dandy," I said. Stanley Fraser was a man with too much around the middle and not enough on top, but he dressed up well. He adjusted his cuff links and straightened his tie. His suit looked expensive; he certainly wasn't making do with worn-out clothes. "Actually, I'm here to ask for your help."

"Do you need a lawyer, Captain Boyle? If not, then I don't see how I can help you."

"Listen, Mr. Fraser," I said, hoping to score points for not calling him Razor. "Let's start over, okay? I'm not here to cause trouble for you. I'm only seeking your assistance."

"All right," Fraser said, sighing and leaning back in his chair. "Tell me what's on your mind."

"I'm trying to identify the body of a man about thirty years old, probably a civilian. He washed up on the beach at Slapton Sands a few days ago."

"What makes you think I would know about a dead body?" Fraser said. "Are you accusing me?"

"No, not at all," I said, shaking my head. "It's imperative that we find out who this person is, in order to rule out any possibility of an enemy agent having gained access to a highly restricted area." That got his attention.

"Did this person drown?" Fraser said.

"Murdered," I said. "Shot." I went over what we knew from the body and the movements of the tides.

"So if this was a German spy, the worry is that others might have been in the restricted area as well?" He leaned forward in his chair, caught up in the drama.

"Exactly. We can't find any record of a missing person who matches his description. The problem we have is obvious, Mr. Fraser. Was this person a spy? If so, we must assume his confederates saw or learned things we don't want the Nazis to know, especially with the invasion of France right around the corner."

"Therefore," Fraser said, steepling his fingers in front of him, "if he was a spy, you'll have to put a lot of man power into the hunt for others. But if you can determine that he was something else, then that takes the heat off you."

"It's for the war effort, Mr. Fraser, not me. The boys who will be storming the beaches."

"Yes, yes, quite," Fraser said, waving away the distinction. "This is where I must say I have no idea why you've come to me, and that none of my clients would be involved in any sinister criminal activity."

"Consider it said."

"You've talked about wanting to identify this body," Fraser said. "Nothing about apprehending the killer."

"That is secondary at this point," I said. I thought Fraser might pick up on that distinction, with his lawyer's gift for legal nitpicking.

"Do you have reason to believe the victim was engaged in a criminal enterprise?" Fraser said.

"It's a guess, but sure," I said. "A civilian, in decent physical condition, not in the military. We're fairly sure of that, since he doesn't match any AWOL reports. I'm thinking a serious criminal conviction when he was younger."

"Any number of medical conditions could have kept him out of the service," Fraser said.

"Sure, but why hasn't anyone reported him missing then? If he were involved in illegal activities, people who knew him would be less likely to report him missing. Being away for long periods would be par for the course."

"I don't disagree with you, Captain Boyle. It is a good guess. But what I think you are asking is quite difficult."

"I'm not asking you to rat out a client," I said. "All I want to know is if you've heard through the grapevine of anyone getting rubbed out within the past three months or so. A turf war, maybe something like that."

"You sound like a gangster film," Fraser said. He tapped his fingers together again and stared past me. He knew something; I could tell.

"Are you branching out into legit clients?" I asked. "Mrs. Fraser said you have an appointment with a regular citizen."

"That would be admitting that my other clients were less than legitimate businessmen," Fraser said.

"Hey, we're not in court," I said. "I'm only asking for some help here. It could save lives; British lives, American, French, I don't know. But that's got to count for something."

"Even to a man like me, you mean?" He was right. I'd had to stop myself from saying it out loud.

"Especially to a man like you," I said. It wasn't time to soft-soap the guy. He knew it and I knew it. He got thugs and killers off the hook. This was a chance to do something decent, something that he could tell his wife in whispers; he could make her promise never to tell anyone that he'd helped catch a spy, or however he spun the story out to her. Yeah, especially to a guy like Razor Fraser.

"There may be something," Fraser said.

"Okay," I said, waiting for him to tell me. He fidgeted and wet his lips, as if he couldn't get his body to go along with this new idea of helping someone in a uniform.

"We are trying to stick to the straight and narrow out here," he said. "Dorothy wanted a change. She threatened to leave me if I didn't get a new clientele."

"Apparently Dorothy doesn't understand the rules," I said. Once you're a shyster for the mob in any country, you don't retire.

"No, she doesn't. But that's part of what I'm trying to tell you. There have been some conflicts. Two of my biggest clients have been killed." He spoke in hushed tones—whether by habit or because his wife's ear was at the door, I didn't know.

"So that frees you up to be a rural attorney?"

"Almost," Fraser said. "I must admit, it would be easier, and it would be nice not to be threatened all the time."

"Threatened?"

"With what would happen if I lost a case," Fraser said. My heart bled.

"Okay. Spill. What do you know?" I thought about threatening him myself, but held off. If he really liked the idea of a change, he had to see me as a safe bet, not another gangster.

"There's a man by the name of Charles Sabini," Fraser said. As soon as the words came out, he slumped back in his chair like a deflated balloon. He had broken the code, and there was no going back. He knew it. "He's half English and half Italian. He had a gang in the thirties, and controlled most of the racecourses in the south of England. He was heavily into gambling, fixing races, extortion, you name it."

"A client of yours?"

"No. My clients were in competition with Sabini. At the beginning of the war, Sabini was interned as an enemy alien, even though he was born here and had an English mother. My guess is that Scotland Yard decided on the internment as a pretext, since they couldn't pin anything on him."

"Sounds reasonable," I said.

"From their point of view, yes," Fraser said. "But the irony is that Sabini's gambling empire was built upon a network of Jewish book-makers operating out of London. When the war began, some of his Italian gangsters wanted to cut ties with their Jewish partners, out of loyalty to Mussolini. Sabini refused, even though it meant being deserted by his men with fascist sympathies."

"I take it he's no longer interned," I said.

"No, he was let out after a year. Scotland Yard probably figured enough damage had been done to his organization by then. They were right," Fraser said.

"And you know that because your clients benefited from his absence," I said.

"Since they are now dead, they can no longer be my clients," Fraser said.

"Understood," I said, a little bothered by the fact that I was following his logic.

"Sabini got right back into the game," Fraser continued. "He was caught fencing stolen property and sent down for two years. Last year he got out and started making up for lost time. He's re-established himself on the horse-racing circuit and branched out into the black market."

"Which means he must have stepped on somebody's toes. Black-market territories are certain to be well established," I said.

"Of course," Fraser said. "Sabini isn't afraid of violent confrontation, but he's also a clever one. He saw the buildup beginning in southwest England. It's not hard to put two and two together and come up with the idea that the area is becoming one big supply dump for the American army as they train for the invasion."

"What about existing gangs? They must be working the ports all along the coast."

"They are," Fraser said. "Sabini cut a deal that he'd stay out of the ports. He's got the inland territory, with men on his payroll who load and unload the trains that haul supplies coming from the ports. He gets his share and then some. The man's got more business than he can handle."

"So what's the connection?" I asked.

"Three months ago, a client dispatched an individual to Newton Abbot, where Sabini is headquartered. The job was to eliminate Sabini. This individual was never heard from again, and never returned to collect the remainder of his fee. Then, within a month, my client cut himself shaving. From ear to ear."

"You don't seem upset," I said.

"A lawyer in my situation learns to keep his opinions to himself and his emotions in check," Fraser said, looking pained in spite of his declaration. "I had to look for a way out. If Sabini thinks I've left my former practice, there's a chance he'll leave me be."

"You think he'd put a hit out on you?" I asked. In the States, legal counsel was usually off-limits, even for hardened gangsters.

"No, Captain Boyle, I'm afraid he'd want me as his attorney," Fraser said, his head bent low and his voice lower. "Neither my wife nor my ulcer would find that acceptable."

Now I understood why Fraser had so readily told me everything. He hoped I'd put Sabini away and all his troubles would be behind him.

"Where does Charles Sabini hang his hat?" I asked.

"At the racecourse in Newton Abbot," Fraser said. "The track sits hard against the River Teign, which flows into the Channel about fifteen or twenty miles from Slapton Sands."

"It fits," I said. "You don't happen to know the name of the guy who was sent to kill Sabini, or where he was from?"

"Captain Boyle, I must caution you," Fraser said, wagging his finger at me, his face turning red. "I never said I was aware of a plot to have anyone killed or injured. If I had been, I would have been duty-bound to report it to the authorities. As it stands, I was aware of an emissary sent to Mr. Sabini, who did not return to my client for reasons unknown. I never knew his name or was acquainted with him in any way."

"Sorry," I said, hands up in surrender, worried that he'd blow a fuse. "I did not mean to imply any knowledge of wrongdoing. I am certain you had no inkling of any criminal activity." That seemed to calm him down. The response was automatic, built up from years of denying what he knew, hiding the truth even from himself. "Is there anything else you can tell me?"

"Yes," Fraser said. "Be very careful. Sabini has vowed never to return to prison, and he has a violent temper. He has also developed a vehement hatred of the British government. Days before he was due to be released from prison, his son Michael, an RAF pilot, was killed in North Africa."

"Thanks for the warning," I said, hoping he was being completely truthful. "If this pans out, how would you and the missus like an invitation to the Mayor's Ball at the Dartmouth Royal Regatta this summer?"

"That would be just the thing," Fraser said, beaming. Respectable. I left him a happy man, which was what I needed. I didn't want him to have any regrets that might prompt a telephone call to his old pals, or worse yet, Sabini himself.

It was a cruel world, I thought as I walked back to the station. Even a crook would be proud of a son fighting in the RAF, but it would take a villain's mind to make his death an affront, turning his grief into anger at a government that had had good reason to jail him. Lots of professional criminals look at what they do as a job, with risks and rewards. They go up against law enforcement, but it's all part of the game. For Sabini, the game had become personal, and that made him dangerous.

The train had passed through Newton Abbot, and on the return trip I watched for a glimpse of the racecourse. It was easy to spot. The train ran along the banks of the River Teign, and as we neared the town it was visible across the river, the oval track fronting the water along one curve, the grandstand and stables at the far end. I had a fleeting glimpse of a small boathouse and dock off a dirt path that led down from the track. A private little spot, if no train was running.

The rail yard was busy. Another set of tracks joined ours at the station, and I could see cars on a siding being unloaded. Maybe some of Sabini's men were hard at work replenishing his stocks, courtesy of Uncle Sam.

The train pulled out of the station, and I watched the river widen into an estuary, the tide running out, a tree branch floating and bobbing on the current, until finally the locomotive picked up speed and we left the Teign behind on its journey to the cold Channel waters.

CHAPTER ELEVEN

KAZ AND DAVID Martindale were waiting for me in Dartmouth.
It was nearly dusk, and I'd spent most of the day on a crowded train
dodging packs and rifles as GIs and Tommies got on and off in droves.
We weren't expected for dinner at Ashcroft, so David suggested the
Dartmouth Arms, which was close by. "They have excellent fish and
ales," he said, which was all I needed to hear.

"Was your trip successful?" Kaz said as we walked to the pub.

"I'll tell you about it after dinner," I said, not certain about what
we should share with David.

We ordered three pints and got a snug booth in the corner. "*Na
zdrowie,*" Kaz said, raising his glass and giving the Polish version of
cheers. We clinked glasses and drank. After a day of train travel and
talking with a crooked lawyer, it went down smooth. As we drank, I
watched David and Kaz. It was easy to see them as chums at school.
Both good-looking—war injuries notwithstanding—with thin features, sharp eyes, and easy grins. I could visualize them up to their
elbows in books, discussing the finer points of Romanian grammar
or some rare book.

I went to see a man about a horse, and when I returned I heard
Kaz speaking in a familiar lilt.

"*Nem blong mi Piotr,*" he said.

"No," David said in amazement. "You actually spoke pidgin with
real Solomon Islanders? You should write a paper, Piotr."

"Hey," I said. "We're not supposed to talk about that, Kaz."

"Billy, it is only because David and I studied languages together. It is quite fascinating, and he's promised not to repeat this to anyone."

"Listen, just don't do it while I'm around. I never heard a thing, okay?"

"*Tenkyu*, Billy," Kaz said, and they both erupted in laughter. I went to get another round, and by the time I returned to the table they were whispering like two Solomon Islanders. I didn't want to spoil their fun, but I didn't want to chance a stretch in Leavenworth either. We'd kept that little jaunt a secret, as we'd been instructed, and it was best that it stayed that way, college buddy or not. I set down the glasses with a hard thump, getting their attention.

"Sorry, Billy," Kaz said, sticking to English this time.

"Cheers," David said. "Don't worry, Billy, I am discretion incarnate. I'm happy to simply enjoy this evening out. Ashcroft can be a little narrow, if you know what I mean."

"Narrow-minded?" Kaz asked, drawing David out.

"No, not at all," he said. "I mean as though the walls are closing in. I hadn't really got to know Helen's family very well, and now I have nothing but time to spend with them. I'm afraid we don't have much in common."

Did he mean Helen or her family? Or both? It was a revealing admission, either way.

"How long will you stay?" Kaz asked.

"That's just it, Piotr, I don't know. The RAF doctor refused to release me for duty. I've got a checkup in two weeks' time, but I doubt that will make any difference. There is no improvement to be had."

"Any further surgeries?" Kaz asked, his voice hesitant.

"No," David said. "They've done what they can. Saved my eye, but it's not worth much, except to balance things out." He worked up a smile, but like all his others, it was crooked, the shiny skin on the right side of his face barely moving.

"Will you stay at Ashcroft if the RAF won't have you back?" Kaz said.

"Good God, no," David said. "I couldn't imagine it, living off Sir

Rupert's kindness. Helen wouldn't mind though, she loves the place. I've got no family left myself, nowhere to go home to."

"Perhaps you could find work," Kaz said, without much hope in his voice.

"And do what? Teach languages at some boarding school? With this face I'd frighten the children, or be the butt of their jokes," David said, waving his hand along his cheek. "I really don't know what I could do to hold down a decent job."

"What happened?" I asked, surprising myself. "I mean, were you shot down or did you crash-land?" Kaz glanced at me, and I knew it was bad form to be so direct.

"A bit of both. We were on our way back to base," David said, his voice steady but quiet. "Four of us. It had been an uneventful patrol, for a change. We were jumped by a dozen or so Fw 190s as we began our descent. They must have been circling high above our airfield, waiting for aircraft to come in. I wish I could say I got any of the bastards, but it happened too fast. Much too fast." He took a drink and wiped his mouth, fingers lingering over the sharp line that had once been his lower lip. "My engine was hit, and I was nearly blinded by black smoke. Flames burst through the instrument panel. I put the nose down and headed for the runway, hoping they were done with me and I could get out before the cockpit was engulfed by fire. It was too low to bail out, otherwise I would have. Do you know that in a Spitfire the fuel tanks are directly in front of the pilot? All that high-octane fuel sitting there, inches away."

"No, I didn't know," I said, just to say something. The thought was horrifying.

"At least I was low on fuel, which saved my life, such as it is," David continued. "I thought I'd made it, but one of the Jerries gave me a final burst. Came at me from the left, a bit too high. He put a single twenty-millimeter shell through my canopy. The wind sucked the flames past my face like a blowtorch. They said the goggles saved my eyes, but I don't remember anything after that long tongue of flame. I landed the Spitfire, although I have no memory of it. The ground crew pulled me out seconds before the aircraft exploded."

He drank again.

"You're certain there's nothing more a specialist could do?" Kaz asked.

"Piotr, I have been in the hands of a great physician. Have you heard of Doctor McIndoe and the Guinea Pig Club?" Neither of us had. "Archibald McIndoe, a truly great man. He heads up the burns and reconstructive-surgery section at the Queen Victoria Hospital in Sussex. It's exclusively for RAF pilots and crewmen who have been badly burned."

"Why 'guinea pig'?" I asked.

"McIndoe had to create new techniques and equipment. No one had ever seen so many burn cases before. The medical staff are all members of the club, and I was inducted a couple of months ago."

"But you were injured a year ago," Kaz said.

"Yes," David answered. "But you have to have had at least ten surgical procedures to be admitted. We can't just let anyone in." There was pride in his voice, and I wondered if David felt more at home with the members of the Guinea Pig Club than at Ashcroft. "You'd be laughed out of the ward with that pathetic little scar of yours, for instance."

"It sounds like Doctor McIndoe has the right approach to the job," I said.

"He does. Some men have lost their hands and faces; they come to the hospital thinking they're beyond redemption. And the injuries are nothing compared to the surgeries," David said, clenching a fist as he thought of the pain. "But he does his best to create a bond between the staff and patients, even with the locals. He got some of them to organize visits for home-cooked meals, to help the lads prepare for going out into the world. They were wary at first, both the locals and the men, but now when they walk through town, they're greeted instead of gawked at."

"Did it help you, David?" Kaz said. "To come home?"

"Listen, Piotr—and Billy. There's something I wanted to ask you," David said, ignoring the question and answering it at the same time. "I'd like to go back on active service. As soon as possible. I thought with you being at SHAEF and all, you might be able to pull some strings."

"Can you still fly?" I asked.

"Not in combat, no," David said. "With only one decent eye, my depth perception is off. I wouldn't last a minute in a dogfight. I can still fly a fighter, although I doubt they'll let me. I need to do something useful."

"You mentioned a doctor's appointment in a few weeks. Won't Doctor McIndoe help you out?"

"It's not up to him, unfortunately. The RAF medical section rules on return to duty, and so far it hasn't been promising. It's not the burns—I know of badly burned men who've been given desk jobs. But one bum eye combined with the burns seems to have them in a quandary."

"Perhaps you should wait and see what this doctor decides," Kaz said.

"If he invalids me out of the RAF, my chances are dashed," David said. "I thought if you could put in a word for me now, there might be a place for a bright Oxford chap on someone's staff. They took you, Piotr." David stopped and glanced at me, then back at Kaz. "Sorry, I didn't mean anything by that. I think I'll go mad if I have to sit around Ashcroft on Sir Rupert's charity any longer."

"Don't worry, David. Billy knows about my heart condition. We have no secrets."

"Good, I was afraid I'd said too much. Well, what about it?"

"David is fluent in several languages," Kaz said, looking to me. "He's fit enough to sit at a desk, wouldn't you say?"

"As well as any staff officer," I said. What else could I say? "I'll talk to Colonel Harding and see what he can do. No promises, though. There might be nothing. Or it could be a job as a glorified file clerk."

"I don't care," David said. "I've had my time in the air. I've got five victories, which makes me an ace, you know. Three Germans and two Italian aircraft. I can be proud of that, but I don't think I can stand being given my walking papers. I want to see this thing through in uniform. Perhaps I can help with translations, or photographic interpretation. I did a bit of that before North Africa. My good eye still has perfect vision."

"We will do our best," Kaz said, resting his hand on David's shoulder. I was glad to see Kaz happy to help out his pal. But there was something else driving David's desire to stay in the service, I was sure of it. Not being stuck at Ashcroft would be at the top of my list.

Our food came. First was fish chowder, then smoked haddock with carrots and parsnips. Root vegetables were big when it came to English cuisine under wartime rationing. Easy to grow and store, they were on every menu.

"Not quite the same as fresh peas," I said.

"But no Great Aunt Sylvia to rap your knuckles," David said.

"Is she always so outspoken?" I said.

"From what I've seen," David said as he took a drink. "As I understand it, Ashcroft belonged to the Pemberton family for hundreds of years. As Sylvia mentioned, she lost both her husband and her son in the last war, so no heirs there. She was the sister of Lord Pemberton, Louise Pemberton's father. Louise being Sir Rupert's deceased wife. Louise had a brother, but he died in the influenza outbreak after the war. That left Louise as the only heir. She inherited the estate when Lord Pemberton died."

"And Great Aunt Sylvia comes with the inheritance?" I said.

"Yes, exactly," David said. "Lord Pemberton put a clause in his will stipulating that Sylvia—she's entitled to be called Lady Pemberton—be provided for at Ashcroft for the remainder of her life. I don't think anyone thought she'd be around so long. She turned ninety last winter."

"Who owns the place now?" I asked.

"Sir Rupert. He inherited it from his wife, and is required to maintain Sylvia in the same manner. I don't believe he begrudges her, but she never passes up an opportunity to mention how well the Pembertons maintained the estate before the Sutcliffes came along. Of course with all the new taxes, it is much harder these days."

"Did you find out anything useful today, Billy?" Kaz asked, after a momentary lull. He was giving me an out in case I didn't want to discuss it in front of David, but this wasn't exactly classified. I didn't want Fraser's name to get around as a stool pigeon, so I left him out of the story.

"There's a gangster by the name of Charles Sabini," I said. "He's been big in gambling and extortion for years, and since he's half Italian, the government interned him at the start of the war. Put a crimp in his business. He did some time after that, too, but lately he's been rebuilding his criminal organization. He has a reputation for violence."

"Where is he?" Kaz asked.

"He works out of the racetrack at Newton Abbot," I said.

"I was there once," David said. "Nice place, overlooks the river."

"The River Teign," Kaz said. "A tidal river."

"Oh, right," David said. "You thought your dead chap may have gone in and out on the tides. The River Teign would do it. It turns tidal close by the racecourse."

"Do you have any reason to connect this gangster to the killing?" Kaz said.

"Apparently a competitor felt Sabini was encroaching on his territory and sent an assassin after him. This was three months ago. But Sabini must have turned the tables, since the killer was never heard from again."

"That fits," Kaz said. "The timing and the reason why no one filed a missing persons report."

"Everything points to it," I said.

"You don't sound terribly convinced," David said, whispering as he checked to see if anyone was listening. He was definitely enjoying himself. Dinner at Ashcroft was never half as exciting.

"I think it's likely," I said. "But we need to check it out. I'd like to hear Sabini's side of the story to see if it matches up with what my contact told me. And I want to see exactly where the tides start in the River Teign, to be sure we have a reasonable case."

"He's not going to confess, do you think?" David asked.

"I don't need him to confess. That's up to Inspector Grange," I said. "Our assignment is to make certain we know who the man on the beach was."

"How are you even going to get him to talk to you?" David said.

"That's where you come in," I said. Kaz raised his eyebrows inquisitively. I told them about Sabini's son Michael in the RAF and how he'd been shot down and killed. "Do you think you could come with us, and give your condolences? Tell Sabini you knew his son?"

"If it would help, certainly," David said.

"Are you sure?" Kaz said. "It could be dangerous. This man has killed before."

"So have I, Piotr," David said. "I have sent men crashing down from the sky in a ball of fire. I am the very face of death."

CHAPTER TWELVE

I'VE BEEN TOLD plenty of times by the English that Americans don't know how to make tea, or even drink it properly. I don't disagree. But try explaining to a Brit that the thin brew they serve as coffee is truly horrible, and nine times out of ten they'll say it tastes just fine and look at you with faint bemusement, as if a desire for strong joe, cold beer, or tea without milk was a testament to colonial depravity.

So I said the java was fine when Meredith inquired at breakfast, saying she understood Americans were particular about their morning coffee. As if the English were nonchalant about tea.

"Was your day successful?" she asked as she spread marmalade on her toast.

"Yes, I think so," I said. "We might be close to wrapping up the case, for our purposes, anyway. We'll turn over our findings to Inspector Grange when we're done." I'd called the inspector and briefed him on what we'd found. He hadn't sounded impressed, but he'd agreed to allow Constable Quick to accompany us. He was from Newton Abbot and would know the lay of the land. If Sabini was so overcome by remorse that he confessed his guilt, we could make an official arrest. Mostly, I was curious about Tom Quick.

"At least the victim's family can be thankful his body was recovered," Helen said from across the table. "It's terrible to think of him floating about in the Channel for so long. Do you think the fishermen were right, about the tides carrying him out?"

"It seems likely," I said, trying to be polite but hoping for a shift in the morning's conversation. I was trying to enjoy breakfast. I was in no hurry to get to Newton Abbot; in my experience, criminal bosses weren't early risers. "David told us about the Guinea Pig Club last night. It sounds like Doctor McIndoe is a remarkable man."

"Guinea pigs?" Helen said. "Whatever do you mean?"

"At the hospital," I said, then realized he must never have told her. Or she didn't want to know. "Never mind, it was only a joke."

"It's nothing to joke about," Helen said in a small voice as she studied the crumbs on her plate.

"Oh, Helen, really!" Meredith said. "At least you have a husband who's done something positive. All Edgar ever did was cause trouble for everyone, and now he's more useless than ever. Don't be such a twit." She bit into her toast like it was a piece of raw meat.

"Good advice all around," Great Aunt Sylvia said, gliding into the room and taking a seat.

"Good morning," I said, standing. "I hope to see you all later this afternoon."

"No need to leave on my account, Captain," Great Aunt Sylvia said, gracing me with a wrinkled smile.

"Crime doesn't wait," I said, giving her a wink to see how she'd react.

"I think it can wait a very long time, Captain Boyle. Good luck to you."

I strolled outside looking for Kaz and David. Three disconcerting women so early in the morning made the grey misty sky seem inviting. I shivered as I sat in the jeep, the mist turning to raindrops that splattered and popped on the canvas top. My shoulder holster dug into my side; I hadn't worn it when the tailor measured me for my Eisenhower jacket, and now I was paying the price for clean lines.

By the time Kaz and David dashed from the house, the rain was lashing, and they had to clutch their caps to their heads. They piled into the jeep and brushed the water from their coats, dripping like wet dogs. By the time we arrived at the police station, the rain lessened, drops splashing intermittently into puddles.

"Need a tour guide, do you?" Constable Quick said as he climbed into the rear of the jeep. Kaz introduced David to Quick, who seemed cheerful enough, not missing a beat at the sight of David's burn-scarred face.

"We're going to speak to Charles Sabini," I told Quick. "I figured it wouldn't hurt to have the law along."

"Actually, it well might," Quick said. "What makes you think he'll talk to you?"

"Flight Lieutenant Martindale knew his son in North Africa. He was killed there. That's our entree."

"His son's death is common knowledge, as is Sabini's temper and hatred of the government. Quite a coincidence," Quick said, glancing at David, "you finding a chap who knew Michael Sabini."

"Listen, all we need to do is have a word with Sabini. We're not here to arrest anyone, or even gather evidence. I want to confirm, even if it's off the record, the information I've been given about the body on the beach."

"I'm game," David said. "I know all sorts of dead chaps. It won't be hard to convince this fellow."

"So you didn't know him?" Quick said.

"I was far more likely to shoot down a Sabini than to know this poor sod," David said. I was beginning to like this guy.

"We thought it might be best for you and me to wait outside," Kaz said. "To back up Billy and David, and to avoid antagonizing Mr. Sabini."

"All right," Quick said. Then to David, "Spitfire pilot, I'd guess."

"Hurricanes first, then Spits in North Africa. How did you know?" David asked.

"Your attitude says you're a fighter pilot. Your burns say Spitfire. I was on a Lancaster until we got shot up. One of the gunners had his legs badly burned. They sent him to a special hospital up in Sussex."

"That's where I was," David said, and they fell to talking about flying, aircraft, friends alive and dead, as easily as if they were old pals. David was a different man away from Ashcroft. And Tom Quick had forgotten about his limp; I'd noticed when we picked him up.

Tom's directions got us to Newton Abbot in half an hour. We passed a medieval tower stuck in the middle of the road at the town center, then crossed the River Teign and drove to the racecourse. The place was deserted except for a few automobiles, the stands empty, and the track itself quiet. A solitary horse was being taken through his paces, kicking up clods of mud as he passed.

David and I walked ahead, looking for some sign of life. Kaz and the constable trailed behind, keeping tabs on us from a distance. Stables and outbuildings stretched on beyond the track, the faint whinny of a horse echoing between them. The ground was muddy and wet, and the lingering rain fell lightly on our shoulders.

"Where is everyone?" I said, whispering in spite of myself.

"Look," David said, pointing to an open door at one end of a row of stables. A sign above it read SABINI ENTERPRISES. A line of footprints in the mud led inside. None came out. I held David back with one arm and motioned the others forward with my other.

"This doesn't look right," I whispered. "Kaz, you stay here with David." David was the only one of us who wasn't armed. Quick had traded his rifle for a revolver which he un-holstered as I drew my .38 Police Special. While Kaz is deadly with his Webley, I wanted a cop at my back. An open door in a rainstorm and one-way footprints are not a good combination. And if whoever left the door wide open had gone out the back, Kaz would be ready.

We went in.

I smelled it before I saw it. The metallic scent of blood and death.

Pools of congealed red gore.

Two men sprawled on the floor, gunshot wounds to the chest. More than enough.

One man seated at his desk, his head hanging backward, a gaping slash at his neck. Spurts of blood decorated the wall, where it had gushed from the carotid artery before the heart stopped pumping. Flies buzzed around all the men's wounds. A feast.

I pointed to another open door, leading into the stables.

"I'll check," Quick said. "But these men have been dead for some time. The blood's coagulated, and the flies didn't just show up."

"Yeah," I said. I went to the doorway and told Kaz and David what we'd found, retracing my steps and being careful not to step in the blood. A quick glance told me the killers had been pros. Two of them, I figured, imagining how it could have been done quickly. They walk in, shoot the bodyguards, and the first guy holds a gun on Sabini. The second guy walks behind Sabini and lifts his chin. Sabini sees the first guy step aside, perhaps understanding it's to avoid the spray of blood. Then lights out.

Revenge.

"It looks like someone succeeded this time," Kaz said.

"Yeah, they smartened up and sent at least two guys," I said, watching for Quick to reappear.

"Could this have anything to do with the man you saw yesterday?" Kaz asked, still keeping Fraser's name mum.

"No. They've been dead since yesterday, I'd guess. Somebody planned this in revenge for Sabini slitting his competitor's throat."

"Which tells us that the theory of the hit man being our corpse on the beach holds water," Kaz said.

"Like a cast-iron pot," I said. "Where's Quick?"

"I thought he was with you," David said.

"He went through the stables," I said. "You two go around front. I'll circle around back, and we'll meet up." I wasn't worried about the killers still being there, but Tom should have been back by now. I moved around the building, keeping close to the wall, my revolver held by my side. I got to the corner and took a quick peek. The rear of the stables faced a road with a row of houses on the far side—or what had once been homes. Piles of brick lined the street, and except for a few soot-covered walls, everything else had been cleared away. Two craters stood between the remaining buildings, marking the spot where German bombs had hit and taken out six brick row houses.

Tom Quick stood at the lip of one crater, his revolver limp in his hand. I went up to him and looked in the crater, wondering if he'd found something. A body or a clue to the killing. But it was filled with rainwater, and the edges of the blackened soil crumbled beneath our feet.

"Tom?" I said, as Kaz and David came up behind me. "Tom, is there something here?"

"No, there's nothing," he said. "You drop a five-hundred-pound bomb on a house, and there's nothing left. As you can see."

"It looks like this happened a while ago," I said, trying to edge around him and see his face. His eyes were unfocused, seeing nothing, remembering everything.

"A lifetime ago," Tom answered. "So many lives ago."

I slowly curled my fingers around his revolver and took it from him. He didn't notice.

"We usually dropped thousand-pound bombs, fourteen at a time," he said. "Can you imagine?"

"No," I said, trying to comprehend the devastation the moment these bombs hit.

"Blockbuster bombs too," Tom said, his voice rising in pitch. "A four-thousand-pound bomb. Do you know why they call them block-busters? Do you?"

"No."

"Because they destroy an entire city block. And blow off roof tiles from the surrounding buildings. That's why we drop incendiary bombs, small ones, at the same time. They start fires better that way, you see? They have professors who figure all that out, but *they* stay at home. Wouldn't it be funny if one of them lived here?" He laughed, a short, harsh spit of derision.

"Okay, Tom," I said. "We need to go to the local police station and report this. Can you show us where it is?"

"Of course I can," Tom said, turning on me as if I was an idiot. "If you'll tell me why the death of three vile criminals means anything. Who will answer for this? Who will hang for *this*?" He pointed at the blasted houses; the stacks of brick awaiting rebuilding; the wet, muddy holes in the ground; as if the bombers were still circling overhead, high in the same sky where, hundreds of miles away, his Lancaster loaded with fourteen thousand pounds of high explosives had once flown over cities and towns, cratering neighborhoods and ending lives, bringing retribution to the nation that had started this terrible war.

CHAPTER THIRTEEN

"HE'S NO DANGER to anyone," Inspector Grange said. "There are simply times when he stops. Becomes lost in himself, so to speak."

"He seemed fine when we found the bodies," I said. We'd spent most of the morning with a detective sergeant from Newton Abbot, giving our statements and having our stories checked. It helped that he knew Tom Quick and had settled him at a desk with a cup of hot tea, the English cure-all. "It was a charnel house, but he held up fine in there."

"As he would have done had the perpetrators been there to be apprehended," Grange said. "My guess is that he saw the area was clear, but before he could return to you, the bomb damage drew him in."

"How do you know he wouldn't have frozen if we had been confronted by armed killers?" I asked.

"That's not Tom's problem," Grange said, settling back in his chair and stuffing his pipe with tobacco. Quick was upstairs in his quarters, with David Martindale keeping him company. Kaz was on the telephone, reporting in to Colonel Harding. I was stuck trying to understand Tom Quick.

"He kept talking about bomb loads. Blockbusters, that sort of thing," I said.

"That's because he was a bombardier," Grange said. "They called those big bombs 'cookies,' as if they were children at play. I suppose it makes it easier, somehow, to change the name of the thing." He puffed on his pipe, studying the glow of the coals as if it were preferable to thinking about the obliteration of cities.

"So what is it, guilt?" I asked.

"Nothing so simple," Grange said, blowing smoke toward the ceiling. "Tom was a good man on the force, the kind of constable you know will move up the ranks. But then the war came along, and he joined the RAF as soon as he could. Wanted to be a pilot, but washed out for some reason, so he made bombardier instead. He came home on leave after his first five missions. He said they'd been easy, mainly against airfields and other German installations in France."

"Military targets," I said.

"Yes. The RAF hadn't yet begun the nighttime bombing. He came to visit and let slip that they were going to hit Bremen next, as soon as he reported back. He shouldn't have said anything, but he was terribly excited about finally bringing the war home to Germany, after all England had suffered. I scolded him, of course, and swore I wouldn't say a thing."

"Where was home?" I asked. "Not the bachelor quarters here."

"No. Tom had a lovely wife and two children, both little girls. They'd moved to Plymouth to stay with her parents when Tom joined up. It was April 1941 when he had that leave. He returned to duty, and that very night he flew off with his squadron, and they dropped their thousand-pound bombs on Bremen. At the same time, the Germans hit Plymouth. Scored a direct hit on the air-raid shelter in Portland Square. Seventy-two people were killed in that one shelter."

"Tom's wife and children among them," I said, a terrible understanding growing in my mind.

"Yes," Grange said, staring at his pipe. It had gone out. "The night he first dropped his bombload on a German city. He was devastated. Almost broken by it, as any man would be. Others might seek revenge, delight in wreaking havoc on the people who had done such a thing. But there was no sign of that with Tom. He had compassionate leave to bury his family, of course, and we all went to the funeral. Going to funerals was almost a full-time job during the Blitz."

"How did Tom react?"

"Like the man he was. He returned to duty and completed his thirty missions. Then he fell apart, completely. Catatonic for a while. I spoke to his RAF doctor before I took him on here, and he said Tom felt he was murdering his own family every time they bombed a city. Which by then was nearly every mission. It didn't help that he lost a good friend on his last flight. His rear gunner, I think it was."

"Which is why you took him on as a War Reserve Constable," I said, wondering if that was the Freddie he'd mentioned. "But not a regular officer."

"Yes, I owed him that much. I try to pair him up with others, keep him busy. I don't think the county constable would ever take him back as a regular if he saw his medical file. But I have some latitude with the War Reserve fellows, so I did what I thought best. He tells people he was invalided out of the service because of his leg wounds. He did take some shrapnel, but nothing serious. It's a convenient and kind lie we all go along with."

"Will he be okay?" I asked.

"He'll snap out of it; he always does," Grange said. "But if you mean will he ever be the old Tom Quick again? No, that man's long gone."

I left Inspector Grange to his pipe and wandered into the office Kaz had been given to make his call to SHAEF. He was just hanging up the telephone. "Colonel Harding says he agrees, the body is more than likely connected to Sabini. He told us to stay here until at least tomorrow. General Eisenhower may be coming down to Slapton Sands to watch a training exercise. I gave him the number for Ashcroft."

"Okay," I said. "Let's collect David and head back." I gave Kaz the basics about Tom Quick as we took the stairs to the constable's quarters. Quick had a small but comfortable room with a dresser, easy chair, table, and bed. Not a place you'd want to spend every waking hour, but not bad for a good night's sleep after walking a beat. I wondered where he'd go when the war was over—but the way things were going, that was a long time off.

"Sorry I caused such a fuss," Tom said, sitting up in his bed, his tunic loosened.

"Nothing to worry about, Tom," David said. "Rest up. They'll have you back on the job in the morning. See you tomorrow night for a pint, all right?"

"Yes," Tom said. "I'll look forward to it." They shook hands, two scarred airmen. If I had to choose at that moment which scar I'd carry if I had to, the Spitfire would win out over the Lancaster.

WE DROVE BACK to Ashcroft in silence. A cool breeze blew the remaining clouds away, revealing achingly blue skies. A beautiful day. Sabini and his goons were on a police surgeon's slab, Tom was coming out of his stupor, and David had found a new friend, someone who might understand what he'd been through. And we didn't have to worry about German spies sneaking ashore at Slapton Sands.

The day could have gone worse.

"There you are, David," Meredith said as she walked through the door, turning away from a man holding a woven basket heaped with produce. "Helen was asking about you. You should tell the poor girl where you are. Baron, Captain, did you kidnap our David again?"

"We've had quite an adventure," David said. "Are we in time for tea?"

"Just," Meredith said. "I'll tell Mrs. Dudley you'll be joining us. Crawford, I'll take the strawberries." She went off, clutching the basket of bright red berries.

"Crawford, these are our guests, Captain Boyle and Baron Kazimierz," David said, a bit quickly, I thought. Was he taken aback by Meredith's abrupt departure, or her comments about Helen? "They have been quite impressed by our food here. Those strawberries look marvelous."

"Gentlemen," Crawford said, giving the hint of a bow. "I'm pleased to hear it. The greenhouse lets us get an early start on things."

"It must be a change from fishing as a livelihood," I said.

Crawford wore a neatly trimmed moustache on his broad face, his brown hair thick and well Brylcreemed. He was square jawed, with a tan from working outdoors and telltale crow's feet around his eyes from squinting into the sun's harsh glare on salt water. He wore wool pants and an open vest over a blue shirt, and his shoes were scuffed but clean.

"I'd prefer to be out on the water, but the government took my land and my mooring, and I lost my boat in a storm. Got pushed up on the rocks at Start Point in a gale, and that was that. I count myself lucky to have Ashcroft, I do."

"I know the family feels the same," David said. Crawford nodded and left through the front door.

"I applaud the egalitarianism of Ashcroft House," Kaz said. "Many country homes would not allow a member of the staff to use the front door. Nor would it even occur to the staff to do so."

"Well, the Sutcliffe family is not hereditary aristocracy. More hard-working upper-middle-class types. Sir Rupert was knighted for his work in India, but that ends with him. The same with the Pembertons," David said. "It would be sheer idiocy to try to keep Ashcroft in the style of the last century. It would bankrupt the place. The war taxes are hard enough on the old boy."

Tea was served in the sitting room. Helen and Sir Rupert were there, along with Edgar, who sat by himself reading a book.

"Ah, here they are. How did it go today?" Sir Rupert asked, taking an unsteady step and nearly falling onto a couch.

"Eventful," Kaz said. "Are you feeling poorly, Sir Rupert?"

"It's the fever," Sir Rupert said. "It never truly leaves one. Dengue fever, picked it up in the Raj," he said to us by way of explanation. "They call it breakbone fever in India, and I can vouch for the name." He winced as he tried to crack a smile, and took a few deep breaths.

"Were you looking for me, dear?" David said to Helen, a hopeful note in his voice.

"No," she said, busying herself with the tea plates. "Oh, I may have wondered where you were, that's all," she said, moving around to his left side before she actually looked at him. "You were with Piotr and Captain Boyle again, I assume?"

"Yes," David said, and retreated in the face of her indifference.

Meredith came in with Great Aunt Sylvia, and tea was served.

There were scones and cookies, which the English insist on calling biscuits, which makes about as much sense as calling a four-thousand-pound bomb a cookie, I guess.

"Do tell us how things went today," Sir Rupert said. He looked pale, and there was a sheen of sweat on his forehead, but he sounded better. I recounted our journey to Newton Abbot with Constable Quick, and described the discovery of the dead bodies. I left out most of the blood, and all of Tom's reaction to the bombed-out houses. I put David a little more at the center of the action, and watched Helen's eyes widen.

"Really?" Helen said. "You found three dead gangsters? How horrible!" For a moment, she looked at David dead-on, her normal aversion forgotten in the excitement of the story.

"Not as horrible as war, my dear," Great Aunt Sylvia said. "And David has seen much of that, remember." There was a touch of reproach in her voice, and Helen had the sense to murmur her agreement.

"Does that settle your business here, then?" Meredith asked Kaz and me. "Or do you still need to investigate that poor man on the beach?"

"No, we think all the stories match up well enough. He was likely the killer sent after Sabini, who was killed in turn and dumped into the River Teign, which carried him out into the Channel," I said.

"Where the tides and currents tossed him about until he washed up on Slapton Sands," Kaz explained.

"How horrible," Meredith said, in an offhand voice that told me she, like her sister, knew little about the horrible things in life.

"Well, please do stay on if you can," Sir Rupert said. "I haven't seen David look so alive since—well, in quite a while." As pale as he was, Sir Rupert's embarrassment showed in his face.

"We can stay on, as it turns out," Kaz said. General Eisenhower's travel plans had to be kept secret, but I hoped we'd have a few days here before we had to tag along to watch the maneuvers at Slapton Sands.

"Splendid," David said. Meredith smiled politely and stood to pour herself some more tea.

"Excuse me, Sir Rupert," Williams said as he entered the room. "An American naval officer wishes to speak to you."

"One of yours?" Sir Rupert said to me.

"I'm not expecting anyone," I said.

"Very well, show him in. One more for tea is no problem." He pushed himself off the couch with some effort and stood to greet the visitor.

"Lieutenant Peter Wiley, sir," Williams said from the doorway.

"I'm very sorry to interrupt your tea," the young lieutenant said. He looked like he should still be in college, and not even about to graduate. He was outfitted in his khaki dress uniform, which didn't have much in the way of decoration except for his lieutenant's bars. He was a good-looking kid, with light, sandy-colored hair and blue eyes that flickered over each person in the room. "I can come back if I'm intruding."

"Not at all, young man," Great Aunt Sylvia said. "Do join us, and tell us why you've come." She raised her glasses and squinted through them as she studied him from across the room.

"I wanted to ask Sir Rupert for permission to paint the house."

"Paint it?" Meredith asked, dropping a sugar cube into her cup.

"I'm a watercolorist, I should explain," Wiley said hurriedly, perhaps in case they thought he'd brought ladders and buckets. He took a step closer and extended his hand to Sir Rupert. "I'm pleased to meet you, sir. I've heard so much about Ashcroft."

Sir Rupert's eyes widened at the proffered hand, and he promptly fell back onto the sofa.

Meredith followed his gaze and promptly dropped her teacup, which shattered on the floor, milky tea splashing on her shoes as she stared, her mouth open in surprise.

"Wiley, you said? Where . . . where did you get that ring?" Sir Rupert asked, wiping his hand across his face as if the man standing before him might be a mirage. He stood again, Helen standing at his side holding his elbow. She was confused, but she showed none of the shock that Meredith and Sir Rupert had displayed when Wiley had held out his hand.

"Who are you, exactly?" Meredith asked, advancing on Wiley, her narrow eyes studying him. "Why are you here?"

"I'm very sorry," he said, taking a step back. "I didn't mean to cause a disturbance. I only wanted to know if I could come back in the morning to paint. I should leave."

"I said, where did you get that ring?" Sir Rupert repeated, his voice unusually loud.

Great Aunt Sylvia stood at Sir Rupert's side, her hand patting his arm.

"I should think he got it from his mother, Julia Greenshaw," she said. "Isn't that so, young man?"

"My God," Sir Rupert said. There was a confused murmur around the room, and Sir Rupert looked like he was ready to hit the couch again.

"Let's all sit down and let Lieutenant Wiley talk," David said, bringing a chair closer for Wiley. Tea was forgotten as the group— except for Edgar, who stayed in a far corner with his book—hunched forward to listen. Kaz and I backed up, not wanting to get in the middle of this family to-do, but not wanting to miss the story either.

"My mother did live here," Peter Wiley said. "Her name was Julia Greenshaw, and she worked as a maid to Miss Pemberton. Lady Sutcliffe, after she became your wife, Sir Rupert."

"Yes, I remember Julia. Miss Greenshaw," he said, his eyes darting to Great Aunt Sylvia. "She married Ted Wiley and emigrated to America. He was our groundskeeper," Sir Rupert added for our benefit.

"That's right. My mother gave me this ring when I got my overseas orders. It was a gift from Lady Sutcliffe. This is the Pemberton crest, I was told."

"Well, the coat of arms, to be precise," Great Aunt Sylvia said.

"What does it mean?" I asked, leaning over Wiley's shoulder, unable to resist butting in. It was a gold ring with a flat surface engraved with a chevron and what looked like three small buckets.

"This coat of arms comes down to us from Sir George Pemberton of the seventeenth century," Great Aunt Sylvia said. "The buckets represent his service furnishing provisions for the army. Beer, perhaps. Possibly not the most prestigious coat of arms in the Empire, but still, not every family has one." With that, she gave Sir Rupert a withering stare.

"I didn't know Louise had given that ring away," Sir Rupert said, sounding a bit confused.

"Now do you believe me?" Meredith said. Sir Rupert ignored her. Believe her about what, I nearly asked, but managed to keep my mouth shut.

"And how are your parents?" Sir Rupert asked Wiley.

"My father died when I was a young child," Wiley said. "My mother passed away six months ago. I wasn't able to be at the funeral."

"Blasted war," Sir Rupert said, suddenly overcome by emotion. He took a breath and continued. "A painter, are you?"

"Yes, sir. I work in a cartography section for the navy, so at least I can use my skills. But I like to get away when I have a day off and paint in the outdoors. Drawing and coloring maps for days on end in the same room becomes a bit dreary after a while. When I found out how close I was to Ashcroft, I thought I'd ride up. My mother spoke about it so often I wanted to see it in person. I only wish I could have told her I made it here."

"Well, of course you can paint here to your heart's content, my boy," Sir Rupert said. "Terribly sorry about the reception, it was simply a surprise to see that ring."

"I should have written, not just shown up on your doorstep," Wiley said.

"Well, you're here now, and you must stay for dinner," Great Aunt Sylvia said. "Will that be all right, Rupert?"

"Of course, you must stay," Sir Rupert readily agreed. "Where are you billeted?"

"Near Torquay, a place called Greenway House. I've been there a couple of months. This is the first time I've had leave."

"And you came here?" David asked, half in jest. "What about the delights of London?"

"Oh, I knew I had to come here," Wiley said. "It meant so much to both of my parents, I had to see it. It was their home, after all. It's where they fell in love. Besides, it's only about thirty minutes away. I'd spend all my time on trains if I went into London."

"If you're on leave, then do stay the night," Sir Rupert said. "We can show you around the place in the morning, and you can come back to paint whenever you like."

"That's very kind, Sir Rupert. I'd like that."

Sir Rupert then did proper introductions all around. Wiley looked at David several times while they spoke, never once flinching as he looked at the pilot's ruined face. When Helen was introduced, she looked at Wiley with a frank, appraising stare. I wondered, was she thinking about her own behavior? Had this stranger's acceptance of David, as he was, finally given her cause to think?

Maybe. She took David's arm and leaned in to him without stepping around to his good side, her eyes studying Peter Wiley intently.

CHAPTER FOURTEEN

DINNER WAS A curious affair. Sir Rupert did his best to act the genial host, even as he mopped the sweat from his brow, his face pale and his breath short. Meredith was positively chatty with Peter Wiley, asking him about his upbringing in America and his art studies. Helen looked bewildered by it all, but at least she leaned in now and then to speak to David in a low voice, as if he were suddenly a safe refuge instead of a hideous parody of the man she'd married. Edgar ate and drank with his usual gusto, indifferent to the reactions of others, or maybe glad that the new guest drew Meredith's attention away from him. Great Aunt Sylvia smiled quietly and watched the proceedings as if from a great distance. A wistful look passed over her, and for a second I could see the young woman she'd once been, with a pretty, round face and those intelligent eyes. At ninety, they still missed nothing.

Dessert was strawberry cake, the fruit courtesy of the ever-remarkable Crawford.

"What did your father do for a living, Lieutenant Wiley?" Meredith asked as she passed him a slice.

"Please call me Peter, if you don't mind," Wiley said.

"Of course we will, Peter," Great Aunt Sylvia said. Coming from a proper lady like her, that was a stamp of approval.

"My father opened a small hardware store in New York City, on the Lower East Side, as soon as he found a place to live," he said. "He died a few years later. My mother kept it going, even during the Depression. She managed to save up enough to send me to New York University."

"America certainly is the land of opportunity," Meredith said. "Even a groundskeeper can own a shop, and a maid can send her child to university. Remarkable."

"Opportunity is what you make with what you've been given," Sir Rupert said sternly. "Julia and Ted seem to have done well with young Peter here, and he's lucky to have an artistic flair. But opportunity is not limited to the New World, not at all. Our family has done well in the colonial service. A decent income, good investments, and a title. That's where opportunity comes from: hard work. You and Edgar should ponder that, Meredith."

The table went silent, whether from shock at Sir Rupert's words or the fact that he had actually spoken to Meredith, I couldn't tell. I ate a bite of cake and waited for someone to say something.

"It may be, Sir Rupert," Edgar said, his hands flat on the table, "that the greatest opportunity one has in life is to do the right thing, regardless of the cost. Please excuse me." Edgar pushed away from the table and left the room, creating an even deeper silence. Peter Wiley looked at me askance, and I shrugged as if to say, *Don't ask me, pal, I'm just passing through myself.*

The gathering broke up quickly after that. Sir Rupert said he was tired and made plans to show Peter around in the morning. Meredith walked out without a word, leaving Helen and David looking some-what uncomfortable. Great Aunt Sylvia surveyed the remaining group with assured calmness.

"Is there anything else we can do to make you more comfortable, Peter?" Great Aunt Sylvia said.

"No, thank you, you've been very gracious," he said. "Though I would like to put my motorbike under cover. Is there a garage or barn?"

"Stables, garage, barn, take your pick. Then do join us in the library. It's almost time for the nine o'clock news."

David went with Peter, and the rest of us joined Edgar in the library. He was fiddling with the dial on the wireless, tuning in the BBC.

Neither Helen nor Great Aunt Sylvia commented on Meredith's abrupt departure, although Helen did tell Edgar that David had gone with Peter to ensure he didn't ride off in the night on his motorbike, which got a laugh. These people seemed to take their odd interactions for granted.

"Peter rides an old Norton Model Sixteen," David said when they returned. "Same as the motorbike I had before the war. A bit older and more rusty, to be sure."

"You have your own bike?" I said. It didn't sound like it would be on any motor-pool inventory.

"Yes, I bought it when I first came to Torquay. I wanted my own transportation, in case I had any free time," Peter said.

Great Aunt Sylvia hushed us as the announcer declared it was the BBC Home Service's nine o'clock war bulletin. There was an American offensive in the jungles of New Guinea. The Soviets had retaken Sevastopol. We'd bombed Budapest. *With cookies?* I wondered. The biggest excitement was about an RAF raid on Gestapo headquarters in The Hague. A pinpoint strike had destroyed the building, along with files on Dutchmen the Gestapo had planned to arrest and send to concentration camps in Germany.

"Good show for the RAF!" David said when the broadcast was over. "Those Mosquito pilots could drop a bomb down a chimney in heavy fog. Smashing." I agreed. I had more reasons than most to applaud the destruction of a Gestapo prison.

"Peter, what are you drawing maps for in that room of yours?" Edgar asked. "Aren't there maps enough? Michelin and all the others?"

"Yes, I wondered that myself," David said. "I know there are high-quality aerial photographs as well as maps already in existence. And why does the navy need maps anyway? Don't they have charts and navigators and that sort of thing?"

"I'm not supposed to talk about it," Peter said. "And you know the military. Nothing much that they want done makes sense. I was happy when I got an assignment that had anything to do with art, so I didn't ask questions."

"Who else is at Greenway House?" Kaz asked. "If you can tell us."

"We have a small cartographic section, and then there's a Coast Guard unit, the Tenth Flotilla. They pilot LCIs for the navy. That's Landing Craft Infantry," Peter said.

"We're familiar with the terms," David said. "It's hard to live in southwest England these days and not be. Do you expect to serve at sea?"

"I doubt it," he said. "I'd like to, but they keep me pretty busy on dry land."

"Helen and I shall adjourn, gentlemen," Great Aunt Sylvia said as she hoisted herself up and fixed her eyes on Wiley. "I am glad you accepted our invitation to stay, Peter. We will leave you men to talk of war and drink brandy."

Edgar took this statement literally and dashed to the side table, returning with a cut-crystal decanter and glasses. He poured, and then settled down into his leather chair with a satisfied *oomph*.

"What is it you fellows do at SHAEF?" Peter asked us as we settled in the comfortable chairs and sipped the fine brandy. Kaz explained what the Office of Special Investigations was all about, and I filled him in on what had brought us here, the body, the tides, the dead gangsters. Not one of our most impressive cases, but I made it sound like Eliot Ness had nothing on us. David offered a toast to Ike, glasses clinked, and the decanter was brought back into action.

We talked about the war news. David was excited about the pinpoint raid on the Gestapo headquarters, so we toasted the RAF. Then Peter asked about his burns, with typical American bluntness, and David told his story. We toasted the aim of the German pilot who had missed blowing his head off by inches, then we toasted the ground crew that pulled David from the Spitfire, followed by his doctors at the hospital.

We weren't drunk, but the excessive camaraderie of drinking men who are downing someone else's excellent booze caused Kaz to blurt out—and he's not given to blurting—"Edgar, what was that scene at dinner all about?"

"Ancient history," Edgar said, shaking his head.

"Come on, Edgar," David said. "We ought to stick together, the two of us marrying Sutcliffe girls. Not always the easiest thing, eh?"

"Sir Rupert does not approve of me," Edgar said after a long silence. "He thinks I have squandered a great opportunity. He is very fond of opportunity."

"How so?" Kaz asked.

"He enjoyed a number of business transactions when he was with the civil service in India. Very favorable to his bank accounts, at very little risk," Edgar said.

"No, I mean what does he think you squandered?" Kaz said.

"Fill that up, will you, David?" Edgar said, handing his glass over. "It's a long story, and thirsty work telling it." Once he had his hands cupped around the glass of amber, he began.

He and Meredith met in London when Edgar was studying at university and working as a tutor at a private school. Meredith was living with friends and looking for work, without success. She had been brought up in India, where her mother, to whom she'd been very close, had died. She and her father had never gotten along, and at the time of her mother's death, something happened that caused the rift to widen. Rupert Sutcliffe—he had not been knighted yet—worked for the civil service and had spent nearly two decades administering the Raj for King and Country.

Rupert had contracted dengue fever, and he became so ill he was sent home to recover. By the time he and his daughters were back in England, Meredith had vowed never to speak to him again; aged eighteen, she struck out on her own. She had money, at least for a while. She never said where it came from, but she had a good time working her way through it.

Although Edgar's dislike for the man was evident, he admitted Rupert was highly intelligent and skilled at dealing with politics in India. He was often called upon to help formulate ways to keep India in the fight while at the same time denying increasing calls for independence. A tightrope act, to be sure. More than two and a half million Indians were engaged in combat against the Axis powers across the globe, and it was vital for Great Britain that they continue to fight, and die, for the British Empire.

"Edgar, get to the point," David said. "I enjoy a good dose of history as much as the next chap, but when do you enter the scene?" Edgar took a slug of brandy and continued.

Edgar and Meredith married. They had two children, and he secured a teaching position. Their children were sent to boarding school, which along with other expenses made family life difficult for a man in his position to afford. Meredith began to compare him unfavorably with her father, whom she detested. This didn't sit well with Edgar, and they argued over money—over anything, but it mattered little because Meredith invariably won.

The war came, and Edgar tried to enlist, but was turned down because of his flat feet and asthma. He applied for a government position, but with so many academics wanting to do their bit, he received no reply other than an instruction to wait. Meredith did not like waiting, and did not like the life of a middle-class—at best—wife of a second-rate professor, to use her words.

So she went to her father. Figuring he could pull strings for Edgar, she humbled herself and pleaded with him to intervene. She cleverly brought pictures of the grandchildren he'd never seen—but not the children themselves, in case Rupert did not comply fully.

He complied. Edgar received his appointment to the Indian Civil Service, and they departed for the subcontinent within weeks. Before leaving, Edgar and Meredith visited Ashcroft with the children—her payment for services rendered. Rupert gave Edgar advice on how to invest in the export of jute, cotton, coffee, tea, and sugarcane. The clear expectation was that an Englishman in India should do well for himself and his family. Very well.

"That's how I ended up in India," Edgar said, draining his glass.

"But why did you come back here?" Peter said. "What happened in India?"

"Three million people died, that's what happened in India," Edgar said. He continued with his story, this time without asking for a refill.

They arrived in New Delhi in 1940, and at first all went well. Edgar had a decent position in the economic office and was involved in the collection of land taxes, which was the primary source of revenue for the administration of the Raj, as the English called their

Indian empire. Then, in December 1941, the war began between Great Britain and Japan. Supplies from Southeast Asia were reduced as the Japanese advanced in the Pacific. Stocks of rice began to be hoarded as prices rose and speculators held on to tons of the stuff, waiting for prices to increase even further. Bengal, an eastern province, was hardest hit. When the Japanese took Burma in early 1942, all rice imports from Southeast Asia ceased, and food shortages were rife.

"It sounds like everyone should have seen that coming," Peter said.

"With hindsight, yes," Edgar said. "But in 1940 we were focused on the war with Germany. No one thought the Japanese would sweep through Asia as they did. The very idea of Singapore falling was unthinkable. And a famine is not like a riot or a battle. There are no burning cities or marching armies, no shouts of warning. It crept up on us. India is a poor nation, and death is common currency. One day, death simply overwhelmed the province, rolling across it like a tidal wave."

"Don't they grow enough food to feed themselves?" David asked.

"No," Edgar said. "Not everywhere in India, anyway. Each province is very protective of its own food sources. The British governor of Madras banned exports of rice from his province to make sure there was enough for his own people. Then the other provinces followed suit. It was every man for himself."

"It sounds like madness," Kaz said.

"More than you know, Baron," Edgar said, his eyes focusing on something far away. "I went to Bengal, to see for myself. It was ghastly. People were dropping dead in the streets, their arms outstretched as they begged to the last gasp. Those still walking about were emaciated and weak from disease. The worst part was that some speculators had kept their rice stocks locked up for so long that they had spoiled. Moldy bags ripped open by rats were stacked six feet high in one warehouse I visited."

"Couldn't the government have done something? Or the army?" David asked.

"The army had orders not to use their limited supply for famine relief," Edgar said. "If they had, it would have disappeared in a matter of days. Soldiers of all ranks gave food when they could, but it only postponed the inevitable. Others were quite callous. Bengal is mainly Muslim, and as you know Muslims do not eat pork. I saw a convoy of trucks pass through Durgapur, our soldiers throwing pieces of bacon at the starving wretches lining the road, laughing as they did so."

"Why have we never heard of this?" Peter asked.

"Because it would reflect badly on the British government, that's why," Edgar said. "Are all Americans as naïve as you?"

"Don't take it out on Peter," I said. "There are plenty of people in this country who would never believe their government would cover up the starvation of millions." I didn't add that I was not one of them. My Irish ancestors had starved at the hands of the English in the last century, so dying Muslim subjects in this decade came as no surprise.

"Sorry," Edgar said. "I sometimes lose my head over this. It was hard to leave it all behind and return to England, where people complain about rationing, for God's sake."

"But why *did* you return?" David asked.

"I was sacked. I'd given information to a journalist, Ian Stephens, from the Calcutta *Statesman*. He published two accounts of the famine before the censors clamped down."

"How did they know it was you?" I asked.

"No proof, really, other than I was always out of step with the other officials. 'In danger of going native,' one of my colleagues said. And some of the information Stephens had could only have come from a few people, and I was the most likely candidate."

"Meredith must not have been pleased," David said.

"She accused me of throwing away a splendid opportunity," Edgar said. "The Sutcliffe predilection for sacred opportunity seems to have been successfully passed down from father to daughter." He looked into his glass, wrinkling his brow as if he was trying to figure out why it was empty. "The funny thing is, I did manage to make money there, aside from my salary. I followed Sir Rupert's advice and contacted a businessman friend of his. I put what money I had into rice futures, not realizing what was about to happen. Made a bundle." He held out his glass, and I filled it up.

"But not enough to live on, I assume?" David said. "Which is why you're here."

"Of course. Meredith insisted we give it another go with dear Papa. Useless, in my opinion, since what I did goes against everything he believes in. So, that's our dirty little family secret."

"What was it you told the journalist, exactly?" Kaz asked. "The information that gave you away, I mean."

"I gave him the reply from Winston Churchill to a cable sent to him by Viceroy Wavell last year. Wavell had asked Churchill for more food to be shipped in. Churchill's reply was, 'If food is so scarce in India, why has Gandhi not yet died?' He did not care one whit about starving Indians."

"Was it really so brazen?" Peter asked. "At the risk of sounding naïve again, it seems incredible."

"Your Canadian neighbors offered to ship one hundred thousand tons of wheat to India," Edgar said, sitting forward in his chair, his indignation still fresh. "Churchill turned them down. He didn't want to divert shipping from the war effort. All along I had thought saving lives was what this war was all about. So you see, my American friend, I was the most naïve of all."

"What will you do?" I asked.

"When we've worn out our welcome, you mean?" Edgar said. "I can probably find a job teaching again. That was the only work I actually enjoyed."

"What did you teach?" Kaz asked.

"English literature. Elizabethan studies, that sort of thing. I'd rather read and teach Shakespeare than anything else."

"And your wife, how does she feel about that sort of career?" I asked.

"Are you married, Captain Boyle?" Edgar asked in reply. I shook my head. "Then you wouldn't understand," he said.

"'A little more than kin, and less than kind,'" Kaz said.

"Ah, *Hamlet*," Edgar said, nodding in agreement.

He and Kaz began to talk about plays. David drifted away and Peter yawned. I went to bed.

CHAPTER FIFTEEN

I LAY AWAKE, the brandy sitting dully in my gut. I hadn't drunk enough of it to forget the foreboding I'd felt when the BBC announcer had reported the raid on the Gestapo headquarters. Or prison. One and the same, in any case.

A lot has happened to me in this war, mostly things I never would have expected. Like falling in love with an Englishwoman, for one. Lady Diana Seaton, to be exact. I often wonder what it would be like to bring an English aristocrat home to meet my Irish family in South Boston. Then I remember Diana is in the Special Operations Executive, and making it to the end of the war might not be in the cards for her. The last time I'd seen her was a few weeks ago, before she was whisked away to an SOE training camp in Scotland. Or so they told me. For all I knew, she could be parachuting into occupied France at this very moment. Maybe even in the hands of the Gestapo, or on the run from them.

Diana felt she had to do her bit, as the English are fond of saying. The only problem with that comes when you fail to realize your bit has had a good long run of luck, and nothing lasts forever. I imagined Diana in the Scottish Highlands, sleeping in a tent and being awakened before dawn by a nasty sergeant major to endure morning calisthenics in the cold rain. That made me feel better, and sleep eventually overcame worry.

■   ■   ■

IN THE MORNING, Kaz was irritatingly chipper. We went down to breakfast and found Peter Wiley drinking tea and eating toast. As a trained detective, I observed him rubbing his temples and deduced he had a hangover, and that he wasn't used to drinking to excess. Good for him.

David seemed none the worse for wear, and I wondered if serious amounts of liquor on the ground were frequently deployed against the horror of combat in the air. Or if ample doses of gin helped the Guinea Pig Club face the terror of surgeries. Either way, he had an immunity that I envied on that bright and sunny morning. Meredith and Edgar were absent. When I had finished eating, having managed to do justice to eggs, toast, and heaps of marmalade, I stepped out onto the veranda to try some of that fresh air. Sir Rupert was standing on the stone steps leading down to the expansive lawn, hands stuffed in the pockets of his wool suit coat.

"Captain Boyle," he said, turning at the sound of my footsteps. "I was about to come and seek you out. Will you take a short walk with me? The air smells wonderful today, don't you think?"

"Yes," I said, falling in beside him and catching the aroma of lavender from the borders on either side of the gravel path. "How are you feeling, Sir Rupert?"

"Much better, Captain. I never know when that blasted fever will lay me low. The doctors say there's nothing they can do. No cure, but at least most people don't die of it. Some comfort, eh?"

"Is there anything I can do for you, Sir Rupert?" I knew he didn't want to talk about breakbone fever.

"You seem like a decent man, Captain Boyle," he said, clasping his hands behind his back. I waited. "And without connections to our family, which is important. You see, there's something I need to know, but I can't talk to anyone else about it. Do you understand?"

"An outsider provides perspective," I said, guessing.

"Yes, exactly. That is what I need. Perspective. You see, ever since Peter Wiley walked into the room yesterday, I've been haunted by something I thought I'd never confront again. Do I have your confidence, Captain? Will you keep what I say between us?"

"Kaz—the baron—and I are partners. I don't keep secrets from my partner. But otherwise, I'll keep what you tell me in confidence."

"Very well," he said as the path descended to the river below. "I leave it up to you, but I ask that you do not repeat this to the baron unless you feel it absolutely necessary, and in that event, you caution him to keep it confidential." I nodded my agreement, and we strolled, more slowly now, as I waited for him to continue.

"It was during the last war," he finally said. "I served in France with the army and was wounded. Shrapnel in my legs and back. The doctors left some in. Too close to nerves to remove, they said. I was at home, recuperating. Meredith was a young child and Helen not yet born. Meredith's birth was difficult, and Louise—my wife—took quite a while to recover. Physically and otherwise." I could see his face redden, although he kept staring at the ground.

"I understand, sir."

"Yes, well, the thing of it is, Julia Greenshaw, the maid who went to America. She and I became close." Even with my cobwebbed mind, I understood. "Once I had recovered, I found work with the Foreign Office in London. Upon my return to Ashcroft, I found that Julia had been sent away, along with Ted Wiley, our groundskeeper. Louise said she knew all about my indiscretion, and had paid Julia to go to America. She claimed Ted had always cared for Julia, and had proposed as soon as he learned she was leaving. I was distraught, ashamed, and had no idea what to do next."

"Did you try and get in touch with her?" I asked.

"I would have, but no one had an address. So I put her out of my mind, as best I could."

"Until Peter Wiley walked into your house, wearing that ring," I said.

"Yes! You can see now why it affected me so. I was shocked to see that ring, in particular."

"Why?"

"It was Louise's, of course, being from the Pemberton family."

"Could Julia have stolen it? Or Ted Wiley?" I asked. "To get back at Louise, I mean, not for the value of it."

"Oh, I doubt it," Sir Rupert said. "Julia was not the type of woman to steal, especially not from the house that employed her. No."

"What is it exactly you want me to do, Sir Rupert?"

He turned and faced me, this time looking straight into my eyes. "I want you to find out if Peter Wiley is my son."

"How can I do that?" I asked. "Julia and Ted Wiley are both dead. Who would know?"

"I don't know how, Captain. You're the investigator. I assume General Eisenhower has you on staff because you know your business. Investigate, ask people. Please," he added, changing his tone when he seemed to remember he was asking for a favor, not issuing orders.

"Have you thought about asking Peter directly?" I said.

"I have," he said with a sigh, resuming our walk along the path. "But he might not know. And I would be accusing his mother of an affair, not to mention coming off as a cad myself, which is not far from the truth."

"What would you have done if she hadn't left?"

"Good God, that's a question I've asked myself a thousand times." He stopped again, looking across Bow Creek at the small stone cottages on the opposite shore. "Julia and I were happy. I know it was wrong, but it wasn't a cheap, sordid affair, the landowner chasing the maid sort of thing."

"Did you and she talk about a future together?" Until a moment ago, that would have been none of my business. But if I was going to look into the paternity of Peter Wiley, now it was my business.

"Yes, but it never amounted to anything. Louise was depressed, and I was worried about her. A divorce might have pushed her over the edge. Julia and I did speak of going off together, since divorce would have been such a scandal, but it was only a daydream. We cared about each other, which is why it was such a shock when I learned she'd left. Now I think I understand. Louise gave her a way out. Bearing a bastard child would have ruined her."

"You think Louise bribed her to leave? And Ted Wiley?"

"Sadly, I think that might have been the case. Perhaps Wiley did have feelings for her, and took his chance at happiness, even knowing who the father was. It might not have been a bad match, at that. Please, Captain Boyle, I have to know. Will you do what you can?"

Sir Rupert looked as down as a grown man could without shedding tears. The past can rip you apart: the missed chances, the lost loves, the joys that never were—things that gleam like silver in comparison with the daily grind of today, the *now* in which this thickset, grey, middle-aged Rupert Sutcliffe found himself. Youthful daydreams are best forgotten, but his had just walked in on him, and he couldn't give up hope that something was left of those magical days of secret love. A son.

"Okay," I said, hoping I wouldn't regret it. Or fail. "I'll look into it and let you know if I come up with anything."

"Thank you, Captain Boyle. I know it's a lot to ask, but I feel better already knowing you've taken it on." He smiled and clasped my arm for a moment, and then we turned around to walk back to the house.

"What do you think?" I asked. "Is he your son?"

"Look at Peter and Helen next time they are next to each other," he said. "And tell me if you don't see the resemblance." I wondered if Helen had noticed it; that would explain why she'd been so attentive to Peter. Meredith had also given him her full attention at dinner, but perhaps she was simply being kind to an unexpected guest.

"Aren't you giving Peter a tour of the estate?" I asked. "Perhaps you could ask him what his mother told him about Ashcroft. Give him an opening without letting on what you suspect."

"I will, but later," Sir Rupert said. "I have some business to attend to with my solicitor in Dartmouth, and it can't wait. Please give my apologies to Peter and tell him he can set up his paints anywhere he wishes."

We parted as he went off to see his lawyer. The scent of lavender now felt cloying and thick as I puzzled over what to do next. I decided it was time for a visit to the kitchen.

It was at the rear of the house, at the end of a wing that abutted vegetable gardens and the greenhouse. It was a long, narrow room with high ceilings and tall windows, along with two large stoves and a wooden table scarred by years of chopping and hot pans.

"Good morning," I said to the grey-haired woman leaning over the stove, stirring a pot. "You must be Mrs. Dudley. I'm Billy Boyle."

"Good morning, Captain," she said, wiping her hands on a towel. "Can I get you anything?" She was in her sixties perhaps, her shoulders stooped from years bent over stoves and dishes, and her body rounded out from the bounty of her kitchen. Her smile was genuine, but I could see she was busy, eager to politely get me out of her hair.

"No, thank you. I wanted to say how much I enjoyed your cooking, Mrs. Dudley. Dinner was great last night."

"Oh, well, thank you, Captain. I'm glad you enjoyed it," Mrs. Dudley said. "We had to stretch things at the last minute with Lieutenant Wiley coming, but that's all in a day's work." She relaxed, willing to take the time to be complimented.

"Yes, quite a story, isn't it? It's great he had the chance to visit Ashcroft. Were you with Sir Rupert then, when Julia and Tom worked here?"

"Well, it would be more proper to say I was with the Pemberton family, Captain. I began as a very young girl in this very kitchen, as a scullery maid. Worked my way up to kitchen maid and then cook. It was a lively house back then, with footmen and the like. It's much quieter now, of course." Again, I got the message that Ashcroft was a Pemberton house, no matter who owned it now.

"But you knew Peter Wiley's parents?"

"Oh yes," Mrs. Dudley said. "I did."

"Has Peter come to talk to you about them?"

"Not yet, no. Do you think he will? It was a good long time ago, I'm not sure I'd remember very much about either. Nice, both of them. Took us all by surprise when they left for America, but it seemed to work out well."

"How do you know?" I asked. "You haven't talked with Peter yet."

"Oh, they'd send a card at Christmas, that sort of thing. Ted had a shop in New York, imagine that! Seems the three of them settled in quite nicely."

"Mr. and Mrs. Sutcliffe must have been pleased to hear that," I said helpfully.

"Oh, they never asked after Ted and Julia. And I doubt either of them would have written to their betters. It wouldn't be done, leastways not back then."

"I understand, Mrs. Dudley. In case Peter wants to hear about his parents and their time here, is there anyone local who knew them well?"

"No, not that I can think of," Mrs. Dudley said. "Julia came from North Devon, and I don't know about Ted."

"Course you do, Mrs. Dudley," a young girl said, coming into the room with a bucket of coal for the stove. "My own dad was friends with Ted Wiley."

"Yes, dear, I'd forgotten about your father. He and Ted did know each other, didn't they?"

"Yes, Dad and Ted went to school together. They were mates. He's got some stories I'm sure Peter would enjoy hearing," Alice said.

"Where could Peter find your father?" I asked.

"He works at the mill, but he'll have a pint in the evening at the pub in North Cornworthy. Just ask for Michael Withers. I could take Peter and introduce him, I'd be glad to," Alice said happily. I could tell she'd caught a glimpse of Peter Wiley and found him attractive.

"That's Lieutenant Wiley to you, girl," Mrs. Dudley said, her lips set in a scowl. "And right now, we have work to do."

As did I.

CHAPTER SIXTEEN

"LADY PEMBERTON, DO you have a moment?" I asked, finding her in the sitting room, opening letters.

"Not as many as I used to, young man, but the next few are yours. Please, sit," she said, gesturing to a nearby armchair.

"I was thinking it would be nice for Peter to speak with someone who knew his parents. Friends or relatives, I mean. Would you know of anyone?"

"Captain Boyle, although we are an informal household, that does not mean I make it a practice to socialize with staff. It simply isn't done, not in England. Is it commonplace wherever you come from?"

"That would be Boston, ma'am, and I guess not."

"Ah, Boston. And there I thought you had a speech impediment. Irish?"

"I am," I said, trying to contain my anger and stifle a laugh at the same time. "My people are more likely to be working stiffs, and I don't recall the folks on Beacon Hill ever inviting us over."

"Beacon Hill? Is that one of the better neighborhoods?"

"They have more money, to be sure. I come from South Boston, and we like it fine there."

"I suppose that is one of the great differences between Americans and the English," Great Aunt Sylvia said. "It's all about money over there, isn't it?"

"Lady Pemberton, it's all about money everywhere. It's simply a matter of how honest you are about it," I said.

"Point taken," she said, with the hint of a smile. "Although our currency includes titles, breeding, and property handed down over centuries. Still, you are right. The things we value are what we measure ourselves against."

"Ted and Julia must have wanted something different," I said. "Otherwise why go all the way to America?" I watched her, waiting for a split second of hesitation, or for her eyes to flit about the room in search of the right lie to tell me. But there was neither. Instead, she was on me like a hawk sighting a mouse in an open field.

"Indeed. I've often wondered that myself, Captain. I do see the appeal of your supposedly classless society: the chance for any immigrant to work his way up, without regard to the kinds of status we hold so dear."

"All they did was open a hardware shop," I said. "Hardly defying society."

"Yes, but you will find very few sons of servants attending university here," Great Aunt Sylvia said. "Your egalitarian way in America may be for the best, I must admit. Otherwise the educated class tends to become inbred, if only in its thinking. But why must progress come at the cost of decorum?"

"How do you mean?"

"When I see Americans in Dartmouth or elsewhere, they are invariably loud. They walk about with their hands stuffed in their pockets and lean against public buildings, making all sorts of rude comments and chewing gum with their mouths wide open. And why do Americans insist on pushing their caps back on their heads? I can't imagine none of you were ever taught how to wear a hat properly. Were you?"

"I was a policeman in Boston. My father would read me the riot act if he ever saw me with my eight pointer at an angle," I said.

"Good," she said. "I noticed that you were properly turned out when we first met. Shows you were well brought up—at least as well as can be expected in America."

"Thank you. As for the rest, I think it's because most Americans don't like being in the army, and they'll be as informal as they can get away with to prove they're still civilians at heart," I said, then attempted to return to the conversation I'd started. "Were you here when Julia and Ted worked at Ashcroft?"

"Yes, I was. After my husband died, Louise's father—the Viscount Pemberton—invited me to come and live here. He and his brother were close, as was the entire family. He wrote me into his will. Whoever gets Ashcroft gets me with it," she said, and covered her laughter with a wrinkled but dainty hand. "I'm sure Rupert has cursed the man on occasion."

"Did Sir Rupert inherit it?" I asked.

"Not from the Viscount, no," she said. "It went to Louise, as the last surviving Pemberton child. When she died in India, Ashcroft went to Sir Rupert. Ashcroft and myself, I should say."

"Excuse me, madam, sir," Williams said from the doorway. "There is an American officer here to see you, Captain."

"All right," I said. "I'll be right there. Lady Pemberton, thank you for your time."

"Not at all, Captain Boyle. I am glad to help."

As I left the sitting room, I realized that she'd been of no help at all.

"There you are, Boyle," Colonel Samuel Harding snapped at me from the foyer as Williams shuffled off to buttle somewhere else. "That's the first time I've had a butler announce me to a junior officer." Kaz was standing next to him with a big smirk on his face.

"Sorry, Colonel," I said. "I was in the middle of being bamboozled by an old lady."

"Lieutenant Kazimierz was filling me in on your stay. Not too shabby, Boyle," Harding said, surveying the walnut paneling hung with oil paintings, the gleaming polished floors, and the high staircase. Harding was trim and fit, a West Pointer who'd served in the last war and stayed on for another go at the Germans. Not one of the gum-chewing rowdy Yanks. Lady Pemberton would approve. His close-cropped hair was flecked with grey at the temples, his face was pale, and there were dark circles under his eyes. The look of a D-Day planner.

"They invited us to stay as long as we wanted," I said, a bit on the defensive.

"That's good," Harding said. "With maneuvers coming up, every hotel and inn within miles is jammed with top brass. Generals and admirals are a dime a dozen up and down the coast. How are you feeling, Boyle?"

"A bit sore, but healing up," I said.

"Colonel Harding?" We turned to see Peter headed for the door, carrying his painting gear.

"Lieutenant Wiley, isn't it?" Harding said. "I see they finally let you out to do some painting."

"You know each other?" I said, surprised that this map-making lieutenant would know an SHAEF colonel.

"Obviously," Harding said. "Don't let me keep you, Lieutenant. The sun is shining." He stepped aside, and Wiley made for the great outdoors.

"How do you know Peter?" I asked.

"By being involved in top-secret business," Harding said, closing off that line of discussion. "I've come from another briefing in Dartmouth. They're trying the live-fire exercise again tomorrow at Slapton Sands, to make sure they've got things worked out."

"Don't tell me we're going back there," I said. "Sir."

"Today, not tomorrow, Boyle. Inspector Grange said he'd had reports of civilians in the area. He sent several teams out to search early this morning. They didn't find anyone, but we need to lend a hand. Take your Constable Quick and patrol the area this afternoon. Any civilians you find, take them into custody."

"Will do, Colonel," I said, happy for a daylight ride in the country rather than an early-morning bombardment.

"Good. I'll be at Greenway House, outside of Torquay by eighteen hundred hours. Report to me there. Lieutenant Wiley can give you directions."

As Harding drove off, we strolled over to where Peter had set up his easel. He had a view of the house and grounds, sunlight dancing off the windows and giving the old oak trees a warm, green glow.

"So you work with Colonel Harding?" I said as nonchalantly as I could while Peter laid out his paints. I hoped for some indication as to what they were involved in, being snoopy on general principles.

"He'd have to tell you about that, Billy. I'm only a lowly lieutenant who's been told to keep his mouth shut. Sorry."

"Don't mind Billy," Kaz said, studying the contents of his paint box. "He can't help asking questions that don't concern him. You use watercolors?"

"It's what the navy gave me to work with, and I do like the effect. Say, can I ask a favor?"

"Shoot," I said.

"I want to go on one of the exercises, and go ashore on one of the landing craft. The navy won't let me, but I thought if you asked Colonel Harding, he could make it happen."

"Why didn't you ask him when he was here?" Kaz said.

"To be honest, he makes me nervous. I chickened out," Peter said, smiling in embarrassment.

"Hey, I know the feeling," I said. "It can't hurt to ask. We have to meet him at Greenway House tonight. I'll let you know. You'll still be here?"

"Yeah, I'll be here. Thanks, Billy," Peter said.

"One question," I said. "Why? Why do you want to ride the waves in a flat-bottomed landing craft along with a bunch of seasick GIs?"

"Perspective," Peter said, mixing water into his deep blue paint. "It's all a matter of perspective."

He wouldn't say anything else, or even look at us. With deft strokes he began to paint the blue sky over Ashcroft, working in silence, indifferent to our presence, and to the dark clouds rolling in from the north.

CHAPTER SEVENTEEN

WE HAD A passenger on our drive into Dartmouth. Crawford—Roger Crawford, I ought to say, although he was one of those guys who seemed to have been born with only a last name—who was going to take his small fishing boat out for plaice, which was British for "flounder."

"The plaice come into the shallows to rest for the night," he said from the backseat, one hand steadying his bicycle. "The tides are perfect today. They'll bring me out and carry me back, like catching the train."

"It must be hard to get petrol," Kaz said.

"There's an allotment for fishermen, and the fish isn't rationed," Crawford said. "Helps with the prices. Otherwise, there'd be little incentive for any sane man to venture offshore. I sell what I can in Dartmouth and bring what's left to Ashcroft. If I work with the tides, I have more than enough fuel. I was lucky to find a spot near town, so I don't have to motor down Bow Creek from Ashcroft. It's not far, but it saves on petrol to set off with the tide in the estuary."

"You fished full-time before the war?" I asked.

"I did. But when I lost my home to the government, along with my mooring, it was a bad time to sell a boat. Not many people wanted to go out into the Channel with the Germans bombing everything that floated, and fuel was hard to come by. Didn't get much for it. Bought this little one so I could go out on the water, but I have to stay close to shore."

"Ashcroft seems like a decent place to work," I said, knowing that Massachusetts men with fishing in their blood would hate the idea of working on dry land, and as a hired hand at that.

"It's not bad," Crawford said, in a low voice that summoned up the minimum commitment necessary not to insult the family that employed him.

"But not like being your own boss," I said.

"No, thanks to your lot," Crawford said. "Both of you. It was the British army that took my property and the Americans who burned it." His voice was bitter, his anger seething in a harsh, clipped tone. I didn't have to see his face to know his jaw was clenched.

"Hey, don't blame us," I said. "We're just two guys giving you a lift."

"It wasn't right," Crawford said, ignoring my protestation. "Especially setting fire to my house. Yanks did that."

"How do you know?" I asked, downshifting as we climbed a hill. A column of GIs double-timed along the road, packs bouncing on their backs and rifles held high.

"You have to watch things," Crawford said. "There are ways. I saw what they did. Threw a thermite grenade through a window, playing like they was real soldiers."

"You snuck into the restricted area to check your house?" I asked.

"Nothing to it, if you're careful," Crawford said. "I crawled on my belly through no-man's-land in the Great War. Now *that* was a challenge. I was a sapper, setting charges to blow barbed wire or laying mines and booby-traps in front of our positions in the black night. A few roadblocks manned by coppers and green Yanks don't count for much after that. There's paths through the woods only us locals know about."

"Where was your house?" I asked.

"Dunstone. A little village inland from Slapton Sands. A nice little place until the American army showed up."

"I am sorry that happened, Crawford," Kaz said. "Apparently some soldiers thought the houses were all slated for destruction. I doubt it was willful."

"Willful or not, it was wrong," Crawford said. "Stop ahead, that's the path to the river." We pulled over and he hoisted his bicycle out of the jeep. "Wrong, I tell you." With that he pulled his cloth cap tight on his head and pedaled off without throwing a glance or a thanks in our direction.

"Odd chap," Kaz said as we drove off.

"Lots of people carry grudges," I said, knowing the burden myself. "I wonder what he was doing in the restricted area."

"Constable Quick said many people try to get in and check on their property," Kaz said reasonably.

"Yeah, but I bet not many hide out and watch GIs grenade their house," I said.

"Do you think he wants revenge?" Kaz asked.

"Maybe he already took it," I said as we entered Dartmouth, the traffic slowing as we neared the police station. There weren't as many ships in the harbor as before, a sure sign that the exercises were in full swing.

"Billy, I think you are seeing too many conspiracies. Next you will tell me he murdered an American soldier and dumped his body in the Channel after changing his clothes."

"Hey, it's only a theory," I said. "It *could* have happened that way."

"Please don't tell Colonel Harding," Kaz said. "He's nervous enough already."

"Okay," I said. I didn't really suspect Crawford. He had good reason to be angry; I'd likely feel the same in his place. But in the absence of absolute proof that the corpse was Sabini's handiwork, it was hard to stop the ideas from coming. Another occupational hazard. The clothes were a problem, but still, there was a glimmer of a chance Crawford had gone over the edge. He was wound tight enough for it. If he'd been in combat in the trenches during the last war, he was no stranger to violence. I made a mental note to keep my eye on the indispensable Crawford while I relaxed and enjoyed our stay at Ashcroft House. That was the benefit of this excursion, wasn't it?

We wended our way along the waterfront as huge landing craft cast off, propellers churning the estuary waters into foamy currents as sirens *whooped* and patrol boats darted across their wakes. Crawford would have to navigate carefully to get his small wooden boat through this scrum of seagoing heavy hardware.

Tom Quick was waiting at the station, and in no time we were headed out of town toward the coast and the border of the restricted area. At Stoke Fleming the road curved along the cliffs going down to the water, giving a fine view of warships steaming out into the Channel: destroyers, minesweepers, corvettes, and transports, all heading for patrol duties and exercises. One day soon it would be the real thing.

"Inspector Grange said there was another big show planned for tomorrow," Tom said from the backseat, raising his voice over the wind swooping up over the cliff face. It smelled of salt with a chaser of engine oil.

"Yeah, a live-fire bombardment again," I said. "We need to check for civilians in the area."

"Makes sense. Could be a farmer or two out there checking to see if his barn got blown up," Quick said. "I'd do the same, most likely."

"Me too," I said. As we drove, I chatted with Tom about Peter Wiley's surprise arrival, leaving out the part about Sir Rupert and paternity, of course.

We passed through the roadblock at Strete, where the MPs reported all quiet except for truckloads of paratroopers from the 101st Airborne who had been brought in this morning. The wind whipped the surf as it crashed against the stony shore of Slapton Sands, filling the air with a cold, salty spray. The target-practice hotel stood with its blackened, gaping holes, forlorn against the blue sky.

"Do you know the way to Dunstone from here?" I said to Quick, shouting to be heard above the wind and the ocean. He guided us inland, through Torcross, where neatly hedged farmers' fields sprouted weeds instead of crops.

Dunstone was barely a bend in the road, with a few farmhouses and cottages, a couple of shops, and a ruined church. Ruined by time, not the American army. It wasn't hard to spot Crawford's place, with its caved-in thatched roof and windows blasted with soot.

"What's special about Dunstone?" Quick asked as we got out of the jeep.

"Have you ever run across Roger Crawford?" I said. "Former fisherman, now manages Ashcroft House for Sir Rupert Sutcliffe."

"I know of him," Quick said. "And he was known to go out for more than fish."

"What do you mean?" Kaz asked.

"Before the war, we suspected him of smuggling booze and cigarettes in from France. You can make a nice profit selling the stuff without the import tax. Small-scale stuff, we thought, until heroin and cocaine began to show up."

"You never caught him," I said.

"No, but the water guard chased his boat during a fierce storm, and he ran onto rocks trying to get away. She sank, and Crawford barely made it to shore. No evidence was ever found, so there was nothing to do. He claimed the rudder was jammed and he couldn't stop her."

"This was off Start Point?" I asked, realizing that Crawford had told two stories. First he'd said he lost his boat during a storm, and today he told us he'd sold it.

"It was. He blames the water guard for the loss, of course."

"As he blames the army for the loss of his house," Kaz said, pointing to the burned-out cottage.

"Crikey," Quick said, surveying the damage. "Some fellows have nothing but bad luck. But how did you know about this?"

"He told us," I said. "He snuck in and watched GIs burn the place. It sounded like they were using it for assault practice."

"I'm not surprised," Quick said. "He's devious enough. I wonder if he was searching for loot or wanted something from his place."

"If he was a smuggler, maybe he left contraband hidden," I said. "He might have gotten nervous when he heard buildings were being destroyed."

"We'll never know," Quick said, leaning inside the charred doorway. "Nothing but stone walls, soot, and ash here."

"They used thermite grenades," Kaz said. "Anything of value would have gone up in smoke."

"This is a burning war," Quick said, turning away. He knew what he was talking about.

We continued our patrol of the area, driving through villages that looked like ones I'd seen in Sicily. Walls pockmarked with bullet holes, doors hanging off hinges, the odor of smoke, and the stink of excrement wafting out of the shambles.

"I'm glad I'm not waiting to come home to the South Hams," Quick said, summing up our feelings.

On the trip back, we began to run into troopers from the 101st. On the road to Slapton Ley, we found a heavy-weapons squad setting up a machine gun behind a stone wall. I pulled the jeep over and Kaz and I got out, returning their salutes as halfheartedly as I could.

"You fellows know there's a real bombardment planned for the morning?" I asked.

"Sure, Captain," said a corporal. "They're going to plaster the beach on the other side of that water. Our lieutenant said we'd be safe here."

"And where is he?" I asked.

"About a quarter mile back," the corporal said with a knowing grin. "Which is why we're digging in deep."

"Good thinking," I said. "Have you seen anyone around other than your outfit? Locals, maybe?"

"Naw, we haven't seen anyone," another private said. "This whole place gives me the creeps."

"Wait until France, Private. What's your part in the exercise?" I asked.

"We've been dropped here, and we're supposed to defend the road to the causeway that links up with the beach," the corporal said. "Dropped from trucks, that is. A lot easier all around, but not very realistic. They should have scattered us all over Devon instead of leaving units intact."

"Damn straight," I said. "I saw plenty of boys from the 82nd Airborne in Sicily. They were straggling in for days."

"What was it like, Captain?" the private asked. "Sicily." By that he meant combat: death, fear, dismemberment, sweat, blood, and the crystal clarity of the borderline between the living and the dead.

"Hot and dusty," I said, keeping those thoughts to myself. "Noisy too. Keep your head down and follow your corporal's lead. He seems to have half a brain." That got a few laughs. When guys who will soon see the elephant ask what it's like, it's best to gloss over the reality. Otherwise, they'll worry themselves to pieces.

"Do not hesitate," Kaz said, as we walked back to the jeep. "Kill anything in a German uniform. Leave mercy behind." It was good advice, but it left a silence as the troopers took in the scar on Kaz's face and the flat certainty in his voice.

"What about you, Constable?" the corporal asked, trying to lighten the mood. "Any advice from law enforcement?"

"I flew thirty missions in Lancasters, son," Quick said. "I've been to Berlin six times. I've killed more Germans on one raid than you ever will with that machine gun, but you do your best when you get over there. They still owe me."

"Be careful tomorrow," I said, hustling my all-too-honest friends into the jeep before these boys went off looking for the chaplain. "Dig in deeper than you think you need to." The corporal waved his entrenching tool as we drove off, hopefully a sign he was about to take my advice. The margin of error when you're talking about shells fired from a cruiser offshore was pretty damn small.

"At least they'll be fighting men in uniform, not massacring civilians," Quick said. We'd made our circuit of the area and stopped midway along Slapton Sands, watching the grey Channel waters break on the shingle. Army engineers were busy stringing rolls of barbed wire above the waterline, working at making the upcoming exercise as realistic as possible.

"It's the way wars are fought these days," I said. "It's not your fault."

"I know," Quick said. "I did my job, same as some damn Jerry bombardier did his. That's the weight of it, all of us doing our bit. Bomb by bomb, until one side gives in. Sad that it takes so many. I don't understand why the Jerries don't shatter and break just like their cities."

"You've done your share of fighting," Kaz said. "Now it is up to those men and others like them. The war will be won on the ground, no matter how many bombs we drop."

"Thirty missions," Quick whispered into the wind. "The first and the last, they were the worst."

"Grange told us about your first mission," I said. "I'm sorry."

"The odd thing is, I'd hardened myself after a while," Quick said, still staring out over the water, ignoring my words. "By the twentieth mission, I figured I'd be dead soon, and none of it mattered. Then we kept coming home. It was horrifying to think about surviving. What would I do? There was nothing but death in the air and grief upon the ground."

We waited as he paused, the wind whipping my trench coat, the salt spray bitter on my lips.

"My pal Freddie Swales kept my spirits up," Quick went on. "He was our rear turret gunner. Those chaps have an average life expectancy of forty flying hours in a Lancaster. Each night mission took about eight hours, so you can calculate the odds for yourself. By twenty-five missions, Freddie thought he could walk on water. When we took off for our last run, I believed it myself. If Freddie lived through it, there was hope for all of us. Hope for me."

"What happened?" I asked into the silence.

"We almost made it," Quick said. "We'd crossed the Dutch coast and were over the North Sea when a swarm of Me-109s hit us. It was near dawn, light enough to see them as they nipped at the formation, trying to score hits and get a straggler to drop out and fall behind. They got one, and formed up for one last attack before they headed home. One bastard came right at us, dead on from the rear. The whole aircraft shook as he peppered the rear turret with machine-gun and cannon fire. I thought we were going down, but we made it to the closest airfield, one engine belching flames and black smoke. There was nothing left of Freddie, nothing that you could call a man. The turret was smashed, nothing but a gaping hole. The ground crew pulled out chunks of Freddie and tossed them into a wheelbarrow. Then they hosed out what was left. And there was poor Freddie, all bits of flesh, blood, and bone, a pink froth settling into the ground. They told me I tried to gather them up, but I don't remember, thank God."

"No wonder you think the Germans still owe you," I said.

"Some debts can only be repaid in blood," Quick said. He turned away and walked back to the jeep.

"He doesn't understand they are not debts," Kaz said to me. "There is no payment for suffering and grief, no recompense for dead family and loved ones."

"Maybe he hopes he can repay his own debts someday," I said.

"He that dies pays all debts,'" Kaz said, with a shrug.

"Shakespeare?" I guessed.

"Very good, Billy," Kaz said. "I forget which play. *The Tempest*, perhaps. I shall ask Edgar tonight."

We trudged back to the jeep, and as we left the restricted area, I wondered if Tom Quick had ever seen the play.

CHAPTER EIGHTEEN

QUICK WAS FINE on the ride back. If that word can describe a man who feels responsible for the deaths of families like his own and who watched his friend's remains get hosed out of a rear turret. We Americans were paying our own butcher's bill in this war, but the English had been at it so much longer, been so victimized by bombs, loss, and sacrifice that their toll of suffering, horror, and deprivation had to be heavier, an ominous presence felt heavily throughout the land.

We left Tom at Constable Carraher's cottage in North Cornworthy, thinking it best for him to be with a friend, then pressed on to meet up with Colonel Harding. We crossed the River Dart and followed the directions Peter Wiley had given for Greenway House, the headquarters of the US Navy 10th Flotilla. I made a mental note to write my mom and tell her we should name our place in South Boston. It sure was the fashion here.

Greenway House sat on a wooded knoll overlooking the river. The navy knew how to pick its billets. It was north of Dartmouth, not far as the crow flies from North Cornworthy, but a bit of a drive since the first bridge was upriver at Totnes. A small ferry ran across the river at Greenway, but it was only for foot traffic and bicyclists. A stone boathouse stood jutting out over the water, with two navy launches moored alongside. From there it was a short hop to the big vessels docked at Dartmouth harbor.

The house itself was stark white, three stories, in the Georgian style, according to Kaz. Only one story less than my house in Boston, which was in the Southie style: clapboards, front stoop and all, but you could probably fit four of the Boyle homesteads into the Greenway footprint.

Shore patrol swabbies checked our IDs before letting us in. The rooms had all been converted into offices, and we found Harding near the back, in a small room that might have been a pantry back when. We gave him our report, short and sweet.

"The only thing to worry about is some guys from the 101st too close to the bombardment area," I said. "No sign of civilians anywhere."

"Okay, that's about all we can do. It's up to the navy to get it right tomorrow," Harding said, pushing himself back from his desk and gathering up folders.

"Colonel," I said, "has Lieutenant Wiley asked you if he could go on the exercise? He's really itching to get out on the water. He is navy, after all."

"He put you up to this?" Harding asked, shrugging on his jacket.

"He was afraid to ask himself," Kaz said.

"That's because I chewed him out the last two times he asked," Harding said, getting ready to leave.

"Any special reason, Colonel?" I asked. "It's only a short run along the coast."

"Follow me," Harding said. He took us down a hallway to where an armed guard stood in front of a door. "This is Lieutenant Wiley's studio. One guard stands here and another outside the window twenty-four hours a day. What does that tell you?"

"That Lieutenant Wiley deserves a promotion," I said. "Why all the security?"

"Because he's engaged in top-secret work, gentlemen," Harding said, his voice almost a growl.

"He's just asking to be onboard for maneuvers, Colonel," I said. "Can't blame a naval officer for wanting to be on a ship."

"I can blame him for not following orders," Harding said. "He pestered the officer in charge of manifests for the maneuvers so much they got into a fistfight."

"Peter Wiley does not seem suited to fisticuffs," Kaz said.

"Neither of them are," Harding said with a rueful laugh. "Two desk jockeys fighting over paperwork. It was almost funny. Lieutenant Siebert's got a lot on his mind, and I think the stress got to him. It just happened to be Wiley who got the brunt of it. Good thing he's got three days' leave, it should give both of them time to calm down. But when he gets back, he doesn't leave dry land. He's been working hard to complete a major assignment. Another one is coming along soon, and I want him rested, ready, and dry when it does. Understood?"

We understood, at least as much as we had to. Maybe he was painting General Eisenhower's portrait. Whatever he was doing, he wouldn't be going far from it.

"There is one other thing, Colonel Harding," Kaz said as we followed Harding out the front door. He pleaded David Martindale's case, stressing his knowledge of languages, one good eye, desire to serve, and the fact that he'd graduated from Oxford, which in Kaz's eyes carried the most weight. It was only when he mentioned photographic interpretation that Harding perked up.

"Are you certain he can see well enough?" the colonel asked.

"Perfect vision in that eye, sir," Kaz said. "And as an experienced pilot, he is used to navigation and recognizing ground structures." I hoped Kaz wasn't overselling David, but it turned out Harding was in a buying mood.

"Have him here tomorrow," Harding said. "We'll see what he can do."

"One out of two isn't bad with him," I said as we watched Harding drive off.

"I wonder if this has any connection to Peter Wiley's map-making," Kaz said. "He could be making maps of coastal defenses, for instance. They'd need to use photographs from reconnaissance aircraft."

"Pretty good guess," I said. "Let's go give David the good news about his audition."

BACK AT ASHCROFT, we spotted Great Aunt Sylvia walking with Lieutenant Wiley on a path to the side of the house. His easel was set up out front, his brushes and paints left ready for his return. It was perfect painting weather: the trees and lawn were a vivid green in the afternoon sun, the sky a clear and sparkling blue after the clouds had blown off. I parked the jeep on the gravel drive, and we strolled over to the painting to take a look.

"Not bad at all," Kaz said. It was unfinished, but Wiley had captured the house perfectly: a grey granite mass that looked like it had sprouted fully formed from the rocks. The grass seemed to bend in a breeze that you could almost feel.

"The lad's quite a painter," David Martindale said, coming up from behind us. He'd been out hiking, dressed in old tweeds and carrying a walking stick.

"Yes," Kaz said. "He has captured the essence of the place."

"On the outside, at least," David said. "It's even gloomier than usual inside today."

"What do you mean?" Kaz asked his friend.

"Sir Rupert is in a foul mood, and doesn't look well on top of it—or because of it, I can't tell," he said. "Meredith has been arguing with him; there was quite a lot of shouting. It was better when they weren't speaking to each other. Helen burst into tears and ran off, so I decided to get some fresh air and wait for things to calm down. I was hoping you'd be back, so I would have some decent company."

Having decided to avoid going inside, we strolled around back to the terrace and sat admiring the view of Bow Creek where it flowed into the River Dart. To one side, I watched Peter Wiley with Great Aunt Sylvia on his arm, returning from their walk in the gardens, an iron gate covered in ivy behind them.

"She must have been showing him the family plot," David said. "She had markers erected for her son and husband. Louise is there too, shipped back from India, where she died. Helen says her mother insisted upon it. She hated India. Or Rupert, I could never sort out the difference."

"Not a happy marriage?" I asked.

"At the end, apparently not. Who knows what it was like earlier?" David said. "Helen says India got to her mother, but she insisted on staying with her husband. Meredith says Rupert was a horrible cad about something, but she keeps her mouth shut about it otherwise. Could be some truth in both stories."

"It's hard to tell with families," I said. "Everyone has their own version of events and memories of what happened. The farther in the past, usually the less reliable." Meredith must have been referring to her father's affair, but I wasn't about to let that cat out of the bag.

"What did Meredith mean about the ring," Kaz said, "when she challenged Sir Rupert? She said, 'Now do you believe me?' when Peter said his mother had received it as a gift."

"I'm not sure," David said. "Helen once alluded to a rumor about Meredith stealing some family jewels when she ran off to London. I never took much stock in it until last night, when Edgar mentioned her having money to burn when he met her."

"I am beginning to think we should take our leave soon," Kaz said. "If these arguments continue, it could be uncomfortable for us to be here."

"Oh no you don't, Piotr," David said. "Don't abandon your old chum, I beg of you." He said it with an easy laugh, but I knew he was serious. "Tell me, have you talked to your colonel about me? Any chance of a spot at SHAEF?"

"There is some good news, perhaps," Kaz said. He told David the plan for the next day, stressing that it was a long shot.

"Brilliant!" David said. "If I wanted to take my chances inside I'd fetch drinks, or look for Williams to fetch them. It's grand to have a butler, even an old fellow like that."

"If there wasn't such bad blood between the Sutcliffe and Pemberton clans this would be a nice setup," I said, imagining the life of an English country squire. I liked the way they ran things here, not as snobby and pretentious as a lot of other homes I'd visited. But the past and long-buried secrets had a way of ruining even such an idyll as Ashcroft.

"How was Tom today?" David asked, and I was reminded that it wasn't merely secrets that ate away at the heart. The war corroded everything it touched as well.

"We saw another side of him," Kaz said, perhaps sensing that I was struggling with the question. "He's lost so much, but still wants revenge. There seem to be two parts of him: the family man who understands the death he has visited upon others, and the airman who did his duty while hardening himself to the horrors he has endured—that is, until he broke under the pressure."

"They're both shattered men," I said. I told David about Tom's pal Freddie, the rear turret gunner.

"I've heard the rear-gunner position on a Lanc is one of the worst," David said. "An unheated glass bubble, not even enough room to wear a parachute. If the plane goes down, the gunner is expected to open the door behind him, reach for his parachute, and put it on, all while rotating the turret sideways so he drops out backwards."

"A dubious prospect," Kaz said. "But not as dubious as Constable Quick's chances of putting all this behind him."

"So it's worse than we thought," David said tentatively.

"I think so," Kaz said. "A man who mourns his wife, children, and best friend, as well as all those whom he has killed, while at the same time hungering for the blood of his enemies, is unlikely to reconcile those two impulses. Grief or a terrible rage will win out in the end. He cannot live with both."

Kaz was the expert here, so I simply nodded my agreement. We sat in silence for a while, the sun nearing the treetops and the air turning cold. I finally left to find Peter and deliver the bad news about Colonel Harding's orders for him to stay ashore. Kaz and David stayed behind, surveying Bow Creek as it flowed along, a constancy amid the ruins of this century.

As I came around to the front lawn, I saw Sir Rupert heading away from Peter and entering the house. Peter sat at his easel, staring at the canvas, not taking notice of my approach until I was nearly on top of him.

"I talked with Colonel Harding," I said. "I did my best, but it's no go."

"What?" Peter said, blinking as if he'd been daydreaming. "Oh, the exercise. That's too bad. I'll find another way, thanks."

"The only other way is to talk to Harding's boss, but I doubt Ike has time to see you," I said. He was distracted, and I wanted to be sure he understood the situation.

"Yeah, of course," Peter said. "Thanks for asking, Billy, I appreciate it."

"It's important?" I asked.

"It could be. I won't know until I'm there."

"Perspective?"

"I shouldn't have said even that much," Peter said. "Forget about it, okay?"

"I forget stuff all the time," I said. "Lady Pemberton showing you around?"

"No, not really. She showed me the gardens, that's all. Sir Rupert is busy, I guess." He looked away, his eyes hitting the woods, the house, the canvas, looking everywhere but at me. An unpracticed liar.

"Sure," I said. "Don't do anything stupid, okay?"

"I'm not sure I should have come here," he said. It was obvious that something else entirely was on his mind.

"The search for perspective leads us to strange places," I said, hoping he'd explain himself.

He didn't.

CHAPTER NINETEEN

"I DON'T CARE!" Meredith's shrill voice echoed in the hallway as I began to make my way down for dinner. "You can't do this to me, I won't stand for it!"

A door slammed. Hard. I retreated a few steps back to my room, not wanting to collide with her while she was fuming. I heard footsteps stomp by my door and another slam. I hoped Edgar wasn't stuck in the bedroom with her. I stepped out into the hallway, making my way to Sir Rupert's study.

"Is everything all right?" I asked Sir Rupert, leaning into the doorway of his study.

"Sorry about the display, Captain Boyle," Sir Rupert said, leaning back in his chair. "A bit of a long-standing feud. I do apologize." He sighed, looking pale and tired as he patted his damp forehead with a handkerchief. "I will join you shortly. I need a moment."

I left, knowing it must have been embarrassing for a guy like him to acknowledge family discord. I wanted to make sure Meredith hadn't whacked him one, though, given her tone and ferocity.

"I trust he's alive and kicking," Great Aunt Sylvia said, swooping along in her ancient dress, a dark blue floor-length affair with a high collar and a pearl brooch.

"None the worse for wear," I said, offering her my arm on the stairway.

"Good," she said. "I hate to see them fight, but it is sadly nothing new. She fought with her mother too, but over silly things. There she is: Louise." We stopped as she pointed to one of the portraits decorating the staircase wall. A serene expression graced the young face of Louise Pemberton in her flowing white dress. Wide blue eyes; light, flowing hair; porcelain skin; and a thin figure—all probably enhanced by the painter's art, but she was still beautiful. And familiar.

"Helen looks a lot like her," I said.

"I agree," Great Aunt Sylvia said. "Meredith takes after her father, which may be why they disagree so often. It happens quite often, don't you think?"

"I wouldn't have said so when I was younger, but I'm beginning to think that's true," I said, thinking of the times Dad and I had butted heads. My kid brother Danny wasn't anything like him, and they seemed to get along most days.

"And this," Lady Pemberton said, taking another step down, "is me, if you can believe it."

Her portrait was smaller, but striking where Louise's was peaceful. A young woman with auburn hair and large dark eyes stared out from the canvas, her head cocked at an angle as if she were taking the measure of the painter, or perhaps the viewer. The look was piercing, intelligent, and coy at the same time. She wore a black velvet dress tight at the waist and cut low enough that I blushed a bit when I looked at her.

"Seventy years ago, I looked like that, young man," Great Aunt Sylvia said, a smile on her lips.

"It makes me wish I was born in a different century, Lady Pemberton," I said, taking her by the hand.

"You flatter very nicely, Captain Boyle," she said. "You may need all your diplomatic skills at dinner if Meredith has not calmed down."

"I'll do my best," I said, thinking that this family had certainly gone downhill since young Sylvia's heyday. There were no paintings of Helen or Meredith. Had it gone out of fashion, or was it because Meredith had run off before sitting for her portrait? "Sir Rupert was never painted, I see. Perhaps Peter could do a watercolor of him." I watched her for any sign acknowledging a link between the two men, but Great Aunt Sylvia gave little away.

"An interesting idea, Captain. But Peter has other things on his mind at the moment. He seems distressed about not going to sea."

"It's not possible," I said, "because of the nature of his work. And it would only be the Channel, in any case. Not exactly going to sea."

"Still, he keeps muttering about perspective. A valuable commodity, don't you think?" With that, she moved into the library and accepted a glass of sherry from Edgar. David and Helen were seated on the couch; they stopped talking as we entered. Peter and Kaz were at the window, looking out over the lawn in the dusky light. Peter glanced at me, a haunted and uncertain look in his eyes. Was he distressed at Harding's decision? I watched Great Aunt Sylvia sipping her sherry and wondered what exactly she had meant about perspective being valuable. I didn't think she was talking about art. There was something she knew, information she was holding back. Nine decades of life sure gave her the corner on perspective, and I wished she'd be more open about what she knew.

A shriek came from upstairs. Meredith, not angry this time, but surprised, shocked, anguished.

I ran up the steps, heading for Sir Rupert's study, as Meredith bolted out, one hand clasped over her mouth, eyes uncannily wide. We collided at the head of the stairs, and she pointed to the study, telling me to hurry. A letter had dropped from her hand, and she plucked it hurriedly from the carpet and ran to her room. I dashed into Sir Rupert's study, fearing the worst, a small part of my mind noting the three-cent stamp and the wrinkled, yellowing envelope.

I found what I expected. Sir Rupert, dead. From a heart attack, most likely, judging by the bottle of digitalis pills clutched in his hand. I felt for a pulse, knowing it was a wasted effort. His lifeless, bulging eyes concurred.

I left the study and shut the door behind me. Peter, Kaz, and David were in the hallway. Beyond them, I could hear Edgar knocking at a door and asking Meredith to open up.

"He's dead," I told them. "It may have been a heart attack. Stay here, and don't let anyone in. I'll have Williams call a doctor, and the police."

"Good God," David said. "Is all that really necessary?"

"It is," Kaz said. "Best to do everything by the book. You and Peter go and tell the others while I remain here." Kaz waited until we were alone and shot me a look.

"There's a bottle of digitalis on the floor," I said, reading his mind. "The doctor should be able to tell us more." I went off to find Williams, who made the calls, managing to stave off his tears so well that I wondered if he was a Pemberton man first and foremost.

A car pulled up to the front door in fifteen minutes. Ashcroft rated prompt service.

Edgar led Meredith into the library while we waited for the doctor to complete his examination. Constable Carraher had gone in with the doctor, and Tom Quick waited outside.

Meredith took a spot on the couch next to Great Aunt Sylvia, who patted her hand and murmured "there, there" a few times as Meredith stared vacantly across the room. Helen sat on the other side of Lady Pemberton, weeping, and David stood conveniently out of sight behind her, holding a hand she offered up to him.

No one spoke.

Doctor Phillips gave his report a few minutes later, looking suitably somber. "My condolences to you all," he said. "I'm fairly certain it was a heart attack. Sir Rupert had an irregular heartbeat, and I had prescribed digitalis for it. I had been quite worried about the effects of the residual dengue fever on his weakened heart. Williams said he was feeling ill yesterday."

"Yes," Meredith said. "Of course, he did anything but rest. He was busy all day in Dartmouth, meeting with his solicitor and who knows what else. He was quite secretive about it."

"Did he seem under any stress?" Doctor Phillips asked. All eyes flitted to Constable Carraher standing behind him, notebook in hand.

"None at all, other than his war work with the Foreign Office," Great Aunt Sylvia said, the certainty in her voice matched only by the magnitude of the lie. The other family members fell in line, nodding in agreement. For Great Aunt Sylvia, the most pressing matter was to keep family matters private and be rid of the policeman with his pencil poised.

"That would be hard on any man his age," the doctor said. "What with the fever and his heart condition, I'm only surprised it didn't happen sooner. Sir Rupert was not a well man. He wished for the extent of his illness to be kept confidential, but that hardly matters now." With that pronouncement, he left to talk to Williams about removing Sir Rupert's body. The silence was uncomfortable as the family worked at not acknowledging the argument between Meredith and her father moments before his death.

Kaz stared out the window into the darkness, possibly wondering how much time he had left on his bum ticker. Once I'd asked him what exactly was wrong, but he changed the subject so fast that I never asked again. Now would probably not be a good time either. I left for some fresh air and a chat with Tom Quick.

"Too bad about the old boy," Tom said as we stood in the light of the portico. "Wasn't a bad sort, from what I heard."

"Apparently his only fault was not being a Pemberton," I said. "What did folks around here think of him?"

"Hard to say. He was off in India for so long he didn't have a chance to make his mark with the locals. You're right about the Pembertons, though. The story was the old lady didn't like Ashcroft leaving their hands. The Sutcliffes were not quite up to snuff in her eyes."

"Any special reason? Scandal in Sir Rupert's past?" I asked, trying to draw out any gossip Tom might have heard.

"Not that I know of. Dig deep enough, though, and you'll find what any man hides away. His shame, his failings, his regrets. I'm sure Rupert Sutcliffe—with his fortune, land, and title—was not exempt from that," Tom said. "Please give my best to David. We were going to meet for a drink tonight, but that can wait."

"Maybe Kaz and I will make ourselves scarce and leave the family to themselves. If we can get away we'll drop by the pub in North Cornworthy." I didn't mention Michael Withers, the man who'd known Ted Wiley in the old days.

Constable Carraher and Doctor Philips filed out, and Tom fell in behind them. They all crammed into an old Jowett Eight coupé and rattled off, satisfied with the stories they'd been told.

"My God," David said from the open doorway, before allowing a sigh escape his lips. "It's hard to believe he's gone."

"How is Helen?" I asked him.

"Distraught, of course," he said. "She was much closer to her father than Meredith. Obviously."

"And how is Meredith doing? It's got to be hard on her."

"She won't let on. I doubt she'd ever admit to any guilt or blame. Edgar thought it best that we leave the three ladies alone so they can have some time to mourn by themselves. Smart chap," David said, with a rueful grin.

"I have a question for you," I said, shutting the door behind him and stepping off the portico so we wouldn't be heard. "Did Kaz ever tell you what his heart problem was, exactly? He never wanted to go into specifics, and Sir Rupert's death has me worried about him. I thought he looked upset in there, but maybe I'm reading too much into it."

"Well, he did seem rather distracted," David said. "Actually, he was diagnosed while we were at Oxford. He'd been short of breath, winded after climbing a single flight of stairs. He was never terribly athletic, but such weakness seemed to be the symptom of an underlying problem. I helped him find a specialist."

"What did he say?"

"Most likely a congenital defect in a blood vessel near the heart. The doctor said it was inoperable, since it was so close to the heart itself," David said.

"Was there a prognosis?"

"He prescribed rest. He said the academic life was well suited."

"That's hardly the life Kaz has now," I said.

"I must say, I've never seen him looking better. He's keeping himself quite fit."

"Yeah," I said. "Last year I think he decided life was worth living. A non-academic life, at that."

"He told me about the explosion. About Daphne," David said. "This war has robbed us of so much."

"It makes a middle-aged man dying at home of a heart attack seem less of a tragedy," I said.

"It will certainly make life at Ashcroft easier," David said. "It's not pleasant to say, but it's true."

"How so?" I asked.

"Well, with Sir Rupert gone, Meredith and Edgar can stay on. His troubles are over, at least as far as a job goes."

"Assuming she inherits, along with Helen, I suppose," I said.

"Who else?" David asked, and opened the door to go inside. It closed behind him with a solid, satisfying sound, thick wood and old iron sealing off the outside world and all its problems.

Who else indeed?

CHAPTER TWENTY

THE HUNTER'S LODGE was cheerier on the inside than the outside. An old stone fireplace took up most of one wall, a well-stocked bar the other, and in between tables were set on a wooden floor that had been polished by generations of leather soles. The banked fire gave off a warm glow, and the odor of tobacco mingled with the scent of workman's sweat and frothy beer. There were about a dozen or so men in the place, most of them probably from the mill, by the looks of their callused hands and worn leather jerkins.

I carried two ales from the bar to the table Kaz had claimed by the fire. I'd filled him in earlier on the details of Sir Rupert's request to determine if Peter Wiley was his son. We were here to look for Michael Withers, but in a small village pub it was best to bide your time and not shoot your mouth off first thing. Besides, the ale was fine and the fire warm. We were in no hurry to get back.

"You the visitors up at Ashcroft?" one of the men at the next table asked. "Is it true what we're hearing, that the squire's dead?"

"Sir Rupert, if that's who you mean, yes," I said. "He had a heart attack today and died."

"Sad thing, that," he said, and went back to his drink, not entirely grief-stricken.

"Did he ever come to the pub?" I asked, to keep the conversation going.

"Rupert Sutcliffe? Not likely," he said. "Hardly stopped in the village at all. It was India, London, the big house for him. North Cornworthy? No."

"Not like the Pembertons?"

"Ah, they're all gone now, except for the old lady. Cruel swant, they were," he said.

"Pardon me?" Kaz said. "They were cruel?"

"No, no," he said. "Sorry, that's how we say right proper 'round here. Very proper people, the Pembertons. The old viscount would come in here and buy a round of drinks and chat with the fellas, ask about the mill and the crops. Not like the cropeing lot up there now. Never seen one o' them; they don't mang with the common sort."

"Cropeing?" Kaz said, ever the student of language. "Not proper?"

"G'wan, Evan, you're laying it on a bit thick for these folk," another man said. "He means stingy, and they don't mix with the likes of us. Of course, Evan thinks anyone who doesn't buy him a drink is cropeing, eh?" Evan didn't disagree, a mischievous gleam in his eye telling me he'd enjoyed flummoxing the newcomers.

"I'm Michael Withers," our translator said. "My daughter said you might come looking for me."

"Please, sit down," I said, before doing the introductions and heading back to the bar for three refills, not wanting to be thought of as cropeing. I returned to find Kaz deep in conversation with Withers, exploring the Devon dialect.

"Billy, this is quite interesting," he said. "I never knew how much Old English was retained in the West Country dialects. They still use *thee* in everyday speech. Fascinating."

"Ooh arr, we do," Withers said. "But only wi' each other. The rest of the land thinks we're country rustics enough. So tell me now, what can I do for you?"

"Alice told me you knew Ted Wiley pretty well. Grew up with him," I said. "His son, Peter, is stationed nearby and came to visit Ashcroft. I thought he might want to chat with someone who knew his father." Peter had decided on an early night, and I'd told him I'd fill him in on anyone who knew his father. Ted Wiley, that is.

"Ted and I were chums, true enough. It's been a long time since I thought of him. But you know how it is, you grow and go your separate ways. I didn't have much to do with Ted after he went to work up at the house."

"Alice said you talked about him often," I said.

"Sure, stories about youthful adventures," Withers said. "Raiding the orchard for apples, fishing and swimming in the river, that sort of thing. It was a simple time back then: chores, school, and playing outdoors. A good time to be a child. But then the war came, and we both signed up when we became of age in 1917." He took a long drink and set down his glass nearly empty. "Ted and I were the lucky ones. We came home, and in one piece."

"You were changed," I said.

"'Course we were," Withers said. "Ted and I met here now and then, but we'd become men, see? Light-hearted boys no more after more than a year in the trenches. I think it was hard for us to stay pals after the war. Maybe we reminded each other of how much we'd lost, even though we'd survived."

It was time for another drink. I nodded to Kaz and he made the trip to the bar.

"Had Ted always been sweet on Julia Greenshaw?" I asked.

"Yes," Withers said. "From the moment he laid eyes on her. Finally got up the nerve to ask for her hand when she said she was leaving for America. Everyone wondered why he hadn't done it sooner."

"Is she why he went to work at Ashcroft?"

"Well, I think he would have anyway," Withers said. "Ted was the kind of man who wanted to better himself. Had no interest in village life. Now me, I think this is grand. Work close by, a good wife and three kids, and a warm pub to pass the time in. What else could a man want?"

"What did Ted want?" I asked as Kaz returned with our drinks.

"To make something of himself, he'd say." Withers stopped to take a healthy swallow and smacked his lips as he set down the glass. "What that was, I never could pin down. Respect, I think it came down to. Ted was a smart one, even when we was kids. If he saw something he wanted, he grabbed it. Could usually talk his way out of trouble, too. Fitty, he was. Clever."

"His son's an artist," I said. "Paints watercolors."

"He must have got that from his mum," Withers said. "Ted couldn't draw, and his penmanship was worse. I could barely make out the one card he sent from America."

"Maybe I'll bring Peter by in a day or so," I said. "I'm sure he'd want to meet you."

"Do that," Withers said. "I'll tell him a few tall tales. Be a pleasure to meet the boy."

"What about Roger Crawford?" I asked. "Did he know Ted?"

"No," Withers said. "Crawford came here from the South Hams after Ted left. Poor bugger."

"I heard stories about him bringing things in from France," I said.

"Stories, eh? I thought you came here to help Ted's boy, not to ask questions about hardworking fishermen." His eyes narrowed, and I saw Evan turn in his chair, watching us.

"Sorry, no harm meant," I said. "It was only something I heard today."

"Gossip is for old ladies," Withers said. "Now I'll bid you goodnight." He rose and went to sit at Evan's table, where they were soon huddled together, heads close and voices low.

"One question too many, Billy," Kaz said, raising his glass in salute. "Here is to knowing when to stop."

"Better than one too few, Kaz." We finished our drinks and gave up on waiting for Tom Quick. He was probably busy helping the local constable with paperwork and arrangements for the body. We walked past Withers, and I nodded as our eyes met. He looked away, but Evan's whisper was loud enough for me to make out his words without understanding them.

"I tell thee, appen the janner will find the shord as well," Evan said, and laughed coarsely as Withers hushed him.

"I have no idea what he meant," Kaz said as we got into the jeep. "We'll need to find a translator. Perhaps David will know. He'd be interested in local dialects."

"Sure," I said. Appen the janner will find the shord. "Or maybe we had one too many."

■ ■ ■

IT WAS LATE enough that we went around to the back door at
Ashcroft, unsure who might still be up and which doors were locked.
The blackout curtains were all drawn, and not a sliver of light escaped
the house. The kitchen door opened, and we found Mrs. Dudley and
Williams seated at the table, both in their dressing gowns, a bottle of
wine and three glasses between them.

"Thank you for coming in this way," Williams said as he slowly
rose to his feet. "Less noise to disturb the family."

"Please sit," Kaz said. "We do not wish to disturb you. It has been
a difficult night."

"Indeed," Williams said, twirling his wineglass.

"A sad thing," Mrs. Dudley said. "Sir Rupert was such a kind man."

"We talked with Michael Withers tonight," I said. "I'd like to thank
Alice for suggesting we meet. Is she still up?"

"No, she went to bed a while ago," Mrs. Dudley said. "Is there
anything I can get for you gentlemen?"

"No, thank you," Kaz said. "Are any of the family about?"

"I heard footsteps a few minutes ago, but no one has rung for
assistance," Williams said. "I assume someone wished for a nightcap
in solitude."

"Enjoy yours," I said, and we wished them goodnight.

"Did you find that odd?" Kaz asked in a whisper after we left the
room.

"The two of them having a drink? No, why should I?"

"Because it was a 1934 Chateau Mouton Rothschild," Kaz said.
"Not a vintage for the downstairs staff, even in a house such as Ashcroft.
And certainly not a bottle to be shared with a young kitchen maid."

"Maybe they were taking advantage of the situation," I said. "Who's
to know?"

"As you have observed, the staff are loyal to the Pemberton family,
who may now have come back into possession of Ashcroft. Whatever
their married name, Helen and Meredith are Pembertons to the bone.
I doubt Williams would pilfer a fine wine from the Pemberton cellars."

"Then it would be interesting to know who the third drinker was," I said, only out of a mild curiosity. If it didn't help me figure out whether Peter Wiley was Sir Rupert's son, I couldn't get too excited about the help tippling a pricey wine. It may well have been their salute to Sir Rupert, after all.

We entered the main foyer, and as we headed to the staircase I noticed a faint glow coming from the library. It looked like candlelight, and I would have bet on Edgar raiding the brandy. But the low voices were women's, hushed and insistent.

"What did you do?" That sounded like Helen. Worried, anxious.

"Nothing at all. How could you ever think such a thing?" Meredith. Appalled. Horrified.

"I know you, Meredith. And I know what I heard."

"Helen, darling, you have suffered a great shock today. Grief is playing tricks on your mind."

"What about you, for God's sake?" Helen's voice rose, then fell to a whisper. "You found him. Didn't that shock you? Or did you hate him so much you felt nothing?"

"My shock came a long time ago, dear sister. But I did feel something when I found him. Relief. For both of us."

"You're horrible!" Helen said. From the silence, it was obvious that Meredith wasn't horrible enough for Helen to leave.

"No, I'm honest, Helen. At least now I won't have to be dependent upon Edgar to provide for me and the children. And David won't have to worry about facing the world with half a face."

"Meredith! What a terrible thing to say."

"But it's true, you idiot!" I could tell Meredith was working hard to keep her voice low. "*You* can't bear to look at him, you, his own wife! How much confidence do you think *that* inspires?"

The next sound was sobbing. Kaz nudged me, and we walked up the carpeted staircase as quietly as we could.

"What do you think they were talking about?" Kaz asked me as we stopped at his door.

"Meredith was holding a letter when she came out of Sir Rupert's study," I said.

"But she said Helen must have been mistaken," Kaz said. "That implies something other than Sir Rupert's death, don't you think?"

"Makes sense," I said. "Maybe we should tell the doctor to check for poison."

"Because of two distraught sisters having a private late-night talk?" Kaz said. "Helen could have been referring to a number of things. Perhaps Meredith stole something of Sir Rupert's. It seems likely she has before."

"Yeah, could be," I said. "Plus, everything Meredith said is true. David stated much the same to me earlier."

"The truth hurts. Especially when it has been twisted and hidden for so long. And what of your promise to Sir Rupert?" Kaz asked, his voice hushed. "It was obviously important to him. A son, even an illegitimate one, might have some right to a share of the inheritance."

"I'll poke around some more," I said. "But there's little chance of finding proof after all this time, and I have no idea what the English laws are about a bastard son inheriting, especially if he was never acknowledged."

"Surely Sir Rupert would have acknowledged him if he had turned out to be his son. Why else would he have wanted to know?"

"There's no proof of that, logical as it sounds," I whispered. "I wish he'd never asked me about it, to tell you the truth. I almost wish we'd never come here, but the food and the accommodations are well worth it." I smiled to show Kaz that I was joking. Half joking.

We heard footsteps and hushed ourselves, looking a bit foolish standing in the hallway saying nothing. It was Peter. He said he was wide-awake and going for a drink to bring to his room. He seemed jumpy, or excited, I couldn't tell which. In truth, I didn't care. We said goodnight.

In my room, I searched for something to read. The library downstairs was full of volumes on history, science, and all sorts of great literature. But the bedrooms each had a small bookshelf of the stuff regular people actually read all the way through. Mysteries and other popular novels. I grabbed an Agatha Christie. *Lord Edgware Dies.* What's that they say about life imitating art?

I took off my shirt, noticing that one of the cuts on my arm had bled through the bandage. I'd have to see Alice in the morning about that. I changed the dressing and eased myself into bed, but I didn't get far with Lord Edgware before I nodded off. During the night I thought I heard hushed voices and rushed footsteps in the hallway, or maybe it was part of my dream. Lord Edgware and Sir Rupert were being buried, but no one seemed sad at all.

CHAPTER TWENTY-ONE

"THANK YOU, ALICE," I said, finding her in the kitchen. She'd done another spit and washsoap job on my shirt and gotten the recent bloodstains out. My arm had stopped bleeding too, so it was good news all around. "I met your father last night at the pub. Did he tell you?"

"No, I haven't had a chance to talk to him, what with everything going on here. Was he a help?"

"Yes, he was. I'm sure Peter will enjoy speaking to him, even though he didn't seem to stay close with Ted Wiley after the war," I said.

"What, those two?" Alice said. "From the stories Dad told me, they were thick as thieves."

"I must have misunderstood what he meant. Something about how they had different interests when they came home from the trenches."

"Oh, I really wouldn't know. I never met him," Alice said, turning to the dishes piled in the sink. "But you tell Peter the next time you see him I'd be glad to take him around to meet Dad."

"He's not here?" I asked.

"No, he left early this morning, is what I heard," she said as she began scrubbing away. I wondered why Peter had gone, what with one more day of leave, and a gorgeous day for painting at that. Maybe we'd get some answers when we took David to Greenway House today.

"I trust you are well, Captain Boyle," Great Aunt Sylvia said as I walked gingerly into the library, where the family was gathering for breakfast. "Have your injuries fully healed? I meant to ask yesterday."

"I'm fine, Lady Pemberton. Thank you."

"Did you enjoy the pub?" Edgar asked as he piled bacon on his plate. "They have a fine local ale."

"So says the expert," Meredith said as she entered the room. "Good morning, Captain Boyle. Edgar, some coffee please." She used the tone you might with a long-time family retainer. Edgar, perhaps sensing how the roles had changed during the last twenty-four hours, complied, delivering her china coffee cup and saucer as she lounged on the couch, lighting a cigarette.

"I heard Peter left?" I asked into the chilled atmosphere.

"Yes, and without a word to anyone," Great Aunt Sylvia said. "Most impolite, unless we receive a note with the afternoon post."

"He might have been called away suddenly," I offered.

"There have been no telephone calls," Meredith said. "He simply vanished this morning. All he left behind was an unfinished painting."

I downed some coffee and excused myself, feeling an interloper, especially without Kaz to smooth things over. I found him, along with David, already making their way to the jeep.

"Ah, there you are Billy," David said. "I couldn't face them this morning, sorry to have almost left you behind."

"I understand," I said, feeling more sorry for David Martindale than ever before. Not the burns, but the loneliness amidst a house full of people.

AT GREENWAY HOUSE, we delivered David to Colonel Harding's office. He was nervous but eager, and we wished him luck. "Let's find Peter," I said.

No luck. Not in his office, according to the guard at the door. Same for his room. The officer of the day said he hadn't signed in from his leave and still had a day left, so why should he be here?

Sensible guy.

We checked the mess hall and walked the corridors until we

saw a name we recognized. Lieutenant James Siebert had his own office with a nameplate on the door. I knocked and entered, only to find it was a nice-sized broom closet. Kaz could barely follow me in.

"What can I do for you, Captain?" Siebert glanced at my rank, deciding on the level of politeness necessary for one rank above him. He got it about right.

"Have you seen Peter Wiley today?"

"Keep that kid away from me," Siebert said. "He's got a one-track mind, and I've got a mind to take another crack at him." Siebert's khakis were rumpled, and he looked like he might have shaved in the dark. Papers and binders were strewn across his desk and stacked up in the tiny room. He made me think of a monk in his cell.

"One-track in terms of getting on a ship?" I asked.

"Captain, it's probably none of your business," Siebert said. "So let's not get into details. But if he says he needs perspective one more time, I'll deck him again."

"We all could use some perspective, Lieutenant," I said.

"What I could use is another pair of hands and ten extra hours in the day," Siebert said. "Will that be all, sir?"

It was. It was clear he didn't like Peter, and that he hadn't seen him. Neither meant much. We went to the mess and had coffee, then walked out to the jeep, where we found David.

"How did it go?" Kaz asked. Given the dark look on David's face, the question wasn't even necessary.

DAVID SAID HARDING had been gracious, but it had become obvious he was not up to the task. His eyesight was worse than he'd thought, and he couldn't make out many of the photographs even with a magnifying glass. After that he sat in silence for the ride back, and we let him be.

"Best to get it over with," he said as we approached the front door of Ashcroft House. "They're probably in the morning room." We dutifully followed.

"David, is it really too much to ask that you let someone know where you go off to?" Helen said as soon as he entered the room. She blushed, as if she hadn't meant to say it out loud and had been thinking far worse. "I'm sorry," she said, looking at the rest of us. "I was worried, that's all."

"My fault, really," David said, taking Helen by the hand and leaning in for a kiss on the cheek. She leaned away and sat next to her sister. "I wanted it to be a pleasant surprise, but it turned out not to be."

"We could have used a pleasant surprise around here, David," Great Aunt Sylvia said. "Please do entertain us with what might have been."

"You know I held little hope for any assignment with the RAF," David said. "But Billy convinced his colonel to let me have a go at a photographic interpretation job. Would have been perfect, too, at a place called Greenway House, right across the river, where Peter is stationed."

"Did you see him?" Meredith asked.

"No. I didn't. Too busy with Colonel Harding," David said. "Well, no matter. I washed out. Seems my one good eye is not as good as I thought. Couldn't make out fine details. It's very precise work, and I simply missed too much."

"Tough luck," Edgar said. "You're sure about the RAF?"

"Fairly certain, yes," David said, his eyes on Helen, who remained silent, her ankles crossed demurely, lips compressed as if she was working at keeping in another unseemly outburst.

"Perhaps another opportunity will come along," Kaz said as he sat down. "It's a matter of finding the right one."

"Oh, come on, Piotr," David said, loudly, his self-control at the breaking point. "It's not like looking for the right flat. No one needs a one-eyed ex-pilot, certainly not one as grotesque as I am."

"Self-pity does not become you, David," Great Aunt Sylvia said. "It is not how this family behaves."

"Quite right. My apologies to you all," David said, taking a deep breath. "I must admit, I was taken aback by this business about my vision. I can read a newspaper as well as I used to, or at least I thought

I could. But to find out that in fact I see more poorly now is a bit of a shock."

"Quite understandable," Meredith said. "Don't you agree, Helen?"

"Of course," Helen said. "And we shall have plenty to keep ourselves busy here, no matter what the RAF decides."

"Here?" David said.

"Of course," Meredith said. "Who else would Father have left Ashcroft to? There are so many things he left untended during his years in India. There will be much work to do, and Edgar will be busy writing his book, won't you, dear?"

"Indeed I will," Edgar piped up. "A monograph on life and death in the last moments of *Hamlet*. I have been researching it for years. I plan to begin as soon as the funeral is over. Baron, perhaps we could discuss the play later. I'd be interested in hearing your perspective."

"Kaz," I said, recalling that the old king's wife had at least waited a couple of months before moving on to other endeavors, "what was that quote you wanted to ask Edgar about?"

"Oh yes, I had forgotten," Kaz said. "'He that dies pays all debts.' Which play is it from?"

"*The Tempest*," Edgar said instantly. "Act three, scene two. How did that one come up? Not a well-known line."

Great Aunt Sylvia turned to look at Meredith. Was she thinking of Rupert Sutcliffe, and the debts his death had paid?

"Oh, it popped into my mind yesterday and I meant to ask you about it. I'd be quite interested in hearing about your work, Edgar," Kaz said, wisely not mentioning the fact that we'd been discussing Tom Quick and his lust for revenge.

"My thesis is a bit esoteric," Edgar began. "It's about the last lines of *Hamlet*, when he says with his dying voice, 'the rest is silence.' Quite final on the subject of heaven and life after death. But in the 1623 Folio, there is a different final line. 'The rest is silence. O, o, o, o.' As if the poor lad had caught a glimpse of something grand, a thing beyond silence."

"You plan to write an entire book about four *os*?" I asked.

"It may not mean much to the average person, especially in the midst of war, I admit," Edgar said. "But to an Elizabethan scholar, it is very important. I believe this was Shakespeare's own revision, his last statement on the emptiness that lies beyond the grave. *Hamlet* is suffused with guilt and death, perhaps reflecting the Bard's own view of the world. But later in life, I think he saw a greater possibility—the potential for resurrection—and added those exclamations as an antidote to the finality of the preceding line."

"Fascinating," Kaz said. "I had not known of that revision."

"It also appears in a 1603 Folio, so we know it predates Shakespeare's death. I'll show you a copy later," Edgar said, retreating to his chair, looking mildly embarrassed about his brief speech.

David pulled a chair closer to Helen. "What do you think of a future here at Ashcroft House?"

"I'm glad Edgar will finally have a chance to write his book," Helen said with indifference, staring straight ahead.

"You know I mean about staying on here," David said in a low voice, his eyes zeroing in on Helen as if she were a Me-109 in his sights. I could almost feel his teeth clench.

"Where else would we go, dear?" Helen said, turning to face him. "What else can we do?" She said it calmly. Perhaps it was her idea. Or Meredith's. Either way, it had a ring of certainty to it. There was meaning in how she looked at David, without flinching or averting of her eyes. The signaling of a truce? A partnership? I hoped for David's sake it was sincere. But she'd been upset about something a minute ago. What had that been all about? Maybe it wasn't a truce. Resignation, perhaps. To her new life and David's ruined face.

Williams entered to announce a call on the telephone for Lady Pemberton from Doctor Phillips.

"He knows I do not speak through that machine," Great Aunt Sylvia said emphatically. "Meredith, would you?"

Meredith nodded somberly and went to do her duty.

"Doctor Phillips has released the body," she said a few minutes later, standing in the doorway with her hands folded in front of her, as if giving a lecture. "The cause of death was definitely a heart attack. We are apparently free to proceed with the funeral." It was interesting that she used the word "definitely." Had anyone else but me suspected foul play? Not that I'd taken the idea seriously, but perhaps someone else had. The last sentence was dripping with sarcasm, the disdain of the upper class for the procedures of mere officialdom. Meredith had tried on the role of lady of the manor and found it fit her well.

"We should see the vicar," Helen said.

"Certainly," David answered. His eyes darted back to Helen. He seemed surprised that she was still looking in his direction. "Are there any other living relatives?"

"None on the Sutcliffe side," Great Aunt Sylvia said. "There was a cousin in Yorkshire or some other dreary northern place. Died after the last war, I think."

"I will check Father's papers in his study to be sure," Meredith said. "Then, in the morning, Helen and I will call upon the vicar." Great Aunt Sylvia gave her an approving nod. Meredith stood, a solid Pemberton look of satisfaction on her face. There were things to be done, and she was the one to do them.

AT DINNER, DAVID was in fine form, telling stories of North Africa and his mates in the RAF. Nothing about burns, crash landings, or empty bunks after a mission, but rather high jinks and pranks, the kind of thing families like to hear, as if their young men were all delightful scamps away at summer camp. He told a story about a German pilot who'd been shot down and was a guest in their mess before he was taken away to a POW camp. Knights of the sky, that sort of thing. Helen laughed and touched his arm, which was nice to see, but these white lies were almost too much to bear. I wanted to scream, to tell them about the young boys recently killed and maimed on a beach not far away, their bodies cold and decaying as we sat eating whiting with carrots. I caught Kaz's eye, and he gave the tiniest of shrugs before taking a healthy drink of wine. He was glad David was in good spirits, I was sure, but I could tell the sudden change in David was bothering him too. A day or so ago, he'd been desperate to find a job that would keep him in uniform and out of Ashcroft. Today, when he should have been down in the dumps, he was the life of the party. Something was wrong.

"David," Kaz said, taking advantage of a break in the conversation, "I heard something of the local dialect at the pub last night. I had no idea it was so colorful."

"The fellows had a fine time at my expense, first time I went there," Edgar said. "It was good-natured fun, as far as I could tell."

"You didn't bore them with Shakespeare while spending our money, did you, darling?" Meredith said with a roll of her eyes.

"'Dost thou think, because thou art virtuous, there shall be no more cakes and ale?'" Edgar said, with a wink toward Kaz.

"Edgar!" Meredith exclaimed, aware that the barb was directed at her.

"Sir Toby, in *Twelfth Night*, is it not?" Kaz asked, an appreciative grin on his face. Edgar raised his glass to him and then graciously to Meredith, who leveled her eyes at Edgar as she returned the toast. The whole table was in top form tonight.

"What did they say?" David asked, returning to the topic of the local dialect. "I can't say I'm familiar with West Country idioms."

"Something about appen the janner and the shord," Kaz said.

"Appen the janner will find the shord," I said. "That was the gist of it."

"Perhaps the seaman will find the gap in the hedge," Great Aunt Sylvia said from her end of the table. "*Janner* could mean a fisherman, anyone who makes their living from the sea. It's an old word, which has become corrupted to mean almost anyone in Devon, and not in a flattering light."

"Interesting," David said. "But what's that about a gap in the hedge?"

"I believe it refers to one who can make his way through cleverness," Meredith said. "Finding a route no one else has, that sort of thing. David, you should make an appearance at the pub, after the funeral, of course. I'm sure Edgar would be more than pleased to go as well. It's expected."

"Lords of the manor, eh, Edgar?" David said, raising his glass. The white wine leapt within the clear crystal as his hand trembled, and he set the glass down a bit harder than necessary. Edgar made a joke about it and everyone laughed, David's nervousness forgotten. Except by me.

After dinner the ladies left the table and Edgar poured brandies for each of the men, then fired up a cigar.

"One of Sir Rupert's," he explained as he sent a cloud of smoke to the ceiling. "No reason for them to go to waste, I say."

"What would Malvolio think of that?" Kaz said, and I could see a mischievous glow in his eyes.

"Who?" I asked.

"Oh, I take your point," Edgar said. "Rather droll. You see, Captain, the scene I quoted from at dinner is a famous one. Sir Toby Belch is a high-spirited comic creation, a cunning fellow in love with life and good drink. His nemesis is steward to his niece, Malvolio. Malvolio is a bit of a stickler for propriety and looks down on excess, especially when it comes to drinking." He was smiling, apparently happy to be compared to a character from his beloved bard.

"I am sorry if I went too far," Kaz said. "I couldn't help it after you quoted that line."

"Not to worry, Baron," Edgar said, waving his cigar expansively. "Once in a while, I get my say in things. And *Twelfth Night* is one of my favorite comedies. Although I find the plot with the forged letter a tad cruel, it is still quite amusing."

"Speaking of quotes, what was that fisherman stuff all about?" David asked. "I'd like to learn more about the dialect, but what was the context of going between the hedges?"

"It was an offhand remark," Kaz said, not revealing that we'd been discussing the possible paternity of Peter Wiley. "We heard it on our way out, and I was curious."

That satisfied David, and we left for our rooms. Something was bothering me, and as I ascended the staircase I tried to put my finger on it, but it was late, and I was too bushed for hard thinking. I hoped it would come to me, but the residual aches, pains, and twinges from my healing cuts and bruises came on strong instead. It wasn't until much later, lying awake, that it I got it. Two things. The first was the envelope. Edgar mentioning the forged letter must have jogged my memory. When I'd encountered Meredith coming out of her father's study, she'd had a letter in her hand. The stamps were American. Had she taken it from her father? Could it have had anything to do with Peter Wiley?

The other thing was about what was said in the pub. It wasn't "perhaps the fisherman will cut through the hedges." Evan had added "as well" at the end. More than one clever man had slipped through that gap in the hedge. What it all meant, I had not a clue.

CHAPTER TWENTY-TWO

THE SOUND CAME from very, very far away. I tried to roll over, hoping it was a dream, but knowing it wasn't.

"Captain Boyle," an insistent voice came from the hallway as the hand I assumed to be connected to it rapped again on my door.

"Coming," I said, stumbling out of bed, noticing the faintest sliver of light showing at the horizon as I glanced out the window. I opened the door to find Williams, in his bathrobe, a look of disapproval on his face and a candle in one hand.

"A Colonel Harding is on the telephone," Williams said. "He says it is urgent that he speak to you."

I grabbed a robe and followed Williams. Not so long ago, Harding had told me to take it easy. Now what did he want? Kaz poked his head out from his room and followed along as Williams led us to the telephone in Sir Rupert's study.

"You can use the telephone in here," Williams said, switching on a lamp. "I will hang up the receiver downstairs."

"Thank you," I said, but the butler had already closed the door behind him.

"Hello?" I said into the mouthpiece. "Colonel Harding?"

"Boyle, I need both of you in Brixham, soon," Harding said, his voice tight.

"Today, Colonel?"

"This morning, Boyle. Now. You and Lieutenant Kazimierz get in that jeep and don't stop until you get to Brixham harbor. I'll be down by the hards along the breakwater. We have a situation. Ships were lost last night in Lyme Bay."

"Where?" I said, trying to understand what Harding was saying, and what I was supposed to do about it.

"Never mind, just get here, pronto," Harding snapped. "This is bad news."

"How will I find you, Colonel?" I said.

"It won't be hard. Look for LST 289. She's easy to spot." With that, he hung up. The line went silent, then a click, and finally a dial tone sounded. It was a short conversation, so it might have been Williams finally getting to the downstairs telephone to hang up. Or a nosy servant.

"Something's up," I said to Kaz. "Harding wants us in Brixham, at the hards."

"The what?" Kaz said.

"The hards," I said. "It's what they call the paved roads that lead straight to the embarkation points. Hard, paved surfaces and concrete ramps built by the engineers. They're made for tanks and trucks, so they can drive right onto the transports. They're everywhere along the coast."

"Of course," Kaz said. "I've seen them. I should have known Americans would create a short name for them. Did the colonel give any clue as to what has happened?"

"No, other than to meet him by LST 289. He said it would be hard to miss." Sitting in Sir Rupert's chair, I idly scanned his desk, out of habit—or nosiness. Papers were strewn across the top, as if someone had dumped files out and gone through them. I opened a drawer and saw much the same: papers jammed back into cardboard files, a rushed and sloppy search job.

"Billy, we should go," Kaz said. "I will see if Mrs. Dudley is up and will provide a thermos of coffee.

"Good idea, Kaz," I said, getting up and switching off the lamp. Part of me wanted to stay and figure out what the desk search had been all about. Especially the part of me that couldn't face the notion of more early morning hours in the jeep.

"You'll have to excuse Mr. Williams," Mrs. Dudley said in the kitchen a little later, pouring coffee into a thermos and wrapping two ham sandwiches for us. "He has little time to himself and holds his sleep very dear. The telephone woke him early."

"Is that coffee?" said Crawford, coming in the back door and sniffing the air.

"Have a cup with me," Mrs. Dudley said. "These gentlemen have got to fly off to Brixham for some reason. Don't know why anyone would want to go there, especially at dawn. What's the bother, Captain?"

"Something about ships in Lyme Bay," I said, shoving my arms into my trench coat.

"I should call my cousin in Salcombe," Crawford said. "He's with a shore battery crew on the heights above the harbor. They've got a clear view across the bay. I'll not want to go out on the tide this morning if Jerry's still prowling about."

"They probably won't be out in daylight," I said. "But you never know."

"Sounds like real trouble," Crawford said as we made our way out.

"Colonels don't call for much else," I said as we left.

Kaz drove, and I checked the map in between bites of smoked ham on brown bread. We took the bridge over the River Dart, invisible as the early morning fog rose off it like white clouds between low, rolling hills. We got on the Brixham road and took it to the coast, finishing the last of our coffee as we wended our way through the town, down the heights to the harbor below. It looked like a decent little seaside town, and I wondered what Mrs. Dudley had against it.

A small inlet marked the beginning of the harbor area, with small craft and fishing boats moored close in. Beyond them were destroyers, patrol boats, and transports of all sizes. The breakwater was farther out, and we followed the newly widened road as it curved alongside the docks. Harding had been right. LST 289 was tough to miss. The ambulances parked close to the ship, and the frenetic activity all around her would have been signal enough. But as we drove down the hard, the damage was plain to see. The entire stern had been blown off, barely enough of the structure left intact to keep the Channel waters from pouring in and swamping the ship. An open gun mount hung precariously over the gaping hole, wisps of smoke escaping into the clear morning air.

The bow ramp was down, and tanks, half-tracks, and jeeps were driving off, passing us as we pulled over. The men on the vehicles looked straight ahead, silent and grim.

"I can't believe it's still afloat," Kaz said, in a half whisper. Ambulances followed the vehicles, none of them in a hurry. No sirens for the dead. As we got out and walked closer, two MPs quickly came toward us, palms out, ordering us to halt. They tried to give us the bum's rush until I mentioned Harding's name, and then one of them escorted us aboard.

The deck was covered in hoses and shell casings. The LST had put up a fight with its light twenty- and forty-millimeter armament. The damage-control party had had a hot fire to deal with as well, judging by the blackened and blistered paint. Inside, we descended metal steps and found Harding at a table in a small room that smelled of oil and smoke. Opposite him was a naval officer, and between them were clipboards and stacks of paperwork. The walls were steel bulkheads with one grimy porthole.

"Captain Boyle and Lieutenant Kazimierz reporting as ordered, sir," I said, almost at attention. I figured Harding would appreciate some military discipline in front of a navy guy.

"Lieutenant Mettler, Captain of the 289," Harding said, nodding to the officer, who rose and shook our hands. He was short and dark haired, and had soot streaked across his forehead. He looked frantic and exhausted at the same time.

"Good luck, Colonel," Mettler said as he left the room. "I'll let you know if we find the body."

"What body?" I said as he cleared the door. Or hatch, I think they call them in the navy.

"A very special body," Harding said. "I can't say any more right now."

"Is there anything you *can* tell us, Colonel?" Kaz asked.

"LST 289 was part of Operation Tiger, the invasion exercise that began this morning," Harding said. "German E-boats hit the convoy in the night, as it was steaming through Lyme Bay. The 289 was torpedoed. They got off easy. Two other LSTs were sunk." He threw the pencil he was holding onto the stack of papers in front of him.

"Fully loaded?" I asked. Harding nodded.

"How many men?" Kaz asked, looking at the list of names in front of Harding.

"Hundreds," he said. "Too many. Only a few from this ship. They managed to get the Higgins boats into the water and used them to push her into port. Smart move, probably saved most of the men on board. There's probably a thousand soldiers and sailors on each LST. Some have been picked up, but not all."

"You mean there are still men floating in the Channel?" I asked.

"The attack was at zero two hundred this morning," Harding said. "The temperature in the Channel waters is forty-four degrees. Unless they're on a raft, no one's alive in the water."

"Colonel, this is terrible, but I still don't know what we can do to help."

"They found him, Colonel," Mettler said, his head popping in from the companionway.

"Come with me," Harding told us, grabbing a clipboard and following Mettler. We descended farther into the bowels of the ship, boots echoing off steep metal steps, our way lit by jury-rigged lights on electric cables. The companionway ended in a sheer drop where the explosion had blasted clean through the steel and left a gaping hole. Below us was a tangle of wires, twisted girders, and smashed vehicles. Arc welders were glowing points of blinding light in the cavernous opening, and we all instinctively shielded our eyes as we took a ladder down into the hold, where the air smelled of gasoline. If there was a body down here, it was dead ten different ways.

Sky appeared above us through a jagged section of bulkhead, caved in by the force of the torpedo blast. Crewmen leaned in to their pry bars, muscling aside a slab of shorn metal as seawater sloshed against our ankles. Beneath the slab was a pool of oil and blood, the form of a body barely discernible in the gloom. Two bodies, I realized, trapped by the explosion and the section of steel bulkhead that had crushed them.

"You sure?" Harding asked.

"Yeah, that's him," Mettler said, pointing at an arm pinned under the corpse of a seaman, his dungarees soaked with blood. "He cut his hand, and I recognize the bandage." There was a wide, dirty bandage at the base of a thumb, which was the best bet for identifying the body. He was dressed in army fatigues with an uninflated life belt clinched around his waist. I could see he was wearing a pack, but his cracked skull distracted me from any further investigation. Suffice it to say, a combat helmet is no protection against an exploding steel wall falling on top of you.

Harding handed me the clipboard and reached down into the mess of blood, bone, brain and oil to break one of the dog tags from the stainless-steel chain. Standing up, he wiped it on his pants, leaving a smear of black and red.

"Captain Andrew Pritchett," he read. "One down, nine to go."

"Nine what, Colonel?" Kaz asked.

He didn't answer. He stared down at the two dead men, their blood mingling with the oil and salt water. One ordinary seaman and one army captain important enough to have a SHAEF colonel confirm his terrible death. But they were equal partners in this endeavor now, neither one less important than the other, neither likely to be mourned more or less for their rank or standing. Death boils all things down to their essence. Not for the living, but certainly for those who lie on the ground or beneath the sea, indifferent to the struggles they have left behind.

CHAPTER TWENTY-THREE

WE LEFT THE ruined, smoking LST behind as we followed Harding in his staff car a few miles up the coast. We were heading to the Paignton rail station, where he promised secrets would be revealed. All we knew was that a German E-boat had put a torpedo in LST 289 and killed a baker's dozen of soldiers and sailors onboard, one of whom was important enough to make Harding fish around in a bloody soup to snag his dog tag.

"Why attach so much importance to identifying a dead man?" Kaz said as he drove. "And only one of several, at that."

"There have to be more out in the Channel," I said. We'd picked up comments from the crew about seeing other ships torpedoed by E-boats. The E stood for enemy, which was the Allied designation for the fast attack craft. Bigger, faster, and more heavily armed than our PT boats, they could be deadly in the close waters of the Channel. Not could be—had been, only a few hours ago. "I wonder what he meant by 'nine to go'?"

"We may be close to finding out," Kaz said. "Look ahead." A line of MPs waved Harding through a checkpoint a few hundred yards short of the railway station, with us on his tail. He pulled up near two armor-plated coaches guarded by more MPs, and we fell in beside him.

"Bayonet," I said, recognizing General Eisenhower's mobile headquarters, the special train he'd christened himself. It was outfitted with sleeping quarters for staff and an office for the general with full telephone and radio gear. Well protected, it was the perfect place to spill top-secret info.

Plush, too, I was reminded as we entered the stateroom. Thick curtains draped the windows, and the wood paneling was lit by the glow of lamps. At the far end was a single desk, where Uncle Ike sat dictating to Kay Summersby, his chauffeur, secretary, and close companion. How close? "None of your business, pal," is how I usually answered that one. The fact that I had to reply to that question fairly often was hard to take. After all, my mom's family is related through Aunt Mamie, so technically I was closer to her than Uncle Ike. But he and I had been through a lot over here since the early days in 1942, and I'm a loyal nephew, so let's drop the subject.

"William, how are you?" Uncle Ike asked as he stood to greet us and Kay departed. "I heard you were injured in that mess at Slapton Sands."

"A few scratches, that's all, General," I said. I hadn't seen him in a couple of weeks, and they must have been rough ones. He looked pale, and the bags under his eyes were heavier and darker than ever. The invasion had to be weighing heavy on his shoulders, and I didn't want to add to his already fearsome burden. "I'm fine. Ready for whatever you need."

"That's good to hear, William," he said. "You know how much I've come to depend on you. It's so good to have family close by, family I can count on."

"Always, Uncle Ike," I said in a low voice. I didn't like people hearing me call him that. When I first showed up in England, the scuttlebutt went that I was a politically connected relative looking for a plush assignment. Truth be told, it wasn't too inaccurate, and I got the cold shoulder from a bunch of people, including Sam Harding. A lot of water had gone under London Bridge since then, but I was still sensitive enough to whisper.

"You writing your mother regularly?" Uncle Ike asked. I told him I was and promised to give her his best in the next letter. Then he asked Kaz how he was, lighting up one of his ever-present Lucky Strikes. Kay returned with a tray of coffee and set it on a table between a long couch and a line of armchairs in the narrow carriage.

"How've you been, Billy?" she said, giving me a wink. "Have you seen Diana lately?"

"No," I said. "She's off doing some training."

"Too bad," Kay said, with a glance at the general, who was whispering with Harding. "Like they say, the course of true love never did run smooth."

"*A Midsummer Night's Dream*," Kaz said. "It is difficult to escape the Bard, it seems."

"I didn't know that," Kay replied. "I thought it was just one of those things people said. I'm off, loads of work to do." She gave us a wave and departed, a smile on her lips. Kay was a beautiful woman and had the virtue of always being happy and upbeat, or so it seemed. She could light up a room and coax a laugh out of the grumpiest of brass hats. I could see why the general liked having her around. I did.

"Have a seat, boys," Uncle Ike said, taking one of the armchairs. Kaz and I sat on the couch opposite Harding and the general. The aroma of coffee filled the room, and after the long, mysterious morning, it smelled like salvation. I waited until Uncle Ike lifted his cup, then went for mine. He nodded to Harding, who managed to take one sip before he launched into his speech.

"As you can imagine, planning for the invasion of Europe is a huge undertaking; one that requires that hundreds of people know where and when the landings will take place. Some know both, others know pieces of the picture, based on the work they need to do. Everyone with any need to know these details has gone through security clearances and been assigned to the BIGOT list. If you're a BIGOT, you know some or all of the secrets of D-Day."

"Why are they called 'bigots'?" Kaz asked.

"It's a term the British used, even before we were in the war," Uncle Ike said. "Stands for British Invasion of German Occupied Territory. A bit outdated at this point, but it stuck." He lit another cigarette and looked to Harding to continue.

"You two are now on the BIGOT list," Harding said. "Not because we're going to tell you any secrets, but because they may come up in the course of your investigation."

"That's fine, Colonel," I said, "but what are we investigating?"

"You saw how badly LST 289 was hit. Unfortunately, two other LSTs, the 507 and the 531, got it worse. Both were sunk in the Channel out in Lyme Bay as they were headed to Slapton Sands. German E-boats caught the tail end of the Operation Tiger convoy and chewed them up."

"The guy on the 289 was a BIGOT," I said, the truth finally dawning on me.

"Yes," Harding said. "There were a total of ten BIGOTs on the boats that were attacked. We need to be certain none of them have fallen into German hands."

"It would change everything," Uncle Ike said. "It's no secret that spring is invasion season. If the Germans got hold of a BIGOT and made him talk, it would endanger the entire invasion, or force its postponement. Either would be a catastrophe."

"Why were so many BIGOTs on those three LSTs?" I said. "What about the other ships that weren't hit?"

"There were eight LSTs in all," Harding said. "The last three had a preponderance of engineer units like the First Engineer Special Brigade and Amphibious Truck companies. These units are responsible for clearing beaches of obstacles and bringing men ashore. They have to know the exact local conditions of the landings. The forward LSTs had mostly combat infantry units from the Fourth Division. The men in those had less of a need to know."

"Why wasn't the convoy better protected?" I asked. "It's well-known that there are German E-boats stationed all along the French coastline."

"Confusion all around," Harding said. "There was to have been another destroyer escort, but it was damaged in a collision yesterday. Naval command did not deal with it properly, and there was no replacement. On top of that, radio frequencies weren't coordinated. Although a warning of the attack was radioed to the lone destroyer escort, the LSTs weren't operating on the same frequency. But everyone thought they'd been warned, including the destroyer escort. As a result, they steamed in a nice straight line, perfect targets for a night attack."

"Large Slow Target," I said. "That's what the GIs say LST really means."

"They nailed it," Uncle Ike said. "Too many men died needlessly out there." He gestured with his hand, cigarette ash flying to the carpet. "We need the two of you to check the bodies as they are brought in and confirm all BIGOTs are accounted for. It's gruesome work, I know, but necessary. I hope some of them survived and were picked up by our ships, but we simply have to know none of them are in German hands."

"Big Mike is coming down from London to join you," Harding said. "He should be on the next train. And Constable Quick has been assigned to you for the duration of this investigation. Seems like he has a good head on his shoulders."

"He does, Colonel," I said, trying to think through the implications of what Harding was asking. "How many do you think were killed?"

"We don't know yet. I'd guess five hundred to a thousand. LST 515 disobeyed orders and turned back to pick up survivors out of the water. Until we get them sorted out, we won't have an exact count."

"What do you mean, Colonel?" Kaz asked. "What were their orders?"

"To proceed to their destination," Harding said. "Navy protocol is for transports not to linger where there are enemy vessels, until the escorts have dealt with them."

"But there was only one escort," I said. "It couldn't leave the convoy, right?"

"Right," Harding said. "I don't want to criticize the navy, but this is a mess. And one we have to keep as quiet as possible."

"That's going to be difficult," I said. "From the little we learned about tides in the Channel, those bodies are going to wash up all along the coast."

"What about France?" Uncle Ike asked.

"Probably not; the tides don't run that way. In and out of the Channel, but not north or south."

"That's something," Harding said. "There's little chance of a man surviving in the cold water this time of year, but if he was on a raft or piece of wreckage, it might be possible."

"You've got ships out searching, don't you?" I said.

"Yes, they're collecting bodies right now," Harding said. "Word is no survivors have been found since LST 515 went back. We know bodies will end up on the coast. Hopefully most will drift into Slapton Sands and the restricted area. For those that don't, we are saying that one ship was lost to enemy action. That should explain any bodies outside the restricted zone."

"General, I understand how important this is, but why does it have to be so hush-hush? The Germans know they hit our ships," I said. "The locals will know there were casualties when bodies start washing ashore. There has to be something else to it."

"There is, William," Uncle Ike said. "This is your real initiation into the BIGOT list. Tell them, Colonel."

"Without revealing the location of the invasion, I can tell you that the beach at Slapton Sands is a close double of one of the invasion beaches. If the Germans even suspected we were practicing full-scale attacks against that beach, they might deduce the actual location. Even if they don't end up with a captured BIGOT, they could do great harm with that information. If they get both, we're in for real trouble."

"It could mean the invasion is thrown back into the sea," Uncle Ike said. "So I don't want you to think this is a meaningless detail. This disaster has to be kept quiet to protect the secret of the actual invasion area. And we must know those nine other BIGOTs are accounted for, dead or alive."

"Here," Harding said, handing me a file containing sheets of names, ranks, and brief physical descriptions. "As soon as Big Mike gets here, you can head out. Graves Registration is setting up collection points along the coast. Work your way through them. The Royal Navy has patrol boats out picking up bodies. Report back to me immediately when you find a BIGOT. I'll be at Greenway House."

"It might be helpful for us to split up," I said. "I know Kaz doesn't care for boats much, so maybe he and Quick could work the land side while Big Mike and I find a boat to take us into Start Bay."

"Good idea," Uncle Ike said. "You can cover more ground that way. Whatever you need, William, feel free to use my name. I've had specific orders typed up, directing all parties, English and American, to render whatever assistance you require. An admiral couldn't deny you a battleship, at least for the next several days. But then, Operation Tiger needs to be forgotten, at least until after the real invasion."

"Yes, sir," I said, standing. "We'll do our best."

"That's exactly what we need, William. Good luck." He rested his palm on my shoulder, and I felt some of his burden transferred to me. The weight was crushing. I'd complained about being left out of the loop on D-Day, and now here I was, with General Eisenhower telling me the future of the war depended on me finding nine dead men.

AS WE STEPPED on to the platform, the locomotive blew its whistle and the wheels began to turn slowly, the engine releasing a hiss of steam as it pulled the two heavy armored carriages out of the station. MPs climbed aboard or sprinted to their jeeps, ready to speed through the countryside and guard the next crossing.

"He was waiting just to speak to us," Kaz said, his voice betraying an awe that he seldom revealed.

"These orders make us gods for the next few days," I said.

"That's how important this job is," Harding said. "I've got another jeep for you. I figured the four of you would split up at some point. Good idea to go out into the Channel, Boyle. The *USS Bayfield* is anchored at Dartmouth. See the captain there, he's got boats that can take you out."

"Will do, Colonel. Tell me, is Peter Wiley a BIGOT? Is that why you denied him permission to ship out with Operation Tiger?"

"Yes," Harding said. "He failed to convince me he needed to be there, although he felt strongly about it. The other BIGOTs all had to be with their units, but Wiley is pretty much a one-man show."

"What does he do, exactly?" Kaz asked.

"You don't need to know," Harding said. It was a joke with us by now.

"We get it, Colonel," I said. I watched Kaz lift a tarp in the backseat of the new jeep. "What's that stuff?"

"Well, I figured we could requisition that place you're holed up in, since Big Mike will need to bunk with you. Or do it the nice way, by bribery. If they're going to feed him, all this will come in handy."

No kidding, I thought. Big cans of coffee, green beans, canned tuna fish, several bottles of Scotch, sugar, a carton of Chesterfields, and to prove Harding had a sense of humor, four large cans of peaches, heavy syrup. A nod to a case back in London a few months ago. I thought the incident had been forgotten, but apparently not.

"Think that will keep the folks at Ashcroft House happy, Peaches?" Harding asked, a smile cracking his face. It wasn't something you saw very often, so I didn't mind the ribbing.

"Nice to see you remembered, Colonel," I said. "This ought to make them delirious. One question before you leave. What about Big Mike and the BIGOT list? Can he be put on it? It's going to be difficult if we can't tell him everything."

"Big Mike's been a BIGOT for over a month now," Harding said, getting into his jeep and starting it. "He had a need to know." His grin got even wider, and I swear he actually laughed as he drove off.

CHAPTER TWENTY-FOUR

"HEY, BILLY, KAZ, how you guys doin'?" Staff Sergeant Mike Miecznikowski, aka Big Mike, asked as he stepped off the train, stooping to squeeze his six-foot-plus frame through the open door.

"Glad you're here, Big Mike," I said as Kaz shook hands with his Polish compatriot. Big Mike was Detroit Polish, and as different from Kaz as burlesque was from Broadway. That didn't get in the way of them being good friends. Big Mike was pals with the world, at home anywhere. By rights, he should have stopped to salute both of us, but acknowledging senior officers didn't come as second nature to him. Even in the rarified atmosphere of SHAEF, Big Mike ignored rank as much as he could, and as a result of his good-hearted nature, the brass often fell over themselves to be seen as one of Big Mike's buddies. I don't know how he did it, but he had a way with people that made even the powerful and famous want to be in his orbit. Maybe it was his huge biceps, or the way he could always scrounge up whatever was needed without a lot of paperwork getting in the way.

Me, I thought all this saluting was a load of hooey myself, but I thought that about most of the chickenshit stuff in the army. Uncle Ike liked deflating oversized egos himself. Maybe that's why he gave Big Mike free reign at headquarters. Some general officers criticized him—behind his back, of course—for talking to GIs with his hands in his pockets. Apparently army trousers were not meant to have hands stuffed inside them, for whatever reason. That was the kind of thing that really ticked Uncle Ike off. So he stuffed his knuckles in his pockets whenever the press was snapping pictures, and the dogfaces loved it. They knew chickenshit, and this was a signal that their Supreme Commander was not a big fan of it himself.

"Sam didn't tell me much on the telephone," Big Mike said as he tossed his duffel in the rear of the jeep. "Somethin' about finding nine guys."

"Nine dead men," I said.

"Sounds unpleasant," Big Mike said. "What's the deal?"

"It's even worse than it sounds. Why don't you drive with Kaz, and he'll fill you in."

"We headed to the joint where your RAF pal David lives?" Big Mike asked Kaz.

"Yes. We'll drop off your gear and all the contraband in the jeep. That's the bribe for them putting up with you."

"Geez," Big Mike said, inspecting the contents. "Ain't Sam ever gonna forget about those peaches?"

They drove off and I followed, glad for the time alone. Time to think about what had been revealed and what was left unsaid. The time and place of D-Day fit into the latter category, but I didn't really want to know that much. Not that I might shoot my mouth off after a couple of pints. I didn't want to see men training for the invasion and know the likely date of their death. I had read a report about expected casualties a week before. It was no secret that airborne divisions would play a key role, but there was talk that Air Vice-Marshal Leigh-Mallory had predicted up to 70 percent casualties for the 82nd Airborne. As for the GIs in the first assault wave, wherever the invasion planners sent them, it would be the same. The Germans had been fortifying the French coastline like mad, planting mines, pouring concrete, laying out fields of fire. The Atlantic Wall, Hitler called it: a long line of fortifications that the tiny Higgins boats would advance upon through churning surf and blazing steel. So, no thanks; I don't want to know when that's happening. No wonder Uncle Ike looked so pale, his face lined with worries I couldn't even imagine.

From Paignton it was a straight shot to the bridge at Totnes, driving through fields of sprouting crops and grazing cows. I cruised by columns of marching GIs carrying heavy packs and counting cadence. There were more in the distance, spread out on maneuvers, darting up gently rolling hills, disappearing into tree lines and appearing again like an undulating swarm of brown ants. Under the English sky, it all looked so simple.

We crossed the river, and even miles inland it was easy to see how low the water was. Small boats sat on the mud bottom waiting for the tide's return, long ropes securing them to the bank six feet up. Would bodies drift up the waterways, the cost of war washing up against farmers' fields? I shook off the macabre image and slowed as the country lane leading to North Cornworthy narrowed, green leafy branches arching over our heads as we drove. Picturesque. The perfect thing before an afternoon of sorting through the dead.

WE PULLED TO a stop in front of Ashcroft House. Big Mike whistled in amazement as he got out of the other jeep.

"This is where you guys have been shacking up? Not bad," he said.

"Wait until you meet the family," I said, stretching after the jeep ride. "How should we handle this?" I asked Kaz.

"Meredith, first," Kaz said. "She seems to be in charge now. Then a courtesy call upon Lady Pemberton." I was about to ask Kaz to brief Big Mike on how to act around Great Aunt Sylvia when voices rose from around the side of the house. Angry voices.

"Who's that?" I said.

"David, perhaps," Kaz said. It was two men, arguing. David and Edgar? I doubted Edgar would get that worked up over anything. "Wait here," Kaz said, obviously worried about his friend, but not wanting to embarrass him with a whole posse. As soon as Kaz turned the corner, the voices dropped off. In a minute, he was back with David and Crawford, who sported a dark scowl.

"Crawford will deliver the supplies to the kitchen," David said to Kaz, studiously avoiding speaking to or looking at Crawford, who bent to the task and left with an armload. Kaz introduced him to Big Mike, who gave David a casual, "How ya doin'? Nice place." If I hadn't been watching for it, I would have missed Big Mike's eyes lingering on the burned face, studying the taut, shiny skin.

"Not mine, I'm afraid. Not really sure who holds the title, not yet anyway. Come inside, we'll find Meredith. Helen will defer to her in any case; she always does. I am sure we'll be happy to have another guest, these delicacies notwithstanding."

Helen was nowhere to be seen, but we found Meredith in Sir Rupert's study. Or his former study. She was in the classic bill payer's pose, a mass of envelopes and invoices on the desk next to an open checkbook.

"Sorry to interrupt, Meredith," David said. "It seems we're being asked to do our bit for the war effort and house a colleague of the baron's for a few days. This is Sergeant . . . er, how do you pronounce that name again?" David gave Big Mike an apologetic look.

"Staff Sergeant Mike Miecznikowski, ma'am," Big Mike said, stepping forward and offering his huge hand. "People call me Big Mike, though."

"I can see why," Meredith said, tossing down her pen and accepting the shake, her delicate hand disappearing into Big Mike's grip. "What exactly can we do for you?"

"It's got something to do with that ship being sunk," David said. Kaz and I exchanged a quick glance. Had news traveled that fast? "The sergeant works with Billy and the baron, and they all need to stay on a few more days."

"Of course, we shall be glad to help in our small way," Meredith said, smiling as she rose from her chair. "Welcome to Ashcroft House, Sergeant. David, could you show our guest to his room? Will you all be staying for luncheon?"

"No, we need to get going," I said. "Thanks very much. I hope this is not an imposition, considering all you've been through." For a dame who was on the outs with her father when he died, Meredith fit into the role of Ashcroft's head honcho easily enough.

"Not at all, Captain," she said. "I for one am glad of the distraction. We can't seem to get a straight answer from father's solicitor about the estate, and meanwhile, we have creditors whose patience seems to be running out. I'm sending each a small amount from our funds and a note explaining the situation." She shook her head, as if clearing away cobwebs. "I'm sorry, I shouldn't be boring you with our troubles, should I? I'll ask Mrs. Dudley to make some sandwiches for you to take."

"Take a look at what they've brought us, while you're at it," David said. "Food and drink of the gods."

"We'll need to be sure Edgar doesn't keep the drink to himself," she said, leaving the room.

"Very kind of Meredith to be so accommodating," I said to David as he escorted Big Mike to his room. "She seems different now that her father's gone."

"Yes, she does," David agreed. "Odd duck, our Meredith. Here you go, Big Mike," he said, opening the door to a room next to mine.

"How did you hear about a ship being sunk?" I asked as we waited for Big Mike to stow his bag.

"From Crawford," he said. "He mentioned that you and Piotr went out early after receiving a call, something to do with a German attack on a convoy, I think. He was going to go out fishing and telephoned a friend of his on a shore battery to find out if it was safe."

"Yeah," I said, remembering the snatch of pre-dawn conversation. "A cousin, I think."

"That's right," David said as Big Mike shut his door behind him. "I assumed that was still your assignment. All right, let's get those sandwiches organized. So sorry Helen isn't about to meet our new guest. She hasn't been herself lately. I think her father's death has had more of an effect on her than she let on." I followed as David led us downstairs, not wanting to stick my nose in and ask what he and Crawford had been arguing about. Besides, Kaz would do that in his own way.

In the kitchen Williams and Mrs. Dudley were *ohhh*ing and *ahhh*-ing over the rations we'd brought along. Meredith and Edgar were there, too, along with Crawford, who was leaning against a counter smoking a cigarette, having already opened the carton of Chesterfields.

"Sugar!" Mrs. Dudley said, feeling the heft of the package. "I haven't seen this much sugar since before the war. Thank you, gentlemen. Oh, I must finish packing your lunch!" She scurried off, wiping her hands on her apron.

"It wasn't necessary, Baron Kazimierz," Meredith said. "But it is appreciated." It was funny how people in this house usually addressed such comments to Kaz exclusively. Their types much preferred talking to a baron over a mere American captain. Hey, who could blame them? Kaz would always be a baron, but when this war was over, I'd be a cop again, relegated to the back door of any place as fancy as this on Beacon Hill. Still, Meredith had treated Big Mike nicely, reserving her cutting remarks for her own husband, and that had to count for something. Out of the corner of my eye, I watched Edgar inspect the Scotch as Meredith supervised the stocking of the larder.

"Let's leave that for drinks tonight, shall we?" she said, a disapproving eyebrow raised in her husband's direction.

"I'll take the bottles to the library," Edgar said, not exactly agreeing or disagreeing.

"Have you seen Helen?" David asked, pulling Meredith's attention away from Edgar, who was walking away from her, bottles clinking in his hands.

"She went out for some air," Meredith said. "She mentioned something about creditors upsetting her. Well, that's what they do, isn't it?"

"I'm sure it will all turn out fine in the end," David said, directing a reassuring smile at Williams and Crawford. No reason to let the help know about financial problems, even in such a progressive house as Ashcroft, I figured.

"Have you set a date for the funeral?" Kaz asked. "We would like to attend, duties permitting."

"In two days," Meredith said. "Thank you. That is most kind. I know Father enjoyed your company, as well as yours, Captain Boyle. I do hope you can be there."

"Don't worry about that, ma'am," Big Mike said. "You tell us where and when, and I'll make sure they get there on time."

"How nice of you, Sergeant," Meredith said. "Ten o'clock, St. Peter's in North Cornworthy. It's the only church in the village. We're very C of E around here. Church of England, I mean," she added for benefit of us outsiders.

"We'll do our best," I said, noticing that Meredith was warming to Big Mike as easily as any crusty old general at SHAEF. "But now we should see Lady Pemberton and pay our respects. Is she in her sitting room?"

"Yes, go on up," Meredith said. "The poor dear is exhausted, so please don't tire her out. I think the events of the past few days have had their effect on her." She wished us well and returned to her list of US Army rations.

Upstairs, we knocked on Great Aunt Sylvia's sitting-room door. She beckoned us in with a weak voice, and we found her sitting in an overstuffed armchair by the window, a blanket on her lap. She did look tired, and quite pale as well.

"Ah, visitors," she said, her eyes still holding a twinkle of life. "How nice. Baron Kazimierz, Captain Boyle, who do you have with you?"

"Sergeant Michael Miecznikowski, Lady Pemberton," Big Mike said, giving her a bow that wouldn't have been out of place at a society shindig. "I'm afraid I will be taking advantage of your hospitality for a few days. Official business; I hope you don't mind."

"What exactly is your business, young man?"

"Keeping these two officers out of trouble. It's a full-time job, Lady Pemberton."

"So I imagine, Sergeant. What did you say your name was again?" She squinted, as if she was having trouble seeing.

"Don't even try, ma'am. I answer to Sarge or Big Mike, which is what General Eisenhower himself calls me."

"Big Mike," Great Aunt Sylvia said. "If ever a name fit the man, yours does. You Americans always seem so large in comparison to our English boys. Thin and pasty, many of them, while you are so fit and tanned. Even our soldiers often look puny in comparison. Boys of eighteen have been living with rationing since they were thirteen years old, raised without proper foods. There are young children in the village who have never seen an orange. Small wonder that our servicemen are often engulfed by their uniforms." She waved a hand across her face as if banishing the image from her mind. "But my manners—please, sit down, and tell me what happened so early this morning."

"We only have a few minutes," I said, sitting on a couch next to Kaz while Big Mike tested the limits of a chair across from Lady Pemberton. "We're looking for survivors from a ship that was torpedoed out in Lyme Bay. Some senior officers haven't been accounted for yet."

"We hope they've been picked up by one of the rescue vessels," Kaz said, which didn't sound too much like a lie.

"I think Crawford went out in his boat," she said. "I seem to recall seeing him from my window, bicycling out shortly after you left. That was today, wasn't it? I get up before the cock crows these days, and I think I watched all of you leave ... Yes, this morning; it must have been. You'll have to excuse my memory. This isn't one of my better days."

"Crawford didn't mention going out," I said, watching Great Aunt Sylvia furrow her brow, worrying as she tried to remember the early morning events.

"Apparently he heard from some relative who saw the explosion. He thought it was close enough in that he might find men still alive in the water. But the navy turned him away, saying it was restricted. From what Crawford reports, they have enough boats out and about."

"Good of him to try," Kaz said.

"Indeed," Great Aunt Sylvia said, stifling a yawn. "I mustn't keep you gentlemen from your duties. It was very nice to meet you, Big Mike. Good luck to you." Her eyelids fluttered, and she seemed about to nod off to sleep. She managed a wave before her hand dropped limply in her lap.

"Nice lady," Big Mike said as we walked downstairs.

"She's a firecracker," I said, pointing to her portrait on the staircase. "That's her."

"Geez, she was a looker," Big Mike said.

"She did seem tired, and a touch confused." Kaz said. "Usually she's quite energetic and clearheaded."

"She *is* ninety," I said. "We all have our bad days."

We picked up our ham sandwiches and went off on our search for men who would never see ninety. As we drove out on the gravel drive, I spotted Helen on a path coming out of the woods from the family cemetery. Her head was down and her arms folded tight against her breast, quick steps taking her closer to Ashcroft until she stopped and looked up at the house from the driveway. Her body was rigid except for the convulsions of her shoulders. Sobbing for her dear departed father? Or afraid of the future?

CHAPTER TWENTY-FIVE

"CONSTABLE TOM QUICK," I said, introducing Big Mike outside the local police station, a small house on the outskirts of North Cornworthy. Tom had been waiting for us, helmet and rifle in hand.

"It must be important," Tom said. "Inspector Grange sent a bicycle messenger from Dartmouth to tell me to wait for you."

"It is," I said. "Have you heard any news?" I wanted to see how far word might have spread.

"Nothing to warrant two jeeps and the biggest sergeant in the US Army," he said.

"Apparently a ship was torpedoed out in Lyme Bay last night," I said, sticking as close to the truth as I could. "We have to determine if nine specific officers are alive or among the dead."

"That'll be difficult if they're at the bottom of the Channel," Quick said. "What's so special about these blokes?"

"Who knows?" Big Mike said. "Probably all politics. We just follow orders. It was the same thing back in Detroit. I was a sergeant then too, only in blue." Big Mike pulled out his gold Detroit PD shield, which he carried like a good luck charm, his link to another life.

"Our squadron leader didn't explain much besides target, altitude, and airspeed, so I know about following orders," Quick said, inspecting the badge. "All right, so how do we handle it?"

"We'll split up," I said, unfolding a map on the hood of the jeep. "Colonel Harding gave us a list of Casualty Clearing Stations.

Morgues, really, but we don't want to let on how great the loss of life might be."

"How bad is it?" Quick asked.

"They fear up to a hundred," Kaz said, shooting me a quick glance. One lie was as good as another.

"There are clearing stations on the coast near Brixham, Stoke Fleming, Slapton Sands, and at the Start Point Lighthouse," I said, pointing to the arc of coastline in front of Lyme Bay. "Tom, you and Kaz will start with Stoke Fleming and work your way south to Start Point. Big Mike and I are going to get a boat to take us out into the bay. I want to see the operation to recover bodies first hand. If the navy is putting in a major effort, our chances will be better. If not, then I doubt we can account for all nine."

"What about Brixham?" Kaz asked.

"If Big Mike and I have time after we get back from Lyme Bay, we'll head up there. We have a list of the men we're looking for and copies of our orders from General Eisenhower," I said, handing a file to Quick.

"Ike himself?" Quick said, a look of amazement on his face.

"Yep," I said. "And this all has to be kept as quiet as possible. Everyone's nervous enough with the invasion coming up. The general doesn't want people panicking about German ships right off the coast."

"Makes sense," Quick said, nodding as he studied the list. "Odd, though. These aren't all senior officers. Four lieutenants, two captains, a major, one colonel, and even a sergeant. No offense, Big Mike, but what's so important about them? I expected a few generals, at least."

"Ours is not to reason why," Kaz said. It was the kind of truism instantly recognized by any cop or soldier on the low end of the pecking order, and it did the trick. Quick murmured his agreement while reviewing the list and scanning the rest of the paperwork.

"With orders like these, we could detail a regiment to take care of the search and have a few pints while they get on with it," Quick said with a grin, to show he was joking. But he was right. We could probably wave these around and walk off with the army payroll before anyone questioned us.

"Tempting," I said. "And the pints will be on me, if and when we find them. We'll rendezvous at Greenway House and report to Colonel Harding at nineteen hundred."

"Seven o'clock, Billy," Big Mike said. "Speak English, willya?" Civilians in uniform—that accounted for most of us over here, as I'd explained to Lady Pemberton a few days before.

I asked Big Mike to drive because my leg was stiff and my healing cuts and scrapes itched like crazy. We followed Kaz and Quick until they turned off for Stoke Fleming and then we headed into Dartmouth. As we drew closer to the harbor, the American MPs and British sailors standing guard were a bit thicker on the ground than they'd been before. Ambulances sat parked along the quay, drivers half asleep or smoking, killing time until the brass decided there would be no more survivors brought in from the Channel. Other than that, it could have been any day at war along the English coast: men, grey ships, the smell of oil and salt mingling with seaweed and garbage.

Our orders got us onboard the *USS Bayfield* pronto. An ensign named Weber escorted us to the captain's quarters. He looked about fifteen years old. His khakis were pressed and his tie knotted perfectly. The brass on his cap gleamed, and I figured he must be an eager beaver at the ensign business. We passed an array of twenty- and forty-millimeter guns, and I saw bigger five-inch cannon forward and aft. "You've got a lot of hardware for a transport," I said.

"We're an Attack Transport, Captain," Ensign Weber said. "Admiral Moon's flagship, too. We're going to be in the thick of it, that's for sure." He grinned, the foolish smile of a kid who's eager for something he knows nothing about. As he knocked on the captain's door, it swung open, and Weber snapped to attention, his back arched and his eyes wide. A stoop-shouldered naval officer stalked past us, and from the flash of gold on his shoulder boards, I figured he must be Admiral Moon. He didn't seem aware that we were in the gangway, inches from him as he brushed by. The admiral had a strong face, with a nose and chin that looked like they could cut through oceans like a destroyer's bow. But he looked haggard—even more so than Uncle Ike. I caught a glimpse of where he'd missed shaving that morning, a patch of stubble along his cheek. How much of that was due to the Operation Tiger debacle, and how much from the pressure of carrying an entire army to the far shore?

"Enter," came a sharp voice from within the captain's quarters. Ensign Weber held the door and announced us to Captain Victor Spencer, US Coast Guard, commanding. It was all very formal. Spencer didn't look up from the paperwork on his desk. The wood and brass fixtures all sparkled, a testimony to the navy's affinity for busywork.

"Tell the kid to beat it," I said. With men adrift in the Channel, I had no patience for spit and polish.

"Who the hell are you, and what are you doing on my ship?" Spencer said, his words echoing off the steel bulkheads. He had a booming voice, the kind you get when no one except an admiral can tell you what to do, and even he has to be nice, since it's your ship.

"Captain Boyle," I said, answering his first question as I handed him my orders. Then, in answer to the second: "And whatever the hell I want." I watched him read, the fury on his face turning to irritation as his eyes darted back and forth, taking in the name of his Supreme Commander.

"Dismissed, Ensign," Captain Spencer said, and Weber did an about-face that almost spun him off his feet.

"I need a boat to take us out to Lyme Bay, where the transports went down," I said. "Ideally with someone who knows the tides and currents."

"This is a United States Navy vessel, Captain Boyle," Spencer said, his lips compressed as if holding back an order to bring out the cat-o'-nine-tails. "Manned by Navy and Coast Guard personnel. We have a nodding acquaintance with the sea. And I will get you out there and off the *Bayfield* as fast as possible." He bellowed for Weber, who must have been gripping the door handle, he was in so fast. "Ensign Weber, take these men to Lieutenant Raffel." Then, turning his eyes on me, he said, "Raffel can take you out on the PA 12-88. It's already in the water, so you can leave as soon as possible."

"Aye aye, Captain," I said, and followed Weber. Sometimes I wise off too much, I know. But the senior brass—most of them—rub me the wrong way. When a mere captain has the authority of the Supreme

Commander, Allied Expeditionary Force behind him, it's hard to resist letting the shit roll in the opposite direction once in a while.

"What about this lieutenant?" I asked Weber. "Does he know the local waters?"

"Sure, he has a little sailboat he picked up. Goes out when he has time and zips around the bay. He's got a good ship and crew. What's this all about, Captain Boyle?"

"Sorry, kid. Need to know."

"Yeah, and I don't need to know," Weber said. "Same old story." And here I thought it was our exclusive little joke. He led us down a gangplank running alongside the ship. Bobbing in the water, tied to the *Bayfield*, was a small craft, sort of a cross between a Higgins boat and a speedboat that had aspirations to grow up and be a PT boat one day. Winches were lowering other landing craft into the water from the decks where they were stored.

"What is that, exactly?" I asked, pointing to the boat riding up and down on the swells, dwarfed by the five-hundred-foot *Bayfield*.

"Landing Craft Support, Small," Weber said as he led us onto the vessel. And the accent was on small. "It's a rocket boat. See those launchers on either side? They can fire twenty-four rockets each."

"That's what we saw firing at Slapton Sands," I said. "Pretty impressive. I didn't realize the boats were so tiny."

"They pack a lot of punch for their size," Weber said proudly as the crew looked us over.

"Lieutenant Keith Raffel," a guy in rumpled khakis said, holding out his hand. I introduced myself and Big Mike, and Weber gave him the word from Captain Spencer that he was to take us out into Lyme Bay. Raffel was tall and gangly, his face tanned from the days on his sailboat or the open bridge of this odd little craft. "We were just about to head out and shake down our new engine," he said. "Glad to have you aboard."

"You heard about the attack on the convoy last night?" I asked.

"Sure, everyone has. We were told mum's the word."

"Still is, but I want to see how the rescue operation is going out there," I said.

"Recovery is more like it," Raffel said. "But sure, we'll take you out. Can I ask why?"

"We're assisting the army investigation," Big Mike said. "Orders from SHAEF." Raffel shrugged, not all that interested in why the army was investigating a navy catastrophe. He probably knew he had no need to know.

"Okay, we're almost ready to shove off," Raffel said, turning to one of his crew. "Yogi, get these men some lifejackets, willya?"

"Sure, Skipper," a young seaman said, coming up from belowdecks. "All we got are lifebelts. You guys know how these work?"

"Yogi?" I said, taking the lifebelt from him. He was stocky and dark, with a ready smile and sharp eyes. "What kind of name is that? You look Italian, maybe."

"I am," he said. "Gunner's Mate Lawrence Berra, but they call me Yogi."

"Why?" Big Mike asked, taking his lifebelt and trying to cinch it around his waist.

"No, no, that ain't right," Yogi said. "Not around the waist. You put it around your chest, right up under your armpits. Then if you gotta go in the water, you inflate it with these CO_2 cartridges, here. See? If you wear this around your waist, you end up head over heels in the water, which don't work so good as far as breathing goes."

"Okay, got it," I said as I tightened the belt as high as I could. Big Mike managed to get his on, extending it as far as it would stretch. "But what's with the name?"

"I played some baseball with the Norfolk Tars in the Piedmont league right before I was drafted," he said. "I used to sit on the field cross-legged, you know? Like those guys in India? So they started calling me Yogi. A guy from the league was in boot camp with me, so the name followed me into the navy."

"Okay, Yogi," I said. "You been on this rocket boat long?"

"Hang on," Yogi said, as the skipper eased her away from the *Bayfield* and gave her some throttle. "Yeah, I volunteered back in basic. They asked if any guys wanted to get into the rocket boats, and I was readin' a Buck Rogers comic book at the time. I guess I thought it was going to be something like that, you know? But here we are, on dry ground, except it's water. I was kinda disappointed, but I don't mind. The future just ain't what it used to be, you know?"

"But . . ." Big Mike began, and then shook his head, thinking better of it.

"So how do these work, Yogi?" I asked, patting the rocket-launcher tubes as we cleared the harbor.

"Well, you don't have to worry, they ain't loaded," Yogi said. "But when they are, we got twenty-four rockets on each side. All forty-eight go off at once when we get three hundred yards from the beach. They set off mines, blow barbed wire, and generally scare the hell out of the Krauts. Then we got twin fifty-caliber machine guns and two thirty-millimeter cannon, to hit machine-gun nests, or whatever. We go in before the infantry lands, right up front."

"That's why the boat is armored," Big Mike said. The sloping front of the bridge was covered in steel plate, with thin vision slits.

"Yep," Yogi said. "Gettin' killed would make our job a lot harder." There was no arguing with that.

The skipper picked up speed as we got out into the Channel. There wasn't much room aboard with the crew of seven. The boat was maybe thirty feet long, and with the rocket launchers and all that armament, there wasn't much space for sightseers. Big Mike and I hung on to the gunwale as we began to bounce over the chop in the grey waters, leaving the shore behind us. The crew manned their weapons, keeping eyes peeled for the Luftwaffe. The wind whipped us, salt spray feeling like sand against our faces.

After five minutes running at full throttle, Raffel eased up and checked with his Machinist's Mate. The new engine was holding up fine. We proceeded at a slightly slower pace, but fast enough that we still had to hold on as we crested each wave and drove on to the next.

"Port bow," one of the gunners yelled, and Raffel eased the boat into a turn. There were two Royal Navy corvettes about half a mile out, close in to each other. As we came nearer, I could make out nets in the water, as if they were after fish. But the nets weren't filled with fish. There were bodies caught up in the netting, most with packs on their backs and many with rifles still slung over their shoulders. It was a gruesome tangle of the drowned and the devastated, some missing limbs, protruding bones stark white amidst the soaked khaki green.

"Keep going," I said. Raffel turned the boat away, his engine muffled as if the sound might disturb the dead. "What I'm looking for is where the tides might bring the bodies. What do you think?"

"Tide's coming in along the southwest coast," Raffel said. "So this is about right. They would have drifted in from the site of the attack, which is about twelve miles out."

"Okay, let's head along the line the tide would take them," I said. I turned, noticing Big Mike's eyes still fixed on the men in the nets, even as our boat picked up speed and left them behind. I hoped we wouldn't run into any more of that.

We spotted other small craft moving slowly, looking for bodies, some close to shore, maybe watching for corpses on the beach. Others were farther out, and I wondered whether there was a chance of finding a survivor in a raft or on a piece of wreckage. And whether the Germans might come looking too. An hour passed, maybe more. It was like a day out fishing, when you head to where the other boats are in hopes of a good catch, but they disperse before you get there. I was about to suggest we head back when Raffel pointed ahead of us, beckoning me to come up on the bridge.

"Look," he said, his hand outstretched to one o'clock off the starboard bow. "What's that?"

"A debris field?" I guessed. He looked through his binoculars as I tried to focus on what lay ahead. Small specks floated on the water, maybe a hundred or more, and I couldn't make heads or tails of what I was seeing.

"Oh my God," Raffel said, handing me the binoculars. As soon as they came into focus, I saw. Boots. Toes and heels floating along, the tide taking them home. I counted, giving up when I hit fifty, and there were more coming in on the current.

Raffel eased up on the throttle as we drew close, and a crewman reached out with a gaff and pulled a body in. GI boots clunked against the hull as he tried to right the dead weight. The guy had his full pack on, and had put his lifebelt around his waist. With all the top-heavy weight, the lifebelt had turned him upside down as soon as he inflated it with the CO_2. It was the same with all of them. They'd gone into the water with all their gear on, even helmets. With field packs on, there'd been no room to put on the lifebelts properly, even if they'd known how to. If Yogi hadn't told me, I would have put mine around my waist, no questions asked. And I wasn't wearing a helmet and a full pack, with an M1 and ammo belt slung over my shoulder. These guys hadn't stood a chance.

"What do we do, Skipper?" the crewman asked as he pushed the body away from the boat. There were simply too many for us. It was too overwhelming, too awful, too unbelievable.

"We call it in," Raffel said. "And stay on station until they get here." He got on the radio and requested assistance. He cut the engine and we waited, drifting with the tide, bodies keeping pace with us as the Channel pulled them in, ever closer to the shore, a pathetic parade of the dead. The rest was silence.

CHAPTER TWENTY-SIX

IT WAS DARK by the time we made it to Greenway House, well past seven o'clock. Raffel had stayed with the bodies, like a shepherd with his wayward sheep, until a destroyer escort and a tug from Dartmouth had relieved him. We left as they lowered nets, searchlights playing over the grisly scene. The GIs must have gone in the water together off one of the stricken LSTs. In the dark, with machine guns firing and explosions all around, they must have thought it was safest to jump overboard with a lifebelt on. But the water was cold, and the shock was probably instantaneous and disorienting as the inflated belts pushed them underwater. Cold, shock, panic, fear, death. A quick death, I prayed. It had been a slow ride back to Dartmouth as the crew played searchlights on the water, looking for more bodies, dreading finding them.

The guard at the door told us Harding was back in the kitchen with a Polish officer and a bobby. As we walked through the house, I kept my eye out for Peter Wiley, but he wasn't to be seen. Nor was anyone else, for that matter; our footsteps echoed through empty halls. The flotilla must have put to sea. I followed the smell of coffee until I found the three of them seated at a long trestle table. It was a large room, white tiled and cheerful, brightly lit with a double stove of blue enamel. A nice place to have a meal, if the day had left me with an appetite.

"How'd you do?" Harding asked as we entered, tapping the ash from his cigarette and sipping his coffee.

"We didn't identify anyone yet," I said. "But I can report the navy is working hard at recovering bodies."

"They're using nets, like trawlers," Big Mike said, sitting himself down at the table. There was a plate of Spam sandwiches at the center, but he didn't make a move for them. Harding poured coffee for us both and set a bottle of Jameson Irish Whiskey on the table.

"We found maybe seventy or eighty GIs," I said. "All floating upside down." I poured equal parts coffee and whiskey for myself.

"Lifebelts worn improperly," Kaz said. "We have been hearing the same thing all day. No one instructed the soldiers on the LSTs how to use them, or what procedures to follow if torpedoed."

"No one expected it," Tom Quick said, his hands cupped around his coffee as he stared into it. "You never do."

"Expected what?" Big Mike said.

"To have to bail out. Jump into the darkness, whether it's over Germany or in the Channel. That's what happens to the other chaps, not you. It's what I always thought. I'm sure Freddie felt the same way before he bought it. Maybe some men know they're going to die, but I think we really can't imagine it until the last second. Those soldiers, going into the water with all that gear on. They didn't expect it." Tom's eyes didn't move from his cup. "It's worse than you're letting on, isn't it?" He shook his head. "No need to answer. I don't want to know the details." Silence settled over us as Harding gave a small shrug. No reason to deny what was plain as day.

"We did have some luck, if you can call it that," Kaz said. "We found the one noncommissioned officer at the first stop. His body, that is. Sergeant Frank Thompson. Which makes it easier, since we don't have to search through all the enlisted men."

"Anyone else?" I asked.

"Yes, a Major Ernest Anderson," Kaz said, checking his clipboard. "That leaves seven."

"Four lieutenants, two captains, and one colonel," Harding said. "They'll probably be bringing in bodies all night. Make the rounds first thing and report back here." He reached for a sandwich and bit into it, chewing mechanically as he stared at the list of names. Big

Mike seemed to finally take notice of the food and joined in, a bit more enthusiastically.

"Better than bully beef," Tom said, taking a healthy bite and pouring himself another whiskey. "Hardly edible, but better." We all laughed, not that it was so funny, but because we were alive and could. We ate and drank. I didn't drink so much that I couldn't drive, only enough to take the edge off the day. Turned out it was a damned sharp edge that didn't dull easily with fortified coffee.

"When you see him," Harding finally said, forgoing coffee for straight whiskey, "tell Peter Wiley to get his butt back here. He wasn't missed today with all the commotion, but he's AWOL at this point."

"I heard he'd left Ashcroft," I said, turning to Kaz. "Yesterday, right?"

"Yes. Early in the morning. He left an unfinished painting, so perhaps he returned to Ashcroft while we were all busy today, thinking he would not be noticed."

"Maybe he's snuck back in already," I said. "Let's check his quarters before we hit the road."

Harding showed us Wiley's room upstairs. It had a fine view across the lawns and down to the River Dart. The bed was made, and there was no sign of the bag and paints Wiley had brought to Ashcroft.

"His office?" I said to Harding.

"No, I checked. It's off limits for security reasons. But I saw nothing missing or unusual. Look around back at Ashcroft. Maybe he wanted to finish that painting. These Coasties are liable to let things slide if a guy's doing his job. Wiley usually works day and night, so the captain may have turned a blind eye."

"They're all out?" I asked.

"More maneuvers and practice landings," Harding said. "One disaster doesn't stop the war."

"If it did, the war would have been over long ago," Tom Quick said. "Let's go." He tapped his hand repeatedly against his leg as we walked outside.

"Your constable pal seems kinda jumpy," Big Mike said on the ride back. He was driving slowly, the only illumination seeping out of the slit in the taped headlights. Blackout driving was dangerous, especially for pedestrians.

"He is," I said. "He did thirty missions in a Lancaster."

"That would make God Almighty jumpy," Big Mike said. I filled him in on what Tom Quick had been through, losing his family, his friend, and very nearly his grip on reality.

"He used to be a cop, too," I said, after reviewing what had happened at the racetrack.

"Is that why he's one of those Reserve guys? They don't trust him back on the force?"

"Inspector Grange trusts him enough to give him that job," I said. "But he might not be able to swing the real thing once the war's over. Sometimes he can drift off. Lose himself when things get difficult."

"Plenty of times I wish I could do that," Big Mike said. "He seems like a decent guy. Hope he's going to be okay. But it's gotta be hard, losing your wife and kids and then going out to bomb other women and children. What's the difference, you gotta ask yourself? Some days I wonder how any of us will get through this war with our heads screwed on straight." He went a little faster over the bridge at Totnes, the moonlight reflecting off the moving water, running high; the tide must have been coming in. Less than a week and I was already a nautical expert. Big Mike slowed as a trio of GIs staggered across the road, their linked arms the only thing keeping them vertical.

"Must be past closing time. Turn left here," I said, pointing to a narrow country lane that led to the village of Bow, where Bow Creek got its name. Or the other way around. Tree branches shrouded the road, cutting off what light the moon gave.

"What's up with this Lieutenant Wiley you guys are talking about?" Big Mike asked as he ducked a particularly low hanging limb.

"Navy. Some kind of map-maker, from the little he says about his work. Harding knows, but of course he won't tell. He showed up at Ashcroft House, asking to visit and set up his easel since his mother had worked there before she went to America." I told Big Mike about Sir Rupert's request and the few facts I'd had time to ferret out.

"So what are you going to do now that the old guy's dead?" Big Mike asked.

"I still have to look into it," I said. "What if Wiley stands to inherit the place?"

"He won't be very popular, that's for sure," he said. "From the little I've seen, that dame Meredith likes running the show. Her old man's bastard son might be in for a rough welcome."

Big Mike was right about that. An unexpected relation from the wrong side of the sheets would be the last person Sir Rupert's daughters would want showing up at the funeral. And I had an uneasy feeling about Sir Rupert's hasty visit to his solicitor the day before he died. If there were a legal document acknowledging Peter Wiley as his illegitimate son, it would throw a monkey wrench into the works for all concerned. But had Sir Rupert actually changed his will? Maybe, or perhaps there was other family business he rushed off to see his solicitor about hours before he died.

Whatever he'd done, it was time I had a talk with Peter Wiley. The more I mulled it over, the surer I was that he deserved to know the truth, or at least what Sir Rupert had suspected the truth to be. Maybe he wouldn't care about an inheritance.

We pulled into the Ashcroft House drive, with Kaz not far behind after he dropped Constable Quick off at his lodgings. I looked at the stone house on the hill, stars twinkling above the darkened structure. Who in their right mind would walk away from a piece of this action? I needed to talk to Wiley.

Inside, the wireless was on in the library, and we stopped in to see who was still up. Edgar and Crawford sat side by side, their heads bent close in hushed conversation. As Big Mike and I entered the room, they broke apart, relaxing back in their seats as if they were intent on listening to the symphony.

"Good evening," I said. "Crawford, this is Sergeant Mike Miecznikowski. I don't think you were introduced earlier."

"Big Mike to my friends," he said, extending his hand to Crawford.

"I don't have Yank friends," Crawford said, ignoring the proffered handshake.

"Or manners," Big Mike said. He moved in even closer, his big mitt still outstretched.

"Oh, all right," Crawford said, standing up and taking Big Mike's hand, then sitting down again, shaking his head as if it had been a mere misunderstanding. "Been a long day, nothing personal meant by it. Sounds like the American navy took a thrashing last night. How'd you get on looking for those fellas?"

"Pretty well," I said, not interested in going into details. "And from what I heard, it was the Royal Navy that had escort duties, by the way."

"Well, no excuse for letting the Jerries in," Crawford said. "I didn't mean to blame anyone, you know. I only heard from my cousin about American ships being hit. He saw the sky light up all the way from his battery at Salcombe."

"Drink?" Edgar asked, always knowing the right thing to say. We accepted a nightcap, settling into the comfortable chairs by the radio.

"Has Peter Wiley come back, by any chance?" I asked.

"I haven't seen him," Edgar said. "Have you, Crawford?"

"No. Haven't laid eyes on him since he left. Or rather, the day before, since he left quite early. Are you looking to find him, Captain Boyle?"

"No," I said. "I thought he might come back to finish that painting."

"That might not be possible," Edgar said. "Meredith took a dislike to the young man. Now that Sir Rupert's gone, I doubt he'd be welcomed back. His mother was a servant, after all."

"Nothing wrong with being in service," Crawford said, his eyes steady on Edgar.

"Admirable, I say," Edgar declared. "Whatever would we do without those who serve? No offense meant, Crawford."

I finished my drink before I said something I'd have to apologize for. This was a side of Edgar I hadn't seen before. Not quite the henpecked boozehound tonight. A bit more on the snarly side, with that cutting remark about servants. More Meredith than do-gooding Edgar. Big Mike and I left as Kaz came in, and as we ascended the stairs, all I could think about were the floating bodies and the bed waiting for me. A tiny part of my brain wondered what Crawford was doing at ease with Edgar in the library. That was for family and guests, not the help, especially under the new regime. But the thought drifted away, replaced by visions of boots I knew would haunt my dreams.

CHAPTER TWENTY-SEVEN

MEREDITH BUTTERED HER toast in a fury, crumbs flying from the knife's edge, encircling her plate with a dark halo to match her mood.

"I've never *heard* of such a thing," she said, not for the first time that morning. "A formal reading of the will, and not until after the funeral. The nerve of that solicitor!"

"Darling, Farnsworth is simply following instructions left by your father. Don't blame the old boy for doing his job," Edgar said, tossing sugar into his coffee.

"How like Father to make things difficult even after he's gone," Meredith said, snapping off a chunk of toast and sending more charred bits onto the white tablecloth. "I mean, really, how extraordinarily Victorian. No one has a reading of the will these days. The solicitor simply fetches it for one, I believe. Isn't that right?"

"I'm not certain myself," David said. "Never had much business with wills, except the one I had drawn up before I joined the service. Not that I had much to leave to anyone but Helen, but I thought it best to clarify things."

"Exactly my point," Meredith said. "A will should clarify things, not muddy the waters. Don't you agree, Baron Kazimierz?"

"All I know," Kaz said, gulping the last of his coffee, "is that we have our own muddy waters awaiting us. I am sure things will turn out for the best. I am sorry we cannot spend more time with you this morning." Big Mike looked pained by that pronouncement—he had only eaten a breakfast fit for a normal person and had undoubtedly been looking forward to more bacon.

"I hope you'll be back for dinner," David said.

"We can't say for sure. But if Peter Wiley should return," I said as I rose to leave, "could you please tell him to get back to base immediately? His leave is up." I thought it best not to mention it had been up for a while.

"Oh, he's probably off painting somewhere," David said. "Artists, you know, they lose all track of time."

"I was so sorry he hadn't time to finish the painting of Ashcroft," Helen said. "Perhaps he will return and complete it."

"Well, he won't be staying here if he does," Meredith said. "We won't be housing and feeding returning sons and daughters of every servant who has worked here. Not if I have anything to say on the subject." She glared at the others, inviting any opposition. The motion was carried by unanimous silence.

Kaz and Big Mike were already at the front door, ready for another morgue ride. I told them to head out. I had to pick up Tom Quick, but first I wanted to check in on Lady Pemberton. Or Great Aunt Sylvia, as I'd come to think of her. There was something endearing about the woman, and I'd been worried to find her confused and half asleep the day before, so I dashed upstairs for a quick check and to say good morning, hoping to find her ready to come down for breakfast.

It didn't work out that way. I knocked on her sitting-room door and pushed it open. She was slumped over in the same chair by the window she'd been in the day before, a broken cup on the floor, the saucer still on her lap, and tea stains on her robe. Her head was lolling to the side, dried saliva leaving a whitish trail down her chin.

"Lady Pemberton!" I said, taking her hand in mine and supporting her head. The hand was warm, and I saw a flutter of eyelashes. "It's me, Billy. Are you all right?"

"Oh . . . Captain Boyle . . . Billy, yes," she said, her voice distant and faint. "What happened?"

"You fell asleep," I said, taking the saucer and picking up the broken pieces of china. A tray with uneaten toast and a small tea pot sat on the side table. "You dropped your cup. I'll get Alice to come help you get cleaned up."

"Oh dear," she said. "Two cups, and I still can't stay awake. What's wrong with me?"

"You've had a shock, Lady Pemberton. Besides, you spilled most of this one. Don't worry about it. This must be a tough time for you."

"Rupert, you mean? Well, I would not have wished him harm, but I am hardly distraught, young man. Billy," she said, correcting herself and softening her tone. She smoothed her dressing gown and sat up straight, gathering her dignity about her. "I have lost my husband and my son, along with most of my friends, and this is my second major war. I don't count the Boer War, that wasn't a proper affair at all. So you see, it takes a fair bit to rattle this old lady."

"See, you're better already," I said, smiling at her quick recovery.

"Perhaps I needed that sleep," she admitted. "What time is it?"

"Almost eight," I said. "I'll fetch Alice to help you clean up."

"It's odd: I have always risen early, but now I can't seem to stay awake once daylight comes," she said, a distracted look in her eyes. "Nice girl, Alice. There was something I wanted to talk to you about, Billy, but for the life of me I cannot recall what it was. No matter, it will come to me." She rubbed her eyes, the strain of whatever was bothering her evident, no matter how chipper she tried to sound.

"We'll try to be back for dinner," I said. "I hope you'll feel better by then."

"I'm sure I will," she said. "Off you go now, Billy. It was kind of you to come and see me. I haven't had company all morning, except for Meredith bringing my tray. She's trying awfully hard, don't you think?"

"She's trying, that's for sure," I said, and left Great Aunt Sylvia chuckling. She seemed better this morning, if still a bit woozy. Whether she wanted to admit it or not, she was in her nineties, and that was bound to make anyone tired and confused. Me, I hadn't hit the quarter century mark, and I was bushed from everything that had happened over the past few days. I found Alice and asked her to tend to Lady Pemberton. Alice called her a "poor dear" and agreed she seemed more tired than ever.

I PICKED UP Tom Quick a short time later. He sat in the jeep with his helmet firmly strapped under his chin, his rifle held between his knees. His knuckles were white, and he didn't say a word.

"Tom, I could drop you off in Dartmouth if you'd rather not come along," I said.

"Rather not? Who does what they'd rather do these days, Billy?"

We drove toward Brixham, planning to start with the Casualty Clearing Station and work our way south until we met up with Kaz and Big Mike—with our list of names all checked off, I hoped. Outside of Stoke Gabriel there were columns of British Tommies on the road, marching four abreast at a pace that would have been tiring without the heavy packs and Lee-Enfield rifles. They stretched as far as I could see, so we backed up and Constable Quick navigated the back roads, taking us along the coast, skirting the main road and the traffic heading into Brixham.

"Looks like good farming country," I said. Cows were grazing in the green pastures. The aroma of spring manure spread on the fields filled the air, mingling with the tangy aroma of salt water from the Channel not far off. A promise of summer—and plenty, in its own way.

"They say Devon cream is the best in England," Quick said, his voice flat and his eyes scanning the fields and enclosures as if he had little interest in cream, cows, or anything in bloom. I was trying to think of what to say when a man jumped out into the lane, waving his arms. I hit the brakes, swerving in the rutty dirt to miss him.

"Down there! They're down there!" he shouted. A farmer, by the look of his work clothes. His face was flushed from exertion, his eyes wide at what he'd seen.

"Who?" Quick asked.

"Some of your lot," he said, pointing to me. "Eight, maybe ten, washed up on the beach. Dead."

"Show us," I said, turning to tell Tom to stay with the jeep. But he was already out. This was his turf, and he showed no hesitation.

"Down this path," the farmer said. "My dog Sally was barking her fool head off this morning. I thought maybe some of the sheep had got out and wandered down this way. I wish it had been the sheep, I tell you."

He took us down a path winding between small rises of pasture, sheep gathering along the wire fence as we passed. We descended to a small beach, a patch of sand and round, smooth boulders—a peaceful, secluded spot, except for the drowned bodies. Sally paced the waterline, barking into the salt air, knowing something was terribly wrong with these men. The waves nudged each corpse, every roller lifting an arm or a leg a few inches, then retreating, the lifeless limbs falling back into the wet sand as they departed. GIs, their life belts all worn the wrong way. Some had helmets strapped on, a few had M1 rifles slung over their backs, tangled in the full field packs they were burdened with. Their uniforms were sodden, laced with seaweed, their faces and hands a dull grey, matched only by their opaque lifeless eyes.

"Seven men," Quick said in a low voice. "Witnesses always exaggerate, although with good reason in this case. It must have been a shock."

"Not an easy thing to see," I said. "Let's get his name and get to the clearing station. They'll send a truck out." Quick got out his notebook and took down the information. Sally leaned against the farmer's leg, her tail brushing the sand as he absently scratched her ear.

"You're not going to leave them like this, are you?" he asked, after giving Tom the details.

"Of course not, no," I said. "Let's pull them up and out of the water, Constable." We dragged each GI by his shoulders up from the water's edge and onto the dry sand. I took the three M1s and hoisted them over my shoulder. Quick checked the dogtags. There were no BIGOTs among them.

"We'll get a vehicle here as soon as possible," Quick said as we began to walk back to the road. "Can you stay with the bodies?"

"No disrespect intended," the farmer said, "but I've got cows to milk. I've no help now that the young men are all off serving, or dead. The wife helps, but it's more than she can handle. So no, I cannot stand watch over these poor lads. But it looks like Sally knows her duty."

He pointed to the beach. Sally had settled in next to the bodies, her chin resting on her paws, her eyes on the row of corpses. A cross between a baby's cry and an old lady's moan rose from her throat as she lifted her head to the sky. She turned once to look at her master, who gave an approving nod, then returned to her vigil.

"I feel bad for the dog," Tom said as we drove away. "She doesn't understand, only knows that something very bad has come into her world. And no one can ever explain it to her."

"I wish someone would explain it to me," I said. "How could this happen? Radio frequencies mixed up, not enough escort to protect the convoy, no instructions on how to use life belts, orders not to go back to pick up survivors. Things are very bad everywhere, Tom, and no one explains any of it." I envied the dog her oblivion.

We drove in silence to Brixham. The Casualty Clearing Station was located outside of town at the site of an old stone fort on the cliffs above the Channel. There were still a few ancient cannon from the last century jutting out of the embrasures, but they hadn't been ready for action since the Napoleonic Wars. A good location for secret work. The ramparts cut off the view, and there was only one road in, manned by MPs and a couple of constables for good measure. Tom gave the Brixham coppers the farmer's name, and they knew the spot. Knew Sally as well. One MP jogged off to give the report, and the other waved us in.

The old fort hadn't seen this much activity since Admiral Nelson sailed the seas. Inside was a long, flat parade ground, marred only by the ruins of a massive stone building. This army used canvas, not stone, and there was plenty of it. Two long tents were marked with the red cross, others with NO ADMITTANCE on hand-painted signs. The former was for the living, the latter was for us. We headed for the first of them, but two MPs intercepted us. One held his carbine at port arms while the other guy, sporting second lieutenant's bars, stood behind him.

"May I ask your business, sir?" the second louie said, in a tone that said *hit the road, bub*.

"Yeah, Lieutenant," I replied. "None of yours." I flashed my orders at him and watched him gulp as he read through them.

"No one is supposed to go in there, Captain," he said. "But this trumps whatever I've been told."

"We're looking to confirm the deaths of several officers. We'll check the dead. Is this everyone who's been brought in?" I waved at the tents.

"Yes, sir. We've been told to keep all the bodies here. They're going to start getting ripe pretty soon."

"Get used to the smell, Lieutenant. How many wounded do you have here?"

"About a hundred," he said. "We're supposed to keep them all here, too, even the serious cases. They even ordered us not to talk to them. One of the doctors said he was told to treat them as if he were a veterinarian. Meaning patch 'em up, but don't get friendly."

"Who gave those orders?" I asked.

"Dunno, sir. It was a bunch of officers come through here yesterday. They wore coats with no shoulder patches, but all of our brass gave them a wide berth."

"Smart of them," I said. "Now do the same, okay?" He did.

I untied the flap of the first tent. The odor of death was new—on the edge of truly putrid, but not there yet. The cold salt water might have slowed the process of decay, but there was no stopping it. I thanked my lucky stars they hadn't been put inside mattress covers yet. This made it easier to spot the ranks we were looking for.

"One colonel, two captains, and four lieutenants," I said to Quick. He had the list of names and descriptions out. The bodies were laid out in rows, close together. Helmets had been removed and packs piled up at their feet. No one had bothered to separate by rank. No officer's quarters for these men. We found a colonel, but he wasn't a match. Ditto for the lieutenants. As we walked between the rows, milky, glazed eyes stared at us. Their faces were clean, washed by the Channel waters; features calm, even serene—because the muscles relaxed at the time of death, not because their deaths had been peaceful. The most wide-eyed, horror-stricken grimace fades as the brain loses all control over nerve and muscle.

"They look peaceful," Quick said, noticing the look on their faces but not understanding it.

"Yeah," I said, seeing no reason to educate him in such matters. A country constable didn't see much death, not compared to a Boston cop. And all his killing had been done from twenty thousand feet, so how would he know? Better to let him think all the people he'd bombed had ended up with this tranquil appearance amidst the rubble he'd created. "Nothing here."

The next tent was different. It looked as if they'd put all the dismembered and torn bodies together. No one looked serene. A tangle of severed legs and arms was piled on one side, three heads sitting on top, helmets still on. Apparently no one had had the stomach to loosen the chin straps.

The bodies themselves were burned or torn apart by explosions or propeller screws. Packs and belts had been left on. They were probably the only things holding the flesh and bone together. I glanced at Tom, not wanting him to think I didn't trust him to handle it. He was pale, but he stood ramrod straight. As a matter of fact, he looked better than I felt. I tamped down my queasiness and started the search. I knelt and checked dog tags, skipping the enlisted men when I could find a sign of rank. Fortunately, even the headless bodies still had the chains tucked under their shirts.

"Lieutenant Winslow," I said. "Lieutenant Chapman." Tom shook his head no. "Here's a Lieutenant Smith. We have one of those, right?" Tom read the serial number. Wrong Smith. We worked our way through the maimed corpses, finally finding one match. Lieutenant Patrick Sullivan. The serial number was a match, which helped since his blond hair had been burned with the rest of him.

"Thank God we found one," Tom said as soon as we'd closed the flap behind us. "I'd hate to have gone through that for nothing."

The next two tents were better, if any pile of sodden dead men can be better than another. But no BIGOTs.

"That's it," I said. "Let's head down to the next station."

"Perhaps we should walk through the hospital tents," Tom suggested. "A badly injured man might have been rushed in before they started listing the names of the wounded."

"Might as well," I said. A long shot, but we were on the scene, so why not? We entered the first tent, and a white-smocked doctor tried to wave us off. I showed him our orders, which he didn't like one bit.

"We've been ordered to keep these men quarantined," he said, loosening his smock to better show off his major's gold oak-leaf insignia. "And I outrank you, Captain Boyle."

"General Eisenhower outranks everyone," I said. "Take it up with him, Major . . . ?"

"Major Clayton Dawes, surgeon with the Thirteenth Field Hospital. Look, I'm not interested in a pissing match, Captain. If these orders are legit, go right ahead. Please be quiet and don't upset anyone, okay?"

"Just how bad are the injuries here?"

"Everything from a broken arm to severe internal injuries and third-degree burns," he said, back on more comfortable territory. "I got pulled in because I was available. I normally do chest and heart surgeries, and there's nothing much in that line here. We're basically operating as an evacuation hospital. The walking wounded should be released as soon as possible, and the others sent on to the field hospital in Exeter."

"When's that going to happen?" I asked.

"Good question," the major said. "I think the brass is more worried about keeping this whole thing quiet and these boys in the dark than about medical necessity."

"I'm not going to argue the point," I said. "We're looking for anyone who might be unidentified. Unconscious, no identification, that sort of thing."

"There's only one man here like that," he said. "Over there, next to Lawson. Lawson's a sad case himself, but it's the man in the next bed I'm concerned about. Lawson insists it's his buddy from LST 507, but that's not possible."

"How do you know?" Tom asked as the major led us through the rows of beds, white enamel frames set on the dirt floor.

"The only ID we had was his life jacket. It had the name Miller and LST 531 stenciled on it," the doctor said. "Lawson was from the 507. They're both navy." He pointed to a bed where a still form was swathed in bandages. A portion of his face and one leg was all that was visible. The face was mottled purple and red, so swollen from bruising that it was unrecognizable. Across from him another sailor sat on his bed, feet on the ground. He had a cast encasing his upper arm and shoulder and a bandage wound around his head. He stared at the other patient, taking no notice of our arrival.

"How you doing, sailor?" I asked. He had sandy hair and thin features, and his forehead was furrowed in worry. He looked startled at my question.

"What's happened?"

"Don't you know, lad?" Tom said.

"No one's talked to us, not even the nurses. You're the first," he said.

"What do you remember?" I said.

"Something hit the ship. There was an explosion. Smoke, fire, yelling and screaming. It's all a blur."

"Do you know this man?" I said, kneeling at his side and pointing to the inert form on the bed opposite.

"Sure, that's Hal. He's my buddy. We been together since basic."

"What's your name, son?" Tom asked, sitting on the bed next to him.

"George Lawson. Machinist's Mate. Were we torpedoed?"

"You were," I said. "Was Hal with you?"

"Yeah. We were both getting some coffee when there was a blast amidships. I thought maybe we'd hit a mine. It sounded like the ship was breaking apart. We had our life vests on, since they'd sounded general quarters, but we thought it was part of the exercise." He continued to stare at the man he thought was Hal, but his eyes were focused on the memory burned into his mind that night. "The lights went out, and I was thrown against a bulkhead. I guess I dislocated my shoulder and got this cut. Blood was running into my eyes, and I couldn't see a thing. Hal got me up and guided me toward the deck.

We passed a hatch that led down onto the tank deck. Where the Shermans are, you know? All set to roll out over the ramp when we hit the beach. Hal opened it and flames blew out. It lasted a few seconds, then faded. We looked in, but it was no good. Fuel cans were exploding, and men were screaming. I saw one guy on fire, trying to climb the ladder and get out, but he just stopped and fell back. It was like what I'd always imagined Hell to be. A dark pit filled with flames." He stopped, slack-jawed. "Hal dogged the hatch. That's regulation, to keep the integrity of the ship. But it was like we were killing those guys." Lawson stopped, gulping in air as if he'd forgotten to breathe.

"You had to do it," I said. "And you couldn't have helped them."

"That's what I told Hal," Lawson said. "But he was crying. He kept saying he was sorry, and I didn't know if he meant for closing those guys in or because he was crying like a baby. I told him it didn't matter. But I knew it did."

"You made it up to the main deck?" I said.

"We must have, but I don't remember everything. Next thing I know, we're aft and guys are jumping off everywhere. The ship was listing, and the fires were spreading. We had twenty-two DUKWs— you know, those amphibious trucks—lashed on deck. All fueled up. They started to go one by one, huge fireballs shooting into the sky, ammo going off, the whole works." He looked beyond us, his eyes still seeing gouts of flames arcing across the night sky.

"What about lifeboats?" Tom asked.

"Some were lowered, but the davits were rusted on a lot of them. I remember one sergeant fired his M1 at the chain, and that did it. The boat fell into the water, but I think it landed on a few guys."

"What did you and Hal do?" I said, trying to keep him focused on his pal. Maybe this was him, but it looked doubtful.

"I tried to get Hal to jump, but he was scared. Said he couldn't swim, that he'd always been afraid of heights too, and it was a good distance to the water. But we had to go. The fire and the explosions were getting closer. I told him the ship was sinking, which was good news since we wouldn't have so far to fall, you know? Making a joke about it. But it didn't work. I dragged him to the railing but he grabbed on with both hands and wouldn't let go. He begged me to stay with him, even when I told him we'd both die right there. He was crying again, saying, 'Please doesn't leave me alone,' and I even tried slugging him, but nothing worked. Finally I said I was going over, and he had to follow me."

"Did he?" I asked.

"I didn't look back," Lawson said. "I jumped and must have hit my shoulder. The pain was something awful. I looked all around for Hal but couldn't see him. The water was cold, really cold, and my teeth were chattering. Then the whole ship blew. It was like the biggest fireworks display you ever saw. I hope Hal saw it, it was really something."

"How long were you in the water?" Tom asked.

"I don't know. I tried not to look at all the soldiers floating upside down. I don't know why no one told them how to use those life belts. And why did they go in with those heavy packs? It doesn't make any sense . . ." His voice trailed off as he tried to come to grips with the illogic and ineptitude of Operation Tiger. He stopped, head bent, and I wondered if he'd passed out.

"What happened next?" I prompted him.

"What? Oh yeah. I drifted for a while and finally found a wooden hatch with two other men on it. There wasn't room for me, but they let me hang on. I lost consciousness, I think, then all of a sudden I was being pulled aboard a small vessel. An English fishing boat, I think. There were a couple dozen guys they'd picked up, maybe more. There were nets and the crew was civilian, so I figured they'd seen the explosions and come to help. I asked everyone about Hal, but no one knew anything about him. Then I woke up here, right next to him. What luck, huh?"

"Yeah, sure," I said. "And you're lucky to be alive, Lawson, remember that. Now relax. The doctor said you'll all be transferred to a real hospital soon."

"Good," he said. "Hal too?"

"Of course, my boy," Tom said with a forced grin. "All of you."

"There was nothing else to say," I told Tom as we exited the tent.

"No," Tom Quick said. "He needed that lie, and we were just the people to give it to him."

CHAPTER TWENTY-EIGHT

WE WALKED IN silence to the jeep, the shadow of death and lies following us from the tents. Tom got in, adjusting his tin-pot helmet so it hid his eyes, or perhaps so he wouldn't have to look at me. I thought about driving him back to Inspector Grange but didn't bring it up. Tom had been right when he'd said no one got their druthers these days, so I started the jeep, ready to head out to our next grisly stop.

"Look," Tom said, pointing to a truck coming through the gate. "More bodies coming in?"

"Probably the GIs from the beach," I said. But I stopped the jeep and watched as the truck backed up to the tents—thankfully not the one for dismembered corpses. Three bodies came off and were man-handled none too gracefully into the tent by GIs wearing gloves and masks. "Let's take a look."

Inside the tent, the three new arrivals were laid out at the end of a row. Two GIs, a sergeant and a PFC. No packs, rifles, or life belts on those two. Maybe they went into the water dead, or drowned the old-fashioned way, right side up. The third man was navy, by the look of his khakis. He had on a US Navy life vest and wore lieutenant's bars. I didn't pay much attention to his face, since the dead had all started to look alike to me, but as I reached for his dog tags, I noticed the sandy-colored hair and the blue eyes, and a gasp escaped my throat.

It was Peter Wiley.

I stood up, shocked. It was someone I knew, a man who I'd seen alive a few days before. A boy, really. His slight frame and fine features looked out of place among the soldiers girded for combat with their heavy boots and field jackets. All Peter had were his summer khakis and low-quarter shoes. He must have been cold going into the water. He looked cold even now.

"That's Peter Wiley," I said.

"The lieutenant Colonel Harding was looking for?" Tom Quick said. "He's supposed to be at Greenway House by now. What's he doing here?"

"I'm not sure. He wanted to go on the exercise but couldn't get permission. Looks like he found his way onboard one of the LSTs."

"Worse luck for him," Tom said. "He should have stayed ashore. We'd best move on, we've still got names to cross off our list."

Then it hit me. Peter Wiley was a BIGOT. But he wasn't on the list. How did he get on an LST without authorization, especially given his top-secret status? You didn't simply stroll onto a ship heading off to a secret invasion exercise, with or without a top security clearance. Did Harding know about this? Doubtful, since he'd been adamant that Wiley stay ashore. I couldn't mention the BIGOT classification to Tom; even mentioning the name was forbidden. But I needed to work out what had happened here.

"Give me a minute," I said, kneeling at Wiley's side. Tom moved off, giving me privacy to pay my last respects. It was a cop's respect I gave him, checking his pockets for anything that might give me a clue as to what he was up to. Nothing. I unbuckled his life vest and looked for anything that might have been secreted inside. Again, nothing. Stenciling proclaimed the vest PROPERTY OF THE US NAVY, but that was it.

Nothing. Which was odd. A lot of guys didn't carry wallets, since they carried their IDs around their necks and Uncle Sam didn't care about driver's licenses. It was nothing but another thing to lose when you shipped out. But most usually carried cash, maybe a money clip, or a picture of a wife or sweetheart in their breast pocket. Peter Wiley had none of that. No wristwatch, ring, or even a pencil, which I wouldn't have been surprised to find on an artist.

I removed the bulky vest and laid it under his head. He was past caring, but it seemed wrong to let it drop to the ground. As I did so, my fingers felt a bump at the base of his skull. I turned his head, brushing aside the hair to reveal a sizeable bruise.

"What did you find?" Tom said, stepping closer.

"Looks like he hit his head at some point," I said. "It might have knocked him out."

"Might have killed him, too. He had a life jacket not one of those belts that turned fellows upside down. Would have been a mercy, since he wasn't found soon enough. Cold water will kill you sure as a bullet, but not as fast."

"Or maybe he went into the water unconscious," I said. "Or was hit by debris once he was in. Hard to tell."

"Impossible," Tom said. "And it hardly matters, does it? Sorry, but I didn't know the lad, so he's only another corpse now. I don't mean to sound heartless, but there are plenty of poor souls here we could cry over. We've a job to do, haven't we?"

"Yeah, we do. I need to have a word with Major Dawes before we go. Wait in the jeep if you want, I won't be long."

I found Dawes and waited while he finished checking a patient. As ordered, he didn't speak to the man, simply checked his wound and left a nurse to re-bandage him. I asked Dawes to look at Wiley's body, and we went to the tent.

"What am I looking for?" Dawes asked as we stood over the body.

"What killed him," I said. "There's a sizeable lump on the back of his head." He knelt and felt the skull, turning the neck each way.

"Without opening him up, I couldn't say for certain, but it doesn't seem to be a fatal wound. Could easily have knocked him out and left him with a concussion. But if there was bleeding into the brain, that would be deadly."

"Can you tell if he drowned?" I asked. "Water in the lungs?"

"It's not really definitive, unfortunately," Dawes said. "When a drowning victim first takes in water, the vocal cords can constrict and seal up the air tube. Ten percent of the time this seal holds until the heart stops. So water in the lungs tells us that the person was alive at the time of immersion, but the absence of it confirms nothing."

"Does the condition of the body tell you anything at all?" I asked.

"Why? What's so special about this man?" Dawes asked, not unreasonably, since we were surrounded by dozens of dead men.

"He's not supposed to be here," I said.

"No one was supposed to die out there," Dawes said. I didn't bother to explain, waiting for him to continue. "Rigor mortis hasn't set in yet, although the cold water can slow that process. Some of the boys who were brought in first are stiff already."

"I was told the temperature in the Channel waters was around forty-five degrees," I said.

"That would do it," Dawes said. "Here's something interesting." He had pulled one of Peter's eyelids fully open.

"What?"

"Do you see the line?" He pointed to the eyeball, and sure enough, there was a horizontal border between a clear area of cornea and a cloudy one. "Water keeps the eyeball glistening. When a body comes out of the water, the eyes are lifelike, but the cloudiness sets in with exposure to air."

"Everyone I've seen has cloudy eyes," I said.

"Not those two," Dawes said, pointing to the bodies that came in with Peter Wiley. I looked, and he was right. Their eyes were clear. "They'll start to cloud up soon, but that's how a drowning victim's eyes initially appear."

"Then what's with the line on Peter's eyes?" I asked, beginning to understand.

"I'd wager he died out of the water with his eyes partially open. The air dried out the exposed portion."

"What if he died from the blow to his head during the torpedo attack, and went into the water shortly after?"

"There probably wouldn't be enough time for the pupils to dry," Dawes said. "Even with the life vest on, his head would naturally fall forward into the water, and the action of the waves would keep his face and eyes soaked. But once the drying takes place, there's no reversing it."

"So how long was he dead before he went into the water?" I asked.

"Impossible to tell, really," Dawes said. "Depends upon conditions. Humidity, condition of the tear ducts, a whole host of variables that makes it difficult to say anything other than he likely did not go into the water alive. Perhaps he fell and died from the blow, or complications, some hours before the attack. I can't really say. Sorry."

"Can we get this body to a morgue and keep him in cold storage?" I asked. "Maybe you could perform an autopsy."

"Normally, yes," Dawes said. "But with the security precautions in place, I don't know. I've heard talk that all these bodies are going into a common grave very soon. What I can do is write up a report on what we've found, in case you need a statement. And I'll try to get him to the morgue at the field hospital."

"Good," I said. "I'm going to radio this in to my boss, see if he can do anything. You'll need to go over this with Constable Quick, too. It may involve the local police."

I sent Tom to be briefed by the doctor and went to the radio tent. I radioed a quick message to Harding, saying that Peter Wiley was among the dead, under suspicious circumstances, and we needed his body on ice. I gave Major Dawes as the contact and said he was writing up his findings.

"A mystery on top of a tragedy," Tom said, shaking his head as he got into the jeep. "What do we do now?"

"I've notified Harding," I said. "We should head to the next Casualty Clearing Station and try to wrap things up. Then we need to determine which LST Peter Wiley was on."

"When he wasn't supposed to be on one at all," Tom said. "Might be tricky, that."

"There has to be someone in charge of who was allowed on board," I said, "outside of the major units assigned to take part in Operation Tiger. Wiley was on his own. There has to be a list of observers, anyone who wasn't assigned to any major formation."

"Any idea why he wanted to go? He must have had a pressing reason if he disobeyed orders to do so."

"Perspective," I said. "When we talked about it, that's what he said.

But it was almost like he hadn't meant to say it out loud. He clammed up right after that."

"Maybe he meant a painter's perspective?" Tom suggested. "Or he could have been thinking about a different viewpoint on things. Some incident at Ashcroft House, perhaps, that he wanted to get away to think about."

"Could have been either," I said as we drove through the guard's station and left the ramparts behind, the old iron cannon zeroed in at our backs. "And speaking of artwork, where is his painting gear?"

"Right," Tom said. "It wasn't in his room at Greenway House. Perhaps you should check the bedroom he used at Ashcroft."

There was a lot to check up on at Ashcroft House, now that a potential heir had turned up dead. I was suddenly much more interested in attending Sir Rupert's funeral. Yesterday going was a courtesy. But tomorrow's burial would now be a duty.

CHAPTER TWENTY-NINE

THE SMALL STONES of Slapton Sands slid out from under my boots as breaking waves clawed at them, drawing the smooth, glistening pebbles back into the Channel with a rocky clatter. Two Higgins boats were making their way to shore, where idling trucks and bored GIs waited. Out in the Channel, vessels cut through the waves in all directions, the search for floaters still in full swing. The wind stung my face, the air cold and damp under darkening clouds.

We'd driven from Brixham and found no sign of Kaz and Big Mike here. Maybe their search was over and they'd headed back to Greenway House. If we didn't find them soon, I'd try to raise them on the radio again. For the moment, I was content to watch the boats come in as I thought about what to do next. It all depended on what Harding thought was more important: the dead BIGOT who wasn't supposed to be there, or a full body count of those who were.

"Look over there," Tom said, pointing to a pile of debris above the high-tide mark. Life belts, packs, and a few helmets lay in a heap. Evidence that bodies had recently been collected.

"I wonder if Big Mike and Kaz have been here already," I said.

"Maybe they went out on those Higgins boats," Tom said. "They'd be good for a slow search."

"Kaz? Never. He gets seasick, and he hates to admit it," I said, launching into my impression of Kaz's precise Polish-accented English. "*I do not like boats.*" We both laughed.

Until the Higgins boats hit the shingle, their engines revving, and their bow ramps dropped.

They were filled with the dead.

They hadn't been searching as much as collecting.

"Christ," Tom said, the curse hissing through clenched teeth. "Will it never end?"

No, not for a good long time, I thought, but I didn't say it. This pile of corpses was only a small down payment. When the Higgins boats went in under fire and the ramps went down, German machine gunners could have a field day, their deadly twenty-five-rounds-per-second MG-42s filling a single Higgins boat with enough hot lead to wipe out a platoon in the time it took to draw your last breath. It would look much like this, but with blood, not water, drenching the uniforms.

I shook the vision off. There was too much at stake for the D-Day planners to have left that to chance. Wherever they hit the beach, concrete emplacements and bunkers would have to have been obliterated by bombers, fighters, battleships, and rocket boats. We had the firepower, and there was no reason in the world not to use every shell, rocket, and bomb stashed in ammo dumps across southern England. I kept telling myself that, but I still had to look away, as if I were scanning the strand for Kaz and Big Mike, blinking against the wind. I could almost hear the MG-42, the machine gun the Germans gleefully called the Bonesaw. With good reason. It fired so fast that it was impossible to hear single bullets being fired. Some guys said the sound was like canvas being quickly ripped apart. All I knew was that it was a noise from the depths of Hell. But now, as I stood in front of corpses stacked three deep, there was only silence. Even the waves quieted, as if in deference to the dead. I felt dizzy and stepped back, fear rising in my gut as if the guns were here and it was happening right now. My face went hot, and I jumped when I felt a hand on me.

"Billy," Tom said, shaking my arm. He was looking at me with a worried expression, and I realized he'd called my name several times. His voice sounded like a distant echo, but I heard him. The wind returned, as did the *click clack* of the stones rolling in the water. "We should check these men now."

"Sure," I said, unsure of where all the sounds had gone. I thrust my trembling hand into a jacket pocket. I'd seen the Bonesaw at work in Italy. Some days I didn't think about it. Most nights I still dreamt about it. We walked closer to where sailors were carrying the dead off the Higgins boats to the waiting trucks. Men, Tom had called them. Respectful, but these were no longer men. They'd joined the ranks of the war dead, that long line of final sacrifice, before they'd even had a chance to storm that far shore.

"Read me the name, Billy," Tom said, clipboard in one hand as he placed the other on my shoulder. It struck me as funny that Tom Quick, a man so haunted by his own loss and the losses he'd inflicted on others, was comforting me, leading me by the hand like a wayward child. I grinned, then laughed, and kept laughing until I got it under control, my sleeve pressed against my mouth. The situation was so bizarre that no one even took notice, or they pretended not to, at any rate.

"Okay," I said, checking the dog tags of the lieutenant at my feet. "Greenberg, Phillip." Tom shook his head. Not one of ours. I shuffled sideways, kneeling on the wet stones, pulling chains from officers' necks. Finally we got a hit. Captain Roger Malcolm, from Pawtucket, Rhode Island. Almost a neighbor. Tom checked him off the list, the last of the officers from the landing craft. We followed the trucks as they drove off the strand once the bodies had all been loaded. Since this was a restricted area, there was no need to hide anything. The Casualty Clearing Station was off the road behind Slapton Ley, on a rise above the empty village of Torcross. The view was stunning, not that it mattered to most of the residents. The thatched roofs of Torcross were scattered on the hillside below us, beyond them the curve of the beach stretching out, the grey Channel on one side and the waters of Slapton Ley, rippled by the wind, on the other. Torcross held the only road off the landing area, and from here it was easy to see why they'd simulated an airborne drop behind the beach. If the enemy held that single road, everyone would be stuck in the landing area with nowhere to go but six feet under.

We turned our attention to the tents laid out in rows on the grassy field. Two long hospital tents faced three unmarked pyramidal tents, with a scattering of others beyond, probably a command post, judging by the antennas and jeeps, and a field kitchen, based on the woodsmoke and the odor of burnt Spam.

"Let's have another go," Tom said, then stopped as Big Mike and Kaz exited the tent nearest us.

"Billy, we've finished here," Kaz said, waving as he spotted us. "We found the colonel and a lieutenant. How did you fare?"

"A captain and two lieutenants," I said. "Well, three, actually. Peter Wiley is dead."

"How did *that* happen?" Kaz said.

"Not entirely certain," I said. "We found him with the bodies at Brixham."

"I thought Sam ordered him to stay behind," Big Mike said.

"He did," I said. "Harding was damn clear about that. I don't know how Peter managed it. I left a radio message for the colonel at Greenway House."

"Ask him right now," Big Mike said. "He's grabbing some coffee in the mess tent. He got here about an hour ago to see what we'd come up with." Thunder rumbled in the distance, and rain began to fall. To the northwest, I saw lightning crackle between thick grey clouds that were tumbling closer. A lot of the weather here rolled in from the northwest, swooping over the Channel before hitting France. I sent up a quick prayer to Saint Clare of Assisi, patron saint of good weather, to intercede when the invasion came, and to ease up on this bit of nasty weather while she was at it.

"What?" Harding nearly shouted when we sat down and told him about Peter Wiley. "That's impossible. He wouldn't make it on board without authorization." He slammed his coffee cup down hard enough for the hot joe to jump ship.

"Colonel," I said, casting my eyes around the mess tent to be sure no one could hear, "this whole exercise was screwed up six ways to Sunday. One guy getting on an LST by hook or by crook isn't that hard to imagine."

"You both saw the body?" he asked, still not wanting to believe it. "Drowned, like the others?"

Tom and I both shrugged. "The surgeon at the Brixham clearing station wrote up a statement about what he found. I asked him to keep Wiley's body secure, but he wasn't sure he had the clout to get that done. From his quick exam, it looked like Peter may have been killed before he went into the water."

"You mean when the LSTs were attacked?" Harding said.

"He can't say for certain. I asked him to get the body to the morgue at his hospital and take a closer look, do a full autopsy if he had to. Is that something you can make happen? Major Dawes said the bodies were going to be taken away soon. We've heard rumors they're going to be dumped in mass graves."

"I'll head there now and look up this Dawes. Between the two of us, we should be able to get the body released. But there's a lot of pressure to wrap this up and keep a tight lid on it, so I can't promise anything. This thing is being handled way above my pay grade. And there are no mass graves. Every man will get a decent burial."

"Could you ask Ike to intervene, just to make sure?" Big Mike said. "Otherwise we got no *corpus delecti*."

"No. He's too busy working on the real invasion. He put us in charge of finding these officers for security reasons, but other than that, he's focused on the real thing. It's up to us. What's the status on the missing men?" Harding asked, gulping the dregs of his coffee.

"We found all but one lieutenant and one captain," I said, going over our checklists.

"Okay," Harding said, tapping his fingers on the wooden table as he calculated how best to proceed. "Constable Quick, you and Big Mike continue the search. Go back to Start Point and see if any more bodies have been brought in."

"That's where we bagged the colonel," Big Mike said to Tom.

"Then work your way north. My guess is that by tomorrow all the bodies will have been accounted for, unless the fish or the Germans got to them. Boyle, you and Lieutenant Kazimierz go to Greenway House. Lieutenant James Siebert is the officer who was responsible for keeping the manifests for all observers. He went into the water, but he had all his papers in a waterproof bag. He got a little banged up, but he'll be back on duty tomorrow morning. See what light he can shed on how this happened." Rain splattered the canvas above us, a crash of thunder not much farther away.

"Tomorrow morning is the funeral of Sir Rupert Sutcliffe," I said. "Since everyone who spent time with Peter will be there, it might be worth our while to attend. Maybe he confided in one of them."

"Worth a shot," Harding said, giving us a curt nod. "But get to Siebert right after that. There's no telling what may happen to any evidence connected with this debacle." The rain became fiercer as wind gusts sent the tent flaps flying.

"Is the search going to proceed in this storm?" Kaz asked, a peal of thunder punctuating his sentence.

"It probably shouldn't," Harding said. "But then again, we may have to launch an invasion in weather not much better than this." A loud, sharp *crack* whipped through the air as a bolt of lightning hit a nearby tree, the wood cracking and crashing to the ground seconds later. Saint Clare must have been busy elsewhere.

Harding went off to the command tent to radio Brixham and tell Major Dawes he was on his way, while the four of us waited for the worst of the storm to pass. Big Mike resupplied himself with doughnuts, and Kaz went in search of a cup of decent tea, a foolish venture in a US Army mess tent. Tom Quick and I stood at the open flaps, watching the rain fall on the sodden field.

"It's a hard thing to see," Tom said. "Even if you're used to it."

"It is," I said. "I don't think you ever get used to it, though."

"You've been in combat," he said. A statement, not a question.

"North Africa. Sicily. Salerno. How can you tell?"

"A man unused to carnage will throw up at the sight of it," Tom said. "A man who has seen too much gets the shakes. And a man who tries to hide the fact stuffs his hands in his pockets."

"You don't miss much," I said.

"I'm a trained constable," he said. "Most days, all a village constable does is watch people. Little things tend to stand out. And I do know something about carnage. From a distance."

"Does that make it any easier?" I said, turning to face Tom. For some reason, I had to know.

"I've no idea," he said. "That's like asking a one-legged man if losing a leg is easier than losing an eye, or a hand. How can he know? All he's aware of is his own misery. What I do know is, it doesn't get any easier when you're confronted with more and more misery. It comes at you from every direction, no matter what you do. And it's likely to keep doing so until this war is over. God knows when that'll be."

"It could be soon," I said. "If the invasion goes well."

"Jerry isn't going to roll over once we get to France, you mark my words. It's going to be a long haul. Some of the chaps I served with are starting their second tour of thirty missions. Nowadays they give them a few months' rest with ground duty, then back for another go. Start the clock ticking all over again. Hard to fathom going through that twice."

"I don't know if I could ever do that," I said. "I was in a bomber, once. We were jumped by fighters over the Adriatic. That was enough time in the air for me."

"You can do anything once you've made your mind up about it. That's what I've found, for what it's worth. So go easy on yourself, Billy. You gave me a fright back there, laughing like a lunatic."

"Thanks, Tom," I said. "Looks like the rain's clearing up." We walked back to the jeep, and I flexed my fingers, working at not shoving my hands into my pockets. I still had a jittery sensation in my stomach, but the trembling was gone. Tom looked at ease, swinging his arms at his sides, whistling an unfamiliar tune. I worked to match his optimism, lunatic that I am.

CHAPTER THIRTY

"A SUCCESSFUL DAY, Captain Boyle?" Meredith inquired when we entered the library, where Edgar was busy manning the drinks tray. "It must have been dreadful being caught in that storm."

"Busy," I said. "Not to mention wet. How about you? It must be a difficult time, with the funeral to arrange and a houseful of guests."

"Quite. Which is why we are so glad to have the three of you, really. It provides a distraction and lets us think we are doing our part in some small way."

"Billy," Edgar said. "I daresay you could use some of this fine Scotch you brought us. Good for warming a man after that cold rain." He handed me a glass with an ample supply of Colonel Harding's whisky, and I didn't argue. We'd come in soaked to the bone, courtesy of a renewed downpour when we'd been in sight of Ashcroft House. They'd run hot baths for us, and Alice Withers had taken our uniforms to dry out and press as best she could.

Since water was rationed as well as food, a hot bath in England was not as commonplace as back in the States. Soap was tough to come by as well. The limit for water was supposed to be four inches. Many hotels had a line painted in the tub to mark the level. But Ashcroft House bent the rules for three soldiers in need of a decent soak, and I didn't complain. The regulation was unenforceable, but most people went along with it, even though it meant a decrease in cleanliness and an increase in bodily odors. A running gag among GIs was that the tents and Quonset hut enclosures for American troops were nick-named Spam Town after the prevailing odor, and everything outside the wire was Goat Town, for the same reason.

"You asked about Lieutenant Wiley this morning," Meredith said as Edgar continued to pour drinks. "I'm afraid he hasn't returned. Have you had word of him?"

"No, we have been too busy to check on Peter," Kaz said, sipping his drink and giving me a quick glance. We'd agreed not to say anything about finding Peter's body. I felt we might learn more if people weren't shocked at the news of his death. No one does like to speak ill of the dead, unless the deceased was a louse through and through, which did not sound like the Peter I had come to know.

"Perhaps I should return his painting to Greenway House," Meredith said, "if he does not possess the common courtesy to retrieve it himself."

"Meredith," Helen said, joining our circle. "He meant it as a gift. That would be rude."

"It's unfinished, dear," Meredith said. "Although nicely done, I must say. Baron Kazimierz, perhaps you would be so kind as to return the painting when you can. Your superior officer is based at Greenway House, is he not?"

"Indeed," Kaz said, keeping up the pretense of Peter ever finishing anything. "It would be my pleasure."

"Sorry I'm late," David said, entering the library behind Big Mike.

"Did you find anything?" Meredith asked.

"No," David said. "I went through his papers, as you did. No sign of a living relative. It appeared his cousin John had none as well. I telephoned the local constable, who said he was the last of the Sut-cliffes in that county. He died last year."

"Father and he were never close," Helen said. "I asked him about it once, and he said he had nothing in common with the man other than blood, but that might serve well enough if John had any children. I thought it rather odd."

"When was this?" Meredith asked, her eyebrows raised.

"A few months ago, I think," Helen said. Meredith furrowed her brow, thinking through the information as the rest of us tried not to notice.

"Your father never seemed interested in family members," David said. "Distant ones, I mean. Not you two." He laughed, to cover up the uncomfortable truth.

"Our fair ladies are quite enough themselves," Edgar said, rejoining the group and handing Big Mike a drink. "Don't you think?" The moment was forgotten in a well-timed toast to Meredith and Helen.

"How was Lady Pemberton today?" I asked.

"Still a bit down, poor dear," Helen said. "I hope she'll be back to her old self when things get back to normal. Although we don't quite know what that will be, do we?"

"Who knows?" Edgar said. "Perhaps Great Aunt Sylvia will inherit the lot and toss us all out on our ears, and we shall have to make a living shining boots for the Americans."

"Why that particular occupation?" Kaz asked.

"Oh, it's just something Crawford says now and again," Edgar said. "I pay him no mind, but it stuck in my head. Silly."

"We know his story," I said. "I might feel the same way if I were in his shoes. But do you feel comfortable employing a smuggler? We heard he was involved in bringing in contraband until he lost his boat."

"Captain," Meredith said with a sly grin, "you have to remember where you are. This is the southwest coast. This has been home to pirates, privateers, and smugglers for centuries. There are plenty of locals who never minded buying goods that had been smuggled in from France. No one likes paying excessive taxes, do they?"

"Think of your own experiment with Prohibition in the States," David offered. "How many people refused a drink because bootleggers had smuggled it in from Cuba or Canada?"

"No one in Detroit," Big Mike said. "The Purple Gang ran a pipeline under the Detroit River from a distillery in Windsor, Ontario. Went straight into a bottling plant downtown. There was a blind pig right across the street from police headquarters, above a bail bondsman's office. Free lunch and bootleg booze."

"A 'blind pig'?" Kaz asked, always interested in American slang.

"Yeah," Big Mike said. "A speakeasy."

"The Purple Gang," Helen said. "What a colorful name."

"They were colorful, all right, and dangerous too," Big Mike said.

"Smuggling has always gone on along this coast," David said. "Not by cutthroat gangs but for the most part by fishermen and anyone with a fast boat and a need for money. No one suffered except for the tax man."

"Which means you don't hold it against Crawford," I said.

"He was never convicted, mind you," Edgar noted. "But I should think the answer would be no in any case. Am I correct, dear?"

"As always," Meredith said. An answer open to interpretation.

AT DINNER I found myself next to Helen, who was next to her husband on his scarred side, smiling demurely. It must have been a relief for David, but I had to wonder, why the sudden change? Same for David himself, for that matter. First he couldn't wait to get back on active duty, then all of a sudden it didn't matter. Maybe a wife not shuddering every time she looked at you changed your outlook. Or did he know something about the inheritance?

Food was passed around, and I ate without tasting much. It occurred to me that since I'd arrived at Ashcroft House, *everything* had changed. David and Helen, not to mention Meredith becoming friendly and Edgar—even though he was still drinking at every opportunity—no longer sitting morosely in a corner. Sir Rupert was dead. Peter Wiley was dead. Lady Pemberton was confused. Not to mention Williams and Mrs. Dudley drinking the good booze late at night, although maybe they had a tradition of that going way back. Crawford was likely his usual self, which was none too agreeable, but consistent. Alice Withers? Still a pleasant young girl, far as I knew. She'd take the news of Peter's death hard. Who else would even care?

Lady Pemberton, I decided. She'd taken to Peter, and her mourning would be sincere. But should she be burdened with more sad news? Not that she'd cried a river over Sir Rupert's death, but a promising young lad like Peter was a double tragedy. Sudden death and a life cut short. And for what? *Perspective.* I wished I knew what he'd meant by that.

"I say, Captain, please pass the peas," Edgar said, loud enough to get my attention. I sent the bowl down the table, aware that I'd drifted off again. Occupational hazard. "Do you think young Peter will return and finish the painting?"

"I for one hope he doesn't," Meredith said, not giving me a chance to respond, which was just as well. "It's a bit much, you know, having some servant's offspring knock on your front door." She twirled her wineglass as she watched the others at the table.

"You have to understand our American friends, dear," Edgar said with a smile that was intended to soften the bluntness of Meredith's statement. "They are not as sensitive to these things as we are. I'm sure young Peter approached us in total innocence."

"Of course," David added. "And don't forget, it was Sir Rupert himself who invited him to stay."

"I'm sure you're right," Meredith said. "I didn't mean to sound high-handed about it."

I was pretty sure she did, and that she had her own suspicions about Peter's paternity. That would explain why she didn't want him back at Ashcroft House. Maybe she had more than suspicions. What was in that old letter from America she had clutched in her hand the night she argued with Sir Rupert? Would she tell me? I wonder where she kept it. A lot of women would stash something like that in their underwear drawer, figuring no one would go through their unmentionables. But Alice probably did the laundry and put things away, so that wasn't a good bet. Maybe a peak in Meredith's bedroom was in order. Not the best behavior for a houseguest, but I still felt an obligation to Sir Rupert, and until the reading of his will, it was still his house.

CHAPTER THIRTY-ONE

SMALL BRANCHES AND green leaves littered the cemetery, tokens of the previous day's storm. Sunlight glittered on dewdrops as pallbearers carried the coffin out of the church to the waiting grave. The Pemberton name was prominent on many gravestones; on others, it was barely legible after several centuries of wear and weather.

Attendance was sparse. Alice's father, Michael, was there, along with Evan from the pub and one older woman. Meredith and Helen walked with Lady Pemberton, each of them lending an arm for support. Edgar and David followed, then Williams, Crawford, Mrs. Dudley, and Alice. Kaz and I followed the small group out of the church. The sunshine was refreshing after the cold stone interior, still damp from the rains.

There had been no eulogy, no tears. The vicar had trotted out the usual stuff: the Lord's Prayer, a psalm, a droning hymn. Then finally the hired hands from the funeral parlor had carried the coffin to the cemetery. More prayers as the casket was lowered into the ground. Family members each took a handful of soil from the pile beside the grave and tossed it in, tiny stones making a harsh rattle as they bounced off burnished wood.

"We now commit the body of Sir Rupert Sutcliffe to the ground," the vicar intoned. "Earth to earth, ashes to ashes, dust to dust, in the sure and certain hope of the resurrection to eternal life."

I watched as the family departed. Meredith's steely eyes seemed satisfied with the dust-to-dust part, less so with any notions of her father's resurrection. The ladies got into an automobile with Crawford at the wheel. A horse cart sufficed for the help, and Kaz volunteered to go with them. A quick nod told me he planned to quiz them about Peter. It would likely be the only time he could talk to the three of them without drawing attention. I gave Edgar and David a ride back.

"I believe Sir Rupert's solicitor is coming tomorrow morning," Edgar said, leaning in from the backseat. "Meredith wanted him here today, but I thought that a bit rushed."

"That's for the best," David said with a wry smile. "No reason not to wait a barely decent interval."

His attitude was refreshing, but it made little difference to me. I was looking forward to chatting with the staff and family over whatever kind of feed they put on after a Church of England funeral. It wouldn't be Irish style, but I still counted on tongues being loosened and maybe at least one family secret being spilled before the day was out.

I knew that wasn't going to happen as soon as I spotted Big Mike. He'd left earlier to pick up Tom Quick and continue the search for the last two BIGOTs. But here he was, parked in front of Ashcroft House with a worried look on his face.

"What's wrong?" I asked, pulling him aside as the others filed into the house.

"Tom wasn't at the constable's house in North Cornworthy," Big Mike said. "Apparently a police car stopped by last night and Tom hitched a ride into Dartmouth. I called and spoke to Inspector Grange. He said you should come right away."

"Did he say anything else?"

"No. But it didn't sound good, Billy."

"Damn," I said. I went inside and found David, trying not to think about what might have happened.

"We've been called away," I said, catching him as the group filed into the sitting room. "Sorry to leave so suddenly. Please give my apologies to the family."

"Will you be back soon?" Meredith asked, turning when she heard me. "I hope it's nothing too terrible."

"I don't know," I said, which pretty much summed up the state of affairs.

"Good luck, Billy," David said, walking me to the door. "Let us know if we can help in any way. And if you find Peter, please do let us know. Meredith is actually concerned, for all her talk."

"Listen, David," I said as Big Mike sat at the wheel of the idling jeep. "We got a message from Inspector Grange in Dartmouth about Tom Quick. I don't know any details, but he told us to get right over there."

"Good God," David said. "I hope . . ."

"Yeah," I said. "Me too. I'll contact you as soon as I can."

"Perhaps I should come along," David said, worry creasing his brow. "If he's in a bad way, it might help."

"You should stay with your family," I said. "We might need you later, after we find out more." What I didn't say was that my gut told me Tom was not in one of his distant moods. No need for a police inspector to call about that. Big Mike and I got Kaz off the horse cart, still plodding its way back to the house, and filled him in on the little we knew.

"I hope Inspector Grange is merely overreacting," Kaz said, getting in the backseat of the jeep.

"Did you learn anything from the servants?" I asked a few minutes later as Big Mike sped down the narrow country lanes.

"I think Alice is a bit afraid of Williams," Kaz said. "He gave her a stern look when I asked about Peter, and she went silent."

"Could be he's a tough boss," I said.

"Perhaps," Kaz said. "Williams did say it served no purpose to speak of the past and staff who had left Ashcroft. He definitely didn't want to discuss Peter Wiley."

"Why?" Big Mike asked, pressing his heavy foot on the accelerator once we had a straightaway.

"Perhaps he knew the truth about Peter's father," Kaz said. "In my experience, butlers can be worse snobs than their masters. Mrs.

Dudley said it was poor manners for young Peter to leave as he did, but what can you expect from an American who doesn't know how to act proper-like, in her words."

"It doesn't help that everyone's in a tizzy about the reading of the will. The thought of money makes people nervous. I wonder who's getting what," Big Mike said.

"I'm pretty sure everyone else is wondering the same thing but trying not to show it," I said.

A minute later we parked in front of the police station in Dartmouth. We entered, expecting the worst.

We found it.

"I've left things as they were," Inspector Grange said, telling us without words. "I wanted you to see the note. Perhaps you can explain what he meant."

We followed him up the stairs to the bachelor police officer's quarters. I knew Tom had come back here the night before, and now I knew why. Inspector Grange opened the door to Tom's room.

He had come here to kill himself. His blue uniform jacket hung on a chair. He hadn't wanted to leave the tunic bloodstained. The wall was splattered red. Tom lay sideways on the bed, feet planted on the floor, rifle between his legs. The back of his head was gone, his face misshapen from the bullet.

I studied the body, my cop instincts kicking in. Big Mike leaned over as well, keeping clear of the mess but going over every inch of the scene. Nothing to indicate it was anything but suicide.

"I'm sorry," was all I could say.

"The note is where he left it," Inspector Grange said, pointing to the table by the window.

I set my hands on the chair, feeling the blue wool of Tom's jacket under my fingers as I read his last words.

There is too much death to go on. I am content with this decision. I have made up my mind to join my wife and children and to leave this terror behind me, and it has left me quite happy. Happier than I have been since the last time I saw them alive. Death is everywhere, and I cannot face it another day. There is no escaping it, no running away, so I will accept and embrace it. I would ask God to forgive me, but there is so much more than this single act I must answer for, it hardly seems right.

"What is it he cannot face another day of?" Inspector Grange demanded of me. "What have you been using him for?"

"Identification of the dead," I said, looking him in the eye. "You know what happened." Or some of it.

"Yes, but how many, for God's sake? He called it a 'terror,' said he couldn't face it another day. I thought he was well enough for police work, but is that what you've been up to? Did you make him a grave-digger?"

"What do you mean, Inspector?" Kaz said, stepping between us.

"We've heard about bodies washed ashore, secret burials, that sort of thing. Didn't you think about what might happen if Tom was confronted with all that?" Grange was red in the face, breathing heavily, and I understood his only purpose in calling us here had been to share the blame and spread his own guilt around.

"I'm sorry, Inspector," I said, "but I can't share the details. It was important work, and we needed his help. It did have to do with the bodies in the Channel, yes, but he wasn't involved in burying anyone." I left out the part about our visits to the charnel-house tents. And the fact that Grange had approved Tom fit for duty.

"So this note makes sense to you?" Grange said, a bit calmer now.

"Yes. We needed to find certain men, and we had to view a good number of the dead to do so. I wish I'd seen a problem with Tom, but he was actually in a fine mood yesterday." In better shape than I'd been, or so I'd thought, watching him jauntily swinging his arms, telling me you could do anything, once you made your mind up about it.

And he had.

CHAPTER THIRTY-TWO

IT WAS A quiet ride back to Ashcroft House. What was there to say? I'd been wrong about Tom Quick, plain and simple. I should have realized back at the racetrack that a sea of bodies would be more than he could bear. The sight of bombed-out buildings had been too much for him; why should I have expected anything less from visions of the dead and dismembered? We slowed to a halt, and David was out of the house moments after the sound of tires on gravel faded away.

"Well, what happened?" he asked. "How is Tom?"

"He shot himself," I said, getting out of the jeep and placing my hand on David's shoulder. "He's dead."

"No," David said, stepping away from me and the finality of the news. "No." His one good eye went wide, and his scarred mouth formed a half O of astonishment. There were times when David's burns seemed to be simply part of his face, an awful tragedy, but still *him*. Other times, like now, the burned skin was a rigid mask that was unable to show emotion, while the undamaged side crumbled at the news and the attempt to deny it. I turned away as Kaz led his friend inside, but I felt Big Mike's hand on my shoulder, pushing me after them. I'd have preferred to stay outdoors, letting my invisible scar tissue harden against this latest death.

"That is so sad," Helen said, sitting next to David on the couch and holding his hand after he'd told her the news. "But you did your best as a friend, David."

"Perhaps I did," he said. "But even a fellow RAF officer, someone who understood where he'd been, couldn't help. Don't you see? That's the worst of it. The bloody war drove him over the edge, and he wasn't even . . . disfigured." He wrenched his hand away from Helen's and stalked out of the room. She rose to go after him but was intercepted by Kaz, who shook his head and guided her back to her seat.

"He won't . . . ?" She couldn't finish the question.

Kaz assured her he wouldn't. "He needs to be alone. I'm sure he's embarrassed to have lost his temper with you." Calming words, but there was more to it than that. David had likely entertained thoughts of suicide at some point after sustaining his injuries. To have befriended Tom Quick, believing he'd done the man some good, only to learn Tom had blown his brains out, had to have reawakened those lonely thoughts. Tom had seemed normal to David, who understandably may have focused more on the physical than the emotional scars of war. If Tom Quick had ended his own life, having survived thirty missions and returned to his civilian occupation, what did that mean for David? Especially if the reading of the will turned out not to be to his advantage? I couldn't help but wonder if his father-in-law's illegitimate son might have posed quite a problem for David's future well-being.

"What's wrong with David?" Meredith asked as she entered the sitting room. "He looked quite ashen."

"A friend of his died," Helen said, eyes downcast.

"Who?" Meredith demanded. "Anyone we know?" She sat next to Helen, more curious than concerned.

"No," Helen answered. "A constable. He'd been in the RAF and was working with the baron and Captain Boyle."

"Terrible," Meredith said. "It must have been sudden, if he's been on duty. An accident?"

"Yes," I said, not wanting to go into details. The room was thick with silence.

"Tell me, Captain Boyle, what have you been investigating?" Meredith said, forging ahead with grim determination. "There are rumors upon rumors."

"Of what?" Kaz asked, a polite smile masking his interest.

"Secret burials in mass graves. Most say it's American soldiers; some insist a German invasion was thwarted and is being hushed up, which makes no sense at all."

"A boat did sink in the Channel," Kaz said, as if explaining the obvious to a dull child. "We are helping to identify the dead. People may have seen bodies being collected from where they washed up along the shoreline and jumped to conclusions."

"As they always do," Meredith said. "Any news yet of Peter Wiley?"

"No, we still have not had time to track him down," Kaz said. Meredith sighed, as if that was quite troublesome.

I excused myself and went outside in search of the open air, away from grief and the stale aftermath of death. Big Mike followed me out onto the terrace and stood beside me silently, his hands deep in his pockets.

"What?" I asked, sensing he was waiting for me to say something.

"So you want Kaz to stay here, right? To make sure his pal is okay." He looked out to the river, where David was strolling on the path along the water.

"Yeah, sure," I said.

"And you want me to check the Casualty Clearing Stations on my own," he said. "You know, for the last two stiffs. Or are you coming with me?"

"No, you go ahead," I said, realizing Big Mike was issuing orders to an officer the way only a sergeant can. "I'll go to Brixham when I'm done here. You head south to Slapton. Radio Harding, okay? Let him know about Tom."

"Already done, Billy," Big Mike said. "You okay?" He cocked an eyebrow as he turned his studied gaze on me.

"I'm okay," I said. "I'm alive, aren't I?"

"You seem kinda distracted."

"It's hard to get used to," I said. "The idea of Tom killing himself."

"It's also hard when a guy you count on isn't all there," Big Mike said. "Tom's dead. We're alive. We need you, believe it or not." He turned on his heel and was gone. And right. I was shook up—more than I wanted to admit—about what had happened in the Channel.

I couldn't erase those terrible visions of drowned men, upside down, floating in on the tide. And in Tom's room, I'd been scared, just as David was scared. What would become of us, those who lived through this carnage, after it was over? I had no idea. Death had become a way of life, and it was going to be one helluva shock when Johnny went marching home.

Toughen up, I scolded myself. Kaz and Big Mike deserved better. I had a job to do. I made for the jeep and started it up as Big Mike was driving away in his. He gave me a nod, a sign I was doing the right thing, and I realized the hardest part of a noncom's job had to be telling officers how to lead their men.

I MADE IT to the outskirts of Brixham, and this time there were no marching soldiers or convoys to get in my way. I got lost, since it had been Tom Quick who'd gotten us here on back roads yesterday. I stumbled upon the coast road outside of town and drove up to the old fort, set high on the cliffs overlooking the Channel. I slowed, waiting for the sentries to step out and check my papers. The ramparts were empty except for the ancient rusting cannon. I drove through the entrance into an eerie silence, the flat parade ground empty. Not a soul, living or dead.

The grass was still flattened where the tents had been. Dark stains on the earth that might have been blood revealed where the dismembered bodies had been stacked. The wind blew off the water, cold and salty, whistling through the windows of the crumbling stone buildings. All that remained was a single tent peg protruding from the ground. Not even a cigarette butt had been left behind.

It was as if it had never happened.

Where had everyone gone? Harding had said he was going to check with Dawes about Peter Wiley. Had he come here and found the place like this? Or had he ordered everyone to disperse? Perhaps the last two bodies had been found, and now the big hush-up was in process. Where had Dawes said he was stationed? Exeter. The 13th Field Hospital. I checked the map and found it, maybe an hour north. Time to see the doctor. I thought about radioing in to Harding, but I didn't want to get ordered back to London right now. If the search for the missing BIGOTs was over, there was nothing to keep us here, but I needed to find out more about Peter Wiley and how he ended up in the drink. Maybe he deserved recognition as Sir Rupert's son, legit or not. Maybe he really was Ted Wiley's son. Whoever his father was, Peter shouldn't have died. Everyone else in that ill-fated convoy had been there because they were ordered to be. Peter went for his own reasons, and until those reasons made sense, I was going to stay on the hunt.

I'd been through Exeter before. It had been bombed heavily back in '42, when the Luftwaffe conducted their Baedeker raids, so-called because they chose targets from Baedeker guides to England, selecting only those cities that had been awarded three stars for architectural and historical significance. The RAF had gone first, bombing the medieval city of Lübeck and starting a competition to see which side could incinerate or blow up the oldest buildings. I wasn't keeping track, but I knew the rubble was still knee-deep in parts of town. I didn't want to inch my way through miles of backed-up traffic, so I pulled over when I came to an encampment and asked the MP at the gate where the 13th Field Hospital was. He gave me directions, and for once luck was on my side. It was close, and I didn't have to drive through bomb-damaged Exeter.

I drove around the encampment, rows and rows of canvas tents surrounded by barbed wire, green fields on the outside, mud and green khaki the predominant colors on the inside. Goat Town and Spam Town.

A road sign marked the turnoff for the field hospital, and I followed a curved drive that led to a large, three-story brick house. It made Ashcroft look like a cottage. Ambulances and jeeps were parked on one side; in the field opposite were rows of tents with red crosses painted over the olive drab.

Inside, two MPs stood behind a clerk seated at a table. I asked where I could find Major Clayton Dawes.

"Why?" one of the MPs said. The clerk, a skinny Private First Class, fiddled with his pencil and looked down at his paperwork.

"Beat it, kid. Go get a cup of coffee," I said, and the PFC was gone so fast his swivel chair rolled back against the wall. "Now, let's start over. Take me to Major Dawes, and show me you're bright enough to handle basic military courtesy."

One of the MPs kept chewing his gum like a contented cow. The other, who was trying to appear intimidating but instead looked increasingly nervous, tried to rethink the situation.

"Why, Captain?"

"You're almost there," I said. "Shows you're not a complete moron. Stand at attention, both of you!" For that last bit, I used my best Sam Harding voice. They jumped. The only thing that made me madder than an MP acting like he owned the world was an MP who made me act like an officer. I'm an easy guy to get along with. Ask anyone. But I don't like to be played for a fool. I stood closer and looked the guy in the eye from about six inches away, waiting. Finally, he got it right.

"Sir! Why do you wish to see Major Dawes, sir?"

"Very good, Sergeant," I said, stepping back. "Since you asked so nicely, I'll give you an answer. None of your goddamn business. But here's the thing: now I want to know why you even care. Tell me as we walk, okay?"

"Sir, you can't see Major Dawes." He relaxed a bit and I stepped closer again, and that put an end to that.

"Two questions, Sergeant," I said. "Is Major Dawes here, and can you read?"

"Yes, sir," he said, deflated.

"Which question are you answering?"

"Both, Captain. He is here, and I can read."

"Good," I said. "On both counts. Read this." I pulled out my orders and waved them in front of his nose. Waved them a good bit, actually, since they were due to run out soon, and I didn't want him looking too closely. I made sure he took in the name Eisenhower and a few choice sentences, then stuffed the papers back in my pocket. "Now take me to Dawes."

"Okay, Captain," the sergeant said, telling his silent partner to stay put. He took me up two flights of stairs and down a hallway flanked by rooms filled with beds, mostly empty, all of them waiting for what was about to come.

"So why'd you pull the tough-guy stuff?" I asked as we strode around a corner, more shining linoleum stretching out in front of us. This place went on forever. "You knew any officer worth his salt wouldn't put up with that."

"Orders, Captain. Straight from Special Agent McLean. He's in this room, with the doctor you wanted." He halted, pointing to a closed door with a painted sign that said CHIEF SURGEON.

"Special Agent? CIC?" I asked.

"Afraid so, Captain." He knocked on the door. The US Army Counter-Intelligence Corps was a secretive bunch, but one thing they were well known for was operating in civilian clothes or plain uniforms with no indication of rank. I always figured it was because most of their operatives were noncommissioned officers, and it helped to shield them from the kind of routine I had used on the MP.

"What?" a voice barked out from the office. The MP opened the door.

"This captain wants to see Major Dawes, Special Agent McLean. And he's got the orders to prove he can." With that, the MP shut the door behind him, probably glad to be out of the cross fire.

Dawes sat in a chair across from McLean. A second agent lounged against the wall behind him. Both CIC men wore unadorned uniforms, no rank insignia except for the "U.S." brass collar insignia, which at least told those who knew about these things that the agents were not enlisted men.

"I need to talk with Major Dawes," I said. "Alone. What's your beef with him?"

"Security precautions," McLean said. He was thin and wiry, scraggly brown hair beating a retreat from his forehead, small eyes too close together, and nicotine stains on his fingers. He drew on a butt with about an inch of life left in it and ground it out in an overflowing ashtray. He looked like a man who enjoyed his work. The other Special Agent was dark, silent, and grim faced. He looked like he didn't enjoy a damn thing. "What do you want the good doctor for?"

"I have a headache," I said. Dawes looked up at me, panic in his eyes. Maybe he thought he was going from the frying pan into the fire. "How much longer are you going to be?"

"Long as it takes," McLean said. "What's your name and unit?"

"Boyle," I said. "SHAEF." I handed him my orders, canning the wiseacre routine. He didn't seem the type to fall for it.

"Let's talk outside," McLean said. Once we were in the hallway, he folded his arms across his chest and jutted his chin in my direction. Not the most welcoming posture. "Tell me, Captain, are we working the same beat here?"

"You tell me," I said. "You've seen my orders. They're from Ike himself."

"Yeah, pretty impressive," the Special Agent said. "But they don't say what you're investigating."

"You first," I said. "General Eisenhower would want it that way."

"Fair enough," McLean said, nodding as if he thought the Supreme Commander might have a point. "Operation Tiger. Heard of it?"

"I wish I never had," I said. "What's your angle?"

"You first, Captain."

"Okay. I met Major Dawes at the Brixham Casualty Clearing Station. I was identifying bodies."

"There were a lot of bodies there, Captain."

"I didn't say all the bodies. And that's all I won't say."

He laughed and unfolded his arms. A good sign. "CIC has been ordered to provide security for the aftermath of Operation Tiger," McLean said. "We got the go-ahead last night to close down the clearing stations. I guess they've recovered all the bodies, dead or alive, by now."

"So your job is to remove all evidence it ever happened," I said. That seemed right up CIC's alley. Back in the States, CIC informers had been recruited among soldiers to report on their fellow servicemen, passing along tidbits about politics and lack of enthusiasm for army life. Supposedly they'd halted that program and were now busy preventing sabotage, investigating military personnel given access to classified information, and generally snooping.

"Basically, yes," McLean said. "Which is what I'm busy with right now. Why do you want to talk to Dawes?"

"It's about a particular body," I said.

"That wouldn't be a naval lieutenant, by any chance?"

"Peter Wiley," I said. McLean nodded, and I began to sense why Dawes was in hot water. "You were a body short, and you found out Dawes had Wiley here in the morgue."

"Yeah," McLean said, his eyes narrowing in suspicion. I could tell he didn't like the idea of losing a corpse, or being blamed for blowing the cover-up. "The deceased are being buried today, and Brixham was missing one. We checked with the ambulance drivers, and one of them admitted to bringing Wiley here."

"He'd been ordered to by Major Dawes, who was acting on my behalf. I hope you didn't send the poor slob to Leavenworth to split rocks."

"Naw, he's cooling his heels downstairs. He gave us the major's name and we were just having a discussion with him about why he stole a corpse. He didn't mention you."

"Are you shocked that he didn't rat me out to CIC? Not everyone caves in to you guys," I said.

"Easy, Captain, I'm just doing my job. What was so special about Lieutenant Wiley?"

"He wasn't supposed to be part of Operation Tiger." I couldn't talk about him being the eleventh BIGOT. Counter-Intelligence Corps probably was not privy to that security classification. "I asked Dawes to keep Wiley's body on ice and do an autopsy."

"Okay, makes sense," McLean said. I could see the wheels turning. He could wrap this up, take Wiley to wherever they were secretly burying the victims of Operation Tiger, and be done with any suggestion he'd screwed up. "You mind talking with Dawes with us in the room?"

"Promise me he won't be punished. Him or the ambulance driver."

"If he was acting under your orders, which were signed by Ike, then there's no reason for punishment. Same goes for the driver." We shook on it and went back into the office. He whispered something to the other agent, who pushed himself away from the wall and lumbered out of the room.

"Captain Boyle has explained what you were doing with Wiley's body, Major Dawes," McLean said. "We weren't privy to his investigation, but now our questions have been answered."

"I'm not in trouble?" Dawes asked me.

"Nope. We have Special Agent McLean's word on that," I said, trying to keep any sense of doubt out of my voice. I didn't want Dawes to get nervous and clam up. "Did you perform an autopsy?"

"Yes," Major Dawes said. "I was finishing when these two showed up." His distaste for the CIC men was evident in his tone. "Lieutenant Wiley was murdered, sometime before his ship was hit."

"Murdered?" McLean said. "You mean someone on board killed him before the Germans attacked?" Dawes ignored him.

"There was evidence of lividity. Blood pooling, you know about that?" Dawes asked me.

"Sure. I was a cop in Boston before the war. That's when the blood settles to the lowest part of the body after death," I explained for the benefit of the CIC agents.

"Right," Dawes said. "In Wiley's case, the blood settled to his back and buttocks and the rear of his legs. You know what that means."

"What?" McLean asked, looking back and forth between us.

"It means Wiley was laid out flat on his back after he died. If he'd gone into the water and died from exposure, or anything else, the blood wouldn't have pooled that way," I said.

"So he was killed on board," McLean said, happier now that he understood things.

"Yeah, but on which ship?" I asked.

"No idea," McLean admitted. "The paperwork is a snafu. Orders changed so many times there's no way to be sure."

"Have you checked?" I asked. By which I meant put in hours of boring police work, checking manifests and personnel lists. I could tell from his expression it was a foreign idea.

"We don't have the time for that," McLean said, shaking his head.

"There's something else," Dawes said. "I think he was burked."

"Now what the hell are you talking about?" McLean demanded.

"I thought you couldn't tell," I said to Dawes, remembering the famous deadly duo of Burke and Hare. A hundred or so years ago they had made good money selling cadavers to medical schools in Scotland. Then they decided to hurry the process along and began murdering people by suffocating them, after giving them drink or drugs. The idea was to sit on the chest of the victim while holding the nose and mouth shut, keeping the diaphragm and ribcage from moving, hastening the moment of death. They got sixteen cadavers that way, then Burke was sentenced to hang and had his name turned into a verb.

"Usually you can't tell," Dawes answered. "But there were small fractures on the fourth and fifth ribs, and the soft organs were congested with blood. Not definitive proof, but indicative of the burking method."

"Captain, please explain what this means," McLean said, giving up on Dawes. I gave him the low down on burking.

"I'm surprised you don't know the term," Dawes said, finally speaking directly to the agent. "It has also come to mean covering things up quietly, suppressing the truth as Burke suppressed breath. It fits your operation perfectly."

"I'll take that as a compliment," McLean said. "Anything else?"

"Yes. We need the body kept in the morgue," I said.

"Too late," McLean said, obviously enjoying himself. "It's already on its way to the burial site. The location of which I am under orders not to disclose. To anyone." Now I knew what he'd whispered to his pal, who had left the room in time to get Wiley out of the morgue and into a truck bound for the ground.

CHAPTER THIRTY-THREE

WE DID THE dance of authority and rank, and ended up right where we had started. So I decided not to waste time flapping my yap about Wiley's body. Dawes was free to go, and I agreed to stop snooping around the hospital. I wrote out the address for Ashcroft House and gave it to Dawes, telling him to look me up. Inside the folded piece of paper, I'd scrawled the word autopsy. He'd given me a wink on the way out, saying we'd have to get together for a drink. He was a smart guy, and anyone who disliked the Counter-Intelligence Corps agents as much as I did would make a good drinking buddy.

I shook hands with McLean to show we were all in this together and went off thinking we'd each pulled one over on the other guy, which wasn't the worst outcome I could have predicted. Just to be certain, I took the stairs to the basement and found the morgue. I asked a corporal mopping the floor if they'd come for Peter Wiley yet, as if I was checking up on my men. He consulted a clipboard and said they had. Well, it had been worth a shot, in case McLean had been bluffing.

I went out the main door in time to see the two MPs and the CIC agents hustling Major Dawes and a GI, probably the ambulance driver, into a staff car.

"Hold up," I yelled, running over to them. "What the hell are you doing? You said no punishments."

"No one is being punished, Captain Boyle," McLean said, nodding to the MPs, who put Dawes and the driver in the rear seat, cop style, pushing down their heads as if they were handcuffed.

"Then what are you doing with them, goddamn it?"

"Giving them a lift," McLean said with a self-satisfied grin. "Their transfers came through. The army transfers people all the time. It's not a punishment at all."

"Where to?" I asked.

"Cairo. Their ship leaves Bristol at dawn, so we have to hit the road."

"Let me talk to Dawes. I want to apologize for getting him into this mess," I said.

"There's no mess, Captain," McLean said. "Simply routine army procedures, but sure, say your piece." He nodded to an MP, who opened the door.

"Sorry, Major Dawes," I said. "You too, Private."

"Well, look on the bright side," Dawes said. "We're going to see the pyramids." The private almost smiled at that.

"I've been there. It's really something to see," I said. I didn't tell him about the flies.

SPECIAL AGENT MCLEAN had left nothing to chance. The only two men who even knew about a temporarily missing body were going to be shut up in a troop transport for weeks and then end up as far as you could go without finding yourself in the Pacific Theater of Operations. If Dawes managed to mail a letter from Cairo, it would take another few weeks to get to me. McLean was a burker, sure enough.

I knew I should contact Harding, but I was dog-tired and didn't want to have to report on how CIC had outsmarted me. He did need to know about Wiley, but there was no reason to rush. What I needed to do was be at the reading of the will tomorrow and witness who got what and who hated whom for it. I thought about what Dawes had discovered and turned it over in my mind as I drove the now familiar roads. As I often did, I wondered what my dad would make of it. He'd taught me how to work a case and drummed it into my head never to assume what you don't actually know to be true. It was one of the reasons he got me to read the Sherlock Holmes stories. The best piece of advice, in his mind, came from *A Study in Scarlet*, when Holmes stated something along the lines of it being a capital mistake to theorize before one has data. That's when you begin to twist facts to suit theories, instead of theories to suit facts. I realized I had done just that. I needed to focus on pure fact, not assumptions.

The air had turned cold by the time I pulled into the drive leading to Ashcroft House. It held a damned odd bunch of people, but it was beginning to feel like home. Or at least a comfortable place with good food. I parked next to Big Mike's jeep, and as I got out, I spotted David returning from a walk. He was dressed in tweed, looking the part of the country squire. He gave a wave, and I waited as he headed for the door.

"Billy," he said in a low voice, avoiding my eyes. "I must apologize for my behavior earlier today. Shameful that I was thinking of myself instead of poor Tom Quick."

"It's only natural," I said. "He was your friend. We tend to see ourselves in the people we like."

"Yes, quite. And I admired him too, for what he had endured. I do wish I'd seen how deep his despair must have been."

"No one could have seen that," I said, wishing that I had too. "You gave him some moments of friendship and understanding. I'm sure it meant a lot to him."

"Thank you, Billy," David said, his hand resting on my shoulder for a second before I opened the door. Coming from a proper Brit, it was like a bear hug and a kiss on the cheek.

"Captain, how nice that you're back," Helen said when she saw us from the hall. She was carrying a basket of cut flowers. "You will be dining with us, I hope?"

"I look forward to it," I said. "Is the baron here?"

"Yes, he was helping me in the garden. Aren't the flowers lovely?"

"Crawford's green thumb?" I asked.

"Oh, it's not all Crawford. I manage to cultivate a few things as well, Captain. How was your walk, David?" She leaned in for him to give her a peck on the cheek. All in all, Helen's temperament had improved dramatically since I arrived. Or was it since her father's departure?

"Just what I needed," David said. "I walked to the village and back along the river. Bracing. I stopped in at the pub and bought a round. It's the kind of thing the locals like, I'm told."

"Who doesn't like a free drink?" I said. I recalled Helen or Meredith telling David it was his duty to mingle more with the villagers, assuming Ashcroft House stayed with their side of the family. Most importantly, David was feeling good enough about himself to make the effort. Most of the residents of North Cornworthy had likely heard about his burns, but few had actually laid eyes on him.

"Maybe we'll pop in again tonight," David said. "There weren't many fellows there this time of day."

"Wonderful idea, David," Helen said, taking him by the arm. "Oh, by the way, Captain, your Colonel Harding dropped in earlier. I believe he left a message for you with the baron."

I found Kaz and Big Mike in the library. Kaz was reading the newspaper, and Big Mike had his feet up and his eyes closed.

"We have news, Billy," Kaz said, folding his paper and slapping Big Mike's foot with it.

"So do I, but not here," I said in a low voice. "My room, and don't make a big deal of it."

Kaz came in five minutes later, followed shortly by Big Mike, carrying three bottles of Whitbread Pale Ale.

"Here you go," Big Mike said. "Williams keeps his ale in the wine cellar. Said I could help myself. He's not so much of a stuffed shirt downstairs."

"You get anything out of him?" I asked, kicking off my shoes and sitting on the bed.

"Not really. He's rooting for Meredith and Helen to inherit, of course. Job security. So what's your news?"

"Tell me what Harding said first."

"First, all the bodies have been found," Big Mike said, taking a seat in an easy chair. "I got one right away at Slapton Sands, and the other washed ashore by Start Point."

"The colonel said to tell you he'd gone to Brixham," Kaz said. "He found the place deserted, so he never spoke to Major Dawes. He returned to Greenway House to contact SHAEF and determine what had happened. He was told that as soon as there were no more bodies to be found near Brixham, an order was given to shut that clearing station down."

"It was the Counter-Intelligence Corps," I said. "I bet once all ten BIGOTs were found, CIC gave the order to make all the other clearing stations disappear too. Our services were no longer required." I took a long pull on the ale.

"Harding was not happy about it," Kaz said. "He told us to find out whatever we could about how Lieutenant Wiley got aboard one of the ships. But how do you know CIC is involved?"

"I tracked down Dawes and found CIC questioning him. He'd snatched Wiley's body for an autopsy, and the agents didn't appreciate coming up one stiff short."

"That mean trouble for Dawes?" Big Mike asked.

"He's getting an all-expenses-paid trip to Cairo," I said. "He gets to see the pyramids."

"Some guys have all the luck," Big Mike said with a rueful laugh. "Did he do the autopsy?"

"Yeah. The CIC special agent let me talk with him before they hustled him away." I stopped, listening to a sound in the hallway. I slipped off the bed and put my ear against the door. Someone was out there. I turned the knob slowly and opened the door, swiveling my head in either direction. I heard footsteps, perhaps in another room.

"Who was it?" Kaz asked after I shut the door.

"Don't know," I said. "It could have been anyone. Maybe Alice doing her chores."

"Hey, don't leave us hanging," Big Mike said.

"Okay," I said, taking a swig of the cool, sharp ale. "Here's what I know for certain. Peter Wiley had a bruise on his head, but nothing that would have killed him. He was dead before he went into the water.

His blood had pooled on his backside, so he was flat on his back long enough for lividity to have set in."

"Did Dawes have a cause of death?" Kaz asked.

"A theory," I said. "But not a certainty. Have either of you heard of the Burke and Hare murders?"

"Edinburgh, was it not?" Kaz asked. Of course Kaz would know. Big Mike hadn't heard of them. I gave him a quick rundown.

"So instead of digging up corpses, they killed outright," Big Mike said. "More efficient, you gotta admit."

"Dawes said that Wiley sustained injuries to his ribs consistent with Burke's method. Compress the chest, close off the air supply."

"Perhaps Peter was knocked unconscious, hence the bruise," Kaz said.

"Likely," I said. "But we can't prove anything. He could have gotten broken ribs from going into the water. And no water in the lungs does not rule out drowning, which I hadn't known."

"But we know he didn't drown," Kaz said. "Because of the lividity. He must have been killed on board the transport."

"Stick to the facts," I said. "We don't even know for certain if he was on a ship, much less which one."

"It seems obvious," Kaz said. "You don't know for certain that Big Mike drove his jeep here. However, you saw the jeep when you arrived, and here is Big Mike. Rather apparent how he arrived."

"Yes, given that he's not an inanimate corpse, I agree," I said, feeling a bit like Sherlock Holmes himself. "But if Big Mike were found dead, we might be curious as to whether he was killed here, or elsewhere and then driven here."

"All right," Kaz said, "I give up. We need to establish which transport Peter Wiley was on."

"Or failing that, how he got into the water," I said. "What was the name of the officer Harding told us to check with? The one responsible for keeping the manifest for all observers."

"Lieutenant James Siebert," Big Mike said. "At Greenway House."

"Okay, we see him in the morning. After the reading of the will."

"I doubt we're invited, Billy," Kaz said.

"That's what keyholes were made for," I said. "Anyway, I doubt it will take long for word to get out. Just watch Meredith."

"Surely you are not pursuing the issue of Peter Wiley's paternity," Kaz said. "It hardly matters. The two persons involved are both dead."

"I'm taking a lesson from Sherlock Holmes," I said. "Never theorize before you have data. That causes you to twist facts to suit theories, instead of the other way around."

"Ah," Kaz said. "Since we have no absolute proof that his paternity does not matter, we should not discount it."

"Right," I said. "Which is why I'm curious about it."

"And all along I thought you were a plain garden-variety snoop," Big Mike said.

"Gossips, eavesdroppers, and snoops are all the same," I said. "We need to know what the hell is going on."

"David did tell me the solicitor is coming here at ten o'clock tomorrow," Kaz said. "I will ask him if we can sit in. He can always say no."

"Count me out," Big Mike said. "I'm the new guy in town. But you two, maybe they'll buy it."

"Can't hurt to try," I said. "How was David this afternoon? He seemed chipper when he came in."

"Much better," Kaz said. "Mainly embarrassed, I think. You know the English and their stiff upper lips."

"Speaking of stiffs," Big Mike said, "when are you going to tell these people Wiley is dead?"

"Let's break the news at dinner," I said. "I doubt anybody will keel over, but I'll be interested to see if anyone looks relieved." I drained the last of my beer and wondered what I was missing. "How's Great Aunt Sylvia? She didn't look well earlier."

"A little better, I think," Kaz said. "When I checked in on her she seemed coherent. She hoped to come down for dinner." I heard a noise in the hallway again and motioned for Kaz to keep talking. As he went on about Lady Pemberton, I went over to the door and listened. I could have sworn I heard someone breathing. I put my hand on the knob and turned it slowly, hoping not to spook whoever was out there.

The hallway was empty, the echo of footsteps fading in another part of the house.

"I guess I'm hearing things," I said, shaking my head in frustration.

"Just as long as you don't start seeing them too," Big Mike said.

"I DON'T KNOW what came over me," Great Aunt Sylvia said when we gathered for drinks before dinner a few hours later. "I can't quite recall the past few days. It was terribly confusing."

"I'm glad to see you up and about," I said, sharing the couch in the library with her.

"I do not mind saying, Billy, that I was a bit worried," she whispered to me. "I must have had a fever and been a bit delirious. But I think I've snapped out of it. I was still a bit groggy earlier today, but I feel much better now. I am grateful to have a clear head for a change."

"Maybe it was a side effect of some medication," I offered.

"Medication? I haven't been ill a day in my life, young man, and I am not about to let a doctor fill me with drugs now. That is not how I got to this age, I can tell you that."

"Sherry, Great Aunt Sylvia?" Edgar asked. She nodded, and he filled a dainty glass.

"I wonder if they're waiting for me to die too," she said as soon as Edgar was out of earshot. "Then they can sell Ashcroft and be done with it. Get their flats in London or wherever is fashionable these days."

"Ashcroft House would be a poorer place without you, Lady Pemberton," I said.

"You Irish have a way with flattery, don't you? How much longer will you be with us, Billy? I shall miss our talks when you've gone."

"Perhaps a day or two more, ma'am. We've taken care of most of our business here, but we still have one matter to clear up. It's been very kind of everyone to let us stay on."

"Well, the baron is David's friend, and nobility of a sort. One doesn't deny the aristocracy, even Polish aristocracy. But I must say, I am surprised—but not disappointed—at Meredith's hospitality. It was her, you know, who insisted you all stay on as long as necessary."

"She wasn't of the same mind about Peter Wiley, was she?"

"Oh, no," Great Aunt Sylvia whispered. "Quite the opposite. Odd, don't you think? But then the Sutcliffes have never been straightforward about much of anything."

"I'm afraid I have some bad news about Peter, Lady Pemberton," I said. Glancing around, I saw that everyone was in the room and decided this was the best time and place. Great Aunt Sylvia put her hand to her mouth and gasped, perhaps sensing what I was about to say.

"Excuse me," I said, rising from the couch. "I wanted you all to know that Lieutenant Peter Wiley has died. We received confirmation today." A little white lie to buy me time as I scanned the faces gathered close. Edgar wagged his head and gave a *tch tch* before downing the rest of his drink. Meredith sat down, oddly affected by the news, her hand going to her head. Helen took David's hand, and I wondered if the look on her face was sorrow or worry about how her husband would take the news of another death. David looked at her, the burned side of his face giving me no clue as to what he was feeling.

Williams moved through the room clearing drinks, his face a stone. But his hand trembled and he dropped a sherry glass, which bounced on the thick carpet.

"That'll be all, Williams," David said. "Perhaps you should inform Alice and Mrs. Dudley. They will know of anyone in the village who should be told." Williams bowed and left, and the room remained silent with discomfort. To some, Peter Wiley had been an unwelcome guest, a naïve American who didn't know his place, and now Meredith and perhaps others didn't know how to react. He might not have been one of them, but he had been part of Ashcroft House, even if he'd come from downstairs.

"What happened to him?" Lady Pemberton asked, her face ashen.

"Are you all right, Great Aunt Sylvia?" Meredith said, going to her side. "Do you want to lie down?"

"I certainly do not," she replied. "I would like an answer to my question."

"He was on the ship that sank in the Channel," Kaz said.

"Evidently he was not expected on board, which led us to believe he'd gone off somewhere."

"Perhaps that's why he left in such a hurry," Meredith said, patting Great Aunt Sylvia's hand.

"He had such promise," David said. "But then so have so many."

It was hard to argue with that. As we filed out of the room to dinner, Crawford stood in the hallway, hands respectfully held behind his back, eyes darting back and forth, as if he were checking for reactions too. Had he been standing there the whole time?

The meal was subdued. There's nothing like a death notice to put a crimp in the dinner conversation. We had cod, fresh peas, potatoes, and carrots, washed down with a French white wine. Kaz complimented our hosts on the selection, and I wondered if the keys to the wine cellar were getting more of a workout now that Sir Rupert was no longer in charge. Why not? If Meredith and Helen were the big losers tomorrow, they might as well drink up while they could.

Big Mike sat next to Lady Pemberton and kept her amused with his stories of Detroit. But she barely ate, and when Big Mike was busy with a mouthful, her smile vanished. Of the whole bunch, I'd have to say she displayed the most emotion over the news of Peter Wiley's demise. Maybe the death of the young was even more of a tragedy for the old; they know how much of life there is to be missed.

As the dishes were cleared, David announced he was off to the village pub and asked if any of the men would like to come along. "Drinks on me," he said. "It will be either the beginning of a tradition or a farewell to North Cornworthy."

Edgar declined, which was not in character as far as free booze went; maybe he had to reread *Hamlet*. Big Mike stayed behind as well, and I thought he was becoming as protective of Lady Pemberton as I was.

THE HUNTER'S LODGE was cheerier than the Ashcroft House dining room, but only because no death had been announced recently. Crawford was there, sitting at a table with Michael Withers. On our last visit, Withers hadn't liked my asking questions about Roger Crawford, him being an "honest fisherman" and all. If Withers thought Crawford honest, then I had reason to doubt anything he'd told me. They raised their glasses in greeting, but then turned their heads away, no friendly invite to join them.

I recognized Evan, the fellow who'd had fun with us last time using the local dialect. There were about ten others, all workingmen to judge by their clothes, probably from the nearby mill. David asked if he could buy a round for everyone and the resounding cheer told him the answer was yes. The publican began to draw pints, and David chatted with Evan and a few others. No one mentioned his potential as a new squire, but it didn't seem as if anyone would mind.

"Captain, 'ow be?" Evan said, raising his pint.

"I be fine, Evan," I said, taking his meaning. "'Ow be thee?"

"Oh, you've got it down proper," Evan said, laughing. "Are you done counting bodies now? That was a terrible business, it was." On this serious subject, Evan made himself easily understood.

"Yes," I said. "War's full of bad business. How'd you hear about it?"

"Crawford, who works up at the house. He told us how he'd heard from his cousin on a shore battery. Seen it all, he said. Took his own boat out to see if he could find any lads before Jerry or the cold finished 'em off. But the navy turned him back. Too dangerous, they said. Too secret, I say. Who wants to admit to a disaster like that, eh?"

"I can't say I would, Evan. But Crawford's cousin may have exaggerated things a bit. It wasn't as bad as the rumors say."

"Well, Crawford can be a spuddler sometimes," Evan said in a whisper.

"Pardon?"

"Sorry, old butt. Means a troublemaker. He that stirs the pot, understand?"

"All too well, Evan. And if you're ever in Boston, don't call a guy in a bar an 'old butt,' okay?"

"Good one! An old butt's a fine friend," he said with a laugh, clapping me on the back. "And you're one as well, Captain Boyle. Now go and get your pint."

I did, and David was right behind me. As befits the temporary squire, he waited for his until everyone else was served, then raised his glass in a toast.

"To the dead." A dozen voices responded with the same, each with their own memories from the last war, this war, the hard times and grueling mill work, whatever served to put the dead in the ground. The toast put me in mind of the two basic motives for murder: love and money. Both seemed in short supply, but there was no shortage of the dead.

After the conversation faded and men were faced with the prospect of paying for their next round, the room thinned out. David, Kaz, and I got another round and sat by the fire.

"Whoever ends up with Ashcroft will have a lot of work to do," David said. "From what Helen tells me, Sir Rupert wasn't much for upkeep. The outbuildings are in need of repair and filled with useless junk."

"Mrs. Dudley did mention Ted Wiley kept them filled with machinery in the old days. She said he always enjoyed a tinker," Kaz said.

"Probably why he opened a hardware store in New York," I said.

"I think Helen mentioned they had a lot of rusted junk hauled away some time ago for the scrap drives," David said. "I looked around in there yesterday and I did see where a motorbike had been stored. It must have been Peter's."

"That is likely," Kaz said. "But how could you tell it was a motorbike?"

"By the tracks leading out of the barn," David said. "A motorbike leaves a tread mark like a bicycle, only deeper on account of the weight, and slightly thicker. And there were oil stains where it had been parked in the barn. Probably an older model. Lots of people making do with what they had before the war, as we do."

"You ought to be a detective," I said. "You're more observant than most."

"A pilot has to be. Hun in the sun and all that," David said, and then went quiet, perhaps contemplating a life less observant.

The evening at the pub wrapped up not long after, and I was glad to climb into bed after a long day. On the way back, David had asked Kaz if he'd sit in on the reading of Sir Rupert's will as a friend of the family, solving one problem for us. I doubted if anyone would mind my tagging along.

I picked up the Agatha Christie puzzler I'd started and tried to read. Lord Edgware's wife wanted a divorce. Hercule Poirot pleads her case, but Lord Edgware says he's quite ready to grant a divorce. Then someone plugs him, and everyone is stumped as to why. Images of Sir Rupert and his daughters drifted across my mind, until the book fell against my chest, startling me awake.

Why is it you can fall asleep reading with the lights on, but when you awake and turn them off you toss and turn? I was dead tired—no, I take that back. The dead were in for a real solid sleep, and I didn't want to tempt fate. I let my thoughts wander, hoping whatever was keeping me awake would simply fade away.

It didn't. There was a gnawing feeling in my gut. I began to think that I'd heard something tonight that should have set off alarm bells but hadn't registered. I went over the conversations I'd had, trying to recollect the exact wording of each.

I finally gave up, remembering what my dad always said. Trust your unconscious mind. If you don't understand something in the light of day, let your subconscious work on it at night. Generally being in favor of cutting ZZZs and letting another guy do the work, I punched the pillow and called in the third shift for the heavy lifting.

CHAPTER THIRTY-FOUR

MATTHEW FARNSWORTH LOOKED every inch the country solicitor. From the last century, which was when he probably started his practice. The wing-tip collar was from the same long-ago era, but it suited him. He'd asked the servants to be present, and said it would be useful for Kaz and me to attend as witnesses. No one seemed to have a problem with that. Big Mike had gone off to Greenway House to check in with Harding and let him know our plans. Not that there was much to tell.

My subconscious had worked overnight, and I planned to talk to a few people after the reading. Since everyone was a bit on edge this morning, I'd decided it could wait until after the main event, which was about to get underway. Williams, Mrs. Dudley, and Alice Withers filed in to the library and stood behind the family members seated in chairs facing Farnsworth. He had his papers spread out on a small writing table and was busy cleaning his glasses, which gave him an excuse not to look directly at any one person. Crawford had taken a straight-backed chair in a far corner, once again slightly presumptuous without quite overstepping the bounds. Kaz and I leaned against the bookshelves, which afforded us a good view of all concerned.

"I apologize for the necessity of this reading," Farnsworth said, placing pince-nez glasses firmly on his nose. "However, Sir Rupert stipulated that his will be presented, and explained if necessary, in this fashion."

"His will be done," Edgar said, which earned him a few nervous chuckles, as well as daggers from Meredith.

"If there are no objections, I will dispense with a full reading of the Last Will and Testament of Sir Rupert Sutcliffe, and summarize the disposition of his estate." Farnsworth peered over his glasses at the two daughters, their husbands, Lady Pemberton, and the servants. No one had the slightest interest in waiting any longer.

"The first point I was instructed to make was that the stipulation regarding Lady Pemberton's ongoing residence here is to stay in force. This was Sir Rupert's wish and also an obligation of the previous inheritance. To ensure that Lady Pemberton's final years are spent in comfort, he left the sum of five hundred pounds to supplement her income and investments."

Farnsworth looked up and nodded to Great Aunt Sylvia, who smiled and returned the gesture.

"As for the servants, Sir Rupert left the sum of five hundred pounds each to Roger Crawford, Charles Williams, and Beryl Dudley. One hundred pounds is to go to Alice Withers, the lesser amount due to her shorter tenure at Ashcroft House."

"Oh!" Alice exclaimed, then clapped her hand over her mouth. Williams frowned at her, but the two thousand or so bucks he was getting had left him in a good mood, and he reverted to his usual stone face. Crawford smiled, but his expression had a bitter edge to it, as if he'd expected to be remembered with a bit more cash.

"The sum of five thousand pounds shall go to Helen Sutcliffe Martindale," Farnsworth said, giving Helen a polite smile and avoiding eye contact with Meredith.

Farnsworth read off a few smaller sums to go the village church, library, and some local charities. Meredith was kneading an embroidered handkerchief in her hands, and I waited for the stitching to come loose as she became more and more impatient. Helen gripped David's hand, her eyes riveted on the solicitor.

"That concludes the smaller items," Farnsworth said. "The bulk of his estate, Ashcroft House with adjoining properties, and the remaining bank accounts total slightly over two hundred forty-six thousand pounds after the aforementioned dispositions. There is also an annual income from rents totaling six thousand pounds."

"Oh!" This time it was Meredith. She must have been startled at the amount. I was. It was nearly a million dollars, if my arithmetic was right. Oh indeed.

"Sir Rupert's original will stipulated the following," Farnsworth said, clearing his throat and fiddling with his papers. He looked nervous, adjusting his glasses before continuing. I wondered why he'd referred to the *original* document. If there was a new will, why not skip it? Had Sir Rupert known more than he let on about Peter Wiley?

"Original?" Helen said, looking to Meredith with confusion written over her face.

"Yes, that is why I am here, to be certain that the new will is understood and to clarify the circumstances under which it is to be carried out," Farnsworth said. He took a deep breath and began again. "The previous will had Ashcroft House going to the government for whatever purposes it deemed necessary. The monies in Sir Rupert's accounts were to be used for its maintenance. The only stipulation was that any usage was to be appropriate to Lady Pemberton's continuing residence."

"The bastard!" Meredith exclaimed.

"Yes, ahem," Farnsworth said, soldiering on. "However, shortly before his death, Sir Rupert came to me and had a codicil added. The long and the short of it is, he directed that instead of the government being given title to the estate, it should go to Peter Wiley, an American, should it be demonstrated reasonably that the young man was the issue of Sir Rupert, the legitimacy of the birth notwithstanding."

"What? Reasonably? What the bloody hell does that mean?" Edgar said, his face red and his voice tight with rage. Around the room, other voices were raised in confusion laced with anger.

"Please," Farnsworth said, holding up one hand. "I will explain as soon as there is quiet."

"Don't tell *me* to be quiet!" Edgar said, but he managed to nonetheless. I was ready for him to stalk out of the room, but his curiosity overcame his anger, and he relaxed back into his seat. Now I understood why Farnsworth had been eager to have Kaz and me present as witnesses.

"Please, Mr. Farnsworth," Helen said, leaning forward, eyes brimming with tears. "Please tell us what this means."

"It's obvious, isn't it?" Meredith said. "Father had an affair with the maid. Such a cliché."

"How do you know that?" Helen said, turning to Meredith in a fury. "What a horrible thing to say!"

"Wake up, darling," Meredith responded. "Aren't you listening to Farnsworth? When Peter Wiley showed up here, Father must have realized, or at least seen the resemblance. And don't forget the ring the American was wearing. Why else would Julia Greenshaw give it to her son?"

"Be that as it may," Farnsworth said, "Sir Rupert asked Captain Boyle to look into the matter for him, to determine whether Peter Wiley was in fact his son, born of Julia Greenshaw."

"What?" Edgar said. "You mean the maid who married the groundskeeper and went to America? Ah, now it becomes clear."

"Mr. Farnsworth, please continue," Great Aunt Sylvia said. "And excuse the interruption; this has been most difficult for us all."

"Understandably, Lady Pemberton," he said. "Sir Rupert came to me most distraught. He had tried for years to communicate with Miss Greenshaw, or I should say Mrs. Wiley, by that time. She never responded to his letters, and he gave up hope of any news from America. When young Peter Wiley came here recently, he said it was his last chance to do right by the boy."

"Right by him?" Helen said. "What about Meredith? He left her nothing. Is that right?"

"My role here is not to pronounce upon morality, Mrs. Martindale. All I can do is communicate Sir Rupert's instructions. If there is any evidence at all that would indicate his paternity, then the estate goes to Peter Wiley. He left it to my discretion, with the understanding that paternity need not be proved legally, but simply to my satisfaction."

"Peter Wiley is dead," I said. It was about time someone said it.

"I am sorry to hear that," Farnsworth said. "But it does not matter in regard to the will. I am obligated to carry out the wishes of my client. Captain Boyle, have you any evidence to suggest that Sir Rupert Sutcliffe was the father of Peter Wiley?"

"No, I don't," I said. "There is a family resemblance, but I had no time to look into the matter or even speak to Peter about it. I'm sorry."

"I don't see how it matters, but I can give you some proof, if you like," Meredith said. Every eye in the room swiveled in her direction. "I knew Peter Wiley was Father's offspring with that maid. I have known for years. I shall be right back."

The room went silent. The sound of Meredith's heels clattering through the foyer and up the stairs echoed in the stunned silence. Helen looked to David as if he might be able to explain what was happening, but all he could do was shake his head. Only Edgar shook off the shock of Meredith's announcement and stood to speak.

"I think, Williams, that you and the rest of the staff may return to your duties. Congratulations on your good fortune," he said with a good deal of graciousness, which was noteworthy considering his own lack of good fortune. The four of them dutifully trooped out of the library as Meredith hurried down the stairs and back into the room. She sat and took a deep breath, composing herself.

"I dislike airing family issues like this, but it does seem necessary to clear this matter up, distasteful though it may be," she began. "It's no secret Father and I did not get along. The state of our relationship is obvious from his will alone. The source of our discord was his dalliance with Julia Greenshaw. I was only a young girl when Father came home from the last war, but I was not ignorant of the ways in which it had changed him. There was nothing of the carefree mother and father I remembered from before the war. Even though Helen was born within a year of his return, there was a sadness in the house. I have memories of laughter and gaiety before the war, although perhaps they are merely a child's delusion."

"Do you have some proof of the paternity in question?" Farnsworth asked, giving the clock on the mantel a quick glance.

"I'm getting to that, Mr. Farnsworth," Meredith said. "This is quite difficult, you know."

"My apologies," he said. "Proceed."

"I believe it began while Mother was carrying Helen," she said. "I would see Father and Julia together at odd moments. He was never one to interfere with the running of the household, so it was puzzling to me, even as a small child. One day I followed them into the garden, my curiosity piqued. They kissed. I ran away before I witnessed any more. It was horrible, quite shattering." She dabbed her eyes with her handkerchief. "Later he and Mother apparently had a major row. I can still hear them screaming at each other. Do you recall, Great Aunt Sylvia? I remember seeing you in the hall when I ran to find out what the matter was."

"Yes, dear," Lady Pemberton said. "I remember quite clearly. An unhappy time. Even when Helen was born, it did not bring them closer."

"I know," Meredith said. "In my childish way, I had thought it would. But a few months later, Mother said she needed a rest and went to stay with a friend in the Lake District. I begged her to take me, but she said it was peace and quiet she required. Father stayed in London for a while, I think."

"He did," Lady Pemberton said. "We hired a nursemaid for Helen and a tutor for Meredith. We felt it best that they did not witness their parents quarreling or bickering about each other. And Rupert began work with the Foreign Office in London at that time." That jibed with what Sir Rupert had told me the day he died.

"Do you concur that this affair between the maid and Sir Rupert took place?" Farnsworth asked Lady Pemberton.

"Sadly, I must," she said, and gestured to Meredith to continue.

"Mother returned at some point, though I cannot say when," Meredith went on. "That is when Julia Greenshaw discovered that she was with child. Father must have arranged a rendezvous or two during Mother's absence. As I understand it, the marriage between her and Ted Wiley was arranged with a substantial gift of money and on condition that they leave for America."

"Why was the maid not simply sacked?" Edgar asked.

"We wished to avoid a scandal," Great Aunt Sylvia said. "To work things out, discreetly." I'd bet Lady Pemberton was very good at that, then and now.

Farnsworth leaned forward, waiting for Meredith to continue. He'd dropped his impatient demeanor and was caught up in the story Meredith was weaving, as were the others in the room. Kaz idly raised an eyebrow in my direction, which for him meant he was riveted as well.

"Several months later we were preparing for our voyage to India. It was all rather exciting, and I hoped that the adventure of it all would bring Mother and Father closer together. I had lost respect for him, but I still wanted a normal family life, if only for Helen. And I wanted Mother to be happy as well. I could see that she was distraught over the affair."

"When was this?" Farnsworth asked.

"Early 1921," Meredith answered. "I know because this letter came days before we were due to depart." She held up the yellowing envelope with the three-cent stamp. "I was the first to see the post, and I noticed the letter from America, with the name Wiley on the return address. It looked like a woman's writing, so I took it. I couldn't bear the thought of that Greenshaw person writing to Father. Or worse, the possibility that he might answer."

"You kept it all this time?" Edgar asked, leaving unsaid the fact that she had never told him the story.

"I don't know why I did. I don't even know if I should be telling you all about it. Once we arrived in India, I told Father that I had taken the letter and burned it. He was livid. He didn't have their new address, and of course he couldn't ask the servants for it. I taunted him about it, never letting on that I had kept it safe. We fought and of course grew distant. I suppose today I got my reward for being so horrible to him."

"May I see the letter?" Farnsworth asked. Meredith nodded, the handkerchief now held to her face, and handed it to him. Farnsworth withdrew the flimsy airmail paper and scanned the two sheets. "I will not read it all. There is no need to disclose words of a highly intimate nature." He shook his head, as if the mail had been meant for something other than personal messages. "It is from Julia Wiley to Sir Rupert, whom she addresses as 'my dearest Rupert.' There is a return address in New York City, and the postmark is visible. I would say that the critical statement for our purposes is, 'Baby Peter will always remind me of our time together at Ashcroft House, brief as it was.' She also refers to a sojourn in London, but I see no need to go into details." He handed the letter back to Meredith.

"So what does this mean, exactly?" David asked, looking uncomfortable with such revelations.

"First, let me ask when Peter Wiley died," Farnsworth said, turning to me.

"We are trying to determine exactly when," I said. "It was during a training accident, and his death likely occurred in the early hours of the morning on April twenty-eighth."

"After the death of Sir Rupert," Farnsworth said.

"Yes," I said. "The baron and I saw Peter after Sir Rupert died, in the hallway. And then briefly after we came back from the pub, later that night. That was the last time I saw him. Apparently he left early the following day."

"Are there others who can attest to that?" Farnsworth asked, looking at the group. David, Kaz, Meredith, and Helen all concurred.

"I saw him later that evening," Edgar said. "After Captain Boyle and the baron went off to the pub. He was in the library, looking for something to read. He was apologetic about being a houseguest under the circumstances. Perhaps that is why he left so suddenly."

"All that matters for our purposes is that Sir Rupert predeceased Peter Wiley," Farnsworth said. "Whether by minutes, hours, or days, does not matter. Lady Pemberton, can you attest to what has been said here? You are the only other family member who could do so."

"Yes," Great Aunt Sylvia said in a restrained voice. "The affair did occur, and I had suspected that Rupert continued it in some fashion while he was in London. I recall that Miss Greenshaw asked for time off to visit her mother in Taunton. That may have been the case, or she may have gone on to London."

"And the arrangement for Julia and Mr. Wiley to marry and emigrate to America?" Farnsworth asked, his pen poised over his papers.

"I do not recall all the details," Great Aunt Sylvia said, her chin held high. "But I do know there was a payment made."

"Presumably to give the child a name and a decent start in America," Farnsworth said.

"What other reason could there be?" Great Aunt Sylvia said.

"The arrangement was a surprise to Sir Rupert?" Farnsworth said.

"It was," Great Aunt Sylvia said. "But he finally came to see the wisdom of it."

"I take it the child was not born here," Farnsworth said. "Did Julia Greenshaw and Ted Wiley marry before they left?"

"The marriage was recorded in the village church," Great Aunt Sylvia said. "I was not privy to Julia's giving birth. They left immediately after the marriage ceremony."

"Rather abrupt," Farnsworth said.

"That was the point, wasn't it?" Great Aunt Sylvia said, the ghost of a smile on her lips.

"Very well then," Farnsworth said, jotting a final note. "In the light of what has emerged this morning, I conclude that Peter Wiley was indeed the illegitimate son of Sir Rupert Sutcliffe. Therefore, he inherited the bulk of the estate upon Sir Rupert's death."

"But Peter is dead," Helen said, glancing at the others with a confused look. "What happens now?"

"What happens, Mrs. Martindale, is that most likely you and your sister inherit from Peter Wiley," Farnsworth said. Helen looked startled and Meredith gasped. Hard to blame her, with all that dough falling into her lap when seconds ago she'd had nothing. "As half-siblings, you each stand to inherit an equal share from his estate."

"Most likely, you said?" David asked, his hand holding Helen's.

"We must determine for certain that Peter Wiley was not married and had no children or other siblings," Farnsworth said. "From what Sir Rupert told me, that seems to be the case, but we must confirm the facts. We must know whether he left a will himself, although in my experience young men do not consider such things, especially since his mother was still alive when he left America. It will be a simple matter for an attorney in New York City to investigate. Barring any unforeseen developments, the ownership of the property should be established within a matter of weeks. In the meantime, I can provide access to the accounts for any necessary expenditures. I imagine the upkeep of Ashcroft House to be no small matter."

"Yes," Helen whispered, a trace of surprise and shock in her voice. She looked to Meredith, who covered her mouth with the handkerchief, maybe to keep from gasping out loud again, or maybe to keep the whoops of joy contained until the elderly solicitor left. Farnsworth gathered up his papers and said his goodbyes, as somber as an undertaker. I had the feeling he'd found all this talk of love affairs and American bastards upsetting. Not your usual last testament.

Great Aunt Sylvia walked him out, and I heard Farnsworth tell her she could rely on his discretion. No one need know the convoluted route the inheritance took to end up with Helen and Meredith. Hushed tones and dirty secrets, all part of the service.

With some difficulty, I steered David away from the group after giving my congratulations.

"Last night at the pub, you mentioned seeing tire tracks," I said. "Motorcycle tracks, right?"

"Yes," David said. "What of it?"

"Could you show me where? It won't take a second." He agreed, shaking his head in puzzlement. He led me out the rear door and along a lane leading to a large barn with a stone foundation and several oversize doors. A greenhouse jutted out at a right angle, and there was a fenced-in garden nearby.

"Here," he said, pointing to a depression between the lane and an open door to the barn. "You can still make them out, but not as clearly as I saw them just after that heavy rain." He was right. The soil was crumbling, but the tread marks were clear. Inside, he showed me faint oil stains were the motorbike had been parked. "What's this all about, then?"

"You didn't see anything else? Anything odd or out of place?" I asked, avoiding the question.

"No. As I said, I was simply puttering about, looking at what was left in the barn. It was too much of a jumble to bother with, so I gave up." He was right. This section of the barn was filled with junk: broken pieces of furniture, rusted machinery—there was barely enough space for us to stand in.

"Now I must get back, Billy," David said. "This has all been quite a surprise." He didn't know the half of it.

I found Kaz and brought him to the barn to show him what was left of the tire tracks.

"It rained *after* Peter left here, quite hard," Kaz said. "Perhaps he returned?"

"Or never left," I said.

CHAPTER THIRTY-FIVE

WE DROVE TO Greenway House, and I filled in Colonel Harding on Meredith and Helen's windfall and the discovery of the motorbike tracks.

"It could have been anyone," Harding said. "Maybe a visiting local."

"Petrol is pretty hard to come by," I said, taking a seat in Harding's cramped office. "Most folks use bicycles for short trips."

"An overloaded bicycle could have made those impressions," Kaz offered. "Maybe Crawford is selling off produce."

"I don't give a good goddamn about produce," Harding said, slamming his fist on his desk. "Or bicycles or motorbikes. What I care about is that an American officer with the highest security clearance has been killed. Murdered, if Dawes is right about him being suffocated. We're right back to where we started when I first sent you here. We have a single dead body in a top-secret area and too many unanswered questions. Where and why was Peter Wiley killed?"

"One possibility is he returned to Ashcroft House for some unknown reason," I said. "That would explain the tire tracks being intact after the rainstorm."

"It is logical," Kaz said. "But it does not explain how he ended up in the Channel. We should talk to Lieutenant Siebert about the manifest."

"Go ahead," Harding said, lighting a Lucky Strike and tossing the matchstick into an overflowing ashtray. "When you're done, head to

Dartmouth. General Montgomery decided he needed his own investigation and sent an officer to question surviving personnel."

"Montgomery? Why is he sticking his nose in?" I asked. General Bernard Law Montgomery was famous for his disdain for Americans and his extremely high self-regard.

"He's got a right," Harding said. "The landing force will be under his command during the invasion, so he wants to get to the bottom of what went wrong. At least he sent an American officer. You'll find Major Brian McClure onboard LST 289 in Dartmouth harbor."

"There is one other thing we should do," Kaz said, bringing up the subject he and I had discussed on the drive over here. "We need to thoroughly search Lieutenant Wiley's office."

"I told you; I looked and saw nothing out of the ordinary," Harding said. "The same as when you searched his room."

"His room was not a secure location," I said. "If he had anything to hide, something that would be a clue as to where he was, his office would be the safest place to leave it."

"And you think you can find it when I couldn't?" Harding said.

"It's my job," I said. "A cop is naturally suspicious of everyone. You're probably too much of a gentleman to do a proper search anyway."

"Okay, cut out the brownnosing, Boyle. Have a chat with Siebert, then get back here. I'll take you in."

"Thanks, Colonel. Is Big Mike around?" It would help to have another bluecoat in khaki in on the search, if only to distract Harding if he didn't like us pawing through top-secret stuff.

"I had to send him to London earlier this morning with some reports. He should be back in a few hours. Now get out of here. I have more on my plate than one dead naval officer."

Siebert was ensconced in an upstairs room that served as his office, bedroom, and dining room, by the looks of the dirty cups and dishes scattered about. It was even more of a mess than the last time we'd been here. Add hospital room to the list, thanks to the white bandage around his head and another wrapped around his wrist.

"What do you want this time?" Lieutenant James Siebert said. He had files stacked on files on the table in front of him. Wads of carbon paper filled a wastepaper basket, and his hands were grimy with the stuff. He'd evidently rubbed his eyes at some point, and he had the look of an injured raccoon.

"I want you to give us your full attention," I said. "I'm sorry you were hurt, but I need some answers. You're the officer in charge of assigning observers to Operation Tiger, right?"

"Yeah," he said. He gestured vaguely in the direction of two mismatched chairs and winced, holding his bandaged wrist.

"We need to know which ship Lieutenant Peter Wiley was on," I said.

"Wiley's a pain in the ass, like I explained last time," Siebert said. "He told me Harding gave him the okay to go along, and I assigned him to LST 507. Then when I didn't see his name on the orders, I asked Harding about it. He chewed me out for not checking with him first."

"Lieutenant Wiley is dead," I said.

"What? How?" Siebert said, obviously surprised. "Jesus, I didn't know. I wouldn't have said that if I'd known."

"He washed up on the shore with all the other bodies," Kaz said.

"That's not possible," Siebert said. "He wasn't on any list. I made sure of that after Harding got through with me."

"He couldn't have snuck on?" I asked. "The boarding must have been hectic."

"No," Siebert said, leaning back in his chair and working through the possibilities. "Individual observers had to present their orders when they went onboard, and then the names had to be checked against the personnel manifest. I guess he could have gone on with an infantry unit, but a naval officer would look out of place. He'd be spotted right away and questioned."

"When was the last time you saw Lieutenant Wiley?" Kaz asked.

"Right before he went off on leave," Siebert said. "I was glad to see him go, so he wouldn't pester me anymore about Operation Tiger."

"Did he say why he was so desperate to be on board?" I asked.

"No, he just insisted he had to. Said it was important for his work."

"What was his job here exactly?" I asked.

"No idea," Siebert said. "He did it behind a locked door in a guarded room. Not something you ask about around here."

"Why did you go on the maneuver?" Kaz asked. "Was it important for you to be there?"

"Hell, no," Siebert said. "I organized everything ahead of time. I could have stayed warm and dry, but I thought it would be fun. Can you imagine that? I went out on the 507 and ended up floating on a section of decking until a British destroyer came along at dawn. It was not fun."

"Are these all the manifests?" I asked, pointing to the piles in front of Siebert.

"Shipping manifests, unit orders, departure schedules, all the paperwork required to get thousands of GIs onto a convoy of LSTs on time," he answered. "These are the personnel manifests, by ship. All the individual brass and observers not part of a participating unit." He handed a folder to me and I glanced through it. The original list was typed, but names had been lined out and others written in.

"This is a mess," I said. "How do you know who went where?"

"Tell me about it," Siebert said. "I was getting changes up to the day before the exercise. New units were added and squeezed out any room for extra men on some ships. Last-minute orders from generals and their staff, that sort of thing."

"Did you look for Peter Wiley's name in there?" I said.

"No. I would have been the guy who put him on the list. No reason to go searching through all this when I know I didn't."

"You're certain no one else could have added his name?" Kaz asked.

Siebert looked irritated. "I locked this stuff up whenever I left the office," he said. "I even took the manifests with me on that damn joyride, in a waterproof bag. There's no way. I never thought anyone would be dumb enough to go against orders and add their name to the list, but it was a top-secret exercise, so I kept everything secure. Besides, names are checked on each boat as well. They have duplicate lists, so adding a name to my list doesn't ensure you get onboard."

"Listen, Lieutenant," I said. "I have orders that would let me force you to go through those manifests standing on your head. So save us a lot of aggravation and do it, okay?"

"Harding told me about your paperwork from Ike," Siebert said. "All right, even though I don't see the sense of it."

"This is the army," I said. "Nothing makes sense. It's a long shot, but you said yourself that you never envisioned someone sneaking themselves onto the list. Off would have been more likely, right?"

"Yeah," he admitted. "I get it. If I didn't expect it, that's an advantage for Wiley."

We left Siebert glumly checking his lists and found Harding finishing a cup of coffee.

"You are about to be further initiated into the brotherhood of BIGOTs," Harding said, unlocking a desk drawer and grabbing a key chain. "Are you ready?"

"We know how to keep our mouths shut, Colonel," I said.

"Let's get this over with so you can get to Dartmouth and see what Montgomery's officer is up to. Maybe he's even learned something useful."

"If he did, I'd be shocked if he shared it. But as he's a fellow Yank, you never know," I said as we trailed Harding to Wiley's office. The guard stood aside as Harding unlocked the door, ushered us in, and quickly shut and locked it behind us.

A tilted artist's table sat beneath high windows. Paints and brushes stood ready on a side table; a rag hung off the back of a chair where Peter might have tossed it after cleaning up. Against the wall sat a long trestle table covered with reconnaissance photographs taped together to create a mosaic. Fields, villages, beaches, and gun emplacements.

"Colleville-sur-Mer," Kaz said behind me. "I know this place. I drove through Normandy on holiday before the war."

"Omaha Beach," I said, reading the caption on the map. TOP SECRET—BIGOT was printed in large green letters at the bottom. Another map hung next to it. "Utah Beach."

"Sainte-Mère-Église," Kaz said, pointing to an inland town on the Utah Beach map. "I recall a pleasant meal in the town square. Coq au vin, I believe."

"Normandy," I said, taking in what had been revealed to us. "That's a long way across the Channel."

"Exactly," Harding said. "The Germans probably think the same thing. Notice anything familiar about the Utah Beach map?"

I studied it, noting the broad expanse of beach and a flooded area beyond it. Causeways linked the beach to Sainte-Mère-Église and other towns and villages along a north-south roadway.

"Slapton Sands," I said. "Slapton Ley is the spitting image of the water behind the beach."

"The Germans flooded it, to isolate the beach. That's why we needed to practice getting off the beach quickly and moving inland. Slapton Sands was the perfect stand-in for Utah Beach."

"Which is why the German attack on the convoy was doubly disastrous," Kaz said. "If the Nazis knew the destination of Operation Tiger, it would be a simple matter to deduce Normandy as the target, and these specific locations."

"Exactly. Which is why we had to identify all the BIGOTs and make sure no one had been picked up by the Germans. The death toll is staggering, over nine hundred dead so far and some still missing. But it would have been far worse if any of this had been revealed."

I looked at the maps and the photos on the table. It was easy to see what Peter had been doing—creating the maps from the recon photos laid out so precisely. The map was accurate down to the smallest building or path. At the bottom of each map, there was a watercolor painting, a dead-on view of the beach from the water. The watercolor was laid out to correspond to physical features on the map directly above it.

"Perspective," I said, taking in the painstaking detail and beauty of Peter's artwork. "He wanted to see the beach from the perspective of a landing craft."

"He was insistent about that," Harding said. "But as you can see, he did a great job from the photographs alone. He worked in church steeples, towers, bunkers, and even trees. I couldn't take a chance on losing him, and besides, he needed some leave. He'd been holed up in here for weeks, working ten or twelve hours a day. He was exhausted."

On the back side of the maps there were detailed charts showing information about the sun, moon, tide, and currents. Harding showed us an idea Peter had come up with to help navigators get as close as possible to the landing beaches. Using a system of transparent overlays, profiles of landing craft of all sizes were displayed. When you adjusted the sheet over a graph showing the slope of the beach, navigators could see the water's depth and where their specific craft would run aground.

"Very clever," Kaz said. "Peter's death is a loss in many ways."

"The only good news is that he'd finished all the maps before he went on leave," Harding said. "It's a damn shame he died. We were going to start a new project soon. Southern France." He leaned against the door as Kaz and I searched the room, checking drawers and rummaging through stacks of recon photos, old road maps of France, and even a pile of postcards from prewar vacations.

Half an hour later, we gave up. This had been Peter's studio, but he hadn't kept anything personal here. I sat in his chair, looking out the window. His artist's table set at the perfect angle to catch the light. I could imagine him hunched over a sheet, using colored inks to create the map itself and the more delicate watercolors to paint the view of the shoreline below, the brush clutched in his thin fingers.

His fingers. I thought back to when I found his body. Besides his khakis, he'd been wearing nothing but his dog tags. His fingers were bare.

"Where's his ring?" I said, jumping up out of the seat.

"What?" Harding said.

"The ring he was wearing when he first came to Ashcroft House," I said. "It wasn't on his finger when I found the body. He had a watch as well, but that was gone too."

"The Pemberton family coat of arms," Kaz explained. "It had been given to his mother, and she passed it on to him. A remembrance, I would assume, from Sir Rupert."

"Sir Rupert nearly keeled over when he saw it," I said. "He'd suspected his daughter Meredith had stolen it years ago. We should search his room again."

Harding locked up Peter's office and took us back to his quarters.

Nothing much had changed. This time we tossed the place, throwing the mattress on the floor, pulling out all the drawers, turning pockets inside out. Nothing.

"I hate to say it, but it could have been stolen, along with his watch," Harding said. "He always wore one. Nothing fancy, a standard issue A-11 wristwatch."

"You can sell a watch on the black market," Kaz said. "But the ring was unique."

"I remember seeing it while he showed me the drafts, now you mention it. It looked like solid gold," Harding said. "Tempting for anyone with an inclination to thievery. Especially after hauling bodies out of the Channel all day. Dozens of sailors and soldiers would have had a chance to help themselves."

"Maybe," I said. "Or it could have been a civilian, if the body washed up on shore."

All we had were more questions. Possibilities that added up to maybes. Harding and Kaz went to grab a cup of joe, but I begged off. Sitting in a chair amidst the chaos of Peter's belongings, I tried to focus my mind on what we knew for certain and what we were guessing at. Or assuming. There was more guesswork than certainty, which I tried to tell myself was good, since I could boil things down to their essence and move on from there.

Peter Wiley had a ring, a ring that connected him to Ashcroft House. The ring was gone.

Peter Wiley was not approved to go on Operation Tiger.

Peter Wiley showed up among the dead of Operation Tiger.

Peter Wiley was alive the night Sir Rupert died. I never saw him again.

Sometime after that, he took a blow to the head, probably not severe enough to kill him.

What else did I know for certain? Nothing.

It was probable, based on what Major Dawes had said about his cloudy eyes, that Peter died out of the water.

It was possible, also based on Dawes's observation, that Peter had been burked. Suffocated. But that one was iffy. I could imagine a crowded scene on a sinking ship, men surging to escape through a hatchway, pressing Peter against a bulkhead and constricting his breathing. It happened often enough when crowds stampeded. But Peter wasn't supposed to be on a ship, was he? So how did he end up in a navy life jacket, among the dead who were?

The motorbike tracks. How did they fit in? I decided that wasn't even worth pursuing. Too many other explanations presented themselves. Crawford on a bicycle loaded down with . . . what? Alice Withers on the back, getting a ride to town? Crawford didn't seem the type to grant a favor like that. But I was an American, and there was no love lost between us on account of that. Maybe he was a swell guy to his own people.

A knock sounded behind me. I nearly jumped out of my skin.

"Billy," Big Mike said. "You okay? I called your name but you didn't budge."

"I'm fine," I said. "Lost in thought, that's all, trying to figure out what happened to Lieutenant Wiley."

"Well, here's something to cheer you up," he said, handing me an envelope. "A letter from Diana. She sent it to the office, probably figuring one of us would get it to you." With that, he left me alone.

The return address was Seaton Manor. Which meant she was on leave, and released from whatever exile MI5 had condemned her to after my last case. Which also meant I might get to see her soon. Not a bad deduction for a detective who couldn't tell up from down in the Wiley case.

I opened the letter gently, so I could close it again to keep it safe. Diana had two weeks' leave, a third of which was used up, judging by the date on the letter. She'd be in London in two days, then busy with other matters for some time. With the invasion coming and her working for the Special Operations Executive, you didn't need to be a detective to work that one out.

There was some other stuff, this being a love letter. I'll keep that to myself, thank you very much.

CHAPTER THIRTY-SIX

I SAUNTERED DOWN the stairs, patting the letter in my pocket. It meant I'd see Diana soon. It also meant she'd probably be parachuting into Nazi-occupied France next, but this was wartime, and we'd both learned to take our pleasure where we could and not worry about the worst that could happen. Dwelling on the horrors of combat and clandestine operations tended to put a damper on things.

As I made for the kitchen, I heard a loud thump from the room right ahead. I peaked in, pushing the door open all the way. The room was crammed with boxes and packing crates, with barely a spot to stand in. A box of files had broken, and papers cascaded across what little floor space there was. A stout, matronly woman stood over them, shaking her head, one hand pressed to her brow.

"Excuse me," I said. "Can I help you?" She was well dressed, her hair done in curls and a string of pearls around her neck. Definitely not a cleaning woman or domestic. So I framed the question the way you do when someone is where they're not supposed to be. But she took me literally.

"Oh!" she said, giving a start and patting her hand over her heart. "You surprised me, young man. Yes, how nice of you to offer. Could you gather these papers up for me?" She sat down at a table, the only clear spot in the room. "I was looking for a particular document when the whole affair came tumbling down. You are so kind to help."

"Glad to, ma'am," I said, handing her a pile of papers. "May I ask what you're doing in here? This is a naval headquarters, after all."

"My goodness, where are my manners? I am Mrs. Mallowan, the owner of Greenway House. Along with Max, of course. My husband. He's in Cairo with the intelligence service. Can't say any more about that, as I'm sure you understand."

"Captain Billy Boyle, ma'am. Glad to meet you. It was nice of you to give up your home. It's quite a setting." I gathered up the rest of the papers, trying to glance at what was written on them without being too obvious about it. She looked familiar, but I couldn't place her, and I hoped some clue would jump out from the jumble of documents.

"Oh, I didn't give it up. His Majesty's Government took it for the duration," she said. "But I don't mind, what with Max gone. I live and work in London, and I'm glad these nice Americans can enjoy Greenway. They let me have this one room to store my personal possessions. I had to come down from London to find a copy of a contract. Oh, there it is. You've found it, Captain Boyle."

She snatched a stack of papers from my hand, but not before I saw the letterhead. William Collins and Company. Then it hit me. I'd seen this woman last night right before I fell asleep.

"You're Agatha Christie," I said.

"There you have me, Captain Boyle. It's Agatha Mallowan in real life, but in the world of literature, I do confess, I am she."

"I'm reading *Lord Edgware Dies* right now," I said, feeling a little star-struck. "It's great."

"Thank you, Captain Boyle. You are most gallant, helping me and paying a compliment at the same time. What is it you do here at Greenway House? I thought it was mainly naval personnel here."

"Coast Guard, most of them, actually. I'm not stationed here. I'm a detective, or at least I was back in Boston. Now I work for General Eisenhower."

"What a delight to meet a real detective, Captain Boyle. Has someone been murdered at Greenway House?" She smiled conspiratorially, but the look on my face must have told her that I really was here on official business. "Oh dear, is it true?"

"A lieutenant, name of Peter Wiley," I said. "Although I doubt he was killed here." .

"Peter!" Her hand went to her mouth and her eyes widened. "What a sweet, talented young man. I saw him painting in the garden the last time I visited, and we struck up a conversation. I remember his delicate hands. So sad. As are all the deaths, of course, but when you know someone is full of promise, it becomes a tragedy twice again, doesn't it?"

"That's a good way of putting it, Mrs. Mallowan. He had a lot to look forward to." His artwork, not to mention a sizeable and unexpected inheritance.

"It's suddenly very close in here, Captain Boyle. Would you care to walk in the fresh air with me? I would like to hear more about Peter's death, if you're willing."

I was. Who better to consult with than the creator of Hercule Piorot?

We sat on a bench, overlooking the sloping lawn of Greenway House. In the distance, a flight of Spitfires roared their way to the Channel, the snarl of engines echoing off the banks of the River Dart.

"They are so graceful, those devices of war," Mrs. Mallowan said. "It is sometimes hard to imagine how terribly lethal they are."

"That applies to people as well," I said.

"Yes. And of course we make the hardware of war in our own image, don't we? A combination of beauty, brutality, and efficiency. Now, tell me how young Peter died."

"First, I need to tell you about his parents," I said. Her sadness about Peter notwithstanding, I saw a gleam of fascination in her eyes. She understood this would be no ordinary story. I began with Peter showing up at Ashcroft House, shocking everyone with his ring. Went on to Sir Rupert's request for me to determine if Peter was his son. Then I gave her a sanitized version of Operation Tiger, and asked her to keep mum about what little I did tell her. I described the Sutcliffe clan and Lady Pemberton, told her about Sir Rupert's death and all that followed, including the revelations at the reading of the will. I finished up with the discovery of Peter's body among the dead and the missing ring. When I was finished, she remained silent, her brow furrowed in thought.

"The death of Sir Rupert," she finally said. "Nothing suspicious?"

"It doesn't seem so. His daughter Meredith was not exactly heartbroken, but there's nothing to suggest she killed him. The doctor confirmed his heart was bad, had been for a while. He should have been resting, not working."

"It would seem that there are strong emotions lurking within Meredith," she said.

"She wasn't happy being left out of the will," I said.

"No, that's not what I mean," Mrs. Mallowan said. "When she was an impressionable young girl, she discovered her father's betrayal. That left a mark upon her. The proof is that she held on to that letter all these years. What rational reason would she have to do so?"

"To use it against Sir Rupert at some point?"

"No, Captain Boyle. She wanted to keep her anger and hatred alive. Time does heal the wounds of youth, and I'd say Meredith kept that letter to make certain hers never healed. I'd wager she was very close to her mother, which is where her loyalty lay. When her mother died, perhaps she feared a reconciliation with Sir Rupert, which would be a betrayal, and of course betrayal was the very thing she hated her father for. That made it all the more important for her to hold on to her loathing for him."

"I had wondered if she'd taunted him with it the night he died. It wouldn't be murder, but close to it."

"Perhaps the question is, why did she bring it out that night, of all nights?"

"Good question," I said. "She had told him she'd destroyed it years before, so there had to be a point in bringing it out now."

"That may be," she said. "But from the way you described their raised voices, it sounds like a serious argument. And a woman has very few weapons to bring to a fight with a powerful man. Of course, it is easy for me to come up with ideas. That is what I do. The truth, of course, is much more difficult to discern."

"You're right about it being an argument," I said. "She was enraged.

I think she said something about not standing for whatever he was doing to her when she stormed out of his office."

"Perhaps he told her she would inherit nothing," Mrs. Mallowan said. "But then what good would the letter do? She couldn't blackmail him with it if he was intent upon acknowledging Peter Wiley as his illegitimate son."

"Then we're back to rage and revenge," I said. "He must have been hurt to know that she'd kept the news from him all those years. But what does any of this have to do with Peter Wiley dead in the Channel?"

"That is a mystery, Captain Boyle," she said with a pleasant smile. "My detectives always look for the small things. Little inconsistencies that lead to the truth. I've no idea how useful that is in a real murder investigation, I must say. But lies are actually quite difficult to maintain, don't you think?"

"Lies and secrets, Mrs. Mallowan. Like Paris of Troy in *Lord Edgware Dies*."

"Exactly! But remember what happened to the young man who realized what that meant."

"I haven't got there yet," I said. "But I get the idea. I'll be careful."

"Please do, Captain Boyle. I'd like you to catch whoever was responsible for this foul deed. There's death enough in the world today without violence being done by one of our own. Tell me a little more about the men in the household."

I told her about David and his burn scars, and the desire he showed to serve again, which disappeared fairly quickly after Sir Rupert's death. And Edgar's principled stand in India, which cost him his position, not to mention his sobriety.

"But they're only visitors," I said. "Roger Crawford is the estate manager, very efficient at it too. Sir Rupert left him a decent sum."

"But?"

"But he's arrogant. Walks through the house like he owns the place. Apparently Ashcroft House is quite egalitarian, but he always strikes me as having a smirk on his face."

"You don't like the man," Mrs. Mallowan said.

"No, I don't, perhaps because he has a chip on his shoulder about Americans. He had a house in the South Hams, which the government took over. I've seen what's left of it after all the live-fire exercises. Hard to blame a guy for being sore after the American army uses your place for target practice."

"And Edgar—Meredith's husband—takes refuge in the bottle, you said?"

"Pretty much. Booze and Shakespeare seem to be his two passions. I think that one decent act in India was all he had in him. He's planning on writing a book about *Hamlet*, which is the only thing I've seen him get excited about," I said. "David's wife, Helen, couldn't look at his face when I first arrived. But now she manages it, and they seem to be getting along. I tried to get him a position here so he could stay in uniform, but his eyesight is too badly damaged. I thought he'd take it hard, but he shrugged it off soon enough."

"All this after the death of Sir Rupert?"

"Yes," I said. "The doctor saw no signs of poison, and confirmed Sir Rupert's heart condition. A matter of time, he said."

"Hmmm. Let me think," she said, tapping her finger against her lips. A ship's horn sounded in the distance, beyond Dartmouth harbor. A couple of minutes passed. "Let me venture a guess about this Meredith woman. Once Peter Wiley left the house, she voiced her displeasure with him in some way, perhaps even saying he would not be welcome again. Am I correct?"

"Yes, you are. How did you know that?"

"Because it is obvious that she knows more than she lets on. Her argument with her father behind closed doors tells me that. Perhaps she sincerely disliked Peter Wiley, and saw no reason to hide the fact after her father's death, or from the moment Sir Rupert told her about Peter being in the revised will. But it is Helen who interests me. You described her as somewhat sensitive, which would make her reaction to her husband's injuries understandable. It's the change in demeanor that is hard to account for."

"Like her husband's?"

"No. That is easily understandable. A disfigured veteran might well worry about how he will make his way in the world and earn a living. Sir Rupert's death may have seemed heaven-sent to a man with half a face, so it is entirely natural that he would no longer wish for employment. He certainly had reason to believe that Helen would receive a decent inheritance, since she and her father got along. But I wonder what drew Helen closer to David, following her father's death? Mourning, or something else?"

"Are you saying I should treat Helen as a suspect? She doesn't seem the murderous type," I said.

"With your knowledge of the real world of criminals and killers, I should bow to your expertise. But based only on the sketch of Helen you have given me, I note the change in her attitude. Why, I ask? What would cause a young woman who is repulsed by her husband's scars to alter her behavior suddenly? Do you have an answer, Captain Boyle?"

"I understand criminals, and that includes female criminals, Mrs. Mallowan. But women in general? I need all the help I can get."

"That's refereshingly honest of you, Captain Boyle. But she bears watching. Is Lady Pemberton a factor in this mystery?"

"I think she knows more than she lets on," I said. "She's still sharp, and she's seen everything that's happened at Ashcroft House since the Great War."

"Ah," Mrs. Mallowan said, tilting her head back and letting the sunlight fall on her face. "Why does the matriarch keep any secrets at all? Her silence must have a purpose. If you discover that, you will then know what the secret is, and why she keeps it hidden."

"Are you sure?" I asked, after thinking through what she'd said.

"Goodness, no, Captain Boyle!" Mrs. Mallowan laughed, turning her face toward mine and clapping her hands together. "I am sure of so little. These are merely ideas, based on what you have told me. When I am planning a book, I sketch out concepts and characters and let them take me where they will. This is much like that process. I am extrapolating from what you've told me. But if I spent five minutes with poor Helen or ferocious Meredith, I might form an entirely different opinion of them. I only know them at second hand, through your American eyes, after all."

"Fair enough," I said. "You've given me a different way to look at these people, and that's a big help. It's been fun talking shop with you."

"Remember to watch for those small inconsistencies, Captain Boyle. Now, is there anything you've forgotten to tell me about? Something so minor you left it out?" I didn't think so, until I thought of the motorcycle tracks.

"Peter arrived on a motorbike. It hasn't been found. But we discovered tire tracks leading out of a barn at Ashcroft House. The only thing is, it was after that heavy rain. They likely would have been washed away if he'd left when everyone said he did."

"Oh dear," Mrs. Mallowan said, rising from the bench. "That is not good, not good at all."

"We thought it might have been a bicycle, actually, carrying a heavy load." As I watched the worried look on her face, I began to feel guilty for not pursuing this clue more thoroughly.

"It could be. But don't you see? If it isn't, you are in some danger, Captain Boyle."

"I can handle myself," I said, somewhat defensively.

"I'm sure you can, but this is an unusual business. Have you thought about the implications?"

"What do you mean?"

"I mean the motorbike may have been used to spirit away the body of poor Peter Wiley, which means the killer is definitely someone from Ashcroft House. Do you have any idea where the motorbike is now?"

"It could be anywhere. In the river, maybe."

"I don't think so, Captain. You mentioned that an inexpensive watch was stolen from Peter's body, as well as the gold ring. That tells me that the thief—and I assume that the thief and the killer are one and the same—is not one to waste anything. A man—or woman—who knows the value of things, and who has perhaps gone without in life."

"We looked through the barn," I said. "I guess we could do a better search of the property."

"Where do Meredith and Helen live?"

"London. But they'd never get enough petrol to drive a motorbike there, not that I can envision either one of them on one."

"Then that leaves Crawford, the estate manager," she said. "I have two recommendations for you, Captain Boyle. First, check his house in the South Hams. A restricted area makes a fine hiding place."

"Good idea. What's the other?"

"Move out of Ashcroft House immediately. This affair is not yet concluded."

CHAPTER THIRTY-SEVEN

"WHO WERE YOU speaking to?" Kaz asked as I started up the jeep to drive to Dartmouth. Big Mike was stuck with Colonel Harding, doing something hush-hush, and we were detailed to check on Monty's spy. Or liaison officer, depending on how diplomatic I felt.

"Agatha Christie," I said.

"No, Billy, not the voices in your head," Kaz retorted. "The lady on the bench."

"Don't believe your pal, eh?" I accelerated going into the curve leading to the main road, and Kaz held on to his hat and his seat.

"You read enough detective novels that it's easy to imagine you carrying on imaginary conversations with the authors," Kaz said. "Didn't I once see you throw a book against the wall and curse the writer?"

"Yeah, because it was a lousy book," I said. "But it just so happens that Agatha Christie, or Mrs. Mallowan, as she prefers to be called, owns Greenway House. It was taken over by the government for the duration, and she was back to look for some business papers."

"Really?" Kaz asked. "Did you discuss the case with her?"

"Yeah. I gave her the basics. She'd met Peter and was upset to hear the news." I went over what we'd talked about, taking it easy on the curves so he could concentrate.

"Those are interesting insights into Meredith and Helen," he said. "But a bit of a stretch concerning the motorbike. Not impossible though. It's too bad Diana isn't here. She may have come to the same conclusion about the two women."

"That's some other news I have," I said, and told Kaz about Diana's letter.

"Good for you both," he said. "Now, what do you think about the advice to leave Ashcroft House?"

"I think it's time," I said. "We have a lot to look into, and I'd prefer not to investigate people whose roof I'm staying under. Let's find this Major McClure and see if he's come up with anything. I doubt it, but orders are orders. Then we'll pack up and say our goodbyes."

"For now," Kaz said.

"Right," I said. "And I want to put some gentle pressure on Great Aunt Sylvia. She is definitely hiding something. She's afraid of scandal and what it would do to the family's reputation. The Pemberton family, that is."

"Do you think her recent illness was real?"

"She seemed genuinely disoriented, and worried about it too. That's hard to fake." We crossed the river and drove through the small villages on the outskirts of Dartmouth. British Tommies were on the march today, single file on either side of the road, their hobnail boots raising a racket as they double-timed it while carrying full packs and rifles at ports arms. I almost felt guilty as I sped past them.

As we wound our way into Dartmouth through streets choked with bicycles, sailors, military vehicles, and GIs searching for girls, Kaz and I talked about the ring and the likelihood of its simply having been purloined by any of the soldiers or civilians recovering bodies. It wouldn't be the first time greed won out over decency. But I was coming around to the notion that it was somewhere in Ashcroft House, hidden by one of its denizens.

"Why?" Kaz asked when I spoke of my hunch.

"Because of everything Mrs. Mallowan said. Meredith keeping the letter all those years. Helen suddenly getting lovey with David."

"You are suspicious because a wife treats her wounded husband well?"

"No, I'm suspicious because her behavior changed," I said. "I think

Meredith is up to no good, and Helen is going along with it. That's why she's leaning on David; she knows she's wrong and wants some comfort from him. I don't think she's made of the same stuff as Meredith." I pulled over near the docks, where the grey warships and transports were lined up like a wall of steel.

"Do you think David is involved in Peter Wiley's death?" Kaz asked, his voice low and his eyes drilling into mine.

"No," I said, after a few seconds. "It doesn't add up. He did drop the idea of going back on active service pretty quickly, but that could well be because he saw a future for himself at Ashcroft."

"Remember, he was turned down by Harding at Greenway House," Kaz said. "He didn't give up, necessarily."

"No, but he didn't seem disappointed, did he? We both expected him to take it hard." We got out of the jeep and walked to the embankment, looking for LST 289, where Major McClure was running his investigation. Sections of wharf ran out into the harbor, some long and wide enough for trucks to offload supplies and men. Others were smaller, with destroyers, Motor Torpedo Boats, and other craft tied up alongside. The tide was out, and the smell of rotting fish wafted up from the muddy flats.

"No," Kaz said. "I must admit I was surprised by his behavior before the reading of the will. Helen could have been left nothing at all. It would have been very English of Sir Rupert to leave everything to the nearest male blood relative, no matter how distant."

"I hadn't thought about that," I said, then pointed to LST 289. It was easy to spot, with its battle-damaged, blackened hull and the bright pinpoints of light as welders worked the steel. The mooring next to the 289 was empty, and three English kids, maybe ten or eleven years old, ran along the water's edge and climbed up a wooden ladder on the wharf, freezing when they saw us approaching. They were carrying all manner of muddy debris that had washed up at high tide, and by their wide-eyed looks I guessed they'd been chased out of here before.

They were about to turn and bolt when I saw what one of them had slung over his shoulder.

"Hey, wait, want a Hershey bar?" I yelled. They put on the brakes.

"Do you have a Hershey bar?" Kaz asked. He had a point.

"What do we have to do, Yank?" The oldest one came forward, sizing us up. "And there's three of us. We'd need three bars, wouldn't we?"

"Tell you what, kid," I said, fishing the coins out of my pocket and nodding to Kaz, who added his own loose change. "You can have this and buy whatever you want. It's a few shillings, at least."

"Give it here then," he said, holding out his hand. All of them had muddy feet but seemed decently dressed otherwise. Schoolkids, I figured, looking to scrounge what they could from the docks. I flipped the oldest kid one coin.

"The rest after you tell me what you've got there, and what else you've come up with," I said.

"You can't make us give it back," one of the younger ones said. "It's stuff you Yanks throw away."

"Overboard's more like it," the other said, and they all laughed. "You lot do toss a lot of good gear, you know."

"I don't want anything back," I said. "And you're not in trouble. Finders keepers, I say."

"All right then," the oldest said. "I got this here canteen and web belt. It's empty, so it floated. And a denim shirt, hardly a rip in it. Needs a good washing is all."

"I got K-Rations," another said. "They were in a big wooden crate, four packs of them. Came in on the tide, and I seen plenty of Yanks walk right by, not even give 'em a look. My old man might be able to dry out the cigarettes, don't you think?"

"Sure," I said. "What about you?" I asked the smallest boy.

"I got this," he said. "A life jacket. Might be able to sell it to a fisherman. I found a bottle of Scotch once, still half full. Dad liked that, he did."

"How much do you think you can get?" I asked. The life jacket was sodden and grimy, but US NAVY was clearly stenciled along the collar.

"Not much. They come in on the tide often enough. You Yanks are a careless lot, ain't ya?"

"Yeah, but we're no fools," I said, handing over the coins. "Now beat it." They didn't need to be told twice, disappearing into a side street in a flash, their laughter and shrieks of joy bouncing off the walls.

"Well, what was that about?" Kaz asked.

"Solving a murder, I think. The hell with Major McClure. Let's go to Ashcroft House and grab our gear. We're bunking somewhere else tonight."

Kaz was full of questions, but I was still putting pieces together in my mind, and I begged him to let me think in silence. It was the little inconsistencies that were beginning to come together, just as Mrs. Mallowan had predicted. They weren't all in place yet, but I was starting to see where they rubbed up against the truth. We arrived at Ashcroft House and saw Meredith walking from the gardens, a basket of cut flowers in her hand. Already the matron of the manor.

"Baron, Captain," she said, walking briskly our way. "I'm glad to see you. I wonder if you'd think it terribly rude of me to ask how much longer you planned to stay with us? After everything that's happened, I think the family needs some privacy to get used to the new situation here. I'm sure you understand?" I did. It was the polite, English version of *get the hell out.*

"Your hospitality has been most appreciated," I said. "Actually, we've received new orders, and I hoped to find you all here to make our apologies for a sudden departure. So it works out for all concerned."

"You can't stay for dinner then? It would be so nice to have a farewell meal together."

"Sadly, no," Kaz said. "We have pressing business to attend to. Is David here? I would like to say goodbye."

"Yes. He was reading in the library when I came out," Meredith said, the relief evident in her eyes. The dinner invitation was as sincere as her line that the family needed privacy. "I must get these flowers inside, so I shall say farewell now. Please do come again, Baron Kazimierz. Your visit did David a world of good, I'm sure." With that, she trotted off, the cut flowers bouncing in her basket.

"Is there anything you want me to ask David?" Kaz said.

"Yes," I said. "Ask him if he's heard if there were any other letters from America that Meredith or Helen kept. Then tell him we have a suspect in Peter Wiley's death. Go down to the kitchen and tell Mrs. Dudley or Williams the same."

"So that word spreads?" Kaz asked. I nodded. He was getting the hang of this. I went upstairs to speak with Great Aunt Sylvia, hoping to find her awake and alert. I knocked and found her seated at the window, reading an Agatha Christie mystery. I had to smile.

"Billy, come in," she said, closing the book. Mrs. Mallowan looked up at me from the back cover. I told Great Aunt Sylvia we had to depart.

"I am sorry you must leave us. I would have liked a visit with less death and distress, but even so I've enjoyed your company," she said.

"Same here," I said, shutting the door behind me.

She gave me a look that said she understood this wasn't only a social call. "The time has come to talk of many things, of shoes and ships and sealing wax," she said, a smile forming on her face.

"And cabbages and kings," I added.

"I loved *Alice's Adventures in Wonderland* as a young girl," she said. "I still have my childhood copy. I devoured *Through the Looking Glass* as well, and I remember both fondly. Odd, at my age, isn't it?"

"I don't think so," I said. "It's a link to the past. I'd bet the past is almost as important to you as the future."

"Be blunt, will you? I might not have that much future left in me."

"I think—no, I know—that you are holding something back from me. About Meredith and Sir Rupert. About Peter Wiley."

"Why would I do that?"

"To make sure I don't see what's on the other side of the looking glass," I said.

"Well, if I am keeping family secrets, why should I reveal anything to you now, when you are about to take your leave of us?" She tilted her head back, every inch the injured aristocrat.

"Because we have a suspect in Peter Wiley's death. If his killing has anything to do with a family member, it would be best if it came out now. If Inspector Grange finds out later, it could be quite a public scandal."

"I thought Peter was killed by the Germans," Lady Pemberton said.

"That's because you haven't looked behind my looking glass," I said. "When Alice stepped through the mirror, didn't she find a book that you could only read by holding it up to a mirror? That's what a murder investigation is like. Once you've put all the pieces together, sometimes all you need to do is look at them a bit differently and they make perfect sense." I was spinning a tall tale of certainty with damn few facts to support it, but that's what interrogations are all about.

Confusion passed across her face as she calculated what to say. That told me there really was a secret. "I knew Meredith had the letter," she said, her bony hands clutching the spine of the book.

"Of course you did," I said. "You see everything that goes on here. Did Meredith come to you when she intercepted the letter? Had she been confiding in you before then?"

"Yes, ever since she spied her father and that woman kissing in the garden. You see, she idolized him. But that moment changed everything. She went from a delightful young girl to a devil of a daughter. At least to Rupert. She transferred her mighty allegiance to her mother, and from that day on, it was war. But I fail to see what this has to do with Peter Wiley."

"Maybe nothing," I said. "Do you have any idea why she kept the letter for all these years?"

"She liked to taunt Rupert about it. She told him he'd never hear from Julia Greenshaw again. Needless to say, that's one reason why she left, and perhaps why she was not mentioned in the will."

"If she took her mother's side in all this, why didn't Louise Pemberton leave Ashcroft House to Meredith and Helen instead of her husband? Wouldn't Louise reward such loyalty?"

"She intended to," Great Aunt Sylvia said. "In fact she promised Meredith she would. That was when they were in India. But the illness came on quickly, and when she died, she had not changed her will. I understand she had written to Farnsworth, our family solicitor, saying that she wanted a new document drafted. If he sent her one, it did not come in time. Her previous will stood, in which she left everything to her husband. Written in the flush of romance, I suspect."

"Meredith must have been unhappy with that," I said.

"Oh, she was. Meredith accused her father of destroying the new will so he would inherit Ashcroft. He denied it, of course, but that was the final break between them."

"Then she stole some jewelry and went to London," I said.

"The ring was missing, but that has been explained by recent events. She did take a few other old pieces, probably enough to sell and get herself set up properly. Nothing of sentimental value. I never begrudged her that much."

"So she and Helen were both here because of their husbands," I said. "Looking for help."

"Essentially, yes. I had also written to both of them, saying that their father was quite ill. Rupert had confided in me a month ago that the doctors were very concerned about his heart. Actually, this was the second time Meredith had asked Rupert for help. She must have choked on her words. The previous time, after the birth of their first child, it was to secure a position for Edgar in the Indian Civil Service. Rupert obliged, and we know what a hash Edgar made of that."

"Some might say he did the honorable thing," I said.

"Perhaps, but it is hardly honorable to come back a second time to ask for help again. But they were desperate. No prospects, a dwindling bank account, persona non grata at the Foreign Office. It made for an awful scene when they first arrived."

"But he didn't throw them out," I said.

"No, not with Helen and David coming as well. I think Rupert knew these were his last days, and even with all the enmity between them, he did find some solace in family."

"And then Peter Wiley walks through the door," I said.

"Yes."

"It must have driven Meredith crazy," I said.

"That is a bit of an exaggeration," Lady Pemberton said. "But she obviously was not pleased. The only good thing for her was that it proved that she had not stolen the ring."

"But Sir Rupert would have known that all along," I said.

"I imagine so. But he couldn't let on, could he? Louise claimed she had lost the ring, perhaps to protect herself from learning the truth. She defended Meredith against the accusations, telling Rupert her daughter would never steal from her. But still, what does all this have to do with the death of poor Peter?"

"I don't know," I said. "But I do know you saw something, probably early in the morning after Sir Rupert's death. From this very window."

"No!" Lady Pemberton said, rising from her seat, the book tumbling to the floor. "Now let us put an end to this. It is high time you left."

I rose and took her hand. "I'm sorry if I caused you distress, Lady Pemberton. I am sure we'll meet again. Soon."

I went to my room and packed up my duffle bag. Kaz and David were in Big Mike's room putting his gear together, and we walked downstairs together.

"I hope you'll visit again, Piotr," David said. "You too, Billy. Although it seems big things are coming soon. The generals will want to be in France before the summer. Can't be too long now."

"Think you'll miss it?" I asked as we swung the bags into the back of the jeep.

"Yes," David said, his voice low and firm. "Terribly. But at least I'm needed here. Gives me something to do. Listen, good luck with the Peter Wiley case. Hard to believe it was murder, but I am glad you seem to be closing in on the killer."

"We're very close," I said. "A key piece of evidence has turned up. But mum's the word, okay?" David agreed, and we shook hands and drove off.

"Where to now?" Kaz said.

"To see Inspector Grange. Then into the restricted area. The timing ought to be about right."

CHAPTER THIRTY-EIGHT

I HAD ENOUGH of the pieces of the puzzle assembled for it to make sense to Kaz as we drove into Dartmouth. Which was good, since that was a dress rehearsal for Inspector Grange. He thought the idea had sufficient merit to send a car with two constables to assist us. But not so much that he came along himself. It was getting dark, and starting to rain to boot, so he decided to do his inspecting indoors.

We drove to Strete, showing orders at the roadblock and explaining that the bobbies in the other automobile were with us.

"You can go ahead if you want, Captain," the MP at the gate said, shaking his head at the idea as raindrops splattered off his helmet. "But there's an exercise scheduled for the morning. Bombardment at zero four thirty, landings at zero six hundred at Slapton Sands. Where are you headed?"

"Dunstone," I said. "Little place south of Torcross."

"I know where it is," he said. "You'd best be clear of it by zero four hundred. They're sending in those new rocket-firing fighter-bombers to soften up the area around the beachhead. They hauled in some old tanks today for target practice. If a stray shell from a cruiser doesn't get you, a P-47 might."

"Cheery," Kaz said as we set off into the wet, bleak landscape. Heavy black clouds blanketed the setting sun, and the rain came and went in gusty showers. We slowed as we made our way through the ruined village of Stokenham, almost slamming into a tank parked in the middle of the road.

"Hey!" I yelled, looking for the crew. Then I noticed there were no treads. It was a wreck, an old M3 model, one of the targets for tomorrow's exercise. The P-47s would be diving and firing their rockets, testing them out against thick armor plate. Flesh and bone wouldn't stand a chance. I drove on, braking at shadows, afraid of a collision with an immoveable object.

We stopped at a fork in the road on the outskirts of Dunstone. An old farmhouse stood between two roads, a ramshackle barn facing the lane leading to the village. Rows of trees stood like sentinels in the night—it had been an apple orchard once upon a time.

"You fellows stay here," I told the constables as they approached the idling jeep. "Watch each road, and follow anyone who passes. Give them about five minutes."

"Right," Constable Carraher said. "We'll hide the motorcar in the barn and follow by foot or vehicle, depending on how the villain proceeds."

"Good," I said. "Remember that he's gotten in before, and he knows the area. He may stay off the road."

"I know this patch as well, Captain," Carraher said. "We'll come on real quiet like if we spot him." He grinned, and I could see he was looking forward to some excitement.

His younger partner looked nervous, pushing his tin-pot helmet up and wiping the rain from his face. "Is he likely to be armed?" Constable Dell asked.

"I don't know," I said. "Maybe a shotgun from Ashcroft House. Best assume he is, although carrying a weapon would raise suspicions if he were stopped anywhere along the way. The safest bet for him would be to go unarmed, but he may be desperate."

"We'll do our bit," Carraher said. "Two rifles and the authority of the Devon Constabulary, that's more than enough weight, eh?" He clapped the other constable on the shoulder, and the kid did his best to put on a brave face. We left the two of them at the farm, backing the Austin into the barn. I told them to get the hell out of there if we

didn't return by four o'clock. I hoped we'd all be sipping hot tea in the
Dartmouth clink by then, but I didn't want them on the receiving end
of a rocket attack if things went south.

We drove closer to Dunstone, pulling over short of the village to
hide the jeep in a grove of trees. The rain had lessened, but that only
made our tire tracks where we left the road more noticeable. We
grabbed some fallen branches and worked at smoothing over the
gouges in the mud at the side of the lane.

"That may be good enough," Kaz said, surveying our handiwork
and tossing his branch into the thick grass. "But if he is suspicious at
all, he might take note."

"Then we'll have lost our chance," I said. I turned up the collar of
my trench coat and stuffed a .45 automatic into my pocket. I had my
.38 Police Special revolver in a shoulder holster. Kaz patted his raincoat
pocket, the Webley Break-Top revolver ready for action. As rain beaded
up on the leather brim of his service cap, he gave me a wink and we
trotted off, slinking around the first decrepit cottages that made up
the mournful remnants of Dunstone. On the open ground we leapt
like dancers in combat boots, jumping from one tuft of grass to another,
trying not to leave any telltale footprints.

"If anyone's watching, they'll laugh themselves silly," I said to Kaz
as we caught our breath behind a tumbledown stone wall.

"Furtive we are not," he said, pointing down the road. "Look, is
that another tank?"

"Yeah," I said as the hulking form took shape in the gloom. It was
a British Valentine, an older model with the turret gone, volunteered
for one last duty as a stationary target. "Maybe we should hunker down
in there. Crawford's cottage is straight ahead."

"It is probably full of water," Kaz said. "And we will be trapped if
he sees us."

"Okay. Let's move around back and check his cottage, then find a
spot to wait." We crouched low and scurried through an overgrown
field, coming up on the rear of Crawford's burned-out house. Guns
drawn, we darted to one corner. Back to back, we watched our respective walls, listening for any trace of movement within. The heavy rain

had let up, air now full of swirling mist, turning the darkness into a blurred landscape of grey and black. To the left was a small barn, one wall smashed as if a tank had backed into it, timbers leaning at crazy angles as if the whole thing was about to collapse. We worked our way around to the front of the cottage, visibility down to ten yards at best. Good in that we wouldn't be seen by anyone farther away than that. Bad in that closer than ten yards, a shotgun can do a lot of damage.

We went in the front entrance, brushing against the blackened timbers where the door had been burned away. I went left, Kaz right, and we stayed low, our backs to the wall, pistols out and searching for anything that moved.

Silence.

I signaled to Kaz to watch the road while I checked the one back room. Same as the rest of the place. Smashed and burned.

"Looks the same as the last time we were here," I whispered to Kaz as we gazed into the night.

"He's a smuggler," Kaz said, "if not worse. He could have a secret compartment or cellar dug out and hidden under all this rubble."

"Well, let's have him point the way to it," I said. "How about that barn? It gives us a good view of the cottage."

"If this weather doesn't turn to fog," Kaz said. "And if the barn doesn't collapse on top of us. Otherwise an excellent idea. Lead on, Billy." He grinned, his scarred face looking slightly maniacal. I don't much mind maniacal when it's on my side.

It must have been a poor excuse for a barn even before it lost a wall. The place smelled of rotten hay and garbage, the latter probably courtesy of GIs passing through. Empty cases of field rations littered the ground, the familiar crescent-moon symbol marking them as C- or K-Rations. We cleared a spot under the overhanging corner of the roof, which looked like it might lose its fight with gravity at any moment. But it was dry, and it gave us a perfect view of the cottage and the road, not to mention a bit of cover provided by the fallen timbers.

So we waited.

And waited. For hours. The misty rain gave way to fog, rising from the ground in a dark haze that muffled the occasional hoot of a nearby owl. It was well past midnight when we first heard it: the puttering, coughing sound of a small motorbike in the distance.

"Where is it?" Kaz whispered, twisting his head to try and locate the sudden sound.

"There," I said, pointing in the direction we'd come from. "No, over there." It was hopeless. It seemed to be everywhere, the noise and the night playing tricks on our ears. It faded away, then rose again, coming from the opposite end of the village.

"He is suspicious," Kaz said. "I think he's trying to draw us out."

"Or maybe it's his usual routine, to see if the MPs are patrolling. Not that he had a motorbike before, but he could have done the same thing on foot, circling the village until he was sure it was empty."

"I wonder if the constables have given chase?" Kaz said.

"Unless they saw him, it'd be a wild goose chase."

We waited some more, listening for the motorbike, picking it up in the distance only to have it fade away again. It was after two o'clock when we heard it draw closer. Much closer than it had been. We strained to find the direction, the thick fog disorienting our senses and cutting visibility to near zero.

"Over there," I said, keeping my voice low. "Across the road, behind the buildings." The engine was idling, giving off a rhythmic *putt-putt*, almost mesmerizing in the dank night air.

"What's he waiting for?" Kaz asked. "An accomplice?"

"Us," I said. "Let's not disappoint him." I was tired of waiting. If he wanted a fight, he could have one. Besides, the clock was ticking on the upcoming shelling and air attack. A mixture of frustration and practicality drove me forward, making me increasingly desperate for a solution that didn't involve a P-47 strafing run.

I motioned to Kaz to stay low, and we used the heavy fog on the ground for cover as best we could. We slipped out of the barn, pistols in hand, and scurried to the tank in the middle of the road, straining our eyes for any sign of movement. We watched the approach to Crawford's cottage, hoping he'd appear. Nothing. We waited ten, maybe fifteen minutes. The idling engine enticed us to move again.

We darted to the blasted doorway of a cottage across from Crawford's, where we spent another ten minutes waiting for something to happen.

"Maybe he *is* waiting for someone," I whispered. "Let's get closer."

I led and Kaz followed, both of us swiveling our heads like mad, watching for a threat from any quarter. We froze at the sound of movement ahead, only to see a big rat run across our path seconds later. We sprinted to the edge of a wooded patch, the motorbike now sounding only yards away.

We stood still, regaining our breath, waiting for footsteps or a voice. Nothing came, nothing but the steadily idling engine. I motioned Kaz to go flat, and we began to crawl through the underbrush, skirting tangles of vines and branches, finally getting close enough to smell the exhaust fumes. Either my eyes were getting used to the fog, or it was thinning out. Kaz nudged my arm and pointed with his Webley.

There it was. On the edge of a clearing about ten yards out. No one in sight, just the monotonous engine noise filling the empty space. Then it began to sputter and cough. It ran ragged for a few minutes and then conked out. The silence encompassed us, the absence of sound suddenly frightening. Now we had to be really quiet; there was no cover to muffle our footsteps in the forest. We moved apart, circling in on the motorbike. I could feel the warmth from the engine, see where the kickstand dug into the loamy earth.

It was as if we were meant to find it.

"Look," Kaz whispered, pointing to a canvas musette bag hanging from the handlebar. He stepped forward to lift it off, and as he did Crawford's words about his service in the last war flooded my brain.

I was a sapper . . . setting charges . . . laying mines and booby-traps.

Kaz pulled the musette bag by the straps, but it only gave a few inches. I heard a metallic *snap* and rushed at Kaz, leaning in low to hit him with my shoulder, lifting him and rolling into the bushes, keeping his body covered with mine.

The explosion blasted over us, the force slamming my face into the ground as I felt a red-hot sensation in my legs. I opened my eyes to check on Kaz, shaking my head to clear it from the shock and the concussive noise.

"Are you okay?" I managed, grasping him by the shoulders and pulling him up.

"What happened?" Kaz answered, wincing as he righted himself.

"It was booby-trapped," I said. "Are you hurt, Kaz?" I tried not to shout, the ringing in my ears still loud.

"No, I think not. Sore but unhurt," he said, picking up his revolver and checking it. The motorbike was a twisted lump of metal and burning rubber, the smoky flames flickering in the darkness, sending shadows dancing at our feet. I felt warmth in my boot and knew that I'd caught some shrapnel. The back of my trench coat was ripped, and I could feel the tears in my wool pants above the boot. I'd have scars on top of scars before this thing was over.

"Let's go," I said, ignoring the squishing between my toes.

"Billy, you're injured," Kaz said, spotting my leg.

"It doesn't matter," I said. "Now we have an advantage." I took off at a gimpy trot, making for Crawford's cottage.

"What, that our heads were not completely blown off? And thank you, by the way. Mine would have been if you hadn't tackled me."

"Anytime," I said, crouching behind a thick tree trunk. "The advantage is that Crawford thinks we're dead, or close to it. The idling bike was a ruse to draw out anyone watching."

"It is about time we had the upper hand," Kaz said. "Let's make good use of it."

"We need to hurry," I whispered, checking my watch. The sky was beginning to lighten at the horizon, the harbinger of a dawn drawing close.

"I am tempted to leave him here," Kaz said. "To the justice of a naval and air bombardment."

"If we didn't need him, that'd be fine with me," I said. But we did, and I wanted the indispensable Crawford alive and uninjured for the job I had in mind for him. We worked out a plan to approach the cottage from both sides, staying out of his line of sight from the doorway. I figured he had valuables stashed in some secret spot, and it was time to dig them up and hightail it out of here. But all I cared about was one gold ring with the Pemberton coat of arms.

I went left and Kaz went right, each of us in a low, careful duck-walk, scurrying across the lane guarded by the gutted tank. Fog hung close to the ground, rising from the damp earth and making sudden movements dangerous; there was no way to tell if you were about to stumble into a hole or fall across a log. The air was thick with moisture and fear as we moved in on the cottage, flattening ourselves against the whitewashed walls on either side.

I heard sounds from inside. The gritty scraping of a heavy stone being moved. The shuffling of feet, a slight grunt, the exhalation of breath. I signaled with my automatic to Kaz. He leaned out from the corner of the cottage, his Webley at the ready. I glanced at the sky, worried that I could see Kaz so clearly, then gave my watch a glance. Already after three o'clock, according to the luminous dial. Plenty of time, I told myself. As long as nothing goes wrong.

I took the flashlight from my pocket, gave Kaz a wave, then stood up at the edge of the soot-blackened window frame. Automatic held out straight, flashlight held high. I took a deep breath and clicked the light on.

"Crawford! Hands up!" I swept the burned-out room with the light, keeping the .45 steady. He was on his knees at the hearth, or what was left of it. A pry bar had lifted a large flat stone away from the chimney, where Crawford knelt, gripping an open knapsack. He dropped it, one hand going up to shield his eyes from the light, the other scrambling for something on the floor. "Don't do it," I warned.

He did. In spades. Rising up, he hoisted a Thompson submachine gun and let loose a volley in my direction. The muzzle flash was lightning bright, and the noise inside the stone cottage was eardrum shattering. Rounds chewed the window frame, whizzing over my head as I ducked. The first few shots were close, but then he went high, unused to the kick of the Thompson. I fired one wild shot through the window and then pressed myself against the wall a few feet away, listening for movement, my ears still ringing.

Another burst came through the window, then several more through the door and other windows. I hadn't heard Kaz, and Crawford was probably unsure if anyone was with me. The sound of the bolt being worked told me Crawford had loaded a new clip. I went to the corner of the cottage and aimed at the door, then pulled back as I saw Kaz do the same. Great minds think alike, but in this case we were more liable to hit each other than Crawford.

Before I could reorient myself, he flew out the door, twisting and turning, firing the Thompson and sending me diving for cover. I heard two single shots, Kaz firing his Webley, and I rolled out from the protection of the cottage wall, my automatic ready, searching for a target.

Nothing.

Was he hit? Or waiting for us to make a move and get peppered with .45 slugs for our trouble? The fog cloaking the ground was beginning to thin out, providing all of us with lessening cover. I was beginning to feel naked, flat on my stomach in the mud, nothing but swirling grey air between me and a tommy gun. Kaz darted past me and I followed, huddling at the base of the abandoned tank. We waited quietly, maybe fifteen minutes, watching for any sign of movement.

"See him?" I whispered. Kaz shook his head. I motioned for Kaz to stay low and pointed to the stone wall fronting the field to our right. He nodded and I stood, working my way slowly along the other side of the tank, scanning the ground ahead.

The Thompson spat rounds from dead ahead, ricochets zinging off armor plating as I went as flat as I could against the side of the tank, firing my automatic in the general direction of the burst, hoping Crawford would duck for long enough for Kaz to get to the cover of the stone wall. I did my own ducking in time to avoid another volley that stitched a line in the mud inches from where I laid. I stuck my hand up and fired off my last shots, hoping it kept Crawford focused on the tank. I loaded a fresh clip and worked the slide as I backed up, worried about Crawford getting the same idea for a flanking move.

"Crawford!" I yelled. "Come out with your hands up. You can't get away, the area is surrounded." I hoped I sounded more confident than I felt. What I wanted most was a reply, so I could be sure of his location.

Silence.

I stood and fired one shot, then sprinted away from Kaz, making for the cover of a cottage about twenty yards away. The one shot was to make Crawford flinch and give me a few seconds' head start. Darkness was fading into light, and I knew I'd make a decent target if I didn't hustle. I pumped my legs as fast as I could, feeling the sticky blood in my boot with each stride, not to mention the pain of accumulated injuries. I felt my knee buckle and hoped I'd be fast enough.

Crawford fired again, the muzzle flash a white-hot blast in my peripheral vision. Bullets hit the cottage wall in front of me, and as I thought about what a lousy shot Crawford was, I caught a root with the toe of my boot and went sprawling, rolling as best I could to gain the cover of the cottage wall.

I made it, but my .45 didn't. I'd dropped it when I fell, about seven or eight feet from the corner of the house where I lay gasping. I crawled on my elbows, hoping I could reach it before Crawford realized where I was. A shot inches from my head told me it wasn't in the cards. He'd gotten smarter, changing the selector to single shot. Better aim and more control. I slithered back, drawing the .38 Police Special from my shoulder holster. Not as much stopping power as the .45, but that hardly mattered if I couldn't see Crawford well enough to shoot him.

If I couldn't plug him, then the next best thing was to give Kaz a chance. Which meant making myself a target again, and trusting Kaz had found a place to hide and fire from. I gripped the revolver tightly and rounded the cottage, running broken-field style, aiming for a point directly opposite where I guessed Kaz to be.

Crawford squeezed off several rounds, slowly, taking his time. The bullets thrummed through the air, some of them smacking into stout trees behind me. Was Crawford playing with me? Missing on purpose? However he'd acquired the Thompson, my guess was he wasn't familiar with it, not yet anyway. But as a slug whizzed closer to my head, I had to admit he was getting the hang of the thing.

I took cover behind a well, the thick, cold stone reassuring. I waited, hoping to spot Crawford in the open, but he was too clever for that. After several minutes of cat and mouse he sent a couple of shots ricocheting off the stones, to let me know he had me in his sights. I looked to the east, where the horizon showed a reddish hue. I glanced at my watch. Just after four o'clock. Time to be getting the hell out of here.

"Crawford!" I yelled. "This place is going to be shelled any minute. We need to clear out."

"Go to hell, Yank!" Crawford hollered back. At least I had him talking instead of shooting.

"It's true," I said. "Naval bombardment followed by fighter-bombers. There won't be anything left of Dunstone, or anyone in it."

"Your lot's made sure of that already," Crawford said. He sounded closer. The well was excellent cover, but it wouldn't matter if he snuck up on me while I was hunkered down. I eased myself up, pistol at the ready, and looked out from the stonework in time to see Crawford hide behind a thick tree about twenty yards out. He knew how to move quietly, a smuggler's advantage.

The stone wall Kaz had used for cover ended on the other side of the road. A thicket of shrubs abutted it, and that's where I hoped Kaz was hiding. If I could get Crawford to turn a bit, Kaz would have him in his sights. Then it was simply a matter of getting him to drop the tommy gun so we wouldn't have to kill him. My plan depended on that, but I was tired of being shot at, and my leg was starting to hurt like the blazes, so a .38 cross fire sounded pretty damn good.

I aimed and shot, nicking the bark of the tree right where I wanted. I could make out Crawford pulling back, a perfect target for Kaz. Now was the moment of truth. If Kaz was not where I thought he was, this was going to go badly.

"Give it up, Crawford!" I said, standing up. "We've got you covered from two sides."

"Liar!"

Kaz fired, taking off his own chunk of treebark. Crawford swiveled to take aim, then realized he had exposed himself to me. He could take one of us, but the other would get the drop on him.

"I know it wasn't your idea," I said, taking careful steps closer, the .38 cradled in both hands. "You helped them out, was all."

"You don't know a damn thing," he said. If he didn't care about dying, he'd fire any second, I decided.

"So it was your idea? To kill Peter Wiley?"

"I'm not going to hang for that, Yank." Good. He wanted to live. Very helpful.

"Okay, so put the Thompson down. We have a lot to talk about, but we need to get the hell out of here." I glanced for a second toward Kaz, who moved in closer, his Webley aimed square at Crawford's chest.

A distant noise drew closer, and I froze until I realized it wasn't an aircraft or the beginning of the bombardment. It was our two constables in their automobile, disobeying orders and racing toward the sound of gunfire.

"I told you the place was surrounded," I said, moving in on Crawford. "Drop the Thompson."

Crawford stared at the police car, a bitter look of defeat on his face as headlights lit the roadway. He lowered the Thompson, looking for a way out, but he was hemmed in on three sides. He dropped the weapon and the knapsack at his feet.

"At least I'll be taken by proper Englishmen, not a bloody American or Pole," Crawford said, watching Constable Carraher as he stepped out from behind the wheel. His look of resignation changed to puzzlement as he gazed skyward, hearing a faint rumble in the distance, as if thunder had erupted along the horizon.

The screaming sound of naval shells arcing through the air told me it was no spring storm. I ran for Crawford, grabbing his arm before he had a chance to raise the Thompson, and knocked it from his grasp.

"Take cover!" I yelled, and dove for the ground, taking Crawford with me. The explosions came seconds later, hitting the woods on the outskirts of the village, sparing us and what was left of the village buildings. They came again and again, volleys of fire that tore trees into shreds and sent geysers of earth skyward. When the shelling stopped, we all looked at one another, stunned to be alive. Crawford was subdued, the way a lot of criminals are right after being taken. Sometimes the toughest hoodlum falls apart as soon as you get the cuffs on. Others bluster and curse, but Crawford was in the quiet category. I liked to think it was because they were ashamed, but I knew better. Exhaustion, more like.

Kaz hustled off to get our jeep while the two constables searched Crawford. I checked the back of my leg and wasn't surprised to find blood. I was exhausted myself, but I bucked up when Carraher pulled a gold ring from Crawford's backpack. It was Peter Wiley's, complete with the Pemberton family coat of arms. He handed it to me, and I smiled. But it didn't last long. The snarl of P-47 engines rose up in a heartbeat, a flight of four of the fighter-bombers coming in low, rockets slung under their wings. Seconds behind them trailed another four.

We were only a few yards from the tank in the middle of the road. Those P-47s had enough firepower to blow the whole damn village to hell and gone.

"Run!" I grabbed Crawford, again, with the two constables following, and sprinted down the road, toward our jeep, away from the tank hulk. This time, Crawford twisted loose and made a break in the opposite direction, into the village. Maybe it was the familiarity of the place, or maybe he didn't give a damn. But I did. I needed him, so I followed. The noise from the P-47s was deafening as they fired their rockets and peeled off in two directions, rising above the carnage they'd unleashed.

Rockets hit the tank and rocked it, a fireball rising from the wreck. Others hit the nearby cottages as I saw Crawford make for his own place, arms and legs pumping as if nothing mattered but getting home. Then the second group of P-47s fired their rockets, and the cottage blew apart, sending timbers hurtling through the air, scattering debris in every direction. The blast knocked me flat, making me feel like I'd gone a few rounds with Joe Louis.

I tried to clear my head and locate Crawford. The pain in my leg was nothing compared to the ringing in my ears. All I could see was dust and swirling smoke. I heard Kaz asking me if I was okay, sounding very far away. And that's all I remember.

CHAPTER THIRTY-NINE

ASHCROFT HOUSE FELT different. It looked different; a lesser place than it had been. Stepping over the threshold as an investigator, not a guest, I saw the cobwebs and cracks in the ceiling, smelled the mustiness of the lies and secrets that permeated the woodwork, and noticed the shabby, faded curtains. Or maybe it was my imagination; it had been a long night, and the brightness of the blue sky had only made my head ache.

Our jeep had been mistaken for another target and shredded by machine-gun fire as the P-47 pilots amused themselves strafing what they thought was a deserted village. The police car survived with only its windows blown out and got us back to headquarters in Dartmouth, where a police surgeon picked shrapnel out of my legs and bandaged me up. Presented with Peter Wiley's ring and the contents of Craw-ford's knapsack, Inspector Grange agreed it was high time for serious talk with all the residents of Ashcroft House. I gave him the lowdown on what I had planned, and he seemed happy for me to stick my neck out and give it a try. There wasn't a lot of hard evidence other than the ring, and we'd have to do some serious conjuring in order to make a murder charge stick.

Kaz and I downed hot tea loaded with precious sugar, then washed up and changed into clean uniforms. We drove to Ashcroft House in two cars, Kaz and me with Inspector Grange, and Constables Carraher and Dell following. Williams answered our knock and stepped back, looking confused as we paraded into the foyer.

"I will fetch . . ." he managed, probably not knowing who exactly should be fetched, and trotted off to the back of the house.

"What is this?" Edgar said from the stairway, halting as if he'd prefer to retreat upstairs.

"We need to speak to everyone in the house," Inspector Grange said. "Please ask family members and staff to assemble."

"For what reason?" Edgar said, puffing out his chest in indignation.

"In aid of a murder investigation," Inspector Grange said. "Preferable to having you all brought in to headquarters, isn't it?" Edgar sagged at that, looking bewildered.

"I am sure that won't be necessary," Meredith announced, Williams trailing her like an obedient hound. "We shall be glad to assist. I believe Crawford is out, but the rest of the household is at your service." She smiled as if she'd been asked to donate old clothes to the church fete. A duty, but a slightly distasteful one. She nodded to Edgar and Williams, who went off to gather their respective peers.

Constable Carraher stood at the double doors, watching as the residents of the house made their way into the library. Inspector Grange stood silently while I rested my arms on the back of a chair, giving my protesting legs a break. David gave Kaz a questioning look, but his friend ignored him, busy keeping his eyes on everybody else. Couldn't blame him, really, after first arriving as a guest and then returning as Dick Tracy. Williams, Mrs. Dudley, and Alice Withers edged in, their backs to the wall, well away from their betters. Helen sat next to David, her arm through his, her eyes darting nervously back and forth, searching for a clue as to what was about to happen. Meredith followed Edgar in, Lady Pemberton on her arm. Edgar looked grumpy, Lady Pemberton angry.

"Why do we have a guard at the door?" Great Aunt Sylvia demanded as she took her seat. "It is quite enough to be summoned like this, without being glared at by a common constable."

"We mean no offense to you, Lady Pemberton," I said, remembering her dislike of policemen in the house even when jewels had been stolen years before. I gave a nod to Carraher, who stepped back from the entrance.

"We have some further questions regarding the death of the American naval officer, Peter Wiley," Inspector Grange said, giving me a nod. I took a deep breath and stepped forward, one hand on the chair for support.

"Actually, we have very few questions," I began. "We know most of what happened."

"Pray tell, what do you mean?" Meredith said. I wasn't surprised she was the first to speak. She'd be the one to try and steer the conversation her way, to stay in control.

"It's my fault, really," I said, ignoring her. "But I'll come back to that later. First, we knew Crawford would not be here today. We followed him into the restricted area last night, knowing he would go in to retrieve the loot from his home."

"Loot?" Edgar said. "What do you mean by that? And wasn't his house destroyed weeks ago?"

"Some of you may know of Crawford's brushes with the law," I said, watching for a reaction. "Smuggling before the war, for one. He carried on his thieving ways even after that avenue was closed. It seems he was moonlighting as a burglar, responsible for a string of thefts Inspector Grange had been investigating. He had a hiding place beneath the stone hearth of his cottage. Very secure, safer than a bank. We found gold and jewels, some cash, and this."

I held out Peter Wiley's ring with the Pemberton coat of arms. I walked in front of them, letting them see the brightly polished gold.

"But that was Peter's," David said. "Wasn't he wearing it when he drowned?"

"Ah," I said. "Good question. We can't say for certain that he drowned. The doctor who did the autopsy had another theory."

"But how did Crawford come by the ring?" David said. "What did he have to say for himself?"

"Nothing," I said. "He overstayed his welcome. Dunstone was the target of a rocket attack by fighter-bombers early this morning. He didn't get out in time. We almost didn't, either."

"Roger is dead?" Meredith said, her hand shooting up to her mouth. "Crawford, I mean."

"Sorry, I didn't mean to upset you," I said. "He was caught in a rocket barrage."

"Well, it *is* upsetting," Meredith said, lowering her hand and regaining control.

"Of course," I said. "Quite a trusted member of the household, wasn't he? The kind of man you'd look to when things had to be taken care of." I watched the two sisters. Steely eyes from Meredith, a deer-in-the-headlights look from Helen.

"Are you saying Crawford killed Peter?" David asked. "Is that why he had the ring?"

I looked at Edgar, wondering if and when he'd pipe up. But his gaze was on Meredith, his brow furrowed in thought. I wondered if he was thinking of Desdemona. "He wasn't supposed to keep the ring, but then how can you trust a thief and smuggler?" I said.

"We certainly trusted him," Meredith said, sounding indignant. "He had the run of the house."

"He definitely did," I said. "'Appen the janner will find the shord.' That's what old Evan at the pub said. Perhaps the fisherman will find his way through the hedge as well. Meaning he was a sly one, and that he'd make his way where he shouldn't, just as Sir Rupert did years ago." Meredith looked away, and I wondered if there was any real sorrow beneath that rigid surface.

"You claimed to know what has happened, Captain Boyle," Edgar said. "I suggest you proceed with facts and leave the baseless insinuations out. You were recently a guest here, remember."

"If you insist," I said, giving in to the pain in my calves and taking a seat. "Here's what I do know. On the night he was killed, Peter Wiley made the mistake of speaking to someone about what Sir Rupert had said to him: that Peter was Rupert's illegitimate son, and that he stood to inherit the estate. My guess is it was done out of genuine, innocent enthusiasm. Peter had lost his parents in America, Ted Wiley quite early in his life. He must have been overcome with joy to find he was part of this family and this house, which he'd heard so much about all his life.

That may have prevented him from thinking through the implications for Sir Rupert's daughters. I'd guess he blurted it out, unable to contain himself. But it was too much to bear, wasn't it, Helen?"

"No!" she shrieked, burying her head in David's shoulder.

"No, it wasn't too much to bear?" I asked.

"Captain Boyle," Meredith said, her teeth clenched. "Stop bullying dear Helen. It's true that none of us liked the idea of Father's unfaithfulness staring us in the face, but that does not add up to murder."

"Even when Peter would inherit?" I said. "After all, your mother had promised you Ashcroft House. It was rightfully yours, but she died before she could put you in the will ahead of her husband. That must have rankled, after what you'd witnessed. Your father and Julia Greenshaw embracing in the garden. Or was it even more than a kiss and embrace that you saw?"

"Captain Boyle! Remember your manners," Lady Pemberton said. There were no manners in an interrogation, but I thought it best not to lecture her on police procedures.

"Of course I hated Father for what he did," Meredith said, too eager to defend herself to listen to anyone else. "He pushed my mother to an early grave and would have begged that terrible Greenshaw woman to return to Ashcroft if I hadn't kept the letter from him."

"Only that one?" I asked.

"It was the only one she sent, as far as I know," Meredith said. "He even offered to get Edgar a position again, if only I'd give it over. I declined."

"What!" Edgar said, roused. "How could you?"

"Easily," Meredith said. "Why bother? You'd only ruin things again. Now you have your leisure to write your silly book. Even you couldn't ruin that."

"It's true, then," Edgar said. "Crawford. I confronted him about it a few nights ago, but he denied it. I've had my suspicions."

"Our private affairs are of no concern to these policemen," Meredith said, her eyes drilling into Edgar's.

"Why did you accuse Helen?" David said, after an uncomfortable silence had filled the room.

"I think it happened on the stairs," I said, not answering directly. I didn't have the heart to tell him it was the only reason his wife could look him in the face, that she sought solace in him out of guilt, not love. "And probably not on purpose. Perhaps near the painting of Helen. You can see a bit of Peter in that, I think. A push, a shove, a desperate need to get away from the words being spoken by this interloper, this man who might take everything away. Who might toss you all out of Ashcroft House."

"Preposterous," David said, looking to Kaz for vindication. Kaz stood rigidly silent.

"I know you didn't mean to kill him, Helen," I said. "But you couldn't help yourself. It must have been a terrible shock. How could you live with no home and a badly scarred husband?"

"It *was* an accident, I tell you!" Helen exclaimed, blinking back tears as she sat up straight. "I didn't mean for any of it to happen."

"So you called for Meredith," I said. "She and Crawford were together, and they took over. Peter Wiley wasn't dead yet, and he might have been saved. But they decided he was worth more dead than alive. He was worth Ashcroft House."

"I had nothing to do with that," Helen said. David moved away, his eyes narrowing as he watched her face.

"It was all Crawford," Meredith said, jumping in before Helen could say any more. "Yes, I admit it. I had an affair with him. I'm so ashamed, but everything was going wrong, and I made a terrible mistake. It was foolish, I know. After all, he was a criminal, as you said." She spoke with the desperation of a woman willing to bear all to evade responsibility.

"What happened next?" I said.

"Crawford said it would be better if Peter died," Meredith said. "We both tried to stop him, didn't we, Helen?" On cue, Helen nodded. "But then he sat on his chest and put his hands over his mouth and nose. He suffocated him. He threatened to do the same to us if we said anything." That fit with what the doctor had said about Peter being burked.

"Why did he do all this?" I asked, eyeing the staff lined up against the wall. Alice's mouth was wide open at the shocking revelations.

"He was worried about being thrown out. He didn't like Americans at all, you know that. He said he'd take care of things. I never thought he'd be so stupid as to keep the ring."

"He didn't get rid of the motorbike either," I said. "He rode it into the restricted area."

"What a brutal, stupid man," Meredith said. "Edgar, I know you can hardly be expected to believe me, but I am terribly sorry. I never intended for things to get so out of hand. He threatened to kill you if I didn't go along with his awful plan. He was kind at first, but that was only a ruse. He turned into a violent beast." Edgar looked away, his eyes flickering over the bookshelves, perhaps thinking how much better life was on the printed page.

"Then Crawford hid the body in the barn, until we came along and gave him the perfect plan for getting rid of it," I said.

"Yes," Meredith admitted, her voice low and demure. "The tides."

"We first came here telling you all about the body on the beach at Slapton Sands, and how the tides and currents carried it in and out, along the coast. As soon as Crawford heard of a transport going down, he took Peter's body and put a life jacket on it. Then he took him out far enough to slip him overboard and let the tide take him out. I figured that much out when we saw how easy it was to pick up a US Navy life jacket down at the harbor in Dartmouth. Then I remembered Crawford said he'd been turned back when he went out to help recover survivors. But the navy wasn't turning anyone away. We saw a fishing boat in the Channel ourselves."

"We didn't know anything about that," Meredith said. I wasn't so sure. Crawford might have come up with the idea to let Peter drift out on the tide all by himself. Or, it could have been Meredith who suggested it.

"I can't believe this," David said, shaking his head as if trying to wake from a dream.

"David," Helen said, taking his hand in hers.

"You killed your own brother," he said, unable to look her in the face. Talk about a twist of fate.

"It was Crawford," Meredith said. "We would have called for a doctor. It was only an accident, after all. But he hated Americans so, he was glad to see Peter die. He threatened us. We were both so frightened of him, we didn't know what to do. He became so ugly I was worried for my own life, and Helen's."

I looked to the door and gave Constable Carraher a nod. Seconds later, they brought in Roger Crawford in cuffs, a thick bandage around his scalp, but fit enough to have heard it all.

"Is that how it happened?" I asked.

"You bloody bitch!" Crawford said, straining to get closer to Meredith. If Carraher and the other constable hadn't had a tight hold on him, he'd have gone for Meredith for certain.

"They said you'd been killed," Meredith exclaimed. "I didn't know. I didn't mean it, not any of it!"

"It's close enough, Yank. Except *she* wanted him dead. She had the inheritance laws all figured out. If Wiley got the house when Sir Rupert died, and then he bit the dust, the estate would go to the two surviving sisters. Alive, he'd've beat them out of their precious Ashcroft. Dead, he was worth the whole lot. She begged me to kill him."

"What about Helen?" David said, hoping for something decent about his wife to come out.

"She ran off. Said she couldn't watch," Crawford said, sneering. "Not like our dear Meredith. She saw her opportunity there and then. Sir Rupert had told her the Yank was in his new will just before he died."

"You frightened me, Captain Boyle, bringing this man back from the dead," Meredith said, fear putting a quiver in her voice. "I did mean everything I said. Can't you see he's nothing but a common criminal trying to save himself?"

"You drugged me," Lady Pemberton said, her eyes fixed on Meredith. "I thought I was losing my mind, thinking I saw a body in the foyer that night. But I did. It was Peter Wiley."

"Of course I didn't, Great Aunt Sylvia," Meredith said. "Why would I do that?" Her hands clutched at the fabric of her skirt, bunching it up, all her fear on display in those two hands while her face remained impassive.

"Because you knew that I had seen," Lady Pemberton said. "I went to look for you in your room, but you weren't there. By the time I got back to the top of the stairs, the body was gone. But I was certain I had seen it."

"You were dreaming, Great Aunt Sylvia," Meredith said, still clinging to this part of her story. "I told you so."

"You were so solicitous, Meredith," she replied. "Bringing my tea every morning after that until I didn't know what time of day it was. A confused old lady. Inspector, I suggest a search of Meredith's room. You may find sleeping pills or some such thing." Lady Pemberton's mouth was set in a grimace, which might have had as much to do with addressing a policeman as with Meredith's gaslighting her. I'd been wrong about where Great Aunt Sylvia had seen something. It wasn't from her window; it was from the staircase, minutes after Peter had been pushed down the stairs.

"Yes, I have sleeping pills," Meredith said. "It's not uncommon, not against the law."

"I want to go to my room," Helen said. "I have a terrible headache."

"You stay put, Madam," Inspector Grange said. "We haven't finished here yet. Lady Pemberton, you are willing to swear to having seen a body at the bottom of the stairs the night Peter Wiley went missing?"

"Yes," she said, with a firm nod.

"Crawford has already given his statement as to what occurred that night," the Inspector said. "It matches the version given by Meredith Shipton, except of course in regard to his forcing the decision on the ladies."

"This can't be true," David said. "Helen?" She turned away. There was nothing she could say. She wasn't a very good liar.

"This is all Father's fault," Meredith said to no one in particular. "If he hadn't gone and got Julia Greenshaw pregnant, none of this would have happened. He drove mother to an early grave with his duplicity and left us with this intolerable situation. I hate him more than I ever did."

"You stupid, stupid girl," Great Aunt Sylvia said, shaking her head wearily. "You directed all your venom and hate at your father, waving that letter like a knife in his face. But you never read it carefully, did you? Never gave him the slightest benefit of the doubt?"

"Whatever do you mean?" Meredith asked.

"Julia said the child would always remind her of their time together at Ashcroft House," Great Aunt Sylvia said, her eyes clenched shut. Then she opened them. "Which was true enough. But she never said Peter was *her* child. Your hatred for your father clouded your judgment, not allowing you to read between the lines. Rupert was not the father. Ted Wiley was. Your own mother bore him."

"What?" Helen said. "Impossible." Meredith looked thunderstruck.

"Ted Wiley was the one who made his way through the hedge, right into the arms of Louise Pemberton. She didn't leave Rupert because of his brief affair with Julia. She left him so that he would not know of her pregnancy, and returned to forgive him only after the birth. For all the love you profess for your dear mother, you murdered her only son."

Meredith opened her mouth, ready to deny everything, but the certainty of Great Aunt Sylvia's statement had hit her hard. Her shaking hand went to her mouth as tears welled up in her eyes.

"Meredith Shipton and Helen Martindale, I am arresting you for the murder of Peter Wiley," Inspector Grange said with a glance at Constable Carraher. "Take them away."

"I'll call Farnsworth," David said, standing as the women were led away by the arm. "He'll know what to do." As soon as Helen was gone, he stalked off without looking at anyone.

"I'll be back to talk to the butler and Mrs. Dudley," the Inspector said. "We need to determine what they may have known about this affair." With that, the inspector and two constables drove off with their three suspects, leaving Kaz and me alone with Great Aunt Sylvia, Edgar, and three very nervous staff.

"Alice, please return to your duties, that's a good girl," Great Aunt Sylvia said. Alice skedaddled. "Now, Williams, what did the inspector mean?"

"I can only think, Lady Pemberton, that he refers to the night Miss

Meredith came downstairs to tell us this would one day be a Pemberton household again. She had us fetch an excellent bottle, a 1934 Chateau Mouton Rothschild, in fact. She seemed very happy." Williams had the look of a man who was glad to have a reasonable explanation.

"That was the night before Peter was killed," I said. "Her happiness supports Crawford's claim that she planned this all along. Maybe Helen's push simply hurried things along."

"Very well," Great Aunt Sylvia said. "Please pass all of this along to Inspector Grange when he asks. You are dismissed." Edgar took that as his own cue and bolted as well.

"We are very sorry, Lady Pemberton," Kaz said, bowing. "It was not our intention to bring this pain down upon you."

"The truth is painful," she said. "But as I have discovered, no more or less painful for having been spoken. At least I spared them the final truth about their mother. It wasn't illness that took her. It was suicide. There, the last family secret is now told."

"Did she love Ted Wiley?" I asked.

"Yes. Or was infatuated, perhaps. But his love was not as strong. It only took a thousand pounds and steamship tickets to America to break his bonds with Louise."

"What about Julia?" Kaz asked.

"She went along with the plan because she knew there was no future for her with Rupert. She did love him, and she played her part well. Although as you heard, she couldn't bring herself to lie to him directly. She let him think the child was his. A kindness on her part, I suppose. The ring came from me. I thought that even a bastard Pemberton should have some acknowledgment of his birthright."

"You let Meredith think it was Sir Rupert's child," Kaz said, as gently as he could.

"Yes, I did," she said. "I had the Pemberton name to protect, and Louise was born a Pemberton. A sin of omission on my part, but a sin nevertheless. But who among us would not transgress to protect family honor?"

"But it comes at a high price, Lady Pemberton," Kaz said. "If Peter was not Sir Rupert's son, he did not inherit Ashcroft. Which means

Meredith and Helen won't either, correct? That leaves David and Edgar with nothing, and the property with the government."

"Not quite, Baron Kazimierz," Great Aunt Sylvia said, appearing distressed and mischievous at the same time. "I once told you Louise did not change her will. That was not entirely correct. Farnsworth did not complete it, as I said. But Louise had a new one drawn up in India. She sent it to me, along with her suicide note. That is how I learned of her death, and I have kept that secret from Meredith and Helen to this very day."

"The will named Peter Wiley as her child and left everything to him," I guessed.

"Indeed. I have kept it safe all these years. I had no wish for the world to know of these sordid affairs, and I never imagined that the discord between Rupert and Meredith would fester so. However, I also have no wish for the government to take over Ashcroft House. I will take the document to Farnsworth and make certain the family maintains control. Such family as remains. Perhaps there is hope for the next generation."

"Perhaps Edgar will turn out to be a good father," I said, seeing no need to add *without Meredith*. "David needs a purpose in life as well."

"Yes," Great Aunt Sylvia said, nodding. "It was Meredith who wanted to keep the children at boarding school, not Edgar. And David mentioned wishing some of his fellow patients could visit. Perhaps healing will be a fitting role for Ashcroft House for the remainder of this terrible war. I shall speak to them both about it."

"Did you suspect anything?" I asked, taking advantage of her momentary openness. Not that it mattered. I had no desire to put this strong but sad old lady behind bars.

"No, I truly thought I had been seeing things. After all, a minute or so later there was no one there. I must have seen Peter moments before Crawford took him away. I should have questioned Meredith's sudden kindness in bringing me my morning tea, but I had waited so long to see the good side of her that I fear I set any suspicions aside."

"It seems that Helen was not as eager as Meredith in this," Kaz said.

"She was always the meek one. I'm more surprised that she pushed Peter than I am that she went along with Meredith. She always did whatever her older sister said. And it explains her sudden embrace of David, now that I think of it."

"She needed a safe harbor," I said. "He was it, scars and all."

"And now he has another wound to deal with. Gentlemen, I must take my leave of you. I need to consult with David and Edgar about what we will do next. Farnsworth is a reliable family solicitor, but we may need a sharper mind in this matter. Baron Kazimierz, I hope you and David can still be friends. He is a decent man, and he needs what help he can get."

"Perhaps after some time has passed," David said from the doorway. "Not today." He looked away as we passed, leaving us with the memory of his scarred and immobile face.

Outside, Big Mike was waiting for us.

"What happened?" he asked as we climbed into the jeep.

"Mrs. Mallowan was right," I said.

CHAPTER FORTY

IT WAS A long ride back to London. After we'd filled Big Mike in on what he'd missed, Kaz and I managed to sleep, even sitting on Uncle Sam's uncomfortable seats. We got to Norfolk House in Saint James's Square in the late afternoon, and I grabbed a cup of joe and got to work typing up my report.

It wasn't that I liked paperwork. It was because I knew Diana was in town, and this was her last night before her upcoming mission. I had to see her. I did the two-finger dance over the typewriter keys and ended up with three pages of army-style police report, along with two carbon copies, before five o'clock. Seventeen hundred hours, for those who prefer army time.

"Good job, Boyle," Colonel Harding said, standing over me as I put the reports in a file to be stored away where no one would ever read them. "And completed paperwork, too. This calls for a celebration."

At that moment, Diana Seaton entered the office. There were a few rows of desks between us, and the sunlight lit the frosted glass behind her, giving her severe First Aid Nursing Yeomanry uniform an ethereal glow. She stood silently, both of us grinning like schoolkids, neither moving for fear of breaking the spell.

"Sorry, Colonel, I have a date," I said, rising from my seat.

"Hold on, Boyle," Harding said, his hand on my shoulder, forcing me back down, his free hand signaling Diana to stop where she was. "I didn't know Miss Seaton was in town."

"What's wrong, Colonel?" I said. "She wrote me a few days ago. She only has tonight before—before she has to leave."

"That's a problem, Boyle," Harding said, facing me and leaning on the desk. "I know she's leaving on a mission. We have a hard and fast rule here. No BIGOT can have contact with personnel destined for enemy territory prior to D-Day. No exceptions."

"Colonel, I'm not going to spill the beans, don't worry."

"It's my job to worry, Boyle. And I trust you both. But the rule is for everyone. I can't make an exception. It's too important."

"Colonel," I whispered. "She may never come back."

"The answer is the same," Harding said. "I'm very sorry." He left to speak with Diana, who stood rigid, moving only to wipe a tear from her cheek. If I wasn't such a tough guy, I would have bawled my eyes out. But I didn't. I watched her as Harding left and signaled an MP to stand between us. We gazed across empty desks for ten minutes or so until she turned and vanished behind the opaque glass.

Kaz and I were driven to the Dorchester, where another MP escorted us to Kaz's suite and said he had orders to stay outside our room until tomorrow. I got him a chair. Why should this poor slob suffer for enforcing Harding's rule? And I couldn't blame Harding much either. It did make sense, and he and I both knew I'd find a way to break loose and see Diana if I wasn't under guard. Not that Kaz's suite was such a bad lockup. We had a drink and put our feet up.

"Think you'll get in touch with David?" I asked, trying to think about anything except Diana.

"Yes, I think so. If only to see how he and Edgar do with life at Ashcroft House. It will be difficult with the trial, but perhaps he'll find a place where he fits in."

"Both of them. Married life with Meredith couldn't have been a bed of roses," I said.

There was a knock at the door.

"Our jailer?" Kaz said.

"Maybe we should invite him in," I said, heading for the door and making a fist as if to knock him out. Kaz laughed, which I always liked to hear.

"There's a room-service guy here," the MP said. Behind him was Walter, the Dorchester's night manager. A decent guy, and not averse to a little black-market business now and then. He'd been on duty the day I first arrived in England, and he was always good to me, and he practically worshipped Kaz, as most of the staff here did.

"Come on in, Walter," I said, wondering how come he'd pulled room-service duty. And who had ordered it.

"Yes, sir," Walter said, pushing a cart into the room. There was a bottle of champagne on ice and two glasses, along with a vase of roses. The door shut behind him, and Walter winked.

"What's going on?" I asked. Walter only smiled and lifted the white tablecloth. Out from under it emerged two shapely legs, followed by the rest of Diana.

"Thank you, Walter," she said. "It was quite a smooth ride."

"You're welcome, Lady Seaton," Walter said with a gracious bow as he placed the champagne and flowers on the table. "And now, Baron Kazimierz, your chariot awaits. We have another room prepared for you for the night."

"Ah," Kaz said. "Excellent! This is the kind of thinking that will win the war." He gave Diana a peck on the cheek and then a hug, his fingers tightening on her shoulders.

He climbed under the cart and Walter expertly wheeled him out, telling the MP he'd be back with a tray of sandwiches on the house. Exactly the right thing to say, in case he'd had any thoughts about checking the cart. No GI would risk losing out on some decent Dorchester chow.

"Smart," I said, moving toward Diana once we were alone. Even in her brown wool FANY uniform, she looked like a million bucks.

"We are trained to be devious in the SOE," she said, grinning from ear to ear. "Are you concerned about disobeying Colonel Harding?"

"Rules," I said, then kissed her. I never got to *were made to be broken.*

AUTHOR'S NOTE

A LONE BODY washed up on the beach at Slapton Sands, much as described in Chapter One, and was examined by the real Doctor Verniquet. The identity or nationality of the corpse was never discovered.

The friendly fire incident and the subsequent training disaster in Lyme Bay did happen as described. The dates and sequence were slightly altered to fit the demands of the narrative.

Charles Sabini was an actual racetrack criminal, the leader of a large gang specializing in extortion and gambling. He was interred as an enemy alien, but released in 1941. His son, serving in the Royal Air Force, was killed while his father was in prison for three years for receiving stolen goods. Sabini harbored a grudge against the British government for his perceived ill treatment and the death of his son. Charles Sabini died in 1950, in a far more peaceable manner than is depicted in this novel.

Agatha Christie's country home, Greenway House, was taken over by the military early in the war. It was used as a naval headquarters for the 10th Flotilla, transports manned by the US Coast Guard for the Normandy D-Day invasion. Not that far from Greenway House, a young sailor named Yogi Berra served on a Landing Craft Support, Small (LCSS) Rocket Launcher. He and his crew took their thirty-six-foot craft to within three hundred yards of Omaha Beach, unleashing their twenty-four rockets at the enemy emplacements in the early hours of D-Day.

The disaster at Slapton Sands was the most deadly training incident in American military history. A total of 946 servicemen were killed, a total far worse than the approximately two hundred casualties incurred at Utah Beach on D-Day itself. Ten BIGOTs were on the ships sunk or damaged, necessitating a hunt for bodies and survivors, lest plans for the invasion fall into German hands. All ten bodies were recovered; the eleventh body is my fictional creation.

It was not only the potential capture of personnel with the BIGOT classification that worried Allied planners. Slapton Sands shares many of its terrain features with Utah Beach; if the Germans had determined that it was the destination of the transport ships, they may have inferred the location of the invasion. However, the attack occurred too far offshore for them to draw any conclusions about the purpose or destination of the convoy.

The map-making activities of Peter Wiley are based on the real-life contributions of Navy Lieutenant William Bostick, who created maps for both Utah and Omaha Beaches. He also developed a system of transparent overlays showing profiles of large and small landing craft. By adjusting the overlay on a graph of the beach slope, navigators could determine water depth and see where their craft would run aground. This is the "perspective" that Peter Wiley was seeking. William Bostick went on to a career in art and lived into his nineties.